MIND OF A KILLER

MIND OF A KILLER

An Alec Lonsdale Mystery

Simon Beaufort

This first world edition published 2017
in Great Britain and the USA by
SEVERN HOUSE PUBLISHERS LTD of
Eardley House, 4 Uxbridge Street, London W8 7SY.
Trade paperback edition first published
in Great Britain and the USA 2018 by
SEVERN HOUSE PUBLISHERS LTD

British Library Cataloguing in Publication Data
A CIP catalogue record for this title is available from the British Library.

ISBN-13: 978-0-7278-8762-7 (cased)
ISBN-13: 978-1-84751-878-1 (trade paper)
ISBN-13: 978-1-78010-940-4 (e-book)

This is a work of fiction. Names, characters, places and incidents
are either the product of the author's imagination or are used fictitiously.
Except where actual historical events and characters are being described
for the storyline of this novel, all situations in this publication are
fictitious and any resemblance to actual persons, living or dead,
business establishments, events or locales is purely coincidental.

All Severn House titles are printed on acid-free paper.

Severn House Publishers support the Forest Stewardship Council™ [FSC™],
the leading international forest certification organisation.
All our titles that are printed on FSC certified paper carry the FSC logo.

Typeset by Palimpsest Book Production Ltd.,
Falkirk, Stirlingshire, Scotland.
Printed and bound in Great Britain by
TJ International, Padstow, Cornwall.

For Ethel, Gertrude, Ada, Audrey, and Ma

This story could be true.

The quotations from news articles and
many of the events described here were taken
directly from *The Pall Mall Gazette*, *The Times*,
and other London newspapers in 1882.

PROLOGUE

Where do the paths begin that lead two people to come together at a specific moment? How far back in their lives, and in what corners of their minds, lie the origins of their convergent fates? Is the linking of destinies part of an all-knowing master plan, or is it driven by some unthinking, unstoppable evolutionary purpose that we do not yet comprehend?

I, of course, think the latter. And yet I discern no progress achieved from those circumstances that have conjoined our lives. In previous years, our footsteps trod different roads. More recently, however, we looked at each other, lied to each other, mistrusted each other. Yet each moment has led to an encounter that will have its final chapter tomorrow, when this man who has dogged my being ceases to exist. But I still wonder when precisely our destinies became bound together.

Perhaps it began on that early December night in 1869. How clearly I remember the rain pattering gently on the chalky walkway, as I stepped deeper under the cover of the lime trees. It was too dark to see my watch, but I suppose I had been observing the house for nearly two hours. It was not attractive, and had no social or architectural pretensions. Indeed, although the buildings and gardens were obviously well loved, the owner's modifications – a flint-stone wall between house and lane, a hedge around the kitchen garden, and the orchard – had been in the interests of privacy, rather than in the showmanship so frequent in Kent's country houses. This desire for solitude was certainly convenient for *my* plans as well.

The evening schedule was as regular as clockwork – also to my benefit. It must be almost 10.30, I judged, meaning that the backgammon, played each night, would soon be finished, and the couple would retire. Then the study would be mine, as the servants never entered it at night.

The rain had eased by the time the drawing-room lights were

blown out, and the ground floor became dark. Still I did not leave the shelter of the trees, but stood tormented by indecision. I knew that within the study were clues about the work with which *he* was currently concerned – perhaps an unfinished paper, which I could rewrite and publish myself. I smiled, because the master of the house was famous for the slow, methodical process by which he reached his conclusions – I could revamp the article well before he completed it. My career would be made overnight if *I* were the first to express the ideas that came from him.

But then my courage began to fail at the prospect of stealing from a man who had proven to be a colossus greater than Newton or Bacon. Would anyone seriously believe that *I* had developed such theories? But why not? Was I not a Balliol man? Could I not be like its other giants?

I pulled on my gloves against the cold, watching for the upstairs lights to be put out. I had not long to wait – since he rose at 6.30 every morning, the master did not stay up late. But I hesitated – was it an hour or minutes until my desire won out, and I approached the house? The window shutters were open, the owner believing that, sixteen miles from London, his peaceful home served as a citadel against the world. It was over in a moment, the crowbar splintering the soft wooden frame around the rear door beneath the central staircase.

Silently I crossed the hall to his study: the microscope on a board in the window, the revolving drum table with its samples and specimens, the notes and scribblings. I closed the door, lit a candle, and then froze as my feet set the floorboards creaking. Had anyone else heard? I paused, motionless, holding my breath. Then I moved the regency chair towards the table, sat down, and began to go through the papers. A new book was obviously in progress, and I read several paragraphs with mounting excitement. I had to force myself to stop – I could hardly steal an entire book!

I continued my search. And there it was – a copy of a letter written that very day. I read it, then again, and gazed at it with a mixture of wonder and enlightenment. I still smile at the image a photograph taken at that moment would portray: a young man, mouth agape; right hand holding the letter and left pressed against the long Dundreary whiskers that were so popular but so ridiculous; and eyes looking far away, yet inward.

I had just found the central meaning of my existence, for this letter was not just an article or a manuscript, but an instruction, a calling from on high. In it were answers not just about *my* future but that of many others. I put it in my pocket and blew out the candle. But I did not leave. I sat there, the profound awareness of that moment seeping into every part of my mind and soul. That one piece of paper had shown me that I would be a leader of men, a minister of a new calling, in fact, no less than a saviour to future generations.

17 January 1882, near Arras, France

William was dozing fitfully in the otherwise empty second-class compartment when the door from the train's inside corridor was thrown open, waking him with a start.

'Good morning,' said one of the two men at the door. 'I hope seven o'clock is not too early to discuss business?'

William swallowed hard as the man entered the compartment and fastidiously brushed off the seat opposite with a gloved hand. His companion closed the door from the outside; William heard him lean against it.

'So,' said the visitor as he sat down, 'what are we going to do?'

'I received a telegram from a friend who's ill,' blurted William, heart racing. 'I was going—'

'Hush.' The man held William's eye for a moment. 'Let's just sit quietly, shall we?'

William's mind whirled in panic, although he knew he had to stay calm if he wanted to survive. The man facing him was more monster than human, and William had never been so terrified in his life. Of course, he did not look evil. His double-breasted morning coat and vertically striped trousers were impeccably pressed, his short, buttoned boots freshly brushed, and his walking stick shiny and clean. He looked like a man stepping out of his club.

'Why are you here, Nathaniel?' asked William, trying to keep the tremor from his voice.

'More to the point,' countered Nathaniel, 'why are *you* here?'

He smiled; it was not a pleasant expression. 'You bought a coupon from Calais to Brussels, making such a show that even the cretin in the ticket office would remember you. But then you changed destinations at Ghent. Now, why was that? Not to escape from me, surely?'

'I can't do this any more,' whispered William, cornered. 'I shan't try to stop you, but I can't be a part of it.'

'You won't try to stop us?' snapped Nathaniel, his voice increasing in volume. 'Fool! This is the natural course of events. No one can stop it! You entered this business as and when *I* determined, and you will leave as and when *I* decide!'

William drew back at the venom in the words, but then Nathaniel smiled gently. 'Come, my young truant,' he said silkily. 'Neither of us should become overly excited. If you wish to leave, then of course you may. But let's talk first; we owe each other that.'

'But how did you know . . .' began William, not deceived by the sudden show of geniality.

Nathaniel wagged a scolding finger. 'Never try to fool the master, William. It was obvious that France was your destination.'

William hung his head, feeling stupid and wretched. 'So what now?'

'Mr Morgan and I hope that you'll accompany us back to London.'

'No!' said William, trying to press himself back into the seat. 'No, please!'

Nathaniel inclined his head. 'Then we shall travel to Boulogne together and talk as we go. I'll try to persuade you to come home, but if you remain firm in your conviction, then I shall bow to your will. At least you'll be easier of mind, having left with my blessing, rather than having stolen away. What do you say?'

William weighed his options, which he sensed were actually very limited. 'Very well – if I have your word that I may leave if I choose.'

'Oh, I guarantee it,' said Nathaniel. 'If you wish to go, we'll just drop you off somewhere along the line.'

He smiled again, but there was such malice in his eyes that William felt his stomach lurch, and he was suddenly more afraid than ever.

ONE

Alexander Lonsdale blinked soot-laden rain from his eyes as he slogged over the well-manicured but sodden fields of Regent's Park. The downpour came in sheets, beating against the butts as he walked through the area reserved for the Royal Toxophilite Society; on reaching the Outer Circle, the ring road around the park, he followed it to Clarence Gate.

A greasy, grey plume, darker than the clouds, lay across the rooftops in the distance. His assumption that there was a blaze somewhere was confirmed by the clanging bells of a fire engine, audible over the ever-present rumble of traffic. The cold, dreary weather meant London's Fire Brigade was busier than usual for April, as hearths were left burning whenever their owners could afford it. Lonsdale kept moving, feeling rain course down his neck and his trousers stick unpleasantly to his knees.

A row of hansom cabs waited at Park Road, their miserable drays standing with drooping heads and matted coats. Drivers stood in huddles, chatting together, or puffing on their clay pipes, waiting for the inclement weather to push customers their way. They eyed Lonsdale hopefully, and he considered hiring one, but he was already sodden and still indignant at the way he had been dismissed at the Zoological Gardens that morning. Thinking exercise would help alleviate his bad humour, he kept walking, eventually reaching Harewood Square, where imposing grey mansions sat behind smooth stone pillars.

But his thoughts kept returning to the irritating business of his unsuccessful morning. It was the second time that week he had arrived for an appointment with the director of the Zoological Gardens. It was also the second time that, after a lengthy wait, he had been informed that Dr Wilson was unavailable, and would he come back another time. As it happened, Lonsdale was not particularly interested in returning, but a

commission was a commission, and if the editor of *The Pall
Mall Gazette* was prepared to pay for an article on London's
magnificent zoo, then Lonsdale would provide him with one.

More rain found its way down the inside of Lonsdale's collar,
and he increased his pace. He resented being treated in such
an ungentlemanly manner, and he had declined to leave until
Wilson's secretary had put a new date in his diary: between
seven and eight the next evening.

Lonsdale decided that if Wilson was indisposed a third time,
the article would be written without his input. Perhaps he would
include a few home truths: that the lions were mangy rather
than ferocious, that cramped conditions were probably responsible for the bizarre behaviour of the monkeys, and that most
of the tropical inhabitants would probably thrive and would
certainly be healthier if they were ever let outside. Wilson
would be hard pressed to deny these charges, and would heartily
wish he had spoken to the reporter.

Engrossed in his vengeful musings, Lonsdale stepped off the
pavement to cross the road. A sudden yell and an urgent jangle
of bells brought him to his senses, and he leapt backwards as
a fire engine hurtled past, the horses' iron-shod hooves striking
sparks against the cobbles. He watched the engine swing down
one of the side streets, and the clanging faded.

He had just begun to walk again when a shrill cacophony
warned of the approach of another engine. Lonsdale glanced
up at the sky, and saw that the dirty grey streak was now a
thick cloud of smoke, hanging heavy across the rooftops. He
could smell burning, too. As the engine thundered past, its brass
pumps gleaming, he thought how unusual it was for three fire
crews to attend the same blaze.

He hesitated. There were few things he despised more than
ghoulish spectators at the scene of a tragedy. Yet he knew that
if he were ever to be hired full-time – something for which he
desperately hoped – he should take advantage of any opportunity
that came his way.

As he hovered indecisively, he saw others were not allowing
fastidious pretensions of dignity to prevent them from indulging
their curiosity and were converging on the scene of the fire.
Some were servants, cloaks hastily thrown over uniforms, sent

to find out what was happening for their masters; others were chance passers-by. Mentally shrugging, Lonsdale followed them.

The engine turned into Marylebone Road, then jigged right into Wyndham Street. Here, among the solid, unpretentious villas of the city's clerks, shopkeepers, and transport employees, was a row of tightly packed, two-storey terraced houses, each with a tiny, low-walled front garden. Halfway down the road, bright tongues of flame licked out of the windows of two of them, and smoke seeped through their roofs – spiralling upwards.

The reason three engines had been sent was painfully clear – the fire was spreading to the adjoining houses. It was obvious that the two homes were lost, and the firemen were concentrating on their neighbours. Clad in their uniforms of dark serge, they laboured furiously with pumps and hoses, and hoisted ladders to the upper windows to drench the rooms and create a sodden barrier in the hope of preventing the fire from advancing.

Lonsdale watched the tiny spouts of water hiss ineffectually against the leaping flames, before moving among the crowd, storing impressions in his mind and looking for someone to tell him who lived there and how the blaze had started.

Some of the spectators lived nearby, and fear that the fire would take their own homes induced them to scream orders and advice, all of which were ignored by the sweating firemen. There seemed to be a body of opinion that the terrace should be demolished before the fire spread further. This proposal was vociferously contested by a thin-faced, frightened man who stood amid a random collection of chairs, clutching a biscuit barrel. Next to him, a woman dazedly rocked a screaming child in her arms, and said nothing. Lonsdale balked at intruding on their despair, and looked for someone else to talk to.

Near the back of the crowd was a man wearing the distinctive peaked cap of a railway guard and a woman with a beaky nose, her sleeves rolled up and her arms dusted with a film of flour. Lonsdale surmised that, unless she often walked around with dough on her arms, they were residents of Wyndham Street and that she had been baking when the excitement started.

'What happened?' he asked, as hot tiles began to slip from the roof to smash on the ground below. A harried policeman and brigade volunteers tried to prevent onlookers from surging forward to snatch a better look.

The railway guard shook his head, while the woman studied Lonsdale suspiciously, pushing a tendril of wet hair from her eyes and leaving a smudge of flour on her nose. Her gaze turned from his face to his clothes, as if assessing his respectability by the quality of the top frock he wore. Lonsdale waited politely, although he knew that any conclusions she drew from his appearance would almost certainly be wrong.

He had spent most of his adult life in the Colonial Service – one of Queen Victoria's faithful representatives in Africa, where he had passed the better part of nine years. He had then returned to London, where a year later he had horrified his family by informing them that he intended to become a newspaper reporter. So Lonsdale, whose clothes were of good quality but not at the height of fashion, was difficult to assess solely on the basis of his attire. Even so, she decided he was sufficiently respectable to warrant a reply, and began to speak in a nasal, self-important voice.

'I was just putting the bread in the oven when I heard yelling outside, so I went to see what the fuss was about. This is a respectable street, and we don't pry into each other's business, so I didn't rush straight out, like some would have done.'

'What did you see?' asked Lonsdale, when she paused for – he assumed – an acknowledgement of her proper manners.

The woman coughed as a billow of smoke rolled over them. 'Mr Donovan was yelling something about his chimney being blocked and catching fire. Then he rushed back inside again. I didn't believe him – he'd had the sweep, you see, so I assumed he was . . . well . . . intoxicated.'

She pursed her lips in prim disapproval, and regarded Lonsdale with bright little eyes. Lonsdale was bemused.

'He called for help because his house was on fire, and you thought he was drunk? And what does the sweep have to do with it?'

She sighed impatiently, and when she spoke, it was slowly, like an adult to a backward child. 'Mr Donovan had his chimney cleaned last week. People's chimneys don't catch fire after the sweep has been, because he removes the soot that causes fires.'

'I see,' said Lonsdale, although he still failed to understand why Donovan's claim that his house was on fire had led her to conclude that he was drunk. Suspecting they would become pointlessly sidetracked if he pressed the matter, he moved on. 'So Mr Donovan's home is one of those burning?'

She nodded. 'Number twenty-four – the left of the two in the middle. Anyway, I went back in the kitchen and put it from my mind. Then Molly Evans from next door came running and said there was smoke pouring from Mr Donovan's roof. We sent her boy for the fire brigade, while her Bert tried to break down the door to get Mr Donovan out.'

'Did he succeed?' asked Lonsdale. The house now was little more than a dark silhouette among the leaping yellow flames. The breeze sent sparks fluttering towards the crowd, which stepped back with a collective gasp of alarm.

The woman scanned the onlookers, then turned back to Lonsdale. 'I don't think so. I can't see him here, and he wouldn't go off while his house burned, would he?'

'I imagine not,' replied Lonsdale, although experience had taught him that people did all manner of strange things in fraught situations. 'What happened next?'

Her husband took up the tale. He did not look at Lonsdale, but addressed his words to the flames, which reflected yellow and orange in the shiny buttons of his railwayman's uniform.

'I was coming home from work, when I saw Bert kicking at Patrick Donovan's door. By then, flames were pouring out of the windows. Funnily, the door was shut fast – locked or bolted. Then I saw the fire had spread to number twenty-two, so Bert and I ran to help Joe Francis with his chairs.'

He nodded towards the man who stood disconsolately with what he and his neighbours had managed to salvage.

'So Mr Donovan is still inside?' asked Lonsdale in horror, astonished that they should abandon their efforts to save a life in order to rescue furniture. 'What about his family? Are they in there, too?

He gazed at where the flames had seared the paint from the door, and envisaged the hapless residents crawling towards it with cinders and flames erupting all around them, only to find it blocked, and then dying in the knowledge that safety was but a few feet away.

'He lives alone,' replied the woman. 'He isn't married and his father passed away last summer.'

'You said you returned to your baking after Mr Donovan first raised the alarm,' said Lonsdale, considering her story in the careful, analytical way that had proven successful for him, both in the Colonial Service and at his newspaper. 'While he ran back inside his house.'

'Yes,' said the woman. Her voice became unfriendly. 'To salvage his belongings, I suppose. What of it?'

'So where are they?' asked Lonsdale.

The woman scanned the road, saw the proprietorial way each small pile of possessions was jealously guarded by its owners, and shrugged. 'He probably didn't have time to bring anything out.'

'But you suggested there were several minutes between him first shouting for help and Mrs Evans telling you the fire was out of control,' Lonsdale pointed out. 'Surely he should have managed to save something, even if only a painting or a book?'

The woman frowned, disliking his questions. 'Well, obviously he didn't.'

Lonsdale moved away, watching the firemen battle on as the steam engine on their pump spat and hissed furiously. Down the street, more residents were taking the precaution of dragging their belongings outside. Lonsdale went to help an elderly woman with a table, then stood by helplessly while she wept in distress and shock. He stood next to her, knowing he was supposed to be observing, not joining in, and wondered if he would ever possess the cynical indifference that seemed necessary to make a good reporter.

Fires were not uncommon in a city where coal and wood were used to heat homes, and London blazes regularly caused loss of life and possessions. Donovan's tale, though pitiful, was hardly front-page news. Still, W. T. Stead, the flamboyant assistant editor of *The Pall Mall Gazette*, was always on the lookout for thrilling, sensational, or tragic tales that would attract readers away from the dignified morning dailies, so there was generally a place for 'human interest' pieces.

Lonsdale rummaged in his pocket for his pencil and notebook, and began to write:

Tragedy struck today at the home of Patrick Donovan of 24 Wyndham Street, when a blocked chimney resulted in a fire so intense that it not only destroyed the adjoining house but threatened to engulf other homes as well.

He frowned at what he had written. Donovan's neighbour had said the chimney had recently been swept, so the fire being caused by a blocked flue was unlikely. So perhaps the sweep had left a brush in the chimney. It would not be the first time incompetence had brought about a tragedy. He continued writing.

Neighbours valiantly tried to smash through the door to save Mr Donovan's life, but to no avail.

He frowned again. Was Donovan still inside, or had he managed to leave via the back door or a window? That Donovan had escaped seemed more plausible than that he had rushed into the street howling that his house was on fire, and then allowed himself to become trapped inside. And if he had run back to salvage his belongings, the absence of so much as a stick of furniture was puzzling. It seemed unlikely that Donovan would have been completely unsuccessful, especially as the woman had assumed he was drunk specifically because she had seen no evidence of fire.

Lonsdale walked to the end of the street, turned the corner, and looked to his right. Running parallel to Wyndham Street was a narrow alley, where more firemen struggled in the swirling smoke. No belongings stood outside, nor – he ascertained from another neighbour – did Donovan.

Lonsdale returned to Wyndham Street. Dozens of spectators were there now – servants, street vendors, well-dressed gentlemen, and the respectable working classes who lived nearby. They stood elbow to elbow, winter-pale faces lit orange in the flames, their mouths hanging open as they gazed upwards. They oohed and aahed as the flames crackled and snapped. A few cast sympathetic glances at the bewildered victims, but most just watched with fascination.

Eventually, the firemen began to win the battle. The flames were less intense, and there was more steam than smoke. Most of the small, pleasant houses in Wyndham Street would be saved.

'You a reporter?'

The soft voice, close to Lonsdale's ear, startled him, and he turned around quickly. The woman who had spoken flinched away from his sudden movement, and looked as though she might bolt. She cast a fearful glance behind her. Lonsdale glanced at the pencil and pad in his hand and thought the question was spurious. Who else made notes at such an incident?

'I write for *The Pall Mall Gazette*,' he said.

'*The Pall Mall Gazette*? That's not a big paper, is it, not like *The Daily Telegraph*?'

'No,' he replied. 'It's aimed at an evening audience, not a morning one.'

She regarded him sceptically, as if wondering who had time to waste reading a paper at night, when darkness brought the opportunity for more interesting activities. 'Well, it doesn't sound as good for me purposes as one of them big jobs, but I suppose it'll do.'

She glanced around again, making Lonsdale wonder what 'purposes' could necessitate such furtive behaviour.

'Are you one of Mr Donovan's neighbours?' he asked.

It was a question designed to begin a conversation, rather than for information, as he already knew the answer: the Wyndham Street residents were solidly upper working class, decent, clean, and dogged adherents of social convention. The woman before him had a pale, thin face, plastered with make-up; her body emanated a stale, unwashed smell, and her clothes were cheap and ostentatious. She was not the kind of person who could afford a home on Wyndham Street, nor one who would be accepted by its residents.

'Never you mind,' she replied, and fixed hard, calculating eyes on Lonsdale in a way that made her seem older than her years. 'All you need to know is that I got sommat to tell you.'

'About the fire?' asked Lonsdale when she fell silent again.

'Donovan ain't the first,' she blurted. 'He ain't the first to die like this. And there'll be others. You have to do sommat! The police won't listen, so you got to help.'

'You mean other people have been killed in house fires?' asked Lonsdale, bemused by the tirade.

'No!' she cried, and then looked around quickly, as if concerned that her outburst might attract attention. 'In other ways. Donovan is at least the sixth.'

'Donovan may have escaped. Just because he isn't here, doesn't mean he's dead.' Lonsdale felt sorry for her; she was clearly distressed and frightened over something.

'He's dead,' said the woman firmly. 'But I ain't talking here. They're watching me. Meet me tonight. Regent's Park – between the drinking fountain on Broad Walk and the bandstand. Eight o'clock; it'll be dark by then. I'll bring someone who'll answer all your questions, and you can bring this to an end.'

'Bring what to an end?' asked Lonsdale, bemused by the stream of instructions. 'Why can't you tell me now? No one can harm you. It's broad daylight.'

She shot him a look that bespoke utter disbelief, and hurried away, head down. Not sure that meeting the woman and her associate in the dark of Regent's Park was an arrangement he intended to honour, Lonsdale followed, catching her arm.

'I have an appointment tonight,' he lied. 'Can we meet another time? Tomorrow perhaps, during the day?'

She grimaced. 'Tomorrow night then – same time and place.'

'At least give me some indication as to what it's about,' he said, smiling in the hope of reassuring her. 'You'll forgive me if I'm a little . . . cautious.'

A tired, sardonic grin tugged at the corners of her mouth. 'Most men don't baulk when I ask 'em to meet me at night. But if you're too scared to take a chance, while I risk me life, then you ain't a man I want to trust anyway.'

'What do you mean, "risk your life"?' asked Lonsdale. 'Is someone threatening you?'

'You could say that. Will you meet me, then, to hear a story so horrible that you won't believe it?'

'If it's *that* incredible, my editor won't print it,' retorted Lonsdale.

'We'll give you proof. Names, dates, places; whatever you need. Will you come? You won't regret it.'

Lonsdale nodded, although the rational part of his mind told him he was a fool to make an assignation with this fidgety, furtive woman in an area that was usually deserted after dark. She gave the briefest of smiles, then turned to stride away, but collided with a policeman, who had been watching their exchange with interest.

'Now, then, Cath Walker,' he said, regarding her coolly. 'Not plying your trade with me standing right next to you, are you?' He was a large man, broad-chested and heavy-bellied, with a livid scar slicing through one eyebrow.

She gazed at him in horror, backing away until she stumbled. Then she turned and fled, tearing blindly down the lane. The policeman watched her go.

'Brazen,' he muttered.

'She's a prostitute?' asked Lonsdale, although he had assumed as much.

'An *unfortunate*, sir,' corrected the policeman primly, using the expression coined for the thousands of women who sold the last resource they could call their own. 'However, she usually works south of the river. Did she proposition you?'

Had she? In light of the policeman's confirmation, Lonsdale found himself uncertain as to what her intentions had been.

'Not as such,' he hedged.

The policeman wanted to press him further, but was interrupted by calls from outside Donovan's house. Several onlookers were signalling for him to assist three firemen, who were passing something through the gap where the window had once been in the now-smouldering house. A second policeman appeared at the other end of the street and headed for the firemen.

Lonsdale turned back to the first officer, and was startled to see him hurrying away. He turned the corner and disappeared.

Lonsdale blinked. Why would he dart away from a place where he was needed? He considered giving chase, but something was happening in the street – a body being carried from the Donovan house. The crowd fell silent as it was laid on the ground.

'Is this him?' asked a fireman, looking around at them. 'Is this Patrick Donovan?'

'How can we tell?' retorted an elderly woman who clutched a shawl around her thin shoulders. The body – sizzling slightly as rain evaporated upon hitting it – was blackened beyond recognition. Its fists were clenched and raised, like a boxer defending himself, and its legs slightly bent. And the head had been crushed.

'What do you want us to do with him, officer?' the fireman asked the policeman, whose pale, youthful face made it clear that he had not had occasion to deal with such an incident before.

'My sergeant will be here soon,' he replied hoarsely, before stepping forward to cover the body with his cape. 'Then we'll take him to the mortuary.'

'Check his leg,' suggested the old woman. 'Mr Donovan lost a kneecap a few years back, when he was kicked by a horse. If that body has one kneecap, then it's poor Mr Donovan.'

The fireman raised his eyebrows at the policeman, inviting him to do it, but the youngster only produced his pocketbook and began to write.

'One kneecap,' he murmured. His hands were unsteady, and Lonsdale felt sorry for him.

'I'll look then, shall I?' asked the fireman mildly. 'We've got to do it now, because we'll have to look for another body if this isn't him.'

The policeman nodded, with his attention wholly fixed on his writing. 'Go on, then.'

'Which kneecap?' asked the fireman. 'Left or right?'

'Well, Mr North?' asked the old woman of the railway guard, who stood with his sharp-eyed wife at the edge of the crowd. 'You were in and out of his house, when he was laid up with his bad leg.'

North swallowed, uncomfortable with being the centre of attention. 'I don't know,' he muttered nervously. 'It was one of the two.'

The fireman bent to poke about the dead man's legs. Tactfully, he shielded what he was doing with his own body, while the crowd seemed torn between the desire to watch, and an urge to look elsewhere.

Eventually, he stood, wiping his hands on the sides of his tunic. 'Left,' he said, letting the cape fall over the black shape on the ground. 'Patrick Donovan was missing his *left* kneecap.'

*   *   *

'So, you were wrong then, Alec,' said Jack Lonsdale, eyeing his younger brother thoughtfully later that day.

They were in the morning room of Jack's house, a large, airy, first-floor chamber dominated by an elegant, but very scratched, table at one end, and a sofa and several worn chairs near the fireplace at the other. Books lay on the table and the floor, which was partly covered by a handsome red-brown rug. Lonsdale loved the morning room's shabby comfort, although Jack's fiancée loathed it, and he knew its scruffy, masculine décor would be one of the first things to go once she was installed as mistress of the house.

The second thing to go would be Lonsdale himself. He had moved into the house – a fine, six-storeyed affair in Cleveland Square, Bayswater – upon his return to London the previous year, after years of hopping around Africa: Zanzibar, the Gold Coast, the Cape Colony, Natal. Despite Jack's belief that working for a newspaper was an ungentlemanly occupation, he had insisted that his brother stay with him. But Lonsdale could hardly continue to live on Jack's hospitality once his brother was married, and Emelia would no more want him in her home than Lonsdale would want to impose. Lonsdale and Emelia were uneasy together, and only a mutual affection for Jack kept them outwardly civil to each other.

Jack flung himself down in a chair, oblivious to the way it groaned under his weight. The family resemblance between the two men was immediately apparent, although Lonsdale had flecks of grey in his dark hair, while Jack's mop was solidly mid-brown. Their eyes were blue-grey and both had a sportsman's physique, although Jack had recently noticed a thickening around his middle, something he attributed to approaching the end of his fourth decade rather than the frequent and lavish dinners at his club. His fashionable sideburns were the only facial hair either wore.

'You were wrong,' Jack said again. 'You thought Donovan might have escaped through the back door, but he died in his house.'

'So it seems,' said Lonsdale. 'Although it makes no sense – if Donovan knew his house was burning, why did he die inside?'

'That's obvious,' said Jack, using his pompous barrister voice. 'He went to salvage his belongings and was overcome by fumes. This reporter business has affected your objectivity. You look for mysteries, when there's nothing but simple tragedy.'

'Donovan's neighbours said they tried to batter down the front door, but it was locked or bolted. Why would he secure the door when his house was on fire?'

'He probably didn't,' said Jack, picking up a morning paper and reaching for his spectacles. 'Some piece of timber, loosened by the flames, doubtless fell across it.'

'In that case, why didn't he escape through the back door?'

'Maybe he was unconscious,' said Jack, opening *The Times* and shaking it out. 'Smoke can render one insensible very quickly.'

'But Donovan's neighbours didn't notice the fire immediately, so it can't have been so serious when he first raised the alarm. That means that he *did* have time to do something. And if his possessions were so dear to him, why weren't any outside?'

'Just because he didn't succeed in saving his property, doesn't mean to say he didn't form the intent to do so,' said Jack, sounding much as he did in court.

He cast his eye down the morning's news. Lonsdale was sure his brother did not need to wear spectacles, but there was no denying that they lent him an air of authority. Jack looked like a barrister without them, dressed in sober suits and immaculate cravats, but with them he looked like the personification of the Old Bailey itself. Lonsdale supposed that if *he* had committed a crime and saw John Lonsdale QC coming to represent him, he would have high hopes of getting away with it.

'The more I think about it, the more I feel this prostitute really does know something odd,' Lonsdale said, tilting his head to read the back of Jack's paper.

The Times was lowered, and Jack's disapproving face appeared over the top of it. 'What she knows is how to rob foolish men who meet her in dark parks. I'm glad you are dining with me tonight – it saved you from your own stupidity. If I'd known this reporting lark would entail meeting harlots in remote places, I'd have stopped you from starting it.'

Lonsdale was silent. Jack could not have stopped anything of the sort, but he did not want to argue. Jack's nose went back into his paper, while Lonsdale read on the back of it that the fatal shooting of Jesse James was deemed 'cowardly' by much of the American public.

The newspaper was lowered censoriously. 'Either buy your own paper or wait until I've finished,' Jack said stiffly, bringing up an ancient and familiar grievance. 'I can't stand it when you try to read mine at the same time.'

Lonsdale stood and went to the window, where he watched a group of children with their nannies career across the road to the gardens opposite, oblivious to the drizzle. He stared absently at the raindrops on the glass.

Jack was right, of course. There was no reason to suppose that Donovan's death was anything other than accidental, regardless of what Cath Walker had claimed. But it nagged him: a man running into a blazing house does not secure the door behind him if he intends to come out again. Perhaps *that* was it: suicide. But then why raise the alarm?

'Good God!' exclaimed Jack, suddenly sitting bolt upright. 'Have you read the obituaries today?'

'Not yet.' Lonsdale had been up early to visit the site of what was expected to be called Eastcheap Station, as part of a series he was writing on a new underground railway line, and then he had gone to the Zoological Gardens. After the fire, he had only just finished rubbing the smell of smoke from his hair with a scented towel when Jack had arrived home, and he had spent the next hour in an unsuccessful attempt to convince his brother that Donovan's death was suspicious.

'Charles Darwin died yesterday,' Jack said. 'There's a blow! Few men have contributed as much to modern thinking as Darwin.'

'Not everyone would agree.' Lonsdale went to scan the story over Jack's shoulder. 'A good number of churchmen, for a start.'

'Ignorant men,' declared Jack, waving his paper dismissively, at least in part to prevent his brother from reading it. 'Individuals whose faith is too flimsy to withstand intellectual probing.'

Lonsdale tuned out what soon became a tirade and read for himself, reaching out to hold it:

Exactly a year to a day has separated the deaths of two of the most powerful men of this century. On 19 April 1881, the civilized world held its breath at the news of the death of former Prime Minister Disraeli. Not less must be the effect when the announcement of the death of Charles Darwin flashes over the face of that Earth whose secrets he has done more than any other to reveal . . .

'How true this is,' said Jack, tapping the paper for emphasis and jerking it from Lonsdale's fingers in the process. 'Natural selection is one of the most brilliant concepts in the history of science.'

'You approve, then?' asked Lonsdale wryly. For a man of law, Jack's world was remarkably black and white. Theories were either brilliant or worthless, and the men who postulated them either geniuses or drooling imbeciles.

'We shall never see another man of science like Darwin,' averred Jack with utter conviction. 'He was the greatest thinker in the country.'

'What about Charles Lyell?' asked Lonsdale wickedly. 'Or James Clerk Maxwell?'

'Them, too,' said Jack, realizing his brother could probably list another half dozen men, all equally significant. 'But you shouldn't be here – you should be at your paper, writing a piece on Darwin. After all, you met him once, which is more than your colleagues can claim.'

'Did I?' asked Lonsdale, astonished. 'When?'

'At the Royal Geographical Society outing two years ago,' replied Jack. 'How could you have forgotten?'

'Probably because I was in Natal at the time. You must have gone with someone else.'

Jack raised the newspaper again. The silence meant that he knew he had been mistaken, but was unwilling to admit it. Yet he was right about one thing: Darwin's death *was* a major event, and it was indeed time that Lonsdale made an appearance at the office.

The Pall Mall Gazette was located on Northumberland Street, a mean little by-way off the Strand that was more alley than road. Number Two was a tall, grubby building with the name of the newspaper strewn like a banner below the top floor windows. Lonsdale hurried inside, glancing uneasily, as he always did, at the huge lamp that hung over the dingy front entrance. He expected that one day it would fall and kill someone.

A dark, narrow staircase led to the first floor, where there were four offices: the editor's, the assistant editor's, one shared by the sub-editors, and one for all the reporters. The door to the editor's office was open, but the leather seat in which John Morley sat while dispensing orders to his minions was empty.

Next door, assistant editor W. T. Stead slouched with his back to his desk and his feet on the mantelpiece, tossing balls of paper at a stuffed bear head that hung on the wall. He looked as though he were idling, but his reporters knew that some of his most brilliant thinking was done while he appeared to be wasting time. As Lonsdale passed the door, one of Stead's missiles bounced off his shoulder.

'Lonsdale!' Stead leapt to his feet with customary vigour as Lonsdale poked his head around the door. 'The article on the zoo. Can it go in the last edition?'

Guiltily, Lonsdale realized that he had not given it a thought since the fire. 'I'm due to meet Dr Wilson at seven tomorrow evening,' he replied evasively. 'It'll be ready first thing Saturday.'

Stead cocked his head to one side and regarded Lonsdale appraisingly. 'You were supposed to meet him this morning. Did his secretary tell you he was indisposed?'

Stead saw his reporter's surprise and grinned teeth flashing white through the tangle of reddish-brown beard that had been growing wilder since Christmas. He twisted around and tossed one of his paper balls at the bear, scoring a direct hit.

'Wilson will be at his club tomorrow night,' he said, tearing up a well-thumbed copy of *The Morning Post* to make more ammunition. 'If his secretary said Wilson would meet you at the Zoological Gardens at seven on a Friday night, he was being naughty.'

'How do you know?'

'Wilson visits the Garrick Club every Friday,' replied Stead. He grinned again. 'Listen to everything you're told, Lonsdale, and forget nothing. That's what'll make you a good reporter, not the ability to pen a story – any monkey can do that. Make yourself familiar with the people you interview, so you always have the advantage.'

Lonsdale nodded gloomily. 'So I should stand outside the Garrick and ambush him as he enters?'

'No need! Ambrose Harris is a member of the Garrick. He'll sign you in.'

'He won't,' said Lonsdale, startled. 'I know him only slightly, like him less, and he would no more sign me into his club than I would sign him into mine.'

'Now, now,' said Stead cheerfully. 'Poor gauche Harris cannot help not having been raised as a gentleman.'

'Perhaps not, but he can certainly help being employed by *The New York Herald*.'

Stead laughed. 'It's a dreadful rag, I agree, but its sensationalism seems to be what makes a successful newspaper in New York. However, we digress. I shall arrange for Harris to sign you into the Garrick tomorrow, and you can tackle Wilson there. I want this zoo story – wild animals are popular at the moment, and people are of a mind to visit them in their time off.' He saw Lonsdale's distaste. 'I know Harris isn't a decent man's choice of company, but we all must make sacrifices.'

He sat at his desk and waved a hand to indicate that Lonsdale should sit also. There was no other chair, but there were piles of newspapers, so Lonsdale perched on one. Stead watched him thoughtfully.

The Pall Mall Gazette did not have a large staff, and one of its senior reporters had recently announced his intention to retire. It was common knowledge that there were three candidates for the post, but it was likely that the choice would be between Lonsdale and another freelance reporter – or 'liner' as they were known – by the name of Henry Voules. Lonsdale wrote well, was a meticulous researcher, learned fast, and was pleasant company. Voules was none of these things, but was the nephew of the paper's business manager and a friend of the owner, both of whom approved of Voules's social connections through his aristocratic mother. It would be a difficult decision, and Stead was not sure the right one would be made.

While he listened to Lonsdale outline the zoo article, Stead collected spent missiles from underneath the bear. He appeared distracted, but he missed nothing that was said. He liked Lonsdale, and felt his experiences with the Colonial Service lent a unique angle to his writing. He had assigned him to cover several stories in a manner frowned upon by most British papers and that had drawn the derogatory term 'investigative reporter' from Morley, the editor. But Morley wisely allowed Stead ample independence in pursuing stories with social significance, and Stead used the success of these articles to support Lonsdale for the upcoming post.

'What about the weekly progress report on the underground railway?' Stead asked. 'Is it ready?'

'The chief engineer says it will open as planned, despite delays over some skeletons that were found. Apparently, the tunnel went through an old plague pit, and the men refused to work when they were uncovered until the bones had been removed. A whole day was lost.'

'Excellent!' exclaimed Stead ghoulishly. 'Buried corpses make more interesting reading than the tonnage of excavated earth.'

'They were reburied in the nearest churchyard,' continued Lonsdale. 'The vicar held a memorial service for them.'

'This underground train system,' mused Stead, fixing Lonsdale with his unsettling blue eyes. 'Will it supersede the hansom and the trolley bus?'

'Never,' declared Lonsdale with conviction. 'It drops you where there's a station, and you have to take a hansom to get where you want to go anyway.'

'True,' agreed Stead. 'We can safely say that there will always be hansom cabs in London.'

'And we've all been on the Metropolitan underground railway,' Lonsdale went on with a shudder. 'Not everyone likes the noise, steam, dirt, and darkness – especially when there are more comfortable modes of transport.'

'*I* most certainly haven't used it,' announced Stead vehemently. 'And nor shall I. I'm all for progress, but not progress into the bowels of the Earth on an infernal machine that stinks of oil and screams like a banshee. Besides, we must think of the social ramifications: what would our friend the tramcar driver do if his livelihood were stolen by steam?'

'Become our friend the underground-railway driver?'

Stead began lining up his paper balls on the edge of the desk. 'Would you ask them to exchange a life in God's clean air for one labouring in the conditions of Hades?'

Lonsdale saw the gleam of fanaticism in Stead's eyes, and decided not to mention that few places in the world were as afflicted by a lack of 'God's clean air' as London.

'Never!' cried Stead when there was no reply. He slapped the desk with his palm. 'I shall see that such a monstrous thing *never* happens! Don't forget, Lonsdale, the mission of the press is to lead the struggle for the betterment of our society. It should give voice to the aspirations of the inarticulate classes and guide public opinion. That's what God's purpose is for us!'

Lonsdale was used to these tirades. 'Your tram drivers are safe enough. But where is everyone? Out working on pieces about Darwin?'

'Most of them,' said Stead, retrieving the balls of paper that had scattered when he hit his desk. 'Although Milner is inter- viewing Mr Parnell about the prospects of being released from gaol and what is being done to calm Ireland – you know Mr Morley likes to dedicate at least a page a day to the Irish Problem. But returning to you, tell me about the fire you witnessed today.'

Lonsdale blinked his surprise. 'Do you have spies in *every* quarter? Or is there still a smell of burning on my coat?'

Stead laughed. 'You reek of it. Was it a case of arson? I heard there was a tremendous inferno at a warehouse in London Pool.'

'Nothing so exciting – just a house fire in Wyndham Street.'

'What happened to attract your interest? Were there casualties?'

Lonsdale nodded. 'A man called Patrick Donovan died, although . . .'

He hesitated, recalling how Jack had dismissed his suspicions. But Stead nodded encouragingly and listened intently as Lonsdale outlined his thoughts, ending with the invitation by Cath Walker to meet her in Regent's Park.

'Will you honour this mysterious assignation, considering that you risked losing the story by being unwilling to go tonight?' asked Stead. He sounded critical, but he had ceased to collect paper balls, a sure sign that he was intrigued.

'I can't go tomorrow, either, if I'm to meet Wilson at the Garrick.'

'You will meet Wilson at seven and your lady at eight,' determined Stead. 'I'll send a message to Harris, warning him not to be late.'

'So you think I should go? I'm intrigued, but I'd almost decided it isn't worth the risk.'

'Only you can determine how important it is to follow a particular story,' preached Stead. 'Meanwhile, write your account of the fire. Don't speculate on foul play. When you finish, go to the Metropolitan Police mortuary and ask for Dr Robert Bradwell. He'll probably be doing the post mortem. Now go, or you'll miss the deadline.'

Lonsdale opened the door to the reporters' office, and headed for one of the tables. The office was stained brown from years of pipe- and cigar-puffing: its walls were brown, the floor was brown, and the ceiling was brown. It stank of tobacco smoke, wet overcoats, and ink, but a small fire cast a cosy glow around the room.

Lonsdale liked the reporters' office, as well as most of the people who worked in it. It ran on the same schedule as the newspaper. Before each edition was 'put to bed', it was a hive of frantic activity, as writers dashed off last-minute stories, while print-boys waited to snatch them away before the ink was dry, and tear upstairs to the waiting compositors. At other times, it had an air of jovial somnolence, as the reporters relaxed and told tall tales.

That day, only three others were there. Hulda Friederichs was writing furiously, Edward Cook was editing his copy while standing next to the one small window for extra light, and Henry Voules was surrounded by an impressive pile of tomes, through which he was lethargically riffling.

'Our Cambridge man,' sneered Voules unpleasantly. 'Come to make sure we don't split our infinitives, have you?'

Lonsdale declined to rise to the bait and only nodded at the books. 'Catching up on natural selection?'

Voules scowled and failed to reply, so Hulda answered for him. 'He needs to summarize Darwin's scientific achievements in less than a page,' she explained, 'which means he must do something at which he does not excel – original work.'

'Then why don't you do it?' asked Lonsdale, surprised. 'You once told me you'd read most of Darwin's work.'

Hulda looked smug, and pretended not to notice Voules's glower of outrage that he was obliged to spend his afternoon wading though Darwin's works, when she might have dashed off a summary in a few moments. Gloatingly, she waved a piece of paper in the air.

'Do you think readers will be more interested in musings on Darwin's theories or in the confession of the murderer Lamson to his Wandsworth Prison guard last night?' she asked. 'A story exclusive to *The PMG.*'

Voules gaped. 'Is *that* where you were all morning? Interviewing the prison guard? And all the while I was stuck here, slaving away over the lunatic theory that we're all descended from monkeys?'

Hulda gave a superior smile, and flounced from the room to present her article to Stead. Voules watched her go, his expression murderous.

'Why Stead hired her, I'll never know,' he muttered. 'She cannot open her mouth without being rude and aggressive!'

'She's also a gifted writer and an astute, incisive interviewer,' Cook pointed out, drawing a firm line through two of his sentences. 'We're lucky Stead persuaded Morley to hire her.'

Morley had broken new and dangerous ground by taking on a female journalist, but no one could claim that his gamble had been anything but a success. The 'Prussian Governess' or 'The Friederichs', as Hulda was known to her colleagues, seemed well on her way to meeting her dream of becoming the first woman reporter to be paid the same as the men. Even so, ability was no certain passport to success in journalism.

Cook was, if anything, even more talented. At twenty-four, he was the youngest liner on the staff, and had only recently graduated from New College, Oxford. He had already shown remarkable abilities, and was the last of the three in contention for the upcoming position, although Morley was unlikely to hire him because of his lack of experience.

Voules, by contrast, was a careless researcher and an indifferent writer, whose only value lay in his family connections. Lonsdale glanced at him and saw greasy crumbs and a long yellow streak of egg yolk adhering to his cravat, while he moistened his thumb with a wet, red tongue to flick through the pages of the book. Morley's personal copy of *The Descent of Man* would never be the same again.

All three were concentrating on their work when Hulda returned wearing a triumphant smirk – her article had been heartily praised. Lonsdale completed his report about the fire, and left as Voules and Hulda began an acrimonious debate about evolution, which Hulda was certain to win. He glanced at his watch. It was four o'clock, and he decided he had plenty of time to visit the mortuary before returning home to change for dinner.

Raised voices followed him down the stairs, and he heard Stead chuckling as Hulda began a ruthless and systematic destruction of Voules's arguments. He walked briskly to the Strand, where he hired a hansom to take him to the mortuary. Iron-grey clouds dropped a light drizzle, and as the wind blew sooty droplets into his face, he felt as though it were the perfect day for a trip to the House of the Dead.

TWO

The northern branch of the Metropolitan Police mortuary lay near the River Thames, in an area of Westminster dominated by dirty streets and grimy buildings. To the south was Millbank Penitentiary, to the east the chartered gas works, and to the west the run-down Grey Coat Hospital. It never ceased to amaze Lonsdale how such a seedy and unkempt area could be located so close to the homes of the upper classes along Victoria Street.

The mortuary was one of the most ramshackle buildings of all, and Lonsdale wondered whether it would survive another winter without some serious repairs. Black water trickled down its walls from leaking gutters, and its wooden door was flaking and rotten. Had it been anything other than a repository for the dead, he was certain thieves would have smashed the filthy windows in their decaying frames, and stolen everything inside.

The door stood ajar, and an oil lamp within threw a feeble yellow gleam into the gloom of a hallway. Wafts of death and strong chemicals billowed out, ranker than the ever-present stench of rotting horse manure and poisoned river that pervaded the city. When no one answered his knock, Lonsdale walked in, calling Dr Bradwell's name. There was no reply.

The hallway stretched away into blackness. Lonsdale took a few tentative steps, then froze at the sound of scrabbling claws on the stone floor. Rats! He was about to take the lamp to light his way, when it gave a sharp hiss and went out, leaving him in the dark. A quick shake revealed that it had run out of fuel. He considered lighting one of the gas lamps on the wall, but then decided against it, feeling that if they were in as poor repair as the rest of the place, he was likely to blow it and himself to kingdom come.

More rats skittered in the darker reaches of the corridor as Lonsdale rummaged in his pockets for matches – he did not smoke, but he always carried a box of Alpine Vesuvians. He struck one, and began to make his way down the dismal corridor, noticing that the walls glistened with black slime, while insects moved this way and that over the foul, speckled surfaces.

At the end of the hall was a sturdy door, with a line of light gleaming along the bottom. Lonsdale's match went out, leaving him in darkness again. He stepped forward and rapped on the door. There was no reply, and he was just reaching for the handle, when it was flung open. A figure silhouetted against the bright light behind advanced on him menacingly.

'What do you want? We're not in the business of cat food, if that's what you're after.'

'I don't have a cat,' replied Lonsdale, wondering what sort of person usually visited the police mortuary. 'I'm from *The Pall Mall Gazette*. Are you Dr Bradwell?'

'One of Stead's fellows?' asked the shadow, the belligerence fading from his voice. 'And women, of course, because one mustn't forget Miss Friederichs. Is she with you?' He stepped forward to peer hopefully into the gloom.

'I came alone,' said Lonsdale.

'Pity,' sighed Bradwell, stepping aside to allow Lonsdale to enter his domain. 'Miss Friederichs is always welcome here.'

'That must be a comfort to her,' said Lonsdale. 'Do you have a specific slab in mind?'

Bradwell gazed at him blankly for a moment before giving a sharp bark of laughter. He was a stocky man in his late thirties, with neat black hair and lively brown eyes. He sported thick sideburns, and his face was prematurely lined, although with laughter or care Lonsdale could not tell. He wore a thick apron, like the ones favoured by the fish porters at Billingsgate, which was stained with ominous smears.

The mortuary's inner sanctum comprised a large square room with a low ceiling that Lonsdale could have touched – not that he would have tried, as it was dappled with all manner of filth. Pressed along three of the walls were waist-level tables, occupied by human shapes covered with grey blankets. He estimated that there were about thirty in all, although this was insufficient, as several were doubled up with occupants.

In the centre of the room were two more tables, larger than the surrounding ones, with a lever at one end to adjust their heights. A brightly burning gas lamp hung above one, while a trolley bearing a grisly selection of instruments stood to one side. The sulphurous, cloying stench of blood and decay was overpowering, but Lonsdale resisted the urge to cover his nose with his handkerchief, knowing he would grow used to the odour. It was not the first time he had visited such places, and, during his days in Africa, he had grown inured to the sight and smell of violent slaughter.

There was but one other living occupant in the room. He was an unkempt-looking man with a poor complexion, a scraggly brown-and-grey beard, and a head of long greasy hair, parted in the middle of a flaking scalp. He wore an apron similar to Bradwell's, and slouched near the wall, picking his teeth.

'Have you come about the Hackney Road murder?' asked

Bradwell, indicating the waxy-white figure that lay on one of the central tables. There was a wide, deep wound on the victim's throat, and bone and cartilage gleamed through the mess of red and black. 'There's not much to tell, I'm afraid. He was killed by a single slash to the neck. The killer has already been apprehended, so there'll be no hue and cry over the police not catching the culprit.'

Lonsdale opened his mouth to tell Bradwell that he had come about the Wyndham Street death, but the doctor was not easy to interrupt. Lonsdale imagined that the sullen assistant, who still poked at his long yellow teeth, was unlikely to be much of a conversationalist, and supposed the pathologist was taking advantage of different company.

'It's difficult to conceal a murder like this,' continued Bradwell enthusiastically. 'Blood spurts from the neck, and unless you know what you're doing, you'll end up as covered with it as your victim. It makes escape more difficult. Why's Stead interested in this case?'

'He isn't,' said Lonsdale. 'We'd like to know about Patrick Donovan – the man who died in Wyndham Street.'

'Really?' asked Bradwell. He shrugged in a way that suggested he considered Donovan's the last case in which anyone should be interested. He turned to the slouching man. 'Bring in the burned one, please, O'Connor.'

O'Connor gazed listlessly at the covered shapes as though he expected Donovan to sit up and identify himself. Bradwell sighed.

'We put him outside, remember?' He turned to Lonsdale. 'He was making the place smell.'

'Yes, I can see that would be unpleasant,' said Lonsdale, wondering how they imagined Donovan's body might make a difference to the choking stench that already pervaded the building.

O'Connor returned with a clanking trolley. It carried a burden that was an unusual shape under its rough, grey blanket. Bradwell whipped the cover off with a flourish, like a magician removing a handkerchief to reveal a golden egg, and underneath lay Patrick Donovan, fists still clenched, knees still bent, and head still a mashed pulp.

Lonsdale was aware of Bradwell watching him, and kept his expression blank. He knew perfectly well that the surgeon had hauled the blanket away in such a dramatic fashion in the hope of shocking him – as a form of initiation to the morgue that would cause the reporter to run from the room in horror. It was by no means the first time a pathologist had played that particular trick on an unsuspecting visitor.

'So?' Lonsdale asked, meeting Bradwell's disappointed gaze.

'Typical pose for a fire victim,' said Bradwell, turning his attention to the body and pointing at the fisted hands. 'The muscles contract to make the corpse look as though it's ready for a fight. So what do you want to know? It's pretty clear to me how he died.'

'Is it?' asked Lonsdale, surprised.

Bradwell's eyes narrowed warily, as though he thought Lonsdale was trying to make fun of him. 'Surely even a layman can see that he's been in a fire.'

'But did the flames kill him, was he overcome by smoke, or did he die from the injury to his head?' asked Lonsdale.

'Oh, I see what you mean. The police don't usually want that kind of detail. House fires are so common that we tend not to waste much time on them. The inquest will be little more than a formality, and the coroner will record the incident as death by fire.'

'You won't even perform a post mortem?' asked Lonsdale, surprised.

'I didn't say that,' said Bradwell. 'But it won't be the kind of in-depth investigation that I'd do for the Hackney Road murder. I'll look at his heart and lungs, and then I'll assess the degree of burning – which you can see is severe.'

'And that's it?'

'Basically. Whether the cause of death was smoke inhalation, burning, or injuries sustained from falling masonry is irrelevant. That he died in the fire is usually enough for the records.'

'And you say it happens a lot?' asked Lonsdale. 'People dying in fires?'

Bradwell looked grim. 'More often than you'd think. People underestimate fires, and they usually don't live to learn their lesson. The smoke overwhelms them and they end up like your friend here.'

'Is that what happened to him?' asked Lonsdale. 'Death by asphyxiation?'

'I can't say without inspecting his lungs. I was planning to leave him until tomorrow, but as you're here, I suppose I could do it now. I'll be late home, but my wife's used to it.'

He and O'Connor transferred the charred remains to the other central table.

'What's your bet?' asked the surgeon, selecting a short, silver knife from the trolley. 'I'll put ten shillings on smoke inhalation. We might as well have a little fun, if I'm doomed to spend an evening in the frosty silence of a wife who objects to my long working hours.'

'I'll go for the head crushing,' said Lonsdale, wondering how he had ended up in the police mortuary on a wet afternoon betting on the cause of someone's death with a man wearing a fishmonger's apron.

For the next few minutes, the room was silent except for moist sucking sounds and the cracking of bones. Lonsdale watched for a while, then began to wander around the room, first inspecting the rows of gleaming instruments and then studying a stained chart on the wall that showed the major muscles. O'Connor watched him intently, and Lonsdale sensed that if he tried to touch anything, the mortuary attendant would leap to slap his hand away.

'You seem more inured to this than most reporters,' said Bradwell, not looking up from his work. 'Yet I haven't seen you before.'

'I worked in Africa,' replied Lonsdale. 'Violent death is no stranger there.'

'Good God!' exclaimed Bradwell suddenly. 'Look at this!'

Lonsdale leaned over him to see where he was pointing, but could determine nothing from the mass of blackened tissue and bone that had so excited the doctor. He said so.

'Neither of us will be claiming that ten shillings,' said Bradwell, straightening and eyeing Lonsdale soberly. 'This man died from neither smoke inhalation nor a crushing of the head. However, someone *has* made off with part of his brain – his cerebrum.'

* * *

For a moment, Lonsdale was too startled to say anything. He gazed at the police surgeon in astonishment, aware that the mortuary assistant was doing likewise from a shadowy corner near the door.

'*What?*' he gasped when he eventually found his voice. 'You must be mistaken!'

Bradwell pursed his lips in annoyance, as if Lonsdale were questioning his professionalism. 'I assure you I'm not. Can you see a cerebrum in that skull?'

'I couldn't tell you one way or the other,' said Lonsdale, looking down at the mess that had been Donovan's head, 'what with the charring and the crushing. Perhaps whatever bit you mean leaked out or was incinerated.'

'The cerebrum is the largest part of the brain,' said Bradwell stiffly. 'It wouldn't just "leak out" and, even after burning, there should be some of it left.'

'So what happened to it, then?' asked Lonsdale sceptically.

'I have no idea. But it didn't disappear of its own accord. And since it didn't go naturally, I can only assume that someone took it.'

Lonsdale began to laugh. 'Stead! He told you to spin me some outrageous tale, so that I'll write it up and provide him with an endless source of amusement.'

'You don't know him very well, if you think that,' said Bradwell reproachfully. 'He might have an odd sense of humour, but he would never make a joke of someone's death.'

Bradwell was right, yet what the surgeon was suggesting was outrageous.

'But Donovan's neighbours saw him run into the street shouting about a fire,' argued Lonsdale. 'I need no medical expertise to assert that he couldn't have done that without his brain.'

'Then his cerebrum must have been removed *after* he returned to his house,' said Bradwell firmly. 'Intriguingly, the rest of the brain is still there, including the cerebellum, the thalamus, and the brain stem.'

'So you think someone followed Donovan into his burning house – unseen by the neighbours – whipped out his cerebrum, and left?' asked Lonsdale incredulously.

'I'm a physician,' said Bradwell icily. 'I leave that sort of speculation to the police. *I* deal in evidence and facts: and the fact here is that there is *no cerebrum in this skull!*'

Lonsdale rubbed his eyes. Although he had sensed something odd about Donovan's death, he had not imagined it would transpire to be anything as sinister – or peculiar – as a missing organ.

'Are you sure someone didn't take it while the body was out in your yard?' he asked. 'When I first arrived, you thought I was looking for cat food, so you obviously deal with some very odd people.'

'We have a high wall topped by broken glass. If someone were to climb over that, he'd want more than a cerebrum.' Bradwell gestured that the reporter should move closer. 'The skull has been smashed, as you so eloquently pointed out, but if you look here, you'll see that the line of fracture isn't jagged – it's straight. In other words, someone sawed carefully around the top of this man's head, much as I did to the gentleman over there, who died from a fall.'

O'Connor lifted a blanket covering one of the corpses to reveal that a circular disc of skull had been removed from the top of the head, allowing the brain within to be examined.

'This is becoming even more outrageous!' exclaimed Lonsdale. 'Now you're suggesting that whoever did this had a degree of medical knowledge?'

Bradwell did not reply but fetched a magnifying glass for a closer look. 'Hah! I'm right! You can see the striations made by the saw.'

Still sceptical, Lonsdale took the glass and noted that there were indeed marks that looked unnatural.

'But what really convinces me that this didn't happen accidentally,' said Bradwell, 'is that *every* part of the cerebrum is gone. It is normally anchored to the skull by membranes, and it's necessary to detach each one very carefully to remove it in one piece.'

'But what could someone want with a cerebrum?' asked Lonsdale, bemused. 'You can hardly put it on your mantelpiece.'

'The world's a queer place,' put in O'Connor sagely, speaking for the first time from where he leaned against one of the tables, his hand placed without any thought on the chest of the body under the blanket. 'Full of strange folk with strange customs.'

'This is scarcely a custom, O'Connor,' said Bradwell.

'I blame the newspapers, personally.' O'Connor cast a venomous glance at Lonsdale. 'They write about all those peculiar places, and it gives people funny ideas.'

'What sort of places?' asked Lonsdale, searching his memory for a report from one of the Empire's far-flung outposts about corpse mutilation.

'Scotland,' said O'Connor, making it sound more sinister than Hades. 'And Manchester. And let's not forget High Wycombe, that vile pit of filth and corruption.'

'Let's not,' agreed Lonsdale, struggling not to smile.

Bradwell returned to the blackened corpse. 'What I imagine happened was this: your man Donovan was killed, his cerebrum removed, and then his skull smashed so that it would appear as though it had been crushed by falling rubble – a ploy designed to prevent a busy, underpaid police surgeon from looking any closer.'

He picked up a knife and investigated further, while Lonsdale watched, his mind teeming with questions. O'Connor busied himself at a sink. While Bradwell worked, Lonsdale studied him covertly. The tiredness in his face, his inexpensive clothes, and his harried air suggested he was a poorly paid hospital physician, forced to undertake additional duties as a police surgeon to make ends meet. He had mentioned a wife, and might even have children to support. Regardless, Lonsdale felt certain that his mortuary work resulted from necessity rather than choice. Eventually, Bradwell straightened up.

'If Donovan died from smoke inhalation, there would be soot in his lungs. There isn't.'

'I knew there was something odd about this,' said Lonsdale, more to himself than the doctor. 'Right from the start.'

'And I'd have missed it if you hadn't been here with your ten shillings,' said Bradwell. 'I had seven post mortems to do today – this makes eight – and I'm expected at St Bartholomew's Hospital for the night shift. I don't have time to waste on the obvious cases. Lord help us! I wonder how many others I've missed?'

'How many fatal fires have you had recently?' asked Lonsdale, thinking without enthusiasm about exhumations.

'Five or six.' Bradwell brightened a little. 'But I can quite safely state that none had a crushed head, and I'd have noticed if someone had taken a slice from the top of a complete one.'

'So, what happens now?' asked Lonsdale.

'I inform the police about my findings, and you tell them why you suspected Donovan's death was not all it seemed. Then they investigate.'

Lonsdale regarded him for a moment. Yes, he would tell the police what he knew, but he would also meet Cath Walker tomorrow night. There might be credence to her claims after all.

Lonsdale was woken the next morning by the customary tap on his door, which preceded the entry of Hillary, the older, primmer of the household's two maids, with tea and toast. She placed the tray beside the bed and opened the curtains. Lonsdale pulled the sheet over his head to avoid the daylight.

While Lonsdale groaned and muttered his way into wakefulness, Hillary bustled about, brushing ash from the fireplace and lighting a fire. She then went to draw his bath, knowing that, although he invariably grumbled immediately upon awakening, soon he was bursting with energy. Thus, before long, Lonsdale had bathed, dressed, breakfasted, and was striding towards the offices of *The PMG*.

He had intended to spend the day investigating the Donovan case, but life as a reporter was never predictable, and he arrived to learn that one of the sub-editors was ill – and as the first liner through the door that morning, he was assigned to replace him. Lonsdale considered objecting, but not for long – he would not win the contest for a permanent post if he questioned orders. Then followed a day that was so hectic that he had scant time to even think of the man in the mortuary with the mangled head – other than when he took ten minutes to talk to the policeman who came to take his statement at noon.

Late in the day, Stead called to Lonsdale, who stepped into the assistant editor's office.

'You have fifteen minutes,' said Stead, while standing with

his back to the door, warming a glass of stout on some exposed hot-water pipes.

Lonsdale regarded him blankly. 'For what?'

'To be at the Garrick Club, where Harris will be waiting. So go – Voules can finish here.'

Lonsdale did not need to be told twice, as he would need to shift if he did not want to be late. 'You spoke to him?' he asked, brushing off his coat and grabbing his hat.

Stead nodded. 'He is expecting you. Can I assume that you will be meeting Miss Walker afterwards?'

'Most definitely,' said Lonsdale, nodding in a gesture of farewell and making for the door.

The Garrick Club occupied a handsome, twenty-year-old Italianate building near Leicester Square. The area was not the usual venue for such establishments – most were located near Pall Mall and St James's Street – but gentlemen's clubs were becoming increasingly popular, and more were being founded every few years. The Garrick was known for a membership that included actors, journalists, and barristers.

When Lonsdale arrived, Harris was waiting at the porter's lodge. 'You're late,' he said irritably, as he wrote their names on the thick cream paper of the visitors' book.

Harris was a stocky American, who possessed a wide jaw filled with a set of vast gleaming teeth that Lonsdale was certain were false. He had a long-standing bet on the matter with Hulda, who maintained that no one would spend good money on a set of dentures that looked so patently unreal. Several attempts by both had been made to find out the true status of the teeth, but Harris had so far eluded their efforts to solve the mystery.

'I appreciate your invitation,' said Lonsdale pleasantly. 'It's good of you.'

'It is,' agreed Harris gracelessly. 'And you can expect me to call on you for a return favour some day. You *and* Stead.'

Lonsdale raised his eyebrows. Reciprocation went without saying, so it was in poor taste to mention it. He fought down his dislike of the man, although something Hulda had said came unbidden into his mind – that Harris had a reputation for getting young, gullible reporters drunk, then stealing their ideas. Such behaviour – as well as his lack of subtlety and his natural tendency to boorishness – was part of why the American was unpopular among London's press fraternity. But the dislike went deeper than his personal qualities or the natural rivalry between reporters. Harris was seen as the embodiment of *The New York Herald*, a paper with a huge circulation and power in the United States – and that could even be purchased in London. But it was also a newspaper that most of the members of the English press considered to be, as one of Morley's friends wrote, 'cheap, filthy, false, and extravagant . . . appealing to the basest of instincts, with sensational stories about romance, rape, murder, suicide, and improbable tales from exotic lands.'

Despite his reservations about the man, Lonsdale followed Harris inside. The Garrick boasted the same elements as most clubs: a sizeable drawing room lit by tall windows; a more formal, panelled morning room; and a variety of other facilities, including a library and a billiards hall. On the walls of its impressive staircase was a magnificent collection of artwork, said to be the finest of any club in London. On the first floor there was a reading room, a coffee lounge, and a dining hall to cater for men who chose not to return home for an evening meal.

'Wilson will be in the reading room,' said Harris, pointing to a door. 'I've got better things to do than spend an evening in the company of *that* crusty old buzzard, so I'm off to eat. You can sign yourself out.'

'Very well,' said Lonsdale, thinking he would never let Harris loose in *his* club. Moreover, as Lonsdale was about to pester Wilson in the one place normally considered a haven from such encounters, Harris leaving him to his own devices was rather rash, as there were likely to be repercussions for the man who had let him in.

Lonsdale entered the reading room and immediately saw Wilson dozing near the fireplace, chest covered by a copy of that morning's *Standard*. He sat for a moment on a leather chair across from Wilson, to study his prey. The director of the Zoological Gardens possessed an ample belly, wild black eyebrows that looked as though they were trying to escape from him in any direction possible, and a bald crown circled by unruly tufts that had been rumpled into miniature horns. In the midst of his thick-featured face, blubbery lips quivered each time he breathed.

The reading room was almost empty. An elderly gentleman with mutton-chop whiskers muttered to himself next to the window, disturbing a thin gentleman who was trying to read a newspaper, while a third sat and gazed blankly into space. He sat so still that Lonsdale began to wonder if he was dead. Then a waiter arrived with a large glass of brandy and a box of cigars, and the man stirred to avail himself of them. Almost immediately, the pungent stench of the cigar filled the room; Lonsdale had seldom smelled anything quite so rank, even at the mortuary, and wondered why the fellow elected to choose such a brand.

Wilson awoke from his nap choking. 'Good God, man!' he gasped, flapping at the air in front of him. 'What are you burning this time? Nettles soaked in lion urine?'

'An interesting notion,' called his colleague cheerfully. 'Nettles are easy to come by, although the lion urine might prove a challenge. I don't suppose you could procure me a drop?'

Wilson glared at him, then produced his own case of cigars. After a moment's hesitation, he offered one to Lonsdale, who declined.

'These will help cover up the smell of Deacon's foul concoctions,' he said, before stopping and studying Lonsdale with a hard stare. 'I haven't seen you here before, although you do have a familiar look. Are you a new member?'

'A guest of Ambrose Harris,' replied Lonsdale. He proffered a hand. 'Alec Lonsdale of *The Pall Mall Gazette*.'

Wilson's handshake was firm enough to hurt. 'Scurrilous Liberal rag! I have argued not to take it at the Garrick. Much better to have an honest, Conservative evening paper like *The St James's Gazette*.'

'I beg to differ,' said Lonsdale, more calmly than he felt was warranted after such an insult. 'Few newspapers offer more insightful political reviews than *The PMG*.'

'Rubbish,' retorted Wilson. '"Liberal" and "insightful" are mutually exclusive concepts. By the way, I'm Dr Oliver Wilson, secretary of the Royal Zoological Society and director of the Zoological Gardens. No doubt you've heard of me?'

'I've visited the zoo a number of times recently,' replied Lonsdale carefully. 'You've done an admirable job with the great apes.'

'We expect a renewed interest in apes over the next few weeks,' said Wilson, paring off the end of his cigar with a silver pocketknife. 'Darwin's death will resurrect the fascination with them that we had in the sixties.'

'People looking for their great-grandfather?' mused Lonsdale.

Wilson leaned back in his chair and eyed Lonsdale through a pall of smoke that was every bit as foul as Deacon's. 'Not a believer in natural selection? That's unusual in a man of your generation. They usually leap to defend modern science against us older, wiser fellows.'

'I accept most of Darwin's theories,' said Lonsdale. 'But only in nature. I can't agree with Herbert Spencer and those who apply Darwin's ideas to humans. If natural selection is operating in us, then why are there so many poor and sick?'

'Because our society has transcended the principles that apply to nature,' replied Wilson with unexpected vigour. 'We are godlike compared to the rest of the beasts, and we have used our powers to bypass natural selection. Now we need to use that knowledge to force natural selection to operate once again, for the benefit of our species as a whole.'

'How?' asked Lonsdale, not at all sure what Wilson was telling him.

'By not allowing the lower classes to breed indiscriminately, like animals – because we are *not* animals. We must decide who produces offspring, and who does not.'

'An *un*natural selection, you mean?' said Lonsdale coolly. He had heard such arguments before, and considered them unethical and impractical.

'On the contrary, what could be more natural than man using his intellect to improve his race? The greatest minds of all time have supported the notion. Plato's *Republic* idealized a society with constant selection for the improvement of human stock. And the Old Testament makes positive references to such concepts.'

'I'm not sure most experts on the Bible would agree,' countered Lonsdale. 'And those examples don't speak to the reality of today.'

Wilson was becoming angry. 'In savage societies, the weak in body or mind soon die, so the ones that survive are stronger, healthier, more vigorous. But we, the "civilized" society, interfere with this process. We build hospitals for the sick, asylums for the imbeciles, and homes for the maimed. We try to extend life for every moment possible, which means the weak have been allowed to propagate. Anyone who has bred animals will tell you that this is highly injurious to the race of man.'

Lonsdale wanted to ask who, in Wilson's scheme, would decide which individuals were allowed to reproduce, but as he could not use such a frightening interpretation of evolutionary theory in his article, he decided he had better steer the conversation to something less controversial.

'Do you think—?'

'It's obvious,' Wilson interrupted, leaning forward with the gleam of the fanatic in his eyes, 'that the high birth rate among the poor is a threat to our very civilization. You see, morals and criminal behaviour are linked to specific physiological types. If a person possesses these physical features – which are much more common in the lower classes – then it's likely that his behaviour will soon degenerate into the criminal or the immoral. Because both behaviour and physiological types are inherited, these people *must* be prevented from producing offspring. Then we'll have what we all want – a world with no crime and no sin.'

'I don't think it's as simple as that,' Lonsdale objected.

'I've applied such methods in the zoo. I isolate the weak and ugly animals, and only allow the strong and attractive to breed. You must have noticed that all my monkeys are powerful, handsome beasts?'

'But people don't live in monkey houses,' Lonsdale pointed out. 'How do you propose to prevent human beings from breeding – short of putting them in our already overflowing prisons?'

'Something must be done, and it *will* be done,' replied the director. 'You'll see, soon enough.' He raised his paper to indicate that the discussion was over. It most certainly was *not* closed for Lonsdale, however.

'What do you mean?' he demanded, clenching his fists to prevent himself from hauling the newspaper away from Wilson's face.

The paper was lowered impatiently. 'Exactly what I say. We can't go on as we are. Our cities can't provide for a population that continues to increase, and the lower classes – which breed at such a ghastly pace – won't sit idly by and accept the division between rich and poor forever. Disraeli gave them a vote. Gladstone and his cronies gave them education. So now they have aspirations, and if we don't control them, they'll revolt. Now, if you'll excuse me, I must bid you goodnight.'

He tossed his newspaper to one side, and stalked out. Watching him leave, Lonsdale realized that the encounter had left him with nothing he could possibly use in his article.

The visit to the Garrick Club had not only been unproductive, it had made Lonsdale late for his meeting with Cath Walker. The bells had long since finished chiming eight and the light had almost faded when he reached the Gloucester Gate entrance to Regent's Park. He headed toward the huge drinking fountain on the Broad Walk – the wide but poorly lit road that traversed the park from north to south.

As Lonsdale neared the fountain, which was illuminated by its own lamp, he slowed and became more cautious. The path that led to the bandstand, a short distance west, appeared to be deserted. He peered into the darkness, and could just see the outline of the bandstand, eerie in the deepening shadows. He had not realized how few lights there were and how dark the park could be; a lone, unarmed man was an easy target. But he told himself that his experiences in Africa – which had taught him more than a modicum of self-defence – combined with having boxed at Cambridge, made him capable of defending himself reasonably respectably.

He approached the bandstand warily. It had a conical roof supported by wrought-iron pillars and was surrounded by waist-high railings. The chairs on which the band sat were piled in the middle and covered with a tarpaulin. There was no one to be seen.

He was reaching for the railing when a rustle brought him to a standstill. Away to the right was a row of bushes and trees, a pleasant, shady area for those who did not want to sit in the sun to listen to music. Had the noise come from there? He took several steps towards it.

'Miss Walker?' he called softly. For several moments, nothing happened, then there was a dull thud behind him. He had spun round before realizing with disgust that he had fallen for an old trick: someone had thrown a stone behind him to make him turn, so he could be attacked from behind.

He had barely started to whip back around when he was knocked from his feet. He went sprawling onto the wet ground, feeling sodden grass against his face. He rolled, aware that his attacker was already bearing down on him. Against the dark grey sky, he saw something glint before it plunged down.

He squirmed sideways and kicked out, catching his assailant across the backs of his legs. There was a grunt as the man tumbled to the ground, but as Lonsdale struggled to his knees, someone else grabbed him from behind. A detached part of his mind acknowledged that Jack had been right – Cath *had* enticed him to an isolated spot where he could be robbed. Anger at his own gullibility spurred him into action.

He jabbed his elbow backwards into the groin of the man behind him, putting every last ounce of his strength into it. There was a satisfying howl of pain, and the man doubled over. The man with the knife circled, a dim silhouette in the dark. Lonsdale feinted to his left, and then followed with a right cross that connected with the man's jaw with a loud crack. The man went down as though poleaxed and lay still.

Lonsdale swung round quickly, sensing that the knifeman's accomplice had recovered and was preparing another attack, but a well-aimed rock hit him squarely on the eyebrow, making bright lights explode inside his head. He struck out blindly to deter the man from coming too close, but when his vision cleared, he did not see his assailant advancing on him but disappearing into the night. He had fled.

Lonsdale knew that the most sensible course of action would

be to leave, but he surmised that if Cath's friends were there, so was she. And he was going to find her. He ignored the still-prostrate attacker and strode to the bushes, listening intently. There was a soft sound, like a moan, then all was silent. He pushed aside an overhanging branch, but could see nothing. He grabbed a stick and began prodding in the undergrowth, aiming to flush her out.

'Cath! I know you're—'

He stopped as his foot encountered something soft. He knelt and reached out. His fingers encountered something warm and sticky, and he withdrew them with a sharp intake of breath. Blood! He struggled to light a match. It had barely flared into life before he dropped it in shock, plunging him into darkness once more. Cursing his unsteady hands, he lit another. Lying on her side in the long grass was Cath Walker. He reached out and touched her cheek with the back of his hand. It was still warm, although the gaping wound in her throat and the glassy-eyed stare confirmed she was dead.

He sat back on his heels in bewilderment. Then the flame burned his fingers and brought him to his senses. He stood and hurried back towards the place he had been attacked, aiming to lay hold of the second assailant. But the place was deserted.

Hoping to find a constable, Lonsdale ran back to the Broad Walk, as he knew the police patrolled it at night. As he skidded to a halt on the muddy gravel, a man wearing a top hat shot him a nervous look and hurried on. Lonsdale looked around wildly, then spotted the distinctive domed hat of a policeman in the distance. He tore towards him.

'There's a dead woman in the bushes near the bandstand,' he gasped, seizing the constable's arm. 'I think she's been murdered.'

The constable was young, and excitement suffused his face at the prospect of a vicious crime to explore. He whipped out his rattle and whirled it furiously to attract colleagues within hearing distance. Then he raced off towards the bandstand. Not knowing what else to do, Lonsdale followed, although his thoughts reeled and his head ached. He raised one hand to his head and felt a tender spot where the stone had hit him.

'She's dead!' yelled the policeman, when Lonsdale had directed him to the spot where the body of Cath Walker lay.

'Yes,' said Lonsdale tiredly. 'She was a—'

'Murder!' bellowed the policeman, accompanying a frantic and ineffective search of the bushes with more violent shaking of his rattle. Eventually, his colleagues began to arrive. A sergeant took control, while the youngster was posted to the Broad Walk to search for witnesses. Suddenly exhausted, Lonsdale sank down, his back against the metal railing and his chin on his knees.

'What happened, sir?' called the sergeant, swiping through the undergrowth with vigorous sweeps of his truncheon. 'A lovers' tiff that ended in violence?'

'It most certainly was not,' replied Lonsdale indignantly. 'The woman was a prostitute.'

'I didn't mean between you and her, sir,' said the sergeant placidly. 'I meant between her and him.' He pushed back a bush to reveal a second crumpled figure lying in the wet leaves. 'There are two corpses here, sir, not just one.'

Within the hour, one Inspector George Peters – a lean, spare man whose droopy moustache served to enhance his resemblance to an elderly spaniel – appeared. He ordered the area cordoned off and the search of the bushes abandoned until daylight. Then he turned to questioning Lonsdale.

Unfortunately, the attack had happened fast and a long way from the nearest light, so Lonsdale was unable to furnish much of a description of his assailants. All he could say was they were smaller than him, and had worn dark clothes.

'Really?' asked Peters coolly. 'It may have escaped your notice, Mr Lonsdale, but most men wear dark clothes. Unless they are performing in music halls.'

'I'm sorry.' Lonsdale rubbed his eyes. 'It all happened so fast. One minute I was calling the prostitute's name, and the next they were all over me.'

'They had knives, you say?'

'One had a knife. The other threw a stone.'

'And where is this stone now?' asked Peters.

Lonsdale stared at him incredulously. 'I don't know. On the ground, I imagine. Why?'

Peters shrugged, and with a shock Lonsdale realized that the inspector did not believe a word he was saying. He wondered how to convince the man. He had no desire for a sojourn in police custody until he could contact Jack. But even as he fretted, salvation came in the unlikely form of Robert Bradwell, summoned to inspect the bodies *in situ*.

'We meet again,' Bradwell said, shaking Lonsdale's hand warmly. 'Which is more than I can say about my wife. I haven't been home since I saw you and I'm due at the hospital tonight. I'll have to wait until tomorrow to face her wrath.' Without further ado, he headed for the bodies. Peters resumed his discussion with Lonsdale, who was feeling wet, cold, and miserable.

'So, let me summarize,' said Peters, after Lonsdale had related his story yet again. 'You came to meet this unfortunate – Cath Walker – in an attempt to discover more about the murder of Patrick Donovan?'

Lonsdale nodded. 'She said she'd bring someone to answer questions, so we could publish the story in *The Pall Mall Gazette* and put a stop to it.'

'I see,' said Peters. 'Put a stop to what, exactly?'

'I don't know.' Lonsdale sensed that the more he said, the less convincing he sounded. 'She claimed Donovan was at least the sixth to have died, although the only one in a fire.'

'Although remember that Donovan didn't die in the fire,' put in Bradwell helpfully, having finished his duties in the bushes. 'He died because he was strangled.'

'What?' blurted Lonsdale. 'You didn't mention this yesterday.'

'I didn't know it then. After you left, I re-examined the body, and found that Donovan's hyoid was broken, although the other neck bones were intact. That's a classic sign of strangulation – as were faint ligature marks in the charred flesh. So, Donovan was strangled, his cerebrum removed, and his skull smashed and his house burned to make his death appear accidental.'

'Wait,' said Peters, raising his hand. He turned to Lonsdale, and fixed him with stern eyes. 'I hope you're not thinking of printing this in your newspaper?'

'We never publish details of police investigations without consent,' said Lonsdale indignantly. 'We're not *The Echo*, you know.'

'Good,' said Peters. 'You may report that there's been a double murder in the park, but keep this other business to yourself. In fact, I'll make you an offer – stay silent until I have this matter in hand, and I'll give you the details twenty-four hours before I release them to any other papers.'

'Fair enough,' said Lonsdale, thinking that all he really wanted was to go home and soak away the horrors of the night in a hot bath. 'I'll let my editor know.'

'However, do not take this as permission to begin your own investigation,' said Peters. 'That would be most inadvisable.'

'Why would someone go to such lengths over a person like Donovan?' asked Bradwell. 'I can see someone making an effort to disguise the murder of an aristocrat or a politician. But Donovan was a shop assistant.'

'You're asking the wrong question,' said Lonsdale, watching two constables carry Cath away on a stretcher. 'Instead, consider why someone was so determined to have his cerebrum.'

'Good point,' agreed Bradwell, nodding. 'The fire seems to have been arranged specifically to ensure that no one noticed it had been taken.'

Peters looked from one to the other, his expression deeply sceptical. 'But who would have a penchant for . . . a cerebrum did you call it? Whoever it might be, if we believe Walker's claim that Donovan was at least the sixth victim, then he has done rather well for himself. But she was an unfortunate, and, in my experience, such women are not reliable witnesses.'

'Yet it would be rash to dismiss her, just because others in her profession have lied,' argued Bradwell. 'Donovan's death is odd, and she clearly knew something about it.'

'Perhaps,' said Peters, in the bland tone that Lonsdale began to realize was his normal manner of speaking. 'But it occurs to me that Mr Lonsdale has a very good reason for wanting us to believe someone *else* might've killed this potentially valuable witness.'

Bradwell raised his hand to silence Lonsdale's immediate protestations. 'But Lonsdale discussed her claim with me at the mortuary yesterday. He'd hardly have told me he was planning to meet her if he intended to dispatch the woman, would he?'

'Maybe not,' hedged Peters, cautiously.

'I'm telling you the truth,' Lonsdale said quietly. 'She said she'd bring proof. Have you searched her body? Perhaps she has something in her pockets that'll answer your questions.'

'Of course we searched her body – and that of her friend,' said Peters, the edge to his voice suggesting that he did not need Lonsdale to tell him how to do his work. 'There was nothing on either.' He turned to Bradwell. 'She claimed another six victims, but surely you would have noticed the absence of a cerebrum in any of your bodies, yes?'

'I would, of course. However, there is always a possibility that they went to another mortuary. Or were buried secretly. The lack of cerebra in—'

'The lack of what?' came a sharply disapproving voice from behind. 'What in the devil are you talking about?'

'It seems we may have an overlap between cases, sir,' said Peters, turning to nod a greeting; Bradwell promptly made himself scarce. 'Mr Lonsdale, may I introduce Superintendent Ramsey and his assistant, Chief Inspector Leonard.'

Ramsey nodded at Lonsdale but made no attempt to shake hands, although his assistant smiled pleasantly enough. The two officers could not have been more different. The superintendent was tall, aloof and self-important, with a thick, white moustache; his lofty demeanour and elegant dress made him appear more like a member of the House of Lords than a policeman. His assistant was short, thin, and cheerful, and wore a Norfolk jacket and the kind of old-fashioned knickerbockers that Lonsdale was surprised could still be purchased.

'Mr Lonsdale is assisting us with our enquiries,' Peters said. 'Or would you care to take charge of the case?'

'Hardly, George!' laughed Leonard. 'The superintendent has more important—'

'Every murder is important,' Ramsey interrupted pompously. 'It doesn't matter if the victim is a Member of Parliament or an unfortunate. I'll maintain a watch on it, but the case is yours, Peters. Now tell us what happened.'

Both officers listened as Peters gave them a summary. Leonard shook his head in silent compassion, while Ramsey's sallow face remained expressionless. When Peters mentioned the mutilation of Donovan, Ramsey gave a shudder of disgust.

'These damned perverts! You put one behind bars, and another appears. London is a veritable breeding ground for them. We need to nip this one in the bud, Peters. I don't want head-stealing lunatics frightening every decent soul in the city.'

And with that, he turned and strode away, not deigning to acknowledge the salutes of his constables. Leonard shot Peters an apologetic smile and made a hurried offer of help before hurrying after him.

'You may be reading too much into this, Bradwell,' said Peters when Bradwell reappeared, continuing the discussion as though the two officers had not interrupted. He pulled a pipe from his pocket and began to tamp it with tobacco. 'You're trying to intellectualize what might be a simple, brutish crime.'

'Simple?' echoed Bradwell. 'Someone went to a good deal of trouble to try to make me miss the fact that Donovan had been strangled and mutilated. It wasn't simple, Inspector, although I concur it was brutal.'

Peters was thoughtful. 'How about this for an explanation,' he began, puffing billows of white smoke into the still night air. 'Donovan was strangled over some private grudge, and his body mutilated as a bizarre form of revenge. When Walker saw Mr Lonsdale making notes at the scene of his death, she saw an opportunity to lure him here to rob him. But her accomplices decided a four-way division of spoils was less attractive than a two-way split, and killed her and her friend. Mr Lonsdale then fought off the remaining two.'

It was a plausible scenario, and Lonsdale could not deny that he had questioned her motives himself. He did not reply, so Peters began to issue orders to his men, instructing them to find out where she had lived and the identity of her companion. While respectable London would soon be retiring to bed, another side of the city would just be waking. It was among them that Peters would concentrate his search.

'You can give your formal statement tomorrow, Mr Lonsdale,' he said. 'Tonight, I'd rather have my men out on the streets looking for the killers.'

'One of the policemen who attended the fire at Donovan's house knew Cath Walker,' said Lonsdale helpfully. 'He might know where she lived.'

'There are hundreds of police officers in London,' said Peters dryly. 'I don't suppose you could furnish me with a name?'

'No, but I can tell you the number he wore on his collar.'

'Yes?' Peters looked marginally impressed.

'Six-nine-six-D.'

Peters stared at him. 'Are you sure?' he asked eventually.

'Yes, of course,' said Lonsdale, puzzled. 'Why?'

'Police Constable Cyril Iverson, number six-nine-six-D, is no longer with the force,' replied Peters. 'He disappeared six months ago, while on duty, and hasn't been seen since. Well, not by us at least. His antics have certainly been reported by a number of other people, however.'

THREE

T he background buzz of conversation in the Queen's Arms and the warm, slightly humid feel of too many people crammed into one room were making Lonsdale drowsy. He leaned back and gazed up at the ceiling, noting it was stained from decades of smoke. The floor was not much better. What had been a handsome red and gold carpet was dulled where booted feet had tracked the muck of the streets across it. The walls, on the other hand, were a rich brown pine boarding, which looked new. Cigar and pipe smoke enveloped all in a thick, hazy pall.

He had already drunk more than was wise, and it proved difficult to bring his attention back to the discussion. It had been Bradwell's suggestion to continue their conversation in the nearby tavern. Peters had readily agreed, although Lonsdale suspected it was only in the hope of gaining more information. Of course, Lonsdale's motive was the same – he wanted the opportunity to quiz Peters. And Bradwell? Lonsdale had a suspicion that he was eager to avoid his wife.

All the private bars – the screened-off booths in which patrons had some seclusion – had been full, so the three men had taken a table in a corner of the public bar, surrounded by omnibus drivers, shopkeepers, and labourers.

'I told you Iverson was ill months ago,' said Bradwell, as Lonsdale mentally re-entered the conversation. 'I spoke to his wife, and she told me he often talked about suicide. The poor man is deranged.'

Lonsdale took another sip of the bad port that Bradwell had bought him. 'So, you think Iverson may have killed Donovan – then dispatched Cath Walker and her companion?'

'There's no evidence to say so,' replied Peters, although it was clear he considered it a possibility.

'He definitely knew her,' said Lonsdale. 'He addressed her by name and asked if she was soliciting. She ran away; I assumed from a prostitute's natural fear of the police.'

'Fear?' snorted Peters. 'If that were true, our job would be a damned sight easier! These women don't fear us, Mr Lonsdale. Distrust, perhaps. Loathe, certainly. But fear – no. What can a policeman do other than lock a prostitute up for a few nights in a place where she'll be warm and fed?'

'And that's more than most can expect on the streets,' put in Bradwell. 'A policeman's lot might not be a happy one, but a whore's is worse.'

'Cath was afraid,' said Lonsdale firmly. 'She almost fell over in her haste to escape.'

'So describe Iverson,' ordered Peters. 'We need to be sure the man you saw was not just someone wearing a uniform bought cheap in a tavern.

Lonsdale considered carefully before replying. 'He was forty to forty-five years old, and had a large blackish-grey moustache that needed trimming. He had a beer-drinker's paunch and the mottled skin of a man who likes spirits. He had dark eyes that were watery, and a scar that ran into one eyebrow.'

'You're observant,' remarked Peters. 'And you've a good memory for details.'

'I met a good many people of low integrity while I was in the Colonial Service,' said Lonsdale, 'many of them diplomats. It was as important for me to remember their faces as it is for you to know those of thieves and robbers.'

Peters gave what was almost a smile. His moustache twitched and some teeth made a fleeting appearance beneath it.

'Iverson's appearance is very distinctive with that scar,' said Bradwell, snapping his fingers to attract the attention of a tap-boy and order more drinks. 'That's why I'm surprised he hasn't been caught yet. Would you be offended if I suggested that some of your men might be protecting him, Inspector?'

Peters looked at Lonsdale. 'Iverson's scar was earned when he saved another officer from a partially collapsed railway tunnel. Policemen are a loyal breed, and it goes against the grain to betray each other, but Iverson's case is different. We all know he's ill, and I don't think anyone would help him stay free when he should be in a hospital.'

'What do you mean by "ill" exactly?' asked Lonsdale.

Peters answered quickly, as though he did not want Bradwell revealing too much. 'Policemen see some dreadful sights, and he isn't the first to crack under the strain.'

'But Iverson's case is more than just cracking under the strain, isn't it?' fished Lonsdale. 'Earlier, you didn't seem surprised when I told you he'd spoken to Cath, or that he was at the scene of Donovan's murder.'

'His presence in Wyndham Street doesn't mean he killed Donovan,' said Peters.

'Well, I can tell you that he didn't have a cerebrum with him when we spoke,' said Lonsdale, then reconsidered. 'Unless it was in his pocket.'

'The cerebrum is fragile,' said Bradwell. 'Ramming it into a pocket would ruin it.'

'Would that matter?' asked Lonsdale. 'Perhaps he didn't intend to keep it, and the excitement lay in its removal.'

Peters toyed with his glass of four-ale, then raised it to his lips and drained the remainder, standing to leave as he did so.

'I must return to the station,' he said. He nodded his thanks to Bradwell for the drinks, and then fixed Lonsdale with a stern eye. 'You'll remember our agreement? No word of this until I say?'

Lonsdale nodded.

Peters sighed. 'You'd think there was more than enough crime and tragedy in this city to satisfy the press, but they always want more. Take a walk in Whitechapel or Spitalfields, Mr Lonsdale. You'll see enough to keep your newspaper in tales of scandal, vice, and wickedness for a decade.'

'He's a cheery soul,' remarked Lonsdale, watching the inspector thread his way through the crowded bar.

'But a fine detective,' said Bradwell. 'Don't be fooled by that plodding façade. Had he thought you were lying, you'd be in his cells now. I doubt it'll be too long before your audience will be reading this story; if anyone can get to the bottom of it, Peters can.'

'I assume Cath died from the wound to her throat?' asked Lonsdale, deciding he had better collect some facts if Peters was as good as Bradwell claimed.

'There was a single slash to her neck, severing the jugular vein and carotid artery on the left side, and slicing through the trachea,' said Bradwell.

'Is that a common way to kill?'

'Fairly,' said the surgeon. 'Cutting a throat is easy and takes very little power. All too often the police assume a killer is male because of its violent nature, but I'm sure a good many are women.'

'What about a theft of a cerebrum?' asked Lonsdale. 'Was that committed by a man or woman? I suppose it requires no great strength either.'

'On the contrary, the brain is surrounded by a protective layer of bone, and sawing through it is hard work.'

'Did Cath's companion die from knife wounds as well?' asked Lonsdale as they made their way outside, to stand with their hands in their pockets in the cold night.

'No,' said Bradwell. 'He was probably poisoned with arsenic.'

Lonsdale stared at him in astonishment. A crowd of drunken dockers staggered past, cheering and laughing. Behind them were three women with hard, calculating eyes, doggedly keeping pace with men who would soon be in no position to decline an offer of their services. One gave Lonsdale and Bradwell a speculative glance, but evidently decided the pickings would be better with the rowdy wharfmen.

'Arsenic? But that makes no sense!'

'Yet it's true, because the body displayed all the characteristic signs of arsenic poisoning, and I recognized the smell of it in his mouth.'

'But how, for God's sake?'

Bradwell shrugged. 'As I told you before, I present the facts to the police and leave them to do the speculating.' He glanced at his watch. 'I'm taking a hansom to Bart's Hospital. I'd offer you a lift, but I doubt you live Clerkenwell way.'

'Other direction.' Lonsdale held out his hand to the doctor. 'Let's hope that the next time we meet will be in more pleasant circumstances.'

'I doubt it,' sighed Bradwell. 'I seldom meet anyone in pleasant circumstances.'

The next morning, Lonsdale woke with a bruise over one eye and a stiff shoulder to remind him of the previous night's events. He left before Jack could see it, and took a cab to Marylebone Lane police station, where he dictated his statement to a sergeant with the largest handlebar moustache he had ever seen. He then walked briskly to *The PMG*'s offices, ascending the rickety wooden staircase to the first floor in the hope of finding Stead. There was a thick cloud of dust outside the reporters' office, and voices were raised in protest. Intrigued, Lonsdale poked his head around the door.

The formidable Hulda Friederichs stood on a stool in the centre of the room armed with a rag tied to a long stick. She was flailing at the ribbons of cobwebs that hung like stalactites from the ceiling, bringing down flakes of ancient brown paint as she did so. Her colleagues cried their objections, but Hulda was not a woman to be deterred by mere words. And it would be a brave man who attempted to use force.

Watching from a safe distance, arms folded and eyes flashing with amusement, was Stead. He saw Lonsdale, and his merriment faded. Leaving the chaos, he took Lonsdale by the elbow and led him to his own office, closing the door behind them.

'What happened to your eye?' he asked.

'My meeting with Cath Walker,' explained Lonsdale, and quickly described what had happened.

Stead tugged at his bushy beard. 'I had a visit this morning from a Chief Inspector Leonard. Nice fellow. He told me that you had stumbled across more murders. Three in two days, Lonsdale! That's remarkable by anyone's standards.'

'I think Cath and her companion were dispatched to prevent them telling me about Donovan's death,' said Lonsdale, and began to outline his theories. Stead listened, his vivid blue eyes never leaving his reporter's face. When Lonsdale finished, the assistant editor scrubbed at his luxurious beard, and then sprang to his feet, to pace back and forth in front of the mantelpiece.

'*The PMG* always complies with the wishes of the police in the interests of justice,' he said, tossing an egg from hand to hand. 'I told Leonard that we'll go no further than a simple statement saying two people were murdered in Regent's Park last night. He assures me that the park murders and the death by fire are unrelated.'

'But they—'

Stead raised a finger to quell Lonsdale's objections, but the reporter started again.

'But Cath said—'

Seeing the authoritative finger was not going to work, Stead threw Lonsdale the egg, forcing him to scramble to catch it before it smashed on the carpet. It was, Lonsdale supposed as he juggled with it, a novel way to shut someone up.

'It matters not one iota what you think, as nothing will be printed until the case is closed. Leonard promised to pass us all the details a day before releasing them to the rest of the press. Now, a day might be an eternity in journalism, but it isn't long to write a decently researched article containing interviews with the people involved.'

Lonsdale saw immediately what Stead was suggesting. He opened his mouth to speak, but Stead had another egg and it was already sailing towards the grimy glass cupboard on Lonsdale's left. Lonsdale's hand shot out, and the brown missile slapped into his palm.

'Talk to Donovan's neighbours,' ordered Stead. 'Find out what kind of man he was, and discover why anyone should want to kill him. Then go south of the river, and see about this murdered girl.'

'Girl?' asked Lonsdale. 'You mean Cath, the prostitute?'

Stead fixed him with a hard stare. 'She was a girl –
twenty-three years old, forced to sell the one commodity that
someone is always willing to buy, just to have a four-pence bed
for the night.'

'How do you know how old she was?' asked Lonsdale,
recalling that Stead had an unwavering compassion for prostitutes, and often used *The PMG* to highlight their miseries to
the newspaper's readers. 'Because she looked a lot more than
twenty-three.'

'If so, that's more a reflection on our society than on her,'
said Stead. 'But we're wasting time. I managed to squeeze from
a friend in Scotland Yard that she lived in Bermondsey. Go
there – find out about her and the man who died with her.
Learning his name would be a start.'

'So you believe me – that Donovan's death and the murders
in the park are connected?' asked Lonsdale, astonished that
Stead was prepared to let him investigate when the police had
asked for discretion.

'I do,' said Stead. 'Poor Miss Walker and her friend died
trying to tell you about Donovan, so you are under a moral
obligation to ensure that they didn't die in vain. Moreover, it
is significant that this missing policeman, Iverson, was at the
scene of the fire, and that she was terrified of him. He might
be at the heart of the whole affair.'

'He might.'

'Then off you go,' said Stead, selecting a third egg from a
box on his desk and tossing it so high in the air that it almost
hit the ceiling. He turned and caught the egg behind his back.
'Take Hulda with you.'

'Friederichs?' blurted Lonsdale. 'But she's—'

'A woman?' asked Stead, raising quixotic eyebrows. 'Exactly!
You can't let it be known that you're a reporter, or you'll have
people selling you all kinds of lies for the price of a beer. Hulda
will make a splendid foil. After all, who'd imagine that we'd
send a female journalist into the roughest areas of London?
Besides, she needs the experience.'

'Very well,' said Lonsdale reluctantly.

'But before you go, I want the zoo story. Go, go! You have
not a moment to lose!'

In reply, Lonsdale lobbed both eggs he was holding at Stead, who, as he had anticipated, made no attempt to catch them.

'Hard-boiled,' grinned Stead.

Completing the article on the Zoological Gardens was not easy when the Prussian Governess leaned over his shoulder every five minutes to see if he had finished. When she was not demanding to know if he was writing a novel, she was swiping at those cobwebs she had missed earlier. Sensibly, the other reporters had made themselves scarce, Voules trailing an especially repellent, dust-enriched cobweb that everyone noticed, but no one mentioned. Eventually, the article was written, approved, and sent to the compositors on the top floor.

'At last!' exclaimed Hulda, wiping her hands on a manly handkerchief. 'Are you ready now, or do you want to write about the decline of the barter system in rural Bechuanaland? Stead told me you know it well.'

'What an excellent idea!' exclaimed Lonsdale, sitting down again and reaching for his pen. 'It will only take an hour or two.'

She gaped in dismay until Lonsdale flung his pen down and made for the door, laughing at her for being so gullible.

He led the way out of the building and walked towards the Strand, suddenly struck by the dismal greyness of London compared to the vivid wonders of Africa. In what, when he was assigned there, had been known as the West African Settlements, he had seen mounds of red, green, and orange fruits piled on brightly coloured rugs and sold by women in clothes the colours of rainbows. By contrast, the apples and potatoes on the street barrows of London had a tired, wizened look, and the vendors' faces were pinched grey with cold above their filthy aprons.

'I suggest we visit Donovan's neighbours first,' he said. 'We can walk there in forty minutes. Or take a hansom – you choose.'

Hulda put her hands on her hips. 'We could never manage that distance in forty minutes! Unless we ran, which is not something I feel inclined to do. Of course we shall take a cab.'

'A cab it is then,' muttered Lonsdale, flagging one down.

Appointing Hulda had not been a popular decision among

the staff of *The PMG* – not because she was a woman, but because she was Hulda. She was aggressive, spoke her mind without considering the consequences, and was of the opinion that she was a better journalist than most of her associates. She was not someone Lonsdale would have chosen to work with, but no one went against Stead's specific instructions.

He glanced at her out of the corner of his eye. She was pretty, but severe looking. Her thick fair hair was scraped austerely back from her face in a neat, no-nonsense bun. Her blue eyes were icy, but her complexion was fresh and clear. She held herself so erect that she looked down her nose at people, even those taller than her, and her clothes were immaculate. She had not been nicknamed 'the Prussian Governess' for nothing.

The cab was cramped once Hulda had her floor-length skirt, pelisse, and gable bonnet wedged in, leaving Lonsdale barely enough room to sit. Even so, he received a withering look as she freed her skirt from underneath him with an irritable tug.

'Why are we going to Wyndham Street first?' she asked. 'Why not go straight to Bermondsey? That is where the real answers lie.'

'Because of the time,' explained Lonsdale, cramped and uncomfortable in the small space she had allotted him. 'No self-respecting prostitute will be up at eleven o'clock on a Saturday morning.'

'Why are *you* familiar with the daily routines of whores?' asked Hulda, regarding him with a disconcertingly candid gaze. 'Are you a customer?'

It was not a question a decent lady would ask, and for a moment Lonsdale was at a loss as to how to respond. He was saved from a reply – and he suspected that a denial or an affirmation would meet with equal disapproval – by the horse stumbling in a pothole.

'Watch where you're going!' yelled Hulda in stentorian tones to the driver. 'We are not at Ascot, you know!'

Lonsdale cringed, hoping the driver would not be rash enough to answer back, sure that if he did an altercation would follow. Hurriedly, he resumed the conversation.

'But Wyndham Street is solidly respectable. Its residents will be up and awake.'

'Yes, but out working,' Hulda pointed out. 'Not lounging about at home.'

'The men perhaps, but we want to speak to their wives – people who were at home when Donovan's house caught on fire.'

Hulda nodded. 'So, how shall we approach them? Honestly, making it clear we're reporters?'

'Stead said we'd have more luck if we didn't. I noticed that there was a house for rent in Wyndham Street. Across the street and down a bit from Donovan's. We could pose as a married couple considering a move to the area.'

'You mean pretend we're married to *each other*?' asked Hulda, aghast. 'Me to you?'

'I doubt we'd get far if we pretended to be married to other people,' said Lonsdale dryly. 'It would offend their morals if I claimed to be a married man intending to move in with someone else's wife.'

'All right then,' conceded Hulda reluctantly. 'What occupation will you claim? You're too untidy to be a clerk, and your clothes are too good for you to be a menial. How about a glass-blower?'

'We should stick to what we know,' said Lonsdale, wondering how she had come up with such a bizarre choice. 'How about an accountant at the zoo? And you can be a ticket vendor at the Haymarket Theatre.'

'Very well,' agreed Hulda. 'Are you sure they won't remember you?'

'They probably will, but why shouldn't I have been looking for a suitable house alone, before bringing my wife to see it?'

'You'll have to remember to call me Hulda, though. Do you have a match, by any chance?'

'Why?'

'Why do you think?' She took a La Jurista cigar from her bag, waggled her fingers for the matches, and lit up. Acrid smoke began to billow round Lonsdale. He leaned forward, pretending to look at houses, in the vain hope of escaping the stench.

'Please don't ask for a light or a glass of brandy if any witnesses invite us into their homes,' he warned. 'I don't want to miss out on information because you like to smoke and drink.'

'Don't be so fastidious!' she said testily. 'Many women smoke and drink these days.'

'Not the ones who live in Wyndham Street. While we're there, just pretend to be a normal person.'

'But I'm not a normal person,' objected Hulda. 'I'm a very superior person.'

'Your name,' said Lonsdale curiously. 'Is it really Prussian?'

'It is,' replied Hulda proudly. 'I was born in Ronsdorf in Rhenish Prussia. My grandfather once told my mother that unless all of her children were christened with Prussian names, he would exclude her from his will.'

'And did "Hulda" satisfy him?'

'You mean did he leave her an inheritance? Yes, he did, although what was left once his debts had been paid was not a great deal. My family's financial position was one reason I sought a profession in which I could rise to the top, as I am currently doing.'

Lonsdale was spared from having to reply because they were travelling down Crawford Street. He banged on the roof to tell the driver to stop. Hulda regarded him askance.

'We're not there yet. What are you doing?'

'A ticket vendor and an accountant are hardly likely to arrive in a hansom when there's a perfectly good omnibus service,' he said. 'We don't want people to be suspicious before we begin. Come on. It's not far.'

They walked to the blackened ruins of Donovan's house. Most of its roof had collapsed, exposing the timbers beneath. The tiny garden at the front was full of broken glass and soggy, burnt wood. The door was charred, but still firmly closed.

'I want to look at the back of the house,' said Lonsdale, leading the way to the alley. He considered taking Hulda's arm, as a man might do with his wife, but was afraid she would bludgeon him with the hefty bag she carried.

The rear door lay in the back garden, the freshly splintered wood showing where the firemen had smashed it with their axes to enter. Lonsdale crouched next to it and inspected the lock. It was still intact, with the metal bar protruding from it, while the doorframe hosted an impressive gash where the bar had torn through the wood. So, he thought, it had been locked when the firemen had forced their way in.

Glass and cinders crunched under his feet as he walked inside. The walls were expanses of scorched wood and hanging timbers, while the stairs had been burned away completely, and the upstairs rooms had collapsed downwards in heaps of blackened rubble. Dark grey clouds were visible between the remaining roof joists. Lonsdale's foot went clear through a floorboard in the hall, forcing him to grab at the remains of a banister to prevent him from plunging to the cellar below.

'There's nothing to see,' said Hulda, surveying the damage from the door. 'Come out; it isn't safe. The roof will go at any minute.'

'I need to examine the front door,' said Lonsdale, extricating his foot and resuming his journey. 'Stay there.'

When he reached the door, he was not surprised that Donovan's neighbours had been unable to break through, as a heavy chest had been placed across it. The box had been opened by looters, but the unburned floor underneath when he tugged it away suggested he was the first to move it since the fire.

So either Donovan had put it there after raising the alarm, or someone else had done so with the intention of preventing anyone from trying to rescue him. The first solution made no sense. The second, along with the rear door being secured, fitted Lonsdale's suspicion that someone had gone to a good deal of trouble to hide the fact that Donovan's death was no accident.

'Lonsdale!' yelled Hulda suddenly as there was a groan of tearing wood. 'Look out!'

Lonsdale could only cringe against the wall with his arms over his head as several roof tiles slipped from one of the sagging rafters and hit the ground with ear-shattering explosions. Then the beam itself fell, thumping down next to him in a cloud of choking, black dust. Before anything else came down, he scrambled over the beam and aimed for the back door. There was another creak, directly above. Instinctively, he glanced up, and then fell heavily as his foot caught in the hole he had made on his way inside.

The creak grew louder, and Lonsdale struggled to stand, but his foot had snagged on the jagged wood and he could not pull it free. Then strong hands grabbed his collar, the charred floor-boards flew away from his foot, and he was hauled forward. There was an almighty crash as more of the roof collapsed, right where he had been lying, and for a few moments he could see nothing but swirling ash and cinders. The hand tightened on his collar, and he was assisted, none too gently, into the garden. He bent, hands on knees, as he struggled to clear his lungs of the suffocating dust.

'I warned you,' said Hulda tartly, relinquishing her hold and brushing herself down. 'I told you it wasn't safe, and you put me in danger by forcing me to come to your rescue.'

'Not so!' he wheezed. 'I told you to stay outside.'

'Ungrateful wretch! Next time, I'll just stand and watch! You could at least say thank you.'

'Thank you,' said Lonsdale, realizing he had been ungracious. 'I mean it.'

She sniffed to acknowledge his capitulation, and tried to brush some of the ash from his clothes. She was still dusty herself, but to reciprocate was more than his life was worth. When she deemed him presentable, they made their way to the front of the house.

'You do realize we are being watched,' she whispered.

'Where?'

'Number twenty-seven,' said Hulda. 'And now she's coming out.'

'What are you doing?' demanded a harsh female voice. 'There's nothing left to steal. This is a respectable neighbour-hood, so why don't you leave us alone? Oh, it's you.'

It was the wife of the railway guard whom Lonsdale had met on the day of the fire. He recalled her name was Mrs North. He smiled and tipped his hat, while she continued to regard him suspiciously.

'We haven't come to loot,' he explained. 'My wife and I are thinking of moving into number thirty-five. I came the day before yesterday to look around the area. I'm an accountant you see – and I need to be near my work at the zoo.'

The woman's manner softened somewhat, although her eyes

remained wary. 'I remember – I suppose you saw more than you bargained for, then?'

'You could say that,' agreed Lonsdale. 'And my wife is anxious. Was it an accident, do you think, this poor gentleman's death?'

'Of course it was an accident!' exclaimed Mrs North. 'What else could it have been? This is a respectable . . .'

She stopped abruptly when Hulda astonished her and Lonsdale alike by giving a groan and pressing her hand to her stomach.

'It's the baby,' she whispered, in a remarkable change to the local accent, while giving Mrs North a weak little smile.

Horrified, Lonsdale took a step away.

'For heaven's sake!' exclaimed Mrs North, rushing to Hulda's side. 'Don't duck away from her like a cornered rat! Help her into my house.'

'I couldn't possibly impose . . .' said Hulda weakly.

'Nonsense,' declared Mrs North. 'I'll put the kettle on. Everyone feels better after a cup of tea.'

'Yes,' whispered Hulda with pathetic gratitude. 'I think you're right.'

'Bring her inside,' instructed Mrs North, treating Lonsdale to an admonishing glower. 'You should be ashamed of yourself, dragging her here when she should be at home with her feet up.'

Lonsdale slipped a cautious hand under Hulda's elbow, and escorted her into Mrs North's best room, a cluttered parlour at the front of the house. The wallpaper had a dark red floral design on a chocolate background, and the floorboards were polished to a treacherous shine. An enormous pair of brass candlesticks dominated the fireplace, and every available inch of space was crammed with knick-knacks and silver-framed sepia photographs.

Once Hulda had been settled on a lumpy horsehair sofa, and furnished with a plate of Bath Oliver biscuits and a cup of tea, Lonsdale tried to restart the conversation.

'You said the other day that Mr Donovan raised the alarm about the fire, then ran back inside his house,' he began, intending to ask whether she had noticed any visitors before his final appearance.

Mrs North's lips pursed in annoyance. 'I've already told you all I know about poor Mr Donovan. It isn't seemly to dwell on it, and I strongly disapprove—'

Again, the intended tirade was interrupted by a timely groan from Hulda.

'Men!' snapped Mrs North, pouring her more tea and glowering at Lonsdale. 'Your poor wife is carrying your child, and you're more concerned with gossip than in her well-being. You don't deserve her.'

'That's certainly true,' muttered Lonsdale.

'I'm much better now, Mrs North,' said Hulda, with the smile of a martyr. 'And my husband doesn't mean to be callous – he's just concerned that we choose the right house, so our child can grow up with respectable, God-fearing folk.'

'Well, you couldn't choose better than Wyndham Street,' averred Mrs North. 'Bert Evans next door is a clerk for the Board of Works, and earns thirty-five shillings a week, while his daughter brings home another twelve as a waitress in the Royal Hotel. And then there's my Harry. He makes almost thirty-three shillings, while my oldest boy earns ten as an apprentice railwayman, even though he's only fifteen.'

She paused to acknowledge the murmured approvals of her two guests, then continued.

'Mr Donovan worked in Salmon and Eden, the gentleman's outfitters, and must have been earning at least forty shillings a week. More, probably.' Her voice dropped reverently, and Lonsdale could see she was deeply impressed by such heady finances.

'Was he a drinking man?' asked Lonsdale.

Mrs North's eyes widened in shock. 'No! What gave you that idea?'

'You did,' replied Lonsdale, unruffled. 'Two days ago, when you said he seemed intoxicated when he ran into the street shouting.'

'Did I?' she asked, frowning. 'Perhaps I did. He sounded different, you see.'

'Different in what way?'

She gave a shrug. 'Hoarse – although I suppose that could have been the smoke. I don't know why I said he'd been drinking. He'd never done it before.'

'Was he married?' asked Hulda, sipping her tea.

'No,' said Mrs North. 'He wasn't the type. Don't get me wrong – there were few gentlemen as respectable – but he was shy.'

At that moment, there was a tap on the door, and the sound of someone entering the house.

'That's Molly Evans from next door, come to find out who I'm entertaining,' said Mrs North. 'We're all good friends here – always in and out of each other's houses. In a neighbourly way, of course.'

'Except Mr Donovan,' said Hulda, regarding Mrs North with wide, innocent eyes. 'Because he was shy.'

'Front parlour, Molly,' called Mrs North, not happy at being caught in an inconsistency.

Lonsdale glimpsed Molly Evans smoothing her hair down in front of the hall mirror, before entering Mrs North's parlour.

'This nice couple are thinking of moving into number thirty-five,' explained Mrs North. 'So I've been telling them all about us.'

'Are they?' asked Molly, surprised. 'The agent told my Bert just yesterday that it's been let to a family from Wales – a Mr and Mrs Rhys.'

Mrs North's eyes narrowed in suspicion, and Lonsdale wondered whether she would demand recompense for all the biscuits Hulda had scoffed.

'Yes, but the agent prefers us,' said Hulda with remarkable aplomb, reaching for another Bath Oliver. 'Because of our references – from the vicar of St Alfrege's and Sir William Stead, my husband's employer.'

'A vicar, and a knight of the realm!' breathed Mrs North.

Hulda nodded. 'Whereas Mr Rhys is a rag-and-bone collector, and only earns fifteen shillings a week. The agent said he was afraid he'd get behind with the rent.'

'A rag-and-bone man?' echoed Molly aghast. She exchanged a look of horror with Mrs North.

'He plans to run his business from behind the house,' continued Hulda relentlessly. 'He has three ponies, two carts, and three of his four sons work for him. All want to move here with him.'

'Four sons?'

'And five daughters, two of whom are unmarried with children. Moreover, one of the sons has a police record. What was his crime, Alec? Was it robbery with violence or arson?'

'Is there any more tea?' asked Lonsdale, to stem Hulda's flow of lies. The two women ignored him and gaped at Hulda. Molly was positively white.

'You must tell the agent the people on the street favour you,' gulped Mrs North. 'You won't find a better neighbourhood in London. And with the exception of this dreadful business with Mr Donovan, the police have never been here.'

'Poor Mr Donovan,' said Molly. 'He was such an upstanding gentleman. He polished the church brass every Saturday afternoon.'

'He was too set in his ways to marry,' said Mrs North, to ensure that her guests read nothing untoward in the fact that Donovan was a bachelor. 'But then, he looked after his father until the old man passed away last year.'

'Did he have no other relations?' asked Hulda.

'None,' replied Mrs North. 'After his father died, he was quite alone. I said he could come over for tea any time he felt lonely. Of course, he never did.'

'He loved his work,' put in Molly. 'He left every morning at seven-thirty, and was never back before nine. Other than church, his only pastimes were books and walks in the park.'

'It seems a terrible thing to happen to such an upright, Christian man,' went on Mrs North. 'I'd give anything to live Thursday over again, and prevent him from running back into his house.'

'I doubt you could have stopped him,' said Lonsdale kindly. 'But we mustn't keep you. You've been very kind.'

'Please consider number thirty-five,' begged Mrs North, reluctant to let them go without some assurance that they would deliver her neighbourhood from the sinister presence of the ominous Rhys family. 'I can't stress enough how respectable we are.'

'You can't let Mr Donovan's accident put you off,' added Molly. 'It was the chimney sweep's fault, after all.'

'The sweep?' asked Hulda, while Lonsdale recalled that Mrs North had mentioned the chimney being cleaned before.

'The firemen said the flue was blocked, and that's how the blaze started,' explained Mrs North. 'Kendal's getting too old. He left a brush up the chimney, and that was that.'

'I shan't have him again,' said Molly firmly.

'Nor will I,' declared Mrs North.

'That poor woman,' said Lonsdale as they walked away, Hulda remembering to take his arm as a pregnant wife might do. 'She's appalled at the prospect of having your rag-and-bone man in her street.'

'Serves her right for being such a self-righteous bigot,' said Hulda, chin in the air and regular accent firmly back in place. 'What makes her think she's better than a man who earns only fifteen shillings?'

'But now she'll race off to the agent, and learn you've spun her all manner of lies. And we won't be able to question her again. How could you prey on someone's kindness like that, pretending to be pregnant and eating all her biscuits?'

'Because if I hadn't, she wouldn't have given us the time of day,' replied Hulda, snatching her arm back as they rounded the corner. 'Your questioning was clumsy, and she had taken a dislike to you before we'd even started.'

'But surely you didn't have to be quite so inventive?'

'Molly was about to reveal us as a pair of frauds,' said Hulda unrepentantly. 'I saved the day *and* inveigled all the information we needed. And the disguise was *your* idea, so don't get at me for embellishing the theme. You'd better lose those scruples if you want to succeed at *The PMG*. You won't do it by being prissy and squeamish.'

'We can bicker later,' said Lonsdale, aware that people were looking at them, 'but if we want to speak to anyone else, we must do it now, before Mrs North finds out we're imposters. Can you bring yourself to act the part of a respectable woman again?'

Seldom had Lonsdale been treated to a look of greater malevolence than that with which Hulda favoured him. He was grateful she was not armed, or there might have been another murder in Wyndham Street.

With Hulda coldly rigid at his side, they spoke to several

other neighbours, but none had anything more to add. All said kind things about Donovan, but no one had really known him. Furthermore, there was nothing in his life that warranted being singled out for such a brutal attack. If he had been fond of the taverns, or had gambled, Lonsdale would have known how to proceed, but there was nothing.

'I can only see one curious thing in what we've been told,' he said to Hulda later, as they sat in a dingy chophouse at the Great Western Railway Terminus. She was the only woman present and was attracting the interested gazes of several men. Lonsdale was considerably more uneasy about it than Hulda, who treated the admiring glances with contemptuous indifference, concentrating instead on cleaning the greasy cutlery with a scrupulously white lace handkerchief.

'Me, too,' she said. 'Salmon and Eden must have closed by eight o'clock, so why did Donovan never reach home until after nine?'

'No,' said Lonsdale, who had not thought of this. 'I mean, yes. He lived alone, so perhaps he ate out before going home so he wouldn't have to cook. But, I was thinking about something else. Everybody has told us that he left for work every morning at half-past seven. But he died mid-morning on a Thursday. Why was he at home when he should have been at Salmon and Eden?'

'By God, you're right!' exclaimed Hulda, slamming her hand on the table. 'That *is* good thinking, Lonsdale. How could I have missed something so obvious?'

'We should visit his shop,' said Lonsdale, choosing to ignore her condescension. 'We can ask his colleagues why he stayed at home – if he took a day off or was ill.'

'Right,' said Hulda, downing half a glass of stout at an impressive rate, and leaping to her feet. 'Off we go, then. Do you know where it is?'

'Near Oxford Street. But we should go to the office first to tell Stead what we're doing. And can we finish the chops?'

'No,' said Hulda briskly. 'I suppose we should see Stead, but there is another lesson you should learn – you will never make a good reporter if you stop to eat.'

* * *

Had Hulda known what was awaiting them at Northumberland Street, she would have been less willing to return there. The moment they looked through Stead's doorway it was apparent that all was not well.

'Ah, my happily married couple,' he said in subdued tones. 'I hope you've solved your crime, because you may not have another opportunity.'

Lonsdale raised his eyebrows questioningly, while Hulda glowered in a way that would have been intimidating to most people.

'We're on our way to conduct more interviews,' she said firmly. 'Shall we tell you what we learned at Wyndham Street?'

'Yes, and Mr Morley will be interested, too,' said Stead. 'He returned today, rather earlier than expected. You know he's been at home, writing a biography of Richard Cobden—'

'Who?' demanded Hulda.

Lonsdale and Stead regarded each other uncertainly. 'The economist and politician who helped found the Anti-Corn Law League,' said Lonsdale. 'One of the most influential figures of his age.'

'He sounds tedious in the extreme,' declared Hulda. 'I'm not surprised Morley has given up.'

'Well the issue of the moment is not his book, but this,' said Stead, handing Lonsdale a piece of stationery, which, in Morley's firm hand, read:

> *My dear Stead,*
> *Your editorial of last night turned my hair grey. In fact, the entire first six pages were crammed with stories that strike me as downright unseemly, and smack of – dare I say – sensationalism. I find that I must return to once again put a chilly frost on your exuberance.*

Hulda glowered anew. 'But sensational stories sell news-papers. Unlike biographies of economists.'

'I know,' said Stead soberly. 'But Mr Morley is the editor, and if he doesn't like our work, we must change what we do. And I'm afraid that he doesn't want you to look into the Donovan case. Unfortunately, no power on Earth will interest him in such matters – he says they "only excite the British tomfool". He told me to take you to him the moment you arrived.'

He led the way to Morley's office, which was lit by a six-paned window on each side of his writing table. In front of a fireplace were three chairs on what had once been a fine Oriental carpet, before ages of coal cinders had leached it of colour. The austere, stern editor signalled for them to sit, while he remained at his desk, dressed in a single-breasted, navy-blue suit with a crisp white shirt and spotted necktie, his thinning grey hair combed neatly backwards. His expression, as always, was grave and dignified.

'Mr Stead told me what you've been doing,' he began coolly. 'I don't believe such matters should occupy you when there are major issues requiring analysis and discussion.'

Lonsdale heard Hulda stifle a sigh. For Morley, 'major issues' meant the Irish situation, for which he owned a deep and abiding fascination.

'Superintendent Ramsey contacted me,' Morley continued. 'He says the Donovan business is too sensitive to be released, and has asked us to withhold publication.'

'I've already assured the police of our discretion,' said Lonsdale, irked that his word as a gentleman seemed to be in question.

'Ramsey gave two reasons for his request, both reasonable,' Morley went on. 'First, he wishes to avoid alarming the public. Do not forget the garrotting murders of 1862, which caused widespread panic.'

'There are few who will forget those,' sighed Stead. 'It was later claimed that the press and police created such a sense of unease that it discouraged people from coming forward with evidence, helping the murderer escape justice.'

'Second, he feels that publishing details will hinder the course of justice. The police can determine guilt or innocence on the basis of what the suspect knows about the crime, but if everything is public, there's a danger that the wrong man might be convicted.'

'So we forget about the murder?' asked Lonsdale, thinking about Stead's contention that *The PMG* was under a moral obligation to investigate because Cath had died for it.

'We do,' nodded Morley. 'We leave it to the police. Superintendent Ramsey has promised to keep us informed of progress, although whether we will ever cover such a sordid affair is debatable.'

'But what happens if the police fail?' demanded Hulda, standing and putting her hands on her hips. 'Do we forget about justice for Walker? And what if the police take months to solve it? No one will be interested in a crime that happened in the dim and distant past.'

The question she did not ask, but that was clear in the way her eyes flashed with righteous indignation was: is that what you want – for the matter to be so ancient that details about it will never sully the pages of *The PMG*?

Thunderclouds gathered across Morley's craggy features. 'The news with which *you* should be concerned, Miss Friederichs,' he snapped icily, 'is that which deals with great affairs – Ireland or the new reform bill to increase the electorate. *These* are the type of topics we should be writing about in order to help our readership understand them.'

'But will they sell papers?' demanded Hulda, while Lonsdale and Stead regarded her askance, astonished that she should challenge the man who had broken convention by hiring her in the first place.

Lonsdale braced himself for an explosion, but Morley only stood and went to the window, standing with his hands behind his back so they would not see his face. Lonsdale sensed he was struggling to control his temper. 'They will if they are well written,' he said. 'So we shall know where the blame lies if circulation falls. Meanwhile, leave crime to the sensational weeklies.'

'But—' began Hulda.

'I will *not* be gainsaid,' he snapped, turning so quickly that Hulda took an involuntary step backwards. Then, to Lonsdale's surprise, Morley's voice became gentler, and he saw the crusty editor had a soft spot for his passionately outspoken assistant. 'Yet Mr Stead believes that the crime is more important than an unsavoury fallout between robbers and unfortunates, and I trust his judgement. Perhaps we will publish a short account of it later – although not until the police say we may.'

Hulda was glaring. 'So what would you like us to write about today?' she asked, her tone only just avoiding insolence.

Morley smiled briefly. 'There's a performance of Gilbert and Sullivan's *Patience* at the Savoy Theatre tonight. I want a review, because there is a new female lead. Now, if there's nothing else . . .'

On leaving Morley's office, Stead disappeared to the compositors' office without a word. Lonsdale went to the reporters' room, Hulda, fuming silently, at his heels. There was only one person there when they arrived – Alfred Milner, a thin-faced Oxford graduate who had abandoned a career in law for journalism. Lonsdale sensed that the mild-mannered Milner was destined for great things, and *The PMG* would not contain his budding genius for long.

'I assume you have just seen Mr Morley,' he said drily. 'You have a look on your face that would curdle new cream, Friederichs.'

'That man—' Hulda began hotly.

'Is one of the greatest intellects of our time,' interrupted Milner. 'A deep-thinker who has turned *The PMG* into a great bastion of political analysis.'

'But there's more to the news than that,' said Lonsdale, finally voicing his own disappointment at Morley's decision.

'How can he not see how important this story might be?' spat Hulda.

'I doubt it will be *important*,' said Milner, gently reproachful. 'Grisly, certainly. Fascinating, perhaps. But not important.'

'I disagree,' said Lonsdale, while Hulda sat at the desk and slammed a few drawers to vent her ire. 'Donovan's murder was superbly planned, and so was Cath's. This isn't the work of some deranged madman; it shows considerable resourcefulness and a highly organized mind.'

Hulda fumbled for a cigar, although she did not light it. 'I'm not surprised to hear *you* speak on his behalf, Milner,' she said sullenly. 'You being a regular guest at his dull Sunday afternoon tea parties. Thank God we have Stead to balance the man.'

'They do complement each other,' agreed Milner. 'But I can assure you that Mr Morley's parties are far from dull – he entertains some of the greatest thinkers in the country. But on a more immediate note, will you read this, Alec? It's about whether Britain should send warships to Egypt, to quell the anarchy brought about by Colonel Arabi's coup.'

With the deadline approaching for the final issue of the week, Lonsdale spent thirty frantic minutes helping Milner finish his article. When it was done, the pressure turned onto the compositors, and Lonsdale gave a sigh of relief as he heard the clatter of the printing machines start up. Within minutes, the papers would be packed in bales and handed to armies of paperboys.

Milner took a handkerchief from his pocket and dabbed at his forehead. He was not physically robust, and rarely came to work before ten o'clock. He screwed the lid back on the ink bottle and leaned back in his chair.

'Thank you, Alec,' he said, running a hand lightly over his slicked hair. 'I'll do the same for you – if you survive another week.' He cast a meaningful glance at Lonsdale's bruised eye. 'I heard what happened. You shouldn't have gone there alone; you should've taken one of us.'

'Me,' said Hulda, looking Milner up and down disparagingly. 'He should have taken *me*. If you had escorted him, there would have been two of you with bruised faces. I, on the other hand, can look after myself.'

Before Milner could respond, the door to the office opened. It was Stead, the customary twinkle back in his eye, and his irritation at Morley's intervention already a thing of the past. 'I've assignments for you two,' he said, looking at Lonsdale and Hulda, 'and you'll be pleased to know they *don't* involve an evening at the Savoy. Cook will handle that. Hulda, I want you to look into an art exhibit that opens in the East End on Monday.'

'Monday?' asked Hulda, brightening. 'Then in the meantime I can explore—'

'No,' interrupted Stead. 'You heard Mr Morley. It is too late to do more today, so I suggest you go home and read anything you might need in preparation for the art exhibit. But not tomorrow, of course. It's a sin to labour on the Sabbath.'

Hulda opened her mouth to argue, then thought better of it. Clamping her cigar between her teeth, she grabbed her coat and stalked out. They heard her heavy steps going down the stairs.

Stead turned to Lonsdale. 'She has the simpler of the assignments,' he said. 'What I have in mind for you is far more difficult, and may even involve a little danger.'

FOUR

That Sunday, after attending church with Jack, Lonsdale began preparing for the assignment that had been allocated by Stead. Then, the following morning, he slept as late as he could, before starting what he imagined actors went through prior to every performance: he readied himself to play a role. At about nine o'clock on Monday night, an unshaven and deliberately grubby Lonsdale was dropped off by a brougham carriage near the insalubrious Fox and Hounds tavern on a rough backstreet of Lambeth. The first step in the assignment allocated by Stead had been taken.

Stead's idea had developed from a brief report in Saturday's final edition – a snippet of news that had been taken from one of the morning newspapers by a sub-editor and included only because there had been unused space on page five. To Stead, however, it represented the tip of an iceberg in an appalling case of neglect and cruelty:

A coroner's jury yesterday returned a verdict of manslaughter against the master of the Holbeach Union Workhouse in Lincolnshire, for causing the death of a pauper named Bingham. The man had been suffering from a skin disease, and was placed in a fumigating box used to disinfect persons, and apparently forgotten. His cries at length attracted attention, and he was released, but not until he had been so terribly burned that skin and flesh fell from different parts of his body. He died a few hours afterwards.

'We *must* find out what the conditions in a workhouse are really like,' Stead had said. 'How are these men lodged and fed? What goes on when night comes, and the misfits and outcasts crowd around workhouse doors? How can a man be left in a box to die? Bingham deserves such questions to be answered!'

'The New Poor Law is behind it,' Milner had stated. 'The law that says able-bodied persons unable to support themselves should only receive relief in workhouses.'

'Workhouses!' spat Stead. 'Wicked places where the standard of living is obliged by law to be inferior to that of the lowest-paid worker, in order to serve as a deterrent to shirkers and drive them back to honest toil. But such centres repress, not help, the poor.'

Stead's plan was for Lonsdale to spend a night in a workhouse to see what it was like to be treated as a 'casual pauper'. The reporter now shuffled away from the carriage in his filthy boots, dressed in what had once been a snuff-brown coat, but was faded to the colour of imperfectly baked bricks. The coat was too small, and his arms projected beyond the sleeves, with his hands thrust deep in his pockets against the chill of a clear, cold night.

Lambeth Workhouse loomed gloomy and squat over Princes Road. Its thick front door was caked in a greasy patina of soot and grime, and Lonsdale could smell the rankness of unwashed bodies from outside, although it was not nearly as powerful as the reek of despair and hopelessness. It unnerved him, and it took considerable courage to knock and ask for a bed.

Once allowed inside, he was interviewed and taken to a room with three large baths, each containing a liquid that looked so much like mutton broth that he baulked at going near them, let alone immersing himself. But the clerk was waiting expectantly, so Lonsdale gave the man his clothes tied in a bundle and plunged into the water. It was icy cold, with a thin layer of scum across the top, and the bottom was full of grit, perhaps an inch deep in places. Lonsdale made a show of splashing about, and scrambled out as soon as he was sure he would not be ordered back in. It was, he thought, one of the most disgusting things he had ever done.

After drying off with a cloth as coarse as sand, he was given a lump of stale bread and was issued a blue sleeping shirt, a rug to cover himself, and a numbered tag so that he could retrieve his clothes in the morning. He was then sent across an open court to a large shed, one side of which was comprised only of a canvas sheet with a gap of some four feet at the bottom. The floor was flagstone, but so thickly encrusted with slime it could barely be seen, and it was sticky under his naked feet.

Inside were, he estimated, at least a hundred and twenty hay-stuffed bags, almost all occupied by men streaked with filth, despite the baths. In a number of places men had moved the bags close to each other – 'clubbing' they called it in self-denigrating sarcasm – as a feeble measure against the cold. Most were asleep, although a few ruffians squatted on their beds, singing ribald songs or telling obscene jokes, their eyes gleaming in the embers of their foul pipes. The place stank of acrid, fetid bodies, rotting bed-straw, and the foul pools on the floor where men, declining to make the chilly trip to the latrines, had created lavatories of their own.

Lonsdale found a free bag and, despite it having a bloodstain bigger than his hand, lay down, knowing that to baulk would show a degree of fastidiousness likely to make the other lodgers take notice of him. He looked at the bread, thinking he would have to eat at least some of it if he did not want to stand out.

'Not hungry, old pal?' asked one of three lads watching him keenly – a short, thin boy of fifteen or so, with large blue eyes and close-cropped hair. 'Chuck it here, then.' Obligingly, Lonsdale tore the bread in two and threw the larger piece to the lad, who devoured it quickly as his friends tried to grab it from him.

'Aw, Jamie,' grumbled one when it was gone. 'You could've shared.'

Determined to learn all he could, Lonsdale propped himself against a post and pretended to doze, watching as Jamie and his friends lit their pipes. He listened in growing horror as the youth began to relate tales of stealing, sex, and fights. Eventually, they slept, and the noise in the shed subsided, so that by the time the bells from nearby St Mary's Church tolled twelve, all was still. It was not quiet, though, with the flapping of the canvas curtain in the wind, snoring, the sounds of drinkers at the communal water pail, and the scuttle of those who got up to relieve themselves at the latrine or against the wall inside.

For hour after hour Lonsdale sat there, counting the time until seven o'clock – when he thought he would be able to leave. Four o'clock came and went, then five, by which time he was so cold that he doubted he would ever be warm again. At six, factory bells called working men to their jobs, but no one stirred in the workhouse, and the snoring continued unabated. Then it chimed seven. Lonsdale jumped up, relieved that the ordeal was almost over, before realizing he was the only one who had moved. Eventually, two men appeared and began bawling out numbers, so that the bundles of clothes turned in the night before could be exchanged for the borrowed shirts.

When everyone was up and dressed, the boys took the rugs, and the men made a heap of the bags against the wall, turning the shed from bedroom to breakfast room. There followed three-quarters of an hour of waiting for a paltry breakfast – a slice of bread and a pint basin of gruel, which had an unpleasant taste but warmed his numb hands. To Lonsdale, frozen, uncomfortable, and thinking longingly of home, it seemed an eternity. Hardly had he finished – having again given half of the bread to Jamie – before a rough-looking man known as the 'task-master' said in a loud voice, 'Now then, you lot belong to me!'

The sun shone brightly as Lonsdale, his ordeal finally over, walked through the busy streets to where the same carriage that had dropped him off the night before was waiting. His friend Milner, whom Stead had assigned to collect him, was lounging comfortably inside, reading *The Daily Telegraph*.

'You look a sight,' said Milner in distaste. 'I'm not sure I want you in here with me.'

Ignoring the comment, Lonsdale flopped back against the plush upholstery and accepted a gulp of brandy from Milner's hipflask. He relished the warmth as it settled in his stomach.

'I've been waiting two hours,' Milner grumbled, as the carriage moved away. 'It's well past eleven o'clock, you know.'

Lonsdale shuddered. 'There are duties to be performed before the inmates are allowed out. I had no idea they'd take so long.'

'What were they?'

'Today's was turning cranks that work a flour mill. Turning the crank is like turning a windlass. It shouldn't have been too laborious, because only four measures of corn have to be ground each day. The problem was that the taskmaster set us to work, then left. At least half the men immediately stopped working. The miller came in once or twice, and suddenly everyone was at work, but when he left, all was as before. It shouldn't have taken more than an hour, but it took three.'

'The poor laws at work,' mused Milner. 'What do . . .'

He trailed off when he saw Lonsdale had fallen asleep, and they rode in silence until the carriage clattered to a halt outside the tall, elegant Georgian façade of Jack's house. Lonsdale woke when the driver jumped down to tend his horses.

'Do you own this?' asked Milner.

'My brother does,' replied Lonsdale. 'But he'll marry soon, and then I'll be looking for rooms. I don't suppose you—?' His question was interrupted by a thump from behind them. 'What was that?'

'It sounded like someone jumping off the back of the carriage,' said Milner peering out of the window. 'I have a feeling we might just have given someone a free ride.'

Wednesday, 26 April
My dear Lonsdale,

I write to congratulate you on your coming of age, not just as a journalist, but as a crusader in the cause of righteousness. I enclose a copy of today's early edition of The PMG, *which includes the first instalment of your account of a night in a workhouse. Milner told me that he had never seen so great a change in appearance wrought in a single night. He felt that when you went in, you were well disguised, but that after spending fifteen hours in the cold and squalor, you had absolutely become confirmed in the visage of a tramp. The experiences that wrought these changes show in your account. You have written with passion of the filth, immorality, and hopelessness, and you have written so that things might be done, not merely discussed.*

It appears from early comments that your work is creating quite a stir. Representatives from several dailies have asked about carrying extracts of the second and third instalments tomorrow and the following day.

Inspector Peters came to find you. You are required to appear tomorrow morning at nine o'clock at the County Court, Great Portland Street, for the inquest into the death of Miss Walker. Although you'll undoubtedly testify early in the proceedings, you may, if you wish, remain there to see if any new facts have arisen.

Yours cordially,
Stead

The County Court dated from the previous century, but it had none of the attractiveness of most Georgian architecture. It was a grim, ineloquent building and everything about it screamed functionality. Lonsdale was directed to a dirty wood-panelled room on the ground floor, where the coroner sat in a high-backed, tatty red-velvet chair, almost hidden by the pile of papers in front of him. Dr Danford Thomas was a small, grey-haired man, with brown eyes hidden behind thick glasses and nicotine-stained teeth.

To Thomas's left, at right angles to his desk, were twelve uncomfortable wooden chairs, on which sat the members of the jury, while to his right were benches for witnesses. A large Bible marked with greasy fingerprints sat in imposing isolation on its own table so that witnesses might swear on it to tell the truth.

Before Lonsdale could sit down, Inspector Peters approached.

'I have to take the jury to see the body before witness testimony can be heard. While we're gone, Leonard would like to speak to you.'

He nodded to where the chief inspector was waiting by the door. Lonsdale went to join him, and they walked outside for privacy.

'Superintendent Ramsey wants you to understand several things before testifying,' Leonard began after a brief exchange of pleasantries. 'You must, of course, explain how you came to find Walker in Regent's Park, but you cannot mention her connection with Donovan.'

'But that's why I was there!' objected Lonsdale. 'If I'm asked—'

'You won't be,' interrupted Leonard. 'Ramsey has already spoken to the coroner, and . . . arrangements are in place.'

Lonsdale regarded him askance. 'You're asking me to withhold information from a legal inquiry?'

Leonard nodded ruefully. 'There are usually reporters at inquests, and if the issue of Donovan's disfiguring comes up, it'll be in the papers. Ramsey has good reasons for keeping it quiet for now, and Thomas has agreed both to avoid the subject and to postpone Donovan's inquest. I can't tell you more yet, but I can assure you that we have the interests of justice at heart.' He saw Lonsdale's doubtful expression. 'You're being asked to cooperate by a very high-ranking police officer.'

'In my experience, that might mean he has something to hide.' He pondered for a moment. 'Very well, I shall do as you ask,' he said, albeit reluctantly.

Leonard patted his shoulder. 'Good man! Now, when Thomas asks what you were doing in the park, you may say that you were meeting Walker . . .'

'No,' said Lonsdale firmly, not about to give some of his less scrupulous colleagues an opportunity to say he had arranged an assignation with a prostitute in a deserted park at night. 'I shall say that she offered me a story, but that I never learned the details. That's true.'

Leonard reflected, then nodded. 'That should be enough. When this is over, I'll give you the whole story. Then you'll see how important your cooperation was.' He reached out to shake Lonsdale's hand. 'Now I must bid you good day.'

Lonsdale watched him walk away, thinking about Milner's belief that the story would not be important, just sensational. Yet senior police officers were prepared to control how the press handled it. Was there more to the tale than a grisly murder and the slaughter of a prostitute and her accomplice? Did the police know of similar cases? He was inclined to conclude they did, as Ramsey would not be concerned with the random killing of a few friendless Londoners. But how could he find out? And could he disobey Morley's order to leave it well alone?

As he turned to go back into the courthouse, he saw a figure dodge into the nearby Portland Hotel. He frowned, then told himself that it had nothing to do with him, and headed back inside the courthouse.

Shortly after ten o'clock, the jury shuffled into their seats, and the inquest began. The initial witness was young Constable Lamb – the first policeman on the scene – who wore a freshly pressed jacket with buttons that gleamed like mirrors. He described how Lonsdale had approached him and what happened in the ensuing minutes. His testimony was followed by that of his colleagues.

Inspector Peters was the last policeman to testify. He rattled off the oath, then turned his lugubrious gaze on the coroner, waiting with all the cheer of a calf sent for slaughter. Thomas led him through his testimony, then asked why the search for clues – which had initially been postponed until daylight – had not yet taken place. Lonsdale leaned forward – he had assumed it had been completed.

'Inspector Beck of Scotland Yard volunteered the use of bloodhounds,' explained Peters. 'But Chief Inspector Leonard informed me that Superintendent Ramsey had countermanded that order. By the time the matter was resolved – it was an unfortunate misunderstanding apparently – a search of the area would have been futile because of the public nature of the place.'

Lonsdale stared at him. A misunderstanding? Or a deliberate attempt to prevent Cath's death from being properly explored? He listened as Peters recounted what he had learned about the victim.

'She was born Catherine Mitchell, was a Primitive Methodist, and had worked briefly as a calico weaver. She could read. Her arrest record included charges of vagrancy, drunkenness, wilful damage, and prostitution.'

'Has your investigation so far shed any further light that would be helpful to this inquiry?' asked Thomas.

'No, sir,' said Peters. 'But the investigation is ongoing.'

Lonsdale was next, and recounted his meeting with Cath at the fire and her offer of information for a story. He then told of being attacked by two men he assumed were her friends.

'She stipulated the bandstand,' said Thomas in a gentle Welsh lilt, 'but you looked for her near the trees and bushes when she failed to appear. Why?'

'Because I heard a noise in that area when I first arrived, then the two assailants came from that vicinity. I just assumed that Miss Walker might be there.'

'Thank you, Mr Lonsdale. That will be all.'

'He must like you,' whispered Hulda, as Lonsdale sat at the back of the courtroom. He was surprised to see her. 'He could have asked a lot more questions.'

Next on the stand was a large woman of about thirty, who said her name was Mary Lawrence. She wore a jacket and skirt of stiff green material and had clearly gone to some trouble to look her best. She identified the body as that of her sister.

'When did you last see her alive?' the coroner asked.

'A quarter to seven last Thursday evening. She came to Red Lion Street, where I work – I'm a seamstress. She was frightened, but wouldn't say why, and stayed less than an hour.'

'Did you know what she did for a living?' asked Thomas quietly.

'She'd been before the police court magistrates once or twice for . . . selling her personal wares.' Her lips compressed in a disapproving line.

'Do you know why she seemed frightened at your final meeting?'

'No, sir. But I can tell you she wasn't one to scare easily.'

Hulda leaned over to whisper to Lonsdale, disapproval in every word. 'He's making it sound as if she was killed because she was a whore – nothing to do with Donovan.'

'Ramsey's orders,' Lonsdale whispered back. 'Leonard told me I had to be careful with what I said, too.'

'So we're wasting our time here? Then let's leave.'

But Lonsdale was determined to see it through. He stayed, a reluctant Hulda at his side, and heard the testimony of a thin, frail-looking woman named Margaret Tanner, a widow who ran the lodging house where the dead woman often stayed.

'When did you last see her alive?' asked Thomas.

'About six thirty on the night she died. She was in the Dog and Bone public house, on Minto Street. She was a lively soul usually, but she seemed out of sorts that night.'

Thomas pressed her for details, but the woman spoke very cagily, obviously determined to ignore any implications that her lodging house might be of dubious reputation. Finally, Thomas dismissed her with a wave of his hand.

Lonsdale felt hungry, so when Thomas announced a thirty-minute lunch break before the afternoon session, he crossed the road and bought a pie from a street vendor. After making some disparaging remarks about it, Hulda followed suit, seduced by the light yellow pastry and the sweet scent of meat and onions. They sat on a grimy bench in a little park to eat, and had barely started when they were hailed.

'I thought you'd be gone,' said Bradwell. His smiled broadened. 'And of course, it's always a pleasure to see you, Miss Friederichs.'

'Dr Bradwell,' beamed Hulda, offering a hand to the pathologist. 'Would you like some of my pie?'

'No, they're made from cat,' replied Bradwell. 'I dislike eating carnivore.' He turned to Lonsdale. 'I've heard you've been ordered not to investigate Donovan's death. Is it true?'

Lonsdale nodded as he threw the remainder of his pie to the pigeons. Hulda finished hers with enthusiasm. 'Which is a pity, because I'm sure something significant is happening – something deeper than a lunatic with a penchant for cerebra.'

'I agree, which is why I hoped to catch you. Can you meet me after the inquest is over?'

'We shall look forward to it,' said Hulda, clearly assuming she was included in the invitation. She dabbed her lips with a piece of lace and glanced at the pie-seller, as if considering a second piece.

They took their places in the court and listened while Bradwell gave his evidence in a concise, professional tone that suggested he had done it many times before. After describing the scene, the placement of the body, and the details of the long and fatal incision in her throat, he noted that the injuries were beyond the possibility of self-infliction.

'Was any anatomical knowledge displayed by the incision?' asked Thomas.

'I believe so,' said Bradwell. 'There seems to have been some knowledge as to where to cut the throat in order to cause a fatal and quick result.'

Bradwell's testimony was followed by that of several of Cath's acquaintances. When Thomas had dismissed the last of these, he looked at the jury. 'Your task now is to decide whether you have been presented with sufficient evidence to decide the cause of Catherine Walker's death.'

Within a matter of moments, having conferred with other jury members, the foreman returned a verdict of 'wilful murder by person or persons unknown.' Thomas added nothing more, but the way his questions had been asked left the distinct impression that Cath was just another unfortunate killed in the course of her occupation.

'Inspector Peters is adjourning to a coffee house,' Bradwell said to Lonsdale following the inquest. 'Shall we join him there? It would be another opportunity to quiz him.'

Lonsdale was not sure he wanted another encounter with the law, particularly as it went contrary to Morley's instructions. However, Hulda accepted the offer with alacrity, so he trailed after them to a seedy establishment on the other side of the park.

'Will Lonsdale have to attend the inquest on Walker's dead friend?' asked Hulda when they were settled around a grimy table. 'What was his name?'

'We don't know it,' replied Peters. 'Not yet.'

'Really?' asked Hulda, voicing Lonsdale's surprise. 'You've had days!'

'Yes,' acknowledged Peters, reaching into his pocket for a briar pipe and Virginia tobacco. 'But he's not my only active case, and these matters are never easy – this is a city of millions of people, and the Metropolitan Police District is huge. Since Walker is from south of the river, it is likely the man is as well, and that means in theory I should be liaising with my colleagues in Southwark Division. But due to professional jealousies, many officers decline to share information with those in different divisions.'

'Is there no way you can obtain this evidence yourself?' asked Hulda, sounding sceptical.

'It's difficult – one has to be careful not to be seen subverting official channels. I did quietly send a detective to Walker's lodging house and then to trawl several local pubs to ask after her friend. Unfortunately, the police are regarded with suspicion in that area.'

'Can *we* help you?' asked Hulda in her most innocent manner.

'No thank you,' responded Peters, a smile twitching his moustache as he knocked the bowl of his pipe on the table and rubbed a bit of burnt tobacco out with a stubby index finger. 'We may move slowly, but we get there in the end.'

'So tell us what's happening with the Donovan case,' said Bradwell. 'I've been informed that I won't be needed for the inquest, which is odd.'

'That's correct,' said Peters flatly. 'Superintendent Ramsey believes that there's no link between Walker and Donovan, and I've been told to wait until I receive further instructions.'

'How can he say they aren't linked?' demanded Lonsdale. 'Cath met me at the fire and *told* me she knew something about the killing of Donovan.'

'So I understand,' said Peters. He rose, putting his pipe and tobacco in his pocket. 'It is all very curious. However, although Dr Bradwell clearly thinks we should all work together on the case – that *is* why you brought them here, is it not, Bradwell? – it *is* a police matter, and I strongly advise you to leave well enough alone.'

'It *is* curious,' said Hulda. 'And perhaps Dr Bradwell is right.' She smiled at the pathologist, who blushed.

'No,' said Inspector Peters, 'he is not. Come, Bradwell. You should return to your house of the dead and I have work to do.'

Hulda allowed Bradwell to keep her hand rather longer than was strictly necessary as the pathologist took his leave, and then the two men were gone, leaving her and Lonsdale alone.

'One has to try to obtain information however one can,' she said in answer to Lonsdale's questioning gaze regarding her coquettishness. 'Now, tell me why the coroner protected you from any serious questioning.'

Lonsdale obliged, and Hulda sat still, thinking.

'Peters is right: this *is* curious,' she said eventually. 'First, Superintendent Ramsey and Chief Inspector Leonard tell our editors that they don't want us investigating. Then Ramsey has Donovan's inquest suppressed and sees to it that you aren't asked why you were meeting Walker, not to mention the "misunderstanding" that saw the scene of the crime left unsearched. Peters pretends not to mind, but he does – terribly. All this points to one thing: Ramsey is covering something up, possibly to protect the missing policeman, Iverson. Maybe Peters has been told to keep quiet, too. If he has, he'd never say.'

Lonsdale agreed. 'But there's nothing we can do.'

'Oh, yes, there is – we can explore these deaths ourselves.'

'But we've been told to leave it alone – by the police, and more importantly by Morley, who is, after all, the editor of *The PMG.*'

Her blue eyes gleamed. 'He also said we might publish a short account when the murders were resolved – which they won't be unless someone actually investigates. The police are willing to forget about it, but I'm not. How can they object when they've already given up?'

'I cannot see Morley being impressed by that argument,' said Lonsdale.

'This is more important than him,' determined Hulda. 'So first thing tomorrow we shall go to Donovan's place of work, and we will inform Morley what we're doing when we have proof of something odd. Then he'll have to agree to let us continue.'

'Morley would certainly rather we consulted him *before* we go to Donovan's workplace,' said Lonsdale. 'But I agree we need a carrot to dangle in front of him. So I will go with you tomorrow, but only if we agree we won't do anything else until he gives us his permission.'

'Of course,' said Hulda, a triumphant smile playing on the edges of her mouth. 'Would I ever do anything without official approval?'

Salmon and Eden Gentleman's Outfitters was a discreet establishment located at the corner of Oxford and Bird streets. Its windows were spotlessly clean – a remarkable feat in

London – and in each there was a tasteful display of suits and coats and hats. Inside, the atmosphere was reverently hushed.

The shop had been open no more than ten minutes when Lonsdale arrived with Hulda. They were barely inside before an assistant came to offer a seat for the lady and his services for the gentleman. While Hulda sat, Lonsdale inspected shirts and trays of collars.

'Are you new?' the reporter asked nonchalantly of the assistant, a neat, dapper little Welshman with thinning hair, a huge moustache, and the name of Rhys. 'The last time I was here, I was attended by Donovan.'

Rhys's face became sombre. 'Mr Donovan is no longer with us, sir.'

'Really?' asked Lonsdale, inspecting a collar. 'I suppose he left because of his father? He told me the old man was ill, but of course this was over a year ago.'

'The old man died, sir,' explained Rhys. 'And, it grieves me to say, so did Mr Donovan. Just last week, in a tragic accident.'

'How dreadful,' Lonsdale exclaimed. 'How?'

'I don't know the details.' Rhys lowered his voice as one of his colleagues darted forward to greet a tall gentleman in a grey double-breasted reefer, who strolled in asking for collar studs. The newcomer glanced around the shop imperiously, allowing his gaze to settle on Lonsdale briefly, before giving his attention to the proffered box.

'What *do* you know?' asked Lonsdale.

'It was Mr Donovan's half-day,' began Rhys, 'Wednesday a week ago, and he said he was going to Hyde Park to watch the model boats. I told him he'd catch a chill in the rain, but he didn't listen. Model boats were his passion, you see. Then, the next day, he didn't arrive for work, which was unusual.'

'I see.'

'Most unusual,' continued Rhys, shaking his head mournfully. 'Regular as clockwork was Mr Donovan. I assumed he'd got a cold from being out in the wet, and planned to stop off to see him on my way home. But the police came and said there'd been an accident. A fire.'

'How terrible!'

'He must have become chilled watching the boats, and then set his house ablaze accidentally when he lit a fire to warm himself. Dreadful business!'

'Did he go boating alone?' asked Lonsdale.

Rhys looked at him curiously, but answered politely enough. 'I believe so, although he didn't boat himself – he just liked to watch. He was a quiet man, not given to chatter. He must have taken a shine to you, if he told you about his father. None of us knew about that until he asked for an hour off to attend the funeral last year.'

'Poor Donovan,' said Lonsdale, genuinely sorry for a man who should be quite so without friends. 'Was he ill Wednesday? Is that why you advised him against boating in the rain?'

'Never had a day's sickness in his life, and never missed a day of work! He was looking forward to his afternoon in the park, humming and singing under his breath as he always did when boating was planned.'

'Is there a wife or dependants whom I might help with a small donation?'

Rhys shook his head. 'It's a kind thought, sir, but Mr Donovan had no family. He was a very private man, and, even though we worked side by side for almost a year, he only invited me to his house once – just a few days before he died.'

'Gracious,' said Lonsdale. 'Did he have a reason for inviting you then?'

'I saw an advertisement for a house to rent in his road,' said Rhys. 'Number thirty-five. When I mentioned it to him, he invited me to pop by when I'd finished viewing it. I did, but I could tell he was uncomfortable, so I stayed only briefly. In fact, it had been so long since he'd had company, that he had to hunt about for a spare cup and saucer.'

'Number thirty-five?' asked Lonsdale, realizing that this was the Welshman about whom Hulda had spun her tales of rag-and-bone men. He felt a surge of guilt.

Rhys nodded. 'My wife and son liked the look of the place. Affordable homes in decent neighbourhoods are harder to find than you'd imagine, so we wanted to take it. But there seems to be a problem, which the agent says is of an "undefined" nature.' He frowned, his pleasant, earnest face puckering in consternation.

'We will be late for our appointment, dear,' said Hulda, standing abruptly and indicating that she and Lonsdale should leave. 'We must go.'

'I'll take three of these,' said Lonsdale, feeling obliged to buy something, so pointing to the first items he saw. He needed new shirts anyway, and disliked shopping. He jotted down his address. 'And half-a-dozen collars.'

Rhys saw them to the door, and Lonsdale took Hulda's arm until they were out of sight, when she promptly tugged it away.

'And you accuse *me* of leading people astray with lies!' she exclaimed. 'Hypocrite! You even offered to give money to a family you knew perfectly well doesn't exist.'

'To be frank, I seriously considered giving it to poor Rhys, given that you ruined his chances of moving into the house of his dreams.'

She had the grace to look guilty, but still retorted, 'Well, for all I know, *you* gave him a false address to which to send the shirts.'

'I most certainly did not,' objected Lonsdale indignantly. 'I—'

'You barely noticed what you were buying,' she interrupted, clearly spoiling for an argument. 'That obviously comes from having more money than sense.'

'I beg your pardon?' said Lonsdale, startled at her effrontery.

'You are independently wealthy, aren't you? Voules told me that one reason he believes he should get the upcoming job at *The PMG* is that whereas he is not financially independent, your father left you a quarter of his not inconsiderable estate when he died. He said it was a fortune that was divided between you, two brothers, and a sister, and that you want for nothing.' She tipped her head back and regarded him defiantly.

'And how is Voules so familiar with my personal affairs?'

'He has contacts in important places.'

'Well, his contacts are wrong,' said Lonsdale coolly. 'My parents are both alive, and my father is the rector of Raunds in Northamptonshire – a country parson, living in a rectory he does not own. And I have a sister and *three* brothers: Jack, one who is the rector in Withersfield in Suffolk, and one who is a lieutenant in the Royal Navy. The reason I live with Jack is that I don't have independent means, and when Jack marries and I move out, I shall probably be all but destitute.'

'Then let's hope you get the position at *The PMG*,' said Hulda, in what Lonsdale supposed was intended to be a placatory manner. 'I'd rather have you than Voules.'

'Thank you,' said Lonsdale, thinking it was not much of a compliment. 'But we should be discussing Donovan, not my personal finances.'

Hulda nodded. 'He was chilled from the rain, so he lit a fire when he got home from the park. The chimney caught fire, and he rushed into the street to raise the alarm. He went back inside, where the killer strangled him, removed his cerebrum, crushed his head to hide the mutilation, left the fire to destroy any other clues, and escaped unseen.'

'Would a killer just happen to be there when the chimney caught fire?' asked Lonsdale doubtfully. 'And, more importantly, why did he want Donovan's cerebrum—'

'Don't look now, but I believe we're being followed,' interrupted Hulda.

She sighed irritably when Lonsdale glanced behind him, just in time to see the tall man who had been in Salmon and Eden duck through a door. Lonsdale frowned. The man had looked respectable, so why was he heading into the jug-and-bottle room of a pub, where drink was normally fetched for home consumption? He shrugged mentally, realizing that his imagination must be spiralling out of control – and so was Hulda's – if they were beginning to question the antics of complete strangers.

'Are you sure he was after us?' he asked. 'He looked a respectable gentleman.'

Hulda glared at him. 'Not him, Lonsdale – the boy.' The one who . . . damn it! He's gone. You would make a hopeless spy. You should have pretended not to notice him, while I doubled back and nabbed him.'

'A boy?'

'A scruffy one. But never mind him now. You and I are going

to Morley, and we shall convince him that Donovan's death *must* be investigated. Well, don't just stand there with your mouth hanging open – flag down a hansom.'

When Hulda and Lonsdale reached the reporters' office at *The PMG*, they were greeted by Voules, his chubby face split by a lascivious leer. The only other person there was young Edward Cook, who was looking angry, as people often did when obliged to spend any time with Voules.

'Coming to work in the same hansom, are we?' Voules asked, rubbing his hands together. 'A romance! How delicious! It is—'

Hulda instantly advanced so menacingly on him that he stepped back in alarm, the grin wiped from his face as though she had used a flannel.

'If I were having a romance, it would not be with Lonsdale, and it would certainly not be any business of yours,' she hissed dangerously. 'So keep your slanderous opinions to yourself. You lied about Lonsdale and his fabled wealth, and now you dare to gossip about me. You're walking directly towards disaster, and it is a very short path.'

Voules opened his mouth to defend himself, but she turned on her heel and stormed away, leaving him standing spluttering at empty air.

'You're playing with fire, Voules,' warned Cook, who was dressed as smartly as Voules was untidily, his thick hair perfectly groomed. 'No one insults The Friederichs and lives to tell the tale.'

'Why, what will she do?' sniggered Voules, vibrating with unpleasant laughter now his intimidator was gone. 'Call me out? Pistols at dawn?' He turned toward Lonsdale. 'Will you be her second?'

Lonsdale ignored him, thinking such remarks beneath his dignity to acknowledge. Cook was not so sanguine, and flushed with anger.

'Friederichs wouldn't need a second,' he said hotly. 'And if it *were* pistols, you would be wise to stay away. She's said to be handy with guns – rifles, shotguns, *and* pistols.'

'Does she fence, too? Or box?' smirked Voules acidly. He

sat at his desk and pulled out his pipe. 'Nothing would surprise me about her. She probably doesn't swoon at the mention of knickers, either, as any well-bred woman should.'

'And any well-bred *man* would not speculate on a lady's personal life,' snapped Cook. 'By such comments, you reveal that you are no gentleman.'

Voules's flabby cheeks burned crimson with anger at the insult, but before he could reply, Cook stood and stamped out. Lonsdale followed, gratified to see Voules seething with indignation. As he passed Stead's office, he was startled to hear Alfred Milner calling him.

He retraced his steps and saw Milner kneeling on the floor, sifting through a pile of morning papers.

'What are you doing?' he asked. 'And where is Stead?'

'At the House, Alec. The budget is to be announced today.' He smiled. 'Your workhouse experiences have created quite a sensation! We had to print extra copies yesterday because of the demand for the second part of the story, and the print run will be higher yet for the final instalment today.'

'If you have time to chat, Milner, I assume you've found what I asked you to retrieve,' came Morley's icy voice from behind Lonsdale.

Lonsdale knew immediately the editor was in a bad mood, as he never criticized Milner as he did the rest of his staff – Morley liked him, because he not only understood the Irish Question, but was interested in it. He decided to make himself scarce, but Hulda arrived at just that moment, still irked by her encounter with Voules.

'Mr Morley,' she began brusquely. 'I'd like a word with you, please.'

'And I with you,' replied Morley coolly. 'Indeed, I was about to send for you. Lonsdale, too.'

They followed him into his office, where he held out an imperious hand, and Milner hurried forward to place a selection of articles in it; all, Lonsdale read upside down, related to Ireland. Milner backed away quickly, as Morley regarded first Hulda and then Lonsdale with a chilly glare.

'Neither of you produced a review of *Patience* as I ordered – Cook did it. I require my reporters to complete the assignments

I give them, not ones they choose to do themselves. Do I make myself clear?'

'Yes, sir,' said Lonsdale, although Hulda remained silent.

'Good. And now you will redeem yourselves. There is a performance of *The Parvenu* at the Court Theatre tonight, and one of you *will* write a review. That means *going*, Miss Friederichs, not reading what *The Times* has to say and copying it.'

'I would never—' Hulda began indignantly.

Morley overrode her. 'Meanwhile, Miss Friederichs will work on our Occasional Notes section, remembering that they are supposed to give life and smartness to the page. Lonsdale, I want a piece on the miners' riots in Camborne. Plus, there's an intriguing story about a charging sperm whale sinking a ship. Whoever escapes the theatre tonight will investigate that.'

'A sperm whale?' echoed Hulda doubtfully.

'Find the truth and write it,' replied Morley, turning to the first of his articles. They both knew they had been dismissed.

'Do you want the theatre or the whale?' Lonsdale asked as they walked into the reporters' room.

'The whale,' replied Hulda at once. 'I can't abide the theatre.'

'Professor Seeley, my old tutor from Caius, is dining at our club tomorrow night,' Lonsdale told Milner later, as several reporters wrapped up their day after the edition had gone to the press. 'Jack and I will join him, and I was wondering if you would, too.'

'John Seeley was your tutor?' asked Milner, eagerly. 'The greatest thinker on historical issues of Christian doctrine? I had no idea you were so well connected!'

Lonsdale smiled fondly at the thought of his mentor. 'So will you come?'

'I can't,' said Milner with a grimace. 'Stead made me promise to take Harris to the club tomorrow, to thank him for taking you to the Garrick. Damn! I don't see how I can escape now that the invitation has been issued.'

'I suppose he could come, too,' said Lonsdale, although the prospect of introducing the erudite Seeley to a boor like Harris was alarming.

'Don't do it!' warned Cook, laughing. 'Not if you have an iota of affection for your old mentor. Harris is a pig and I cannot imagine why the Garrick let him in.'

'No indeed,' agreed Milner. 'Of course, it could be worse. We could drop into our clubs one day and find The Friederichs there, hogging the best papers and smoking her revolting cigars.'

'Hulda doesn't smoke cigars,' said Cook, ever the gentleman.

Lonsdale said nothing.

'She keeps some on her desk, but perhaps they're just for show,' said Milner. 'Well, why not? There's nothing so healthy or as satisfying as a fat cigar.' He went to Hulda's desk and picked up a La Jurista before grimacing and dropping it in distaste. 'Not one of these! But an El Diamante is one of the great pleasures in life. I always smoke during interviews, as it puts the people being questioned at ease.'

'I can't see Friederichs smoking a cigar, though,' said Cook loyally. 'It would be unbecoming in a woman.'

'True,' conceded Milner. 'In this day of women gaining new legal rights and being allowed to receive a superior education, a cigar is still one of the great benefits of being a man.'

Lonsdale continued to remain silent.

By the time Lonsdale had eaten a quick supper at home, changed into his evening suit, and caught a hansom to the Court Theatre, the performance was about to begin. The theatre was full, at least in part because the Prince of Wales was there, exuding his customary melange of gentility and debauchery. Lonsdale quickly lost interest in the play, and found himself thinking about Donovan, Cath, and the mysterious Constable Iverson. He reviewed his encounter with the prostitute again, in the hope of uncovering some previously overlooked clue.

Did she have a tale to tell him, or had her intention been to rob him? She had promised to bring a witness to prove her claims, and then she and the unidentified man were killed – her with a slit throat and him by poison. Why two such different modes of execution? It all seemed unnecessarily complex.

More to the point, who had killed them? The two men who had attacked him? He pondered the question and decided not, on the grounds that they had been such inept fighters, and the killer of Cath, her accomplice, and Donovan – he no longer doubted that the deaths of Donovan and Cath were related – had been ruthlessly efficient.

Applause from the audience brought him out of his reverie, and he stood for intermission. The theatre stank of perfume, hair lacquer, eau-de-Cologne, and other beautifying potions, all vying with the reek of smoke from cigars, cigarettes, and pipes. The latter grew worse as people collected their refreshments from the foyer. Eventually, it proved more than Lonsdale could bear, and he walked outside for some fresh air.

Or, rather, some cooler air. Smoke from thousands upon thousands of chimneys poured into London's sky. Lonsdale took a deep breath and felt grit between his teeth. He was about to go back inside again, when there was a low rumble followed by the sound of smashing glass and a blast of hot air. For a moment, nothing happened, then people began to scream, and dust billowed through the doors.

Lonsdale's first thought was that it was an attempt by Irish Fenians on the life of the Prince of Wales. He covered his mouth and nose with his handkerchief and raced inside.

In the foyer, a huge chandelier hung by a thread from the ceiling, threatening to drop at any moment. Broken glass was everywhere. A woman shrieked in terror, and another was sobbing. Lonsdale saw that someone had organized a line of people with water buckets to douse the flames. Indeed, most people were leaving in a surprisingly calm fashion, gentlemen even pausing to assist older ladies. Several stewards had manned the cloakroom and were returning hats, cloaks, and capes.

He knelt next to a young doorman, who lay on the floor, clutching his knee. It was messy but not serious, caused when the lad had fallen on some glass. He staunched the flow of blood with his handkerchief and made a crude bandage with his tie.

Above the clatter of heels on the marble floor, whispers told Lonsdale that the Prince of Wales had taken charge, and was overseeing the evacuation. Lonsdale lifted the lad in his arms, and joined the flow of people outside.

'Was it one of those Irish mobs, do you think?' one man

asked as they went. 'They certainly wouldn't hesitate to inflict such an outrage.'

'We were damned lucky,' said another. 'The bell had rung to announce the second act, so people were on the move. Had the explosion occurred five minutes earlier, there would have been a massacre.'

Two firemen informed the white-faced manager that they would not be able to tell whether the explosion was caused by gas or something more sinister until the following morning. Seeing there was no more to learn, Lonsdale decided to go home.

He relinquished the lad into the care of a steward, retrieved his overcoat and gibus hat, and began searching for a hansom. He was about to hail one when he saw a nicely dressed young lad watching him from the kerbside on the opposite side of the road. He was familiar, but it took Lonsdale a moment to remember where he had seen him before.

'Hello, Jamie,' Lonsdale said, approaching the boy he had seen at the workhouse. 'Not your normal area, is it?'

'I get around,' shrugged Jamie. 'Same as you.'

'How did you . . .?' began Lonsdale curiously, but then understanding came in a flash. 'You rode on the back of the carriage when I was collected from the workhouse. You jumped off when I reached home – I heard you.'

Jamie grinned. 'I saw you getting into a big carriage, so I thought to myself, "why don't we see who this feller is?" So I went along for the ride, all the way to Bayswater. The houses kept getting bigger and bigger, and yours was one of the biggest.'

'And you were on Oxford Street this morning . . .'

'Your lady friend spotted me, I suppose. But, yeah, I've been watching you since, seeing if I could figger what you really are. One thing you ain't, is a man that needs to doss at a workhouse.'

'Nor are you, judging by your clothes,' said Lonsdale wryly.

'Just did a bit of snow-droppin', didn't I?'

'You mean you stole them from a line while they were drying?'

Jamie grinned again. 'So now I look like a right little gen'leman.'

'Well then, little gentleman, what do you want from me?'

'It's what *you* want from me, old pal – I can tell you things for your newspaper.' He smirked when Lonsdale's eyebrows rose. 'Yeah, I know you're a reporter. I ain't stupid – you stay at home for a couple of days after you leave the workhouse, and then all of a sudden everyone's talking about what happens there. I guessed right away what you done.'

'But what makes you think I need more information? I learned more than enough the other night.'

'You'll want to hear what I got to say, old pal. But speaking the Lord's truth is hungry work.' He looked at Lonsdale meaningfully.

'All right,' said Lonsdale, laughing. 'There's a café nearby. I'll buy you a meal in exchange for your gossip.'

The Aerated Bread Company cafés were small, respectable, and known for their quick service, clean cutlery, and inexpensive food. The one on Sloane Street was filled with clerks and white-collar workers who had been working late, and the air was heavy with the smell of hot lard from the skillets. Feeling conspicuous in his finery, Lonsdale selected a table at the back.

'So, what can you tell me?' he asked, after Jamie had ordered enough food to fill someone twice his size. The lad had been gawking at the displays of food in walnut cases along the wall, but when he looked back at Lonsdale, his bravado seemed to wilt. He grew sombre.

'You seem a nice man,' he said. 'Maybe you can do sommat to help me. And you got reason to, because the same men who've taken me mates are looking for you.'

'What do you mean?' asked Lonsdale, bemused. 'Who's looking for me? And what happened to your friends?'

'I know lots of people from the workhouses. You stay there long enough, you get to know most. And I've been there for years – since me dad did a runner. Lately, some've disappeared, including two of me mates.' He paused and looked around furtively. 'I see things, but I don't get seen, if you know what I mean. I've seen a number of people being taken away – and they ain't never come back.'

'Taken away?' asked Lonsdale.

'Loo-ered,' said the lad, giving a particularly sinister tone to a word he obviously did not use often. 'Talked into going off with women.'

'Lured away by prostitutes?'

'No. I know dollies, whether they're the fanciest flash-tails, the common dress-lodgers, or the wrens that hang about the military barracks. None of them. These were women that were hired to get men away from the workhouse.'

'Perhaps they're just wives or girlfriends.'

'They ain't, I tell you,' insisted Jamie. He paused as the waiter brought his food, and did not speak again until he had scoffed his first cake. 'The men go away with the women, and they don't come back. It's because of the men who're watching.'

'What men?' asked Lonsdale, bewildered by the flood of information.

'Four or five of 'em, usually a couple at a time.' Jamie spoke from around a massive bite of beef pie. 'The one I've seen the most is older'n you – short, but with big arms, like a blacksmith. He's got thinnish hair and a long beard. And he's got a real swagger, like some lord.'

Lonsdale took out his pocket book and began to write. 'And the others?'

'Another's small, not much bigger'n me. I've seen him walking into a pub once, over in Stepney, and he was cursing to himself sommat vile. He's got a funny moustache – half dark, half grey. And one of those top hats that the killer wore – the cove that was hanged.'

'A Müller cut-down?' Lonsdale asked, giving a name popularly used for a hat that resembled a top hat trimmed to half its height. It was named for a murderer whose penchant for them had led to his eventual identification and arrest.

'That's it. And then there's an older feller. He's big too, but fat. Hands shaking with excitement all the time and a great scar through his eyebrow—'

Lonsdale sat bolt upright. 'What?'

'I said you'd be interested,' said Jamie smugly. 'Saw him following you the other day. You and your lady friend.'

'Where?' demanded Lonsdale.

'Great Portland Street. He was just there, watching. Didn't

know I was watching him – like I said, I see but I don't get seen. And he ain't the only one. There's a gent, too. Dark grey suit, top hat, and nice shoes. Not nearly so good at staying out of sight as Eyebrow is.'

'I've seen him, too,' mused Lonsdale. 'Although I hadn't given him much thought. Do they know each other?'

'Dunno.' Jamie gave him a conspiratorial glance. 'Seems you've been up to more than just going to a workhouse.'

'I think it's the ones following me who have been up to something,' muttered Lonsdale. 'Murder – I think they've murdered people.'

Jamie stopped chewing. 'Then me mates is done for?'

'I don't know yet. Tell me more about what you've seen.'

So Jamie did.

FIVE

Lonsdale was at Northumberland Street early the following morning to write an eyewitness account of the explosion at the Court Theatre. That done, he went to see Stead, whose bright eyes and cheerful smile were due to the continued success of the workhouse story and the subsequent questions that were being asked by influential individuals about urban poverty. Lonsdale poured out all he had learned from Jamie, while the assistant editor listened without interruption. Leaving Lonsdale sitting on a stack of newspapers, Stead went to request an appointment with Morley. Moments later, he poked his head back in. 'Mr Morley will see us now.'

'Us?' queried Lonsdale.

'This requires a united front, Lonsdale. We besiege him together. Come.'

Lonsdale followed him along the hall to Morley's office, where the editor sat at his desk, fingers steepled. He nodded for them to sit, and his sombre gaze settled unflinchingly on his reporter.

'Mr Stead tells me that you wish to continue your investigation into these murders,' he said. 'Pray tell me why, when the police asked us to desist.'

'More information has come to light since we last spoke,' Lonsdale began. 'And to be frank, sir, there's something odd about the police investigation – almost as if they want to deny that Donovan's death is suspicious, and hope that if they obfuscate long enough, all will be forgotten.'

'Go on,' said Morley.'

'There are questions that *should* be asked, but that the police – or rather Superintendent Ramsey – seem unwilling to pose,' Lonsdale continued. 'Such as why Donovan, who never missed work, was at home when he was killed? Why did he run back inside his house and lock his doors after raising the alarm? Did the chimney sweep leave a brush that caused the fire? Who was the man killed with Cath and why was he poisoned?'

Lonsdale then outlined all Jamie had told him about the men being lured away by women and never seen again.

'Tell him about you being followed, too,' ordered Stead when Lonsdale had finished. He glanced at Morley. 'Followed by men involved in the luring, one of whom matches the description of a missing and very dangerous policeman – one Constable Iverson.'

'Miss Friederichs told me yesterday that you were being stalked by a child – not a deadly ex-officer of the law,' said Morley.

'It was both – and more,' said Lonsdale. 'I was not the only one who saw the tall man in the suit – Jamie did, too.'

Lonsdale could see that, although Stead was convinced that something was badly amiss, Morley remained sceptical. He realized he needed to present a stronger case. The inspiration hit him in the form of an article Milner had written, and as Morley admired Milner . . .

'Do you recall Milner's two-part article entitled "British Nomads", sir?' he asked, going to where Morley kept a copy of the back issues and riffling through them to find the one he wanted.

'Of course,' said Morley, pointedly consulting his fob watch.

'There was a bit about marriage, and how some women select

husbands.' Lonsdale found what he was looking for and began to read:

> *We will suppose that a female hawker of small wares is in want of a partner. She has ways of making money, and can maintain herself and a partner in comfortable style, but she would rather not join fortunes with one of her own sort, as such a one would arrogate supremacy in the partnership, and insist on keeping the purse. In short, she would be little better than a drudge. She therefore prefers to pick a man who will allow her to play the leading part – a fellow considerably younger than herself, whom she may rule and regulate according to her liking.*
>
> *Failing to meet the right sort on her travels, she looks elsewhere – the casual ward. Ere many evenings pass she is sure to meet just the sort of person she wants, beckons him aside, and makes a proposal that he can hardly refuse. She wants somebody to carry her baskets; she offers in return food, lodging, drink, and a little money. The work is light, and a shiftless tramp is not likely to refuse such an offer – and the woman carries off her prey.*

'What are you saying?' asked Morley, incredulously. 'That your urchin's friends are being whisked away to become kept men?'

'No – I'm saying that someone is using the *technique* Milner described to ensnare them,' explained Lonsdale. 'Jamie said his friends were "picked up" by women – definitely not prostitutes – near the workhouses. These aren't men with money for prostitutes, and he's seen the same women at workhouses in different parts of the city. And once the men go, they never come back.'

'How do you know they have not been recruited to earn an honest wage elsewhere?' asked Morley, still sceptical. 'Labouring, perhaps? I see no reason to think these "disappearances" are related to your murders.'

With the editor seemingly intractable, Lonsdale decided to play his last desperate hand to convince him.

'There's one other vital piece of information,' he said. 'Jamie's friends who disappeared from the workhouse are named

Joseph Killian, Sean MacDermott, and Eamon O'Sullivan. Add Patrick Donovan to that, and what do you have?'

Lonsdale held his breath, hoping that four Irish names would snag Morley's interest, as there was little about that country that did not fascinate him.

'How can you be sure it's not coincidence?' asked Morley, although Lonsdale saw a glimmer of curiosity flare in his cool, grey eyes.

Lonsdale handed him page five of that morning's *Daily Telegraph*. Circled near the bottom was a small note that read:

> *Yesterday morning the body of John Keefe, a small farmer from Kingwilliamstown, County Cork, was found in a ditch, under circumstances that left no doubt as to his being murdered. A multitude of wounds showed that the unfortunate man had been subjected to shocking violence, and his head had been fractured and crushed to the point that the only way he was recognized was by his clothes.*

'With a head crushed like that, do you think he still had a cerebrum inside?' asked Lonsdale, seeing with satisfaction that Morley's reservations were crumbling at last.

The editor sat in silence for a long time before speaking. 'Lonsdale, you've known me long enough to appreciate that I dislike tales that appeal to the readers of police gazettes and exploitative weeklies. That said, I see you may have stumbled across a crime that might have deeper and wider-ranging consequences. We don't know if there's a connection between Keefe and your murders, but if there is, exposing it is our moral duty. After all, disruption in Ireland is one of the greatest threats our society faces today.'

'I quite agree,' said Stead. 'It is the only ethical decision to make.'

'However,' continued Morley, 'I do not want Miss Friederichs to investigate with you, given the obvious danger of the quest.'

Lonsdale sincerely hoped he would not be the one assigned to tell her, but Stead waved an airy hand. 'We need all our staff to be available for this, but I promise to keep her away from anything risky. Come, Lonsdale – there is not a moment to lose.'

'Stay,' ordered Morley as Lonsdale aimed for the door. 'You cannot explore a case with Irish implications without a clear understanding of the nuances of the Irish situation, and much changed in the years that you were out of the country. It would be dangerous if you proved to be dealing with individuals involved in the armed struggle. So sit. I shall apprise you of the important issues and details now.'

Stead winked at Lonsdale as he left, amused that he should use the editor's obsession to get his way. Lonsdale floundered for an excuse to escape, too, but he saw Morley's determined expression and realized there was none.

Forty minutes later, Lonsdale emerged with his head spinning. He left the building quickly, unwilling to risk being waylaid by colleagues, and eager to begin his investigation in earnest now he had the editor's approval. He decided his first task was to visit the sweep to find out if the man really had left one of his brushes up Donovan's chimney. He remembered from the comments made by Donovan's neighbour, Mrs North, that his name was Kendal.

He walked to the Victoria Embankment and stopped near Cleopatra's Needle, resting his elbows on the low wall and gazing across the greasy, grey-brown swirl of the Thames as he thought about his next move. The river stank, despite the sewer system and its elaborate pumping stations that had been built at great expense two decades before.

While he listened to ships' horns and the scream of gulls, he pondered how he might find the sweep. Then he recalled that Jack had recently employed one. He took a hansom home, and rifled through his brother's desk until he found a card that read:

> *J. Hanker, Chimney Sweep, respectfully begs to inform the Gentry and Inhabitants of Bayswater Road and its Vicinity that he hopes, by his unremitting Attention, to merit liberal Support.*

At the bottom was an assurance that Hanker always used clean cloths.

The card gave an address on Woodchester Street, near the

Great Western Railway, so Lonsdale set off on foot, aiming to ask Hanker for Kendal's address – as there was bound to be some form of fraternity among fellow workers. As he walked, the houses changed from spacious mansions to middle-class semis, to working-class terraces, and finally to grimy hovels. All were located within close proximity of each other, something that upset many of the wealthier inhabitants of the city on those occasions when they let themselves think about it.

Eventually, Lonsdale found Woodchester Street, a road with houses built from dull, charcoal-grey bricks that seemed to leach every speck of colour from their surroundings. An occasional pot of flowers had been placed in brave defiance of the monochrome. Lonsdale's progress was monitored closely by men and boys slouching outside their houses, smoking clay pipes or cheap Early Bird cigarettes. Painfully aware of the less-than-inviting looks, he knocked on Hanker's door until it was answered by a woman holding a screaming baby.

'Mr Kendal!' yelled Lonsdale, above the ear-splitting screeches. 'Where does he live?'

'Why?' demanded the woman. 'My husband John does chimneys better than old Kendal. When do you want him to come?'

'He's already been,' shouted Lonsdale, then added hastily, seeing the woman's lips harden into a thin line, 'and a splendid job he did. We'll most definitely ask him again. But I need to speak to Kendal about something else.'

'I know, you think Kendal can do better,' said the woman bitterly, jigging the baby up and down vigorously enough to make it sick. 'Well, there isn't a finer sweep in London than John. And his cloths are always clean. I wash 'em myself.'

'Then tell him to come to Number Seventeen Cleveland Square next Thursday at nine o'clock,' yelled Lonsdale, to convince her he was not taking his custom to Kendal. 'Now, where can I find Mr Kendal?'

The woman nodded her satisfaction. 'All right, then. He lives on Hatton Street, the other side of Edgware Road. But if I hear you employed him over John, I'll be round to your house – and not with clean cloths!'

Lonsdale believed it. He escaped from her and her shrieking offspring with relief.

Hatton Street was even more downtrodden, and equally popu-
lated with sullen, resentful men who watched him with open
suspicion. Lonsdale asked one where Kendal lived. The fellow
nodded at a house with planks of wood nailed over the glassless
windows.

A young woman with a white face and a tubercular cough
answered Lonsdale's knock and conducted him to a small room
at the back. The sweep sat in the only chair, huddled next to a
miserable fire that produced a pall of choking smoke. Lonsdale
felt like recommending he have his chimney swept. A broken-
down iron bed stood near the window, strewn with covers that
had been coal sacks in a previous incarnation. A wooden table
with a broken leg was pushed against the wall to keep it standing.
The sweep himself was elderly, with red-rimmed and runny
eyes. Gnarled, soot-impregnated hands clutched a dirty bottle
filled with a colourless liquid. He raised it to his lips when
Lonsdale entered and drank deeply.

'Please forgive the intrusion,' said Lonsdale. 'I wondered
whether you might be able to help me.'

Kendal looked him up and down. 'Of course,' he said bitterly.
'I'm sure there's all manner of things the likes of me could do
for the likes of you.'

Lonsdale took a shilling from his pocket and laid it on the
mantelpiece.

'It's about the fire in Wyndham Street—'

'I see!' snarled the sweep, coming unsteadily to his feet.
'You've come to accuse me of killing Mr Donovan!'

'No,' said Lonsdale, standing his ground as Kendal staggered
towards him. 'I just wanted to ask—'

'That fire ruined me,' said the sweep, turning from anger to
self-pity in the way that drunks often did. 'I should be out there
now, working. I had a full week booked. Then Donovan sets
himself alight, and who gets the blame? Everyone's cancelled
me, even the vicarage – and I've been doing them chimneys
for thirty years.'

'I'm sorry,' said Lonsdale quietly.

'The Fire Brigade accused me of leaving a brush up there!'
Kendal gestured to a shadowy corner, where there was a collection of black-headed brooms and poles. 'But you tell me what

you see there. All my brushes, that's what. They're expensive! How do they think I can afford to leave them up chimneys?'

'I see your point.'

'I went back to Donovan's house, you know,' said Kendal, slumping back down in his chair. 'On Friday – the night after the fire. I looked up the chimney.'

'What did you see?'

'Nothing,' said Kendal mournfully. He slumped further down in his chair and studied the reporter blearily. 'You don't get it, do you?'

Lonsdale struggled to understand. 'Nothing? You mean you couldn't see up the chimney? It was blocked?'

The sweep nodded. 'But I could see right up it when I finished cleaning. I got down on my hands and knees, like I always do, and saw a ring of sky like a bright, round penny. I take pride in my work, and if that penny hadn't been round, I'd have had the brushes up again.'

'Yet it was blocked after the fire?' asked Lonsdale.

Kendall nodded. 'I poked about with a stick, and a ball of burned rags came down. I looked up the chimney again, and there was the penny of sky.'

'So, someone deliberately stuffed them up it, so that the fire would be deemed an accident?'

'Why would someone do such a thing to me?' wailed Kendal. 'I've been honest all my life. I've had plenty of opportunities to slip a silver spoon or a few coins in my pocket, or to filch a bit of crockery. But I never did it, not once. Now I wish I had. There's so many sweeps that it's not easy to get work, but I've done all right, because everyone knows I'm honest. But some folks are struggling something cruel.'

Lonsdale glanced around Kendal's grimy, sparsely furnished home, and wondered how those 'struggling something cruel' were forced to live.

'I believe you're innocent of any wrong-doing, Mr Kendal,' said Lonsdale. 'And I'm going to prove it, but I need your help. Will you tell me – with all your knowledge of chimneys and fires – how the blaze started in Donovan's house?'

Hope lit the old man's eyes. 'I think the rags were shoved up the chimney and set alight. Of course, they'd need to have

been soaked in something to make them burn. Oil perhaps.
Then the chimney would catch fire, because the flames would
be fed by the air coming down it. Once a chimney is going,
it's a devil to put out. More often than not the whole house
goes. I told the police all this, but I could tell they thought I
was just trying to save my own skin.'

'Did you catch the names of the officers?'

'No, but I can tell you that the first one I spoke to was older,
with a scar over his eye, while the second had ginger hair and
looked young enough to be my grandson.'

Lonsdale felt his heartbeat quicken. 'Was the first one a large
man, with black hair?'

'I suppose,' said the old man, frowning as he tried to recall.
'Of course, they don't know their arses from their elbows – the
ginger lad told me that the scarred one had never been here.'

Kendal could tell him no more, so Lonsdale took his leave,
promising again to clear his name.

The Oxford and Cambridge Club was a grand building at 71–77
Pall Mall, with a pillared porch and an imposing façade. Its
only requirement for membership was matriculation at – not
necessarily graduation from – one of the two universities. It
had been founded in the 1830s, after the waiting list for the
United University Club had become too long to be tolerated.

Gentlemen's clubs tended to be understated on the outside,
but the Oxford and Cambridge was unique in having a smartly
uniformed porter on the *outside*, and by the time Lonsdale and
Milner reached him, the door was open. They nodded their thanks
and entered the spacious hall. They gave their hats and overcoats
to another porter, and Milner also handed over an umbrella topped
with a finely carved eagle's head with very conspicuous eyes.
He dreaded the possibility of getting wet in a sudden shower.

'Stead got hold of that today,' said Milner, nodding to it. 'He
came to the reporters' room to hold forth. Suddenly, it was in
his hands, whirling around as if he were leading a cavalry
charge.'

'Did you manage to ditch Harris?' asked Lonsdale. The
American was nowhere to be seen.

Milner grimaced. 'He has promised to grace me with his

presence later. I'm hoping that it will be late enough that everyone I know will have gone home.'

They headed up the stairs to the drawing room, a sumptuous wood-panelled chamber packed with comfortable chairs, sofas, and low tables scattered with newspapers. Jack was there, sitting with John Seeley, Regius Professor of History at Cambridge, and the man who had convinced Lonsdale to join the Colonial Service. Lonsdale introduced him and Milner.

'Are you a Cambridge man?' asked Seeley, shaking Milner's hand. 'Or are you from the Other Place?'

'Alfred is too modest to boast,' said Lonsdale, 'but he not only took a double first at Balliol, but won no fewer than four of Oxford's major scholarships.'

Milner blushed, and Lonsdale was amused to see him at a loss for words. Seeley motioned for them to sit down.

'Jack has been regaling me with the most alarming news, Alec,' he said. 'That you've decided to turn your unfortunate interest in journalism into a full-time profession. You were one of my best students . . . and to be telling stories for a newspaper! There must be something we can do to make you return to the Colonial Service.'

'There isn't,' said Lonsdale, shortly. 'This is what I want to do.' He was very fond of Seeley, so had not wanted to respond too forcefully. But before he could change the subject, Seeley turned to Milner.

'Can *you* persuade him to abandon this reckless course of action?' A man of your scholarly background must deplore a squandering of such talents. Alec could someday be a foreign ambassador. Urge him to follow this path.'

'That would be beyond my capabilities,' Milner responded, 'not to mention rather hypocritical if I attempted it, under the circumstances. Besides, journalists *are* ambassadors, are they not? They interpret events and opinions, which they then present to a large body of people.'

'That's an intriguing notion,' said Seeley, contemplating Milner's argument.

'I understand that you have written another book, Professor,' Lonsdale said quickly, hoping to avoid any awkward differences in opinion. 'One to be published next year?'

'Indeed I have,' said Seeley. A discussion of the theories that his new work would propound ensued, and both the professor and Milner were pleased with the challenge of the other's intellect. Finally, there was a pause, and Seeley looked around gloomily.

'The club isn't what it once was. I hardly know a soul here. I recognize Francis Galton, but no one else.'

'Galton?' asked Jack, sitting up abruptly. 'I'd like to meet *him*! His theories relating to natural history . . . well, they are astounding to say the least.'

Seeley gave a sly smile. 'Perhaps I *should* introduce you to him, Alec. He was in Africa, so he might be able to talk some sense into you about the Colonial Service.'

Francis Galton, one of the country's most eminent gentleman-scientists, an expert on travel, and author of several much-acclaimed books on heredity, looked up with rude disinterest when Seeley introduced the Lonsdale brothers and Milner. Galton was a stocky man with thick eyebrows, bald except for a fringe of long, dangling grey hair around the back, and a pair of colossal mutton-chop sideburns. A gentleman in a charcoal grey lounge suit was engrossed in his paper in the chair opposite; he vacated his seat politely when he saw that Galton had visitors, so that they all might sit down together. Something about him was familiar, but Seeley was making introductions, so there was no time for Lonsdale to ponder about him.

'I was hoping you might persuade Alec to rejoin the Colonial Service,' said Seeley amiably once introductions had been made, 'instead of wasting his great talents on newspapers.'

'You're a reporter?' asked Galton, in much the same way that he might have spoken to a dung collector; clearly, there was no difference between the two in his eyes. 'I hope you don't think I shall speak to you about my cousin Charles Darwin. I've had the press pestering me day and night, wanting a eulogy. Well, you shall not have it!'

'I see,' said Lonsdale, taken aback by his vehemence and exchanging an uncomfortable glance with Milner. 'But we didn't—'

'Your work on heredity and intelligence can only be described as brilliant, Mr Galton,' said Jack enthusiastically, breaking into what could have become an embarrassing discussion. 'I can't tell you how much I enjoy your writing.'

Galton's pale eyes immediately softened. 'Of course you do. Any man of breeding and intellect will appreciate the significance of my work.'

Milner caught Lonsdale's eye and raised an amused eyebrow. Lonsdale looked away quickly, not wanting to laugh, although Galton was far too engrossed in himself to notice.

'I'm working on another book entitled *Inquiries into Human Faculty and Its Development*,' he continued pompously. 'It will be a seminal work, admired and consulted by scholars for many generations to come.'

'What's its central thesis?' asked Jack keenly.

Galton preened. 'It builds on my previous work, including *Hereditary Genius* and *English Men of Science*, and it presents the results of several experiments. It begins with an analysis of physical characteristics – such as facial features and physical build. Then it considers energy and sensitivity, both of which are shown to be greater in the intellectually gifted – like me – than in the less able of our species.'

'Goodness!' blurted Jack, showing that even he was taken aback by Galton's boastful manner.

'I have investigated the subject of *character*, perhaps best illustrated in the traits that distinguish the sexes,' Galton went on. 'You see, characteristics found in mankind can also be discovered in lesser species – such as directness in men and a caprice in women.'

'Caprice?' echoed Lonsdale, thinking of Hulda and unable to imagine her ever having a 'capricious' moment in her life.

Galton nodded impatiently. 'Yes. The willy-nilly disposition of the human female in matters of love is also apparent in the butterfly, so it must have been continuously favoured from the earliest stages of animal evolution. Capriciousness has thus become a heritage of ladies, together with a cohort of allied weaknesses that men have come to think admirable in their wives and lovers, but that they would never tolerate among themselves.'

'I would hardly—' Seeley began, but Galton droned on mercilessly.

'The *next* section of my book investigates such matters as fear, revulsion, conscience, and gregariousness. And the last part draws it all together by showing how selective breeding would control these characteristics and benefit our race as a whole.'

'How intriguing,' said Jack nervously.

'Breeding,' announced Galton in a loud voice, 'is the heart of the problem. It should never be done without thought or reason.'

Lonsdale regarded the scientist in genuine horror, thinking his comments were every bit as distasteful as those made by Wilson.

'To no nation is a high human breed more necessary than our own,' Galton brayed on. 'We plant our stock around the world, laying the foundation for future millions of the human race. Yet you've only to walk in Whitechapel to see how the weak are numerically supplanting the strong – and the appalling poverty that accompanies this. It cannot be allowed to continue, and, by denying criminals, the idle, and other undesirables the opportunity to breed, we would abolish much suffering and misery.'

There was a stunned silence before Seeley, with a stricken, apologetic glance at the three younger men, hastened to change the subject. Lonsdale was relieved, having never expected to hear such offensive sentiments in his own club. 'Lonsdale was in southern Africa for a spell,' Seeley said, a little desperately. 'You were there, weren't you, Galton?'

'A spell?' drawled Galton, in distaste. 'And what was your "spell", young man? A couple of weeks? It is my contention that one cannot understand a continent in less than a month.'

'Nine years,' replied Lonsdale, gratified to see the great man's surprise. But good manners got the better of him, obliging him to add, 'I hear you were there in the forties, sir. Your experiences must have been fascinating—'

'I can tell you about them now,' said Galton, glancing at his watch. 'I have a few hours to spare.'

And without further ado, he began a detailed monologue describing every moment of what sounded to be a remarkably dull expedition. His audience listened politely, but all attempts to change the subject or escape were ruthlessly quashed. After an hour, a steward came to say that Harris had arrived, and it was a testament to Galton's tediousness that Lonsdale actually envied Milner for being able to go and greet the obnoxious American. Galton droned on, and Lonsdale looked at Milner with pleading eyes when he returned with his guest a few moments later. Milner took a deep breath and returned to the fray.

'I'm afraid I must take my friends away, Mr Galton,' he began. 'They—'

'Nonsense,' said Galton and continued his story. 'I found the daughter of the king of Ovampoland installed in my tent in her finery – she was covered with red ochre and butter, and as capable of leaving a mark on anything she touched as a well-inked printer's roller. Meanwhile, I was dressed in my one well-preserved suit of white linen—'

But Galton had reckoned without Harris, who, on recognizing him, homed in on him like a bluebottle on rotting meat. He thrust his outstretched hand into Galton's face. 'Ambrose Harris of *The New York Herald*. I wonder if I might ask you a few questions about Mr Darwin for the overseas audience.'

'Young man,' said Galton, brushing the proffered hand away contemptuously, 'a gentlemen's club is for *gentlemen*. It is not somewhere to demonstrate distasteful forwardness.' He stood and addressed Seeley. 'If you ever needed an instrument of persuasion against journalism, that man is it. He has quite put me off my dinner. I shall go home instead.'

'Thank God,' muttered Jack as the scientist gathered up his belongings. 'And thank Milner!'

'You seem a decent enough fellow,' said Galton, turning to Lonsdale before he left. 'I've enjoyed discussing Africa with you. Call on me at home next Friday afternoon, and I shall finish my story, although I appreciate you will find it hard to wait for the denouement. And then I shall show you something you will never forget – my collection of dried grasses from the Trans-Orange region!'

'I can think of little I'd enjoy more,' lied Lonsdale.

'I do enjoy the Reverend Carpenter's sermons,' said Jack the following morning – Sunday – as he and his brother strolled through Kensington Gardens. 'He makes his case about the teachings of the Church with the intellect of a barrister, the precision of an engineer, and the force of an Evangelical.'

'I'm not sure that he would appreciate being called an Evangelical,' said Lonsdale. 'Or worse yet, a barrister.'

'Do not try to vex me – not today of all days,' said Jack mildly. He tipped his hat to a couple strolling the other way. The gentleman tipped back.

'Don't worry. I'll behave when your fiancée and her sister come to dine today.' Lonsdale glanced at him. 'This custom of constantly raising the hat is very odd. Before I left for Africa, it was thought to be foreign and in bad taste. Now everyone is doing it.'

'Emelia likes the respect it affords,' said Jack, tipping to another couple. 'And I aim to please. Shall we go home now to make sure Mrs Webster and the servants have returned from church and are preparing the meal? If it is not ready by two, Emelia will be irked.'

Lonsdale disliked the way Jack was constantly changing himself to please Emelia. The couple had first been introduced a year before at a meeting in support of the Married Women's Property Act, and had become engaged at Christmas. He had dined with her family three of every four Sundays since, and, despite him being twelve years older than her, both families had been supportive of the proposed union.

Jack had hosted Emelia and her family before, but never when Lonsdale had been there. Lonsdale had thus never met any of the clan other than Emelia. Jack was anxious that they – and especially Emelia's sister Anne – should like his brother, and evidently was terrified that Lonsdale might do something to make them think twice about having given him permission to marry their younger daughter. Lonsdale was mildly offended that Jack did not have more confidence in him, and could only suppose that the decision to become a journalist had given his brother a deeper shock than he had realized.

'Don't worry, Jack,' said Lonsdale kindly. 'You have a gem of a housekeeper in Mrs Webster. No one realizes better than she does that this is the first time you have entertained Emelia with only her sister and me as chaperones. Moreover, I am sure Anne will like me and will sing my praises to your fiancée.'

'You sound like Galton,' muttered Jack, eyeing him suspiciously and very nervously.

Shortly after one o'clock, Emilia and Anne arrived by private carriage. They were clearly sisters: tall, dark eyed, slim, and with naturally curly hair brushed back into a bun at the nape of the neck in the popular fashion of the day. Emelia's was dark brown; Anne's was lighter, almost blond. Lonsdale found Anne, the elder by just over two years, not only much prettier but far more charming.

Emelia was also nervous of the first meeting between Anne and Lonsdale, although he could not imagine why, as Anne seemed a rational, intelligent woman, not at all the prim, dull spinster he had feared. Knowing that the affianced couple were more concerned that Anne might not like him rather than the other way around, he went out of his way to be as courteous and pleasing as possible.

Most of the conversation at the meal revolved around the changes that Emelia would make to Jack's house when she became mistress of it. Bored, Lonsdale asked Emelia to describe how she and Jack had met, knowing she loved to recount the tale. However, in the presence of Anne, he learned two things Emelia and Jack had not told him before – that Emelia had only attended the meeting to support the Married Women's Property Act because Anne had begged her to, and that Jack had only been there because a colleague had done the same to him. Lonsdale wondered why Jack had persisted in his courtship, given that he and Emelia had little in common, but saw from Jack's besotted expression that no amount of reasoning or logic would convince him that he could do better.

Even when Emelia rose from the table and began to walk around the room pointing out items that would have to be removed or changed when she was in charge, Jack watched her dotingly, and Lonsdale saw that there was nothing he would not do for her. Yet how dull she was! He glanced at Anne and saw that she had been studying him. Embarrassed to be caught, she quickly looked away.

After the meal, Emelia suggested a stroll around the square onto which Jack's house backed. The engaged couple walked leisurely arm-in-arm, while the chaperones followed behind, Lonsdale with his hands clasped behind his back, and Anne clutching her pelisse.

'Do *you* think my brother's house needs complete renovation?' Lonsdale asked, as he heard Emelia's high-pitched assurance that dark-blue flock wallpaper would look charming in the morning room.

'I wouldn't presume to judge. At the risk of sounding radical, I believe people should decorate the inside of their homes as suits them, rather than as convention dictates.'

'I agree,' said Lonsdale, pleasantly surprised. 'In Africa, houses are designed for comfort, and fashion is a very distant second.'

Anne transpired to be an easy, pleasant conversationalist once away from her silly younger sister, and they soon advanced from Mr Lonsdale and Miss Humbage to Alec and Anne. She and Emelia had spent their early years in India – the daughters of a former brigadier – and she talked intelligently and astutely about it. She listened with fascination as Lonsdale spoke of Africa – the lands, peoples, and wildlife. He was surprised to find he was enjoying himself.

'Your descriptions make me wish to visit Africa,' said Anne. 'It's obvious you care about it, so why did you leave?'

'Because of the actions and attitudes of some of those in charge,' said Lonsdale. 'I was a Colonial Service administrator, first under Bartle Frere in Zanzibar and then General Wolseley in the Gold Coast and Ashanti. I served under both again in southern Africa. But for every gem like Sir Henry or Sir Garnet, there were other governors or commissioners who were morally bankrupt. Eventually, Owen Lanyon's treatment of the Boers and the other Africans became so oppressive and bigoted that I resigned.'

'But I thought Jack said you were at Whitehall after you returned home.'

'When I reached London, I found my resignation had been treated as a reassignment to the Colonial Office itself. I suspect Wolseley was behind that, because by that time he was back in

England, but he's never admitted it. However, it still wasn't what I wanted, so after eight months I resigned again.'

'And now you're a reporter.'

'Yes,' he said, not mentioning that he would not be a real one unless he earned the full-time post. He glanced at her. 'How do you spend *your* days?'

'Wishing I had what you do: the freedom to live my life as I want, without being hindered by social constraints. I want to wear *comfortable* clothes, not silly dresses that are so tight I feel hobbled like a horse. And I want to study at the university, to read philosophy and politics as I please, and to vote for the government that runs my country.'

'That's not unreasonable,' said Lonsdale.

'I'm glad to hear you think so,' said Anne, and smiled.

Lonsdale's stomach did a curious little flip, and he felt not a little irritated that Jack and Emelia should have conspired to keep this pretty, intelligent woman away from him for so long.

SIX

As Lonsdale had been told that he would not be needed until Monday afternoon, he decided to see if the pathologist Bradwell had any new information to share. He pushed open the mortuary door and was startled to see a number of policemen gathered in the hallway. Inspector Peters was there, fiddling with his pipe, while Bradwell leaned nonchalantly against a wall next to him, oblivious to the black mould that stained his coat.

'Lonsdale,' drawled the inspector. 'Ever a man at the scene of a crime, I see. Well, I want a word with you.'

'That sounds ominous,' said Lonsdale. 'Why?'

'You went to see the sweep, Kendal,' said Peters. 'Even though my superiors ordered you to leave Donovan's death for the police to explore.'

'Yes, I did,' said Lonsdale, unrepentant. 'It was an enlightening

conversation, and has convinced me even more that something
is badly amiss.'

He outlined the sweep's discovery of the rags in the chimney
and what they might have meant. When he had finished, Peters
was scowling.

'So why did he say nothing of this to us?' he demanded.

'He did, sir,' said a young policeman with a mop of ginger
hair, overhearing. He hastened to explain himself. 'But he was
drunk – he said he'd already spoken to the police, but that was
a lie because *I* was the first sent to interview him. I assumed
he was trying to worm his way out of being blamed.'

'I see,' said Peters, turning his lugubrious stare on the young
officer, who blushed and began a detailed study of the mud on
his boots.

'The "policeman" Kendal referred to had a scar through his
eyebrow,' announced Lonsdale, unable to resist a touch of the
dramatic.

'No!' gulped the lad in alarm. 'I meant . . . I didn't ask for
a description, but why would I? He was drunk, so I thought he
was making it all up. As I said, I was the only one sent . . .'

Peters pursed his lips. 'Then you'd better go and talk to him
again, lad. Determine for certain if it was Iverson who quizzed
him.'

Eager to make amends, the constable hurried out. 'So
someone deliberately started the fire to hide that Donovan had
been mutilated,' said Bradwell. He glanced at Peters. 'I think
you should take Lonsdale into your confidence, because we
need all the help we can get, and you cannot rely on your
superiors to supply it.'

'No, I can't,' acknowledged Peters, tiredly.

Lonsdale looked from one to the other. 'Has something
happened? Why are all these officers here?'

'Because our killer has just acquired himself another cerebrum,' said Bradwell, 'from here, right under our noses.'

Lonsdale stared down at the body on the dissecting table. The
injury looked like the one Bradwell had shown him on his first
visit, although this victim was older and fitter. There was a
gaping wound in the neck, although the head seemed to be intact.

'I don't understand,' he said. 'Donovan's head was crushed, but this one seems normal enough.'

'Look closer,' instructed Bradwell. Seeing Lonsdale's bemusement, he sighed impatiently. 'No, closer! You won't see anything from back there, and it won't bite.'

Lonsdale was disinclined to pore over corpses just to satisfy Bradwell. 'Just point out what I'm missing,' he suggested. 'It will be quicker.'

Bradwell slipped his hand under the fringe of hair that dropped across the body's forehead and lifted it. Underneath, there was a thin, but distinct incision.

'I take it you didn't do that,' said Lonsdale.

'Why would I look at the head of a body with a slashed throat?' asked Bradwell. 'I don't have time. In cases like this, where the cause of death is obvious, I perform the briefest of examinations and move on. If I performed a complete, extensive examination on every one, we would be drowning in them.'

'Do so many people suffer violent deaths, then?' asked Lonsdale.

'Fortunately not,' replied Bradwell. 'Most die from dysentery, phthisis, children's fevers, or diseases of the heart and lungs – such as heart attacks, pneumonia, and bronchitis – not to mention accidents.'

Lonsdale indicated the corpse on the table. 'So how can you be sure that this cut wasn't made by his killer?'

Bradwell looked indignant. 'I may be forced to work fast, but I always follow specific procedures. I look for stab marks on the torso, look in the mouth for blistering or discoloration from poison, look at the hands and forearms for any evidence of self-defence, and check the skull for dents and bumps.'

Lonsdale raised his eyebrows. 'Even when it's obvious that the person died of a disease or an accident?'

Bradwell nodded. 'I've seen many cases where a family has hastened the end of an ill relative.'

Lonsdale stared down at the body. 'So when was he . . .'

'Some time between when I finished his post mortem on Thursday night and about two hours ago, when the body was due to be released for burial. But I imagine it happened last night, after O'Connor and I had gone home. Sundays are always quiet here.'

'And the cerebrum is gone?'

Bradwell peeled back the scalp to reveal a circular groove in the bone, where the uppermost part had been sliced through, like taking the top off a hard-boiled egg. He eased the detached cap away, and Lonsdale saw a dark cavity coated with a yellowish-grey matter and clots of blood.

'What do you think, Lonsdale?' asked Peters, calmly puffing at his pipe, which, mixed with the smell of death and disinfectant, made Lonsdale slightly queasy.

'That whoever did this must have lost control of his wits. Have any of the other bodies been . . .?' He hesitated. The words savaged, despoiled, or mutilated seemed too brutal for such a clinical procedure.

'No,' said Bradwell. 'I've been uneasy since I was almost fooled over Donovan's death, so I've inspected every corpse as it arrives, then again when it's released. Thank God I did!'

'How did the culprit get in?' asked Lonsdale.

'Through the small window at the back. It's not the first time we've been burgled that way, despite it being seven feet off the ground. Thieves think we keep the personal effects of the deceased here, but few people we house have much worth stealing.'

'That depends on your standards,' said Lonsdale, thinking about the workhouse. 'Have you asked around for potential witnesses?'

'Around here?' asked Peters archly. 'The rule of the folk in this area is "see nothing, hear nothing, know nothing", especially if it's the police who ask.'

'But surely they'd only keep quiet if the culprit was someone they knew,' persisted Lonsdale. 'They wouldn't lie to protect a stranger, would they?'

'Even a criminal has a greater claim on their allegiance than a police officer,' said Peters. 'They—'

Suddenly there was a loud knock at the door to the postmortem theatre, followed by an irate demand to open up at once. Peters turned quickly to Lonsdale and pointed towards a large closet. With a shock, Lonsdale saw he expected him to hide there.

'Superintendent Ramsey might not be as understanding about

your meddling as I've been,' said Peters, when Lonsdale hesitated. 'Hurry, man! He might order you arrested.'

Reluctantly, Lonsdale did as he was told, entering a tiny room containing stacks of reports on shelves. He did not close the door completely, but held it open a crack so that he could watch and listen.

Ramsey strode in like a Shakespearian actor, Leonard at his heels like a faithful dog. The superintendent immediately began a furious diatribe, although Leonard smiled genially and nodded friendly greetings to his colleagues. Lonsdale was wondering how two such completely different individuals could work together, when a vision of Hulda sprang to mind. Leonard probably had no more control over whom he worked with than did Lonsdale.

'This is an outrage!' stormed Ramsey. 'Is nowhere safe? What are you doing about it, Bradwell?'

'There's not much I *can* do,' responded the surgeon with a shrug. 'O'Connor has boarded up the broken window. I'd board up the others, too, but my budget won't allow it. As it was, O'Connor had to use wood taken from a pile near a railway line.'

'You stole wood to mend police property?' breathed the superintendent, aghast. 'What do you think the newspapers would make of that?'

Bradwell's patience was wearing thin. 'I imagine they'd suggest giving me more money,' he snapped. 'The Metropolitan Police pay nothing towards the upkeep of the building. Look in the hall. If you wondered why it's so dark, it's because the gas pipes have been stolen, and your finance department has ignored my requests for replacements for eighteen months.'

'There's no need for light in the hall,' said Ramsey defensively. 'It's not as if the occupants need to see their way out.' He gestured at the gleaming tray of instruments. 'Moreover, you can't possibly need all those knives. One is sufficient, surely? Learn to manage your budget properly, man.'

Seeing the surgeon's face turn white with anger, Leonard stepped forward to intervene. Lonsdale imagined that he probably had a good deal of experience in calming waters troubled by his pompous, acerbic senior officer.

'Perhaps you could tell us what happened,' he suggested gently. He nodded to the body. 'How came it to lose—'

'I haven't finished my examination yet,' said Bradwell, his temper barely under control. 'You'll have to wait.'

He selected the largest knife from his arsenal of weapons and waved it in a way that was vaguely threatening. Hastily, Ramsey suggested he and his officers wait elsewhere, so Bradwell would not be distracted. Before Peters could object, Ramsey strode towards Lonsdale's hiding place.

Alarmed, Lonsdale looked around for a place to hide, and saw that the only possibility was behind a short cabinet at the back. He shot towards it and crouched down just as the door flew open and Ramsey marched in.

'This place is a disgrace,' the superintendent muttered. With horror, Lonsdale saw Ramsey's feet come closer, and realized that he intended to perch on the pile of papers directly in front of him.

'Here is a chair, sir,' Peters said, quickly grabbing one from next to the door and placing it so Ramsey's back was towards Lonsdale.

'I'm not sure Bradwell's appointment was wise,' said Ramsey, once Leonard had closed the door and all three – four including Lonsdale – were crowded inside. Lonsdale was tempted to laugh at the ridiculousness of the situation. 'The man's a fool. We never had problems like this with old Dr Robbins.'

'But Bradwell's reports don't make me want to request second opinions,' said Peters. 'We're lucky to have a man of his calibre. Don't forget that he covers the entire district north of the Thames, and we only pay him for twenty hours a week, regardless of how much time he works.'

'But this place is a disgrace,' Ramsey growled again, kicking at a stain on the floor.

'Very true,' agreed Peters. 'But that's hardly his fault.'

'So what do you plan to do about this stolen brain business?' Ramsey snapped. 'House enquiries around here will be useless. Have you checked the lunatic asylums for escapees? God knows, only a lunatic can be responsible for this outrage.'

'I've two men making enquiries as we speak. Yet I wonder

if this may be the work not of random madmen but someone with a desire for specific human organs.'

Ramsey groaned. 'Lord help us! What depths some folk will sink to! Are there any links between the fellow in the fire and the chap whose body's just been violated?'

'I cannot tell you that, sir. You took me off the Donovan case, if you recall.'

'Besides, there is the matter of jurisdiction,' put in Leonard. 'Peters is in Division D, but the most recent mutilation—'

'Philip Yeats,' put in Peters, causing Lonsdale to blink at yet another Irish name.

'—is in Division M,' finished Leonard. 'Southwark.'

'To hell with that administrative nonsense,' barked Ramsey. 'I want Peters investigating both these corpses – sort it out, Leonard. It's obvious there's a connection between Donovan and Yeats. Forget the other two – the whore and her accomplice.'

'But they're—' began Peters.

'We need to be *seen* on the Yeats murder,' interrupted Ramsey. 'When news that two desecrations have occurred seeps out, the press will be demanding an arrest.'

'Yeats died five days ago,' said Peters placatingly. 'His murder is old news, so there's no reason why this should leak out.'

'Then for God's sake, let's keep it that way. This *must* be kept from reporters. The last thing we want is headlines declaring that we have organ-stealing murderers on the rampage – especially ones who strike at men like Yeats. I'd lose my position for certain.'

'Men like Yeats?' asked Peters, bemused. 'What do you mean, sir?'

'He was a music-hall entertainer,' explained Leonard. 'He's famous in his way.'

'Bastards,' Ramsey snarled. 'We should hang them all.'

'Entertainers?' asked Peters, startled.

'Reporters!' snarled Ramsey. 'I mean the damn reporters! They encourage the lower classes to expect better than they deserve. They disclose secrets they've no business knowing in the first place. And they constantly get in the way of investigations and then tell us how to do our jobs! If this brain-thief was putting reporters in here, I wouldn't lift a finger to stop him.'

'Steady on, sir,' said Leonard, shocked. 'I find them irritating, too, but they're only doing their jobs.'

'And I have occasionally found them very helpful,' said Peters. 'They can offer a fresh perspective and have the advantage of gaining access to people and places denied to us.'

'You are a fool if you trust them,' declared Ramsey, breathing hard. He made an effort to bring his temper under control. 'Now listen, Peters, because I have an avenue I want you to explore. I'm giving you a pointer here.'

'Yes, sir?'

'I was in India for some years, so I am acquainted with the methods of Eastern criminals. I believe these murders might have been committed by a Malay or some other low-class Asiatic, of whom there are many in London. Mutilations are *Eastern* habits intended to express insult, hatred, and contempt. But there has never been an instance of murder and mutilation of this kind by an Englishman. So I think that some Asiatic man has taken the lives of those he holds guilty of injuring him in some way.'

'There's no evidence—' began Leonard, but Ramsey forged on.

'Thousands of them live in London, speak English, and dress in normal clothes. Such a man would be quite safe in the haunts of his fellow countrymen. Unless caught red-handed, being polite and even obsequious, he would be the last to be suspected. But when the villain is primed with opium or gin, and lustful for slaughter, he'll destroy his victim with the ferocity and cunning of a tiger. And past successes will render him even more daring. So we might face the terrors of this wily Asian again and again, unless he has joined a crew of Lascars on a steamer leaving the country.'

'I'll bear this insightful observation in mind, sir,' Peters said flatly.

'Good man. But don't dither, as there are more important matters to take up our time. For example, the Prince of Wales was almost blown up at the Court Theatre on Friday night, and there are rumours that the Fenians did it.'

'Those rumours are false,' said Leonard. 'The report from the Fire Brigade said that faulty gas pipes were responsible.'

'Gas!' spat Ramsey. 'The new miracle fuel! It won't last. You mark my words. No one wants a substance in his home that'll kill him just as easily as light his rooms.'

Before Ramsey could rant further, Bradwell walked in, to report what he had already told Peters and Lonsdale: that someone had removed Yeats's skullcap, sliced out the cerebrum, and concealed his work by carefully arranging the victim's hair. Ramsey responded with an interrogation, quizzing the pathologist about his methods, and even going so far as to intimate that Bradwell might have mutilated Yeats's corpse himself, as a ploy to increase his budget. When Bradwell's expression became murderous, Leonard suggested that he and Ramsey should leave so as not to be late for their next appointment. Ramsey glanced at his watch, his eyebrows shot up, and he hurried from the room without another word.

'I'm sorry, Peters,' Leonard said before he followed. 'But he's right – Yeats and Donovan must take priority. Forget about the prostitute.'

'Walker also deserves justice,' said Peters.

'And she'll have it – as soon as you've caught the maniac who steals brains,' said Leonard, and hurried after Ramsey.

'Bastard!' muttered Bradwell, as Lonsdale stood and emerged from his hiding place. 'Did you hear him accuse me of being the murderer? How dare he!'

'It was no more bizarre than his suggestion that the culprits are thuggees from India,' said Lonsdale.

'I'd be careful, if I were you, Lonsdale,' said Peters. 'When there's pressure to solve a crime, Ramsey usually responds by arresting someone, regardless of guilt or innocence. It could be you.'

'I admire your fortitude, Alec,' said Milner, as he and Lonsdale entered the Victorian Embankment Gardens for a moment's peace late that afternoon. They sat on a wooden bench that was soft with rot, and watched a flurry of pigeons squabbling over a bag of crumbs emptied out by a man in a bowler hat. Dark clouds massed overhead, promising rain, and the wind that sliced up from the river had a keen edge to it. 'To *choose* Hulda to help you, when Stead offered you the choice of all of us.'

'She's meticulous and perceptive. If anyone can find links between past murders and these current ones, it will be her.'

'How will you do that?'

'By looking in *The PMG* archive. Stead has given us his blessing to spend as much time there as need be, so now I'm just waiting for him to give us the key.'

'An interesting approach,' said Milner. 'And if that's what's been dominating your thoughts, then I needn't ask about Emilia's sister. If you meet a woman and all you can think about is murder . . .'

'Oh, I don't know,' said Lonsdale, recalling the fair, pretty features of Anne. 'We got on rather well.'

They walked back towards Northumberland Street, where Hulda was waiting. She brandished a key. 'You're late,' she said, although Lonsdale did not recall setting any particular time. 'I suppose you were talking about sport.'

'Sport?' he echoed, bewildered. 'Why would we be talking of sport?'

'All men do,' she replied authoritatively. 'They can't help themselves. It is a male obsession – whether they would rather shoot birds or mammals; whether they want a shotgun or a rifle; whether foreign animals are as enjoyable to kill as homegrown ones. The scope is endless.'

'Don't take a gun of any description into the archive with you, Alec,' warned Milner as Lonsdale prepared to follow her down the stairs. 'You might be tempted to use it on The Friederichs, confined as you will be.'

The Pall Mall Gazette archive was a claustrophobic basement room with a low ceiling, stone floors, and walls lined with metal cabinets holding copies of most London dailies. The filing was performed irregularly, which, in combination with reporters casually borrowing copies and tossing them back without regard for organization, meant that many were misfiled or lost altogether. It was also exceedingly noisy, as the two Marinoni presses turning out *The PMG* were located only a thin door away.

After only a few minutes on Tuesday morning – his first full day in the archive – Lonsdale felt filthy. Clouds of dust swirled when he shifted the piles of papers to get at those further back. The lighting was from a single hanging lamp that was inadequate, so Hulda was obliged to fetch a storm lantern from the reporters' room. The dry mustiness of the air and the oil fumes combined to make Lonsdale's head pound. It was a depressing place, and he could not rid himself of the notion that he was incarcerated in an Egyptian tomb.

By late afternoon, they were obliged to drink multiple cups of tea to stay awake. He had not realized what a daunting task he had given them – ploughing through each of six London morning dailies, five major evening papers, five quality Sunday publications, and numerous weeklies, including sensational gazettes that specialized in crime. Even with Hulda's help, he realized that he was going to have to spend days there.

However, he did feel they were making some progress. The more he read, the more he became sure that he had led Morley astray regarding the so-called Irish connection. It was true that Jamie's friends, along with Donovan and Yeats, had Irish names, but that was not to say they were Irish themselves. It was coincidence, although he and Hulda agreed to keep that to themselves, lest Morley took them off the case again.

'It's almost seven, and you've been down here all day,' came a voice from the door. 'Come to the club for dinner.'

'Thank you,' said Hulda, standing from where she had been kneeling on the floor. 'I should be delighted.'

'Hulda!' gulped Cook, *The PMG*'s youngest reporter. 'I did not realize you . . . I thought you'd gone home.'

'We'll go to the Oyster Bar,' said Lonsdale, and because he did not want Hulda to begin a rant on the injustice of women being barred from gentlemen's clubs, added, 'We won't be allowed in unless we change – we're filthy.'

Hulda nodded acceptance of the offer and they abandoned the dungeon with relief. Milner joined them, too, and they aimed for Fleet Street together.

Its convenience to the offices of numerous newspapers meant that Craig's Oyster Bar was always packed with reporters. It was open from midday to midnight, and the bustling, deadline-driven nature of its customers gave it a hectic, noisy atmosphere. Most newspapermen were well dressed, wearing clothes that were as suited to the Houses of Parliament or research in the British Library, as to visiting the scenes of accidents or conducting interviews. One man was different, however – a burly fellow wearing a dirty cloth cap. Lonsdale supposed he was an informant, instructed to meet a reporter there.

Hulda, Lonsdale, Milner and Cook ordered oysters for a shilling a dozen, washed down with warm, sweet stout. They talked about Prime Minister Gladstone's announcement that day of the release of Irish nationalist leader Charles Stewart Parnell from gaol, speaking loudly over the ear-shattering yells of other patrons and the crash of crockery and glasses from inside the bar.

When Hulda went to powder her nose, two reporters from *The Standard* joined them, changing the discussion to the explosion at the Court Theatre. They were openly jealous that Lonsdale had been on hand to see the Prince of Wales taking charge. They pestered him for details. Then one of them suddenly leapt to his feet, dragging his colleague with him, and headed for the door. Before Lonsdale knew what was happening, he felt a hand drop on his shoulder with considerable force.

'Glad I've found you lot,' boomed Harris, and sat uninvited. He grabbed a beer that one of *The Standard* men had abandoned, drained it in a single swallow, and wiped his sleeve over his lips. 'I received an official reprimand from the Garrick because of you, Lonsdale.'

'Have you?' asked Lonsdale, not surprised, given his unpleasant interaction with Dr Wilson in the Garrick's reading room.

'They won't say why,' said Harris, 'but a number of people have suddenly taken against me. All I can think is that you misbehaved when you were my guest.'

'You don't think you've done anything yourself, then?' Cook asked mildly. 'Clubs do like a certain air of gentility and elegance.'

'Of course they do,' replied Harris unabashed. 'Which is why I can only think Lonsdale must have done something wrong.'

'We need to be at the House of Commons in half an hour to hear the Opposition's responses to Parnell's release,' lied Lonsdale, aiming to escape, although he was aware that would leave Hulda with the man when she returned. 'Are you two ready?'

'Yes,' said Milner with relief, despite having only eaten half his food.

'You don't want these then?' asked Harris, nodding to the oysters Milner had left on his plate.

'No, but neither do you,' said Milner. 'I think there's something wrong with them. They taste off.'

'Nonsense,' declared Harris, hauling the plate over to where he was sitting. 'Waste not, want not, as they say.'

'We should go,' said Lonsdale, starting to stand.

'Not yet,' said Harris, as he forked an oyster into his mouth. 'Mr Northcote, the Conservative leader, won't speak for at least another hour. You've plenty of time to enjoy more of this warm beer you English love. And I want to talk to you anyway.' Butter dripped down his chin.

'About what?' said Milner, gaping in astonishment as Harris leaned across the table and helped himself to Hulda's stout.

'Wilson – the zoo director,' replied Harris, pushing his hat onto the back of his head and taking another crustacean. 'He told me not to let you near him ever again. I want to know why. Is there a story I should know about?'

'There is,' said Hulda, who had returned unnoticed. She reclaimed her stout, but did not drink it. 'However, it's a secret. Can we trust you not to run with it first?'

'Of course,' said Harris, eyes gleaming. 'What is it?'

'Apes,' replied Hulda. 'Several hundred have escaped recently, and have been hired to work in Shoreditch by the East London Waterworks Company, which likes them because they accept lower wages. Obviously, Dr Wilson doesn't want to be accused of flouting employment laws, so he's keen to keep a low profile.'

Harris gazed at her. 'You're serious?'

'Completely,' said Hulda without the flicker of a smile. 'Go and check for yourself. However, please promise not to report it before *The PMG*. We don't want to lose such a scoop.'

'I promise,' said Harris, scrambling to his feet. 'Good evening to you, ma'am.'

'What?' asked Hulda when he had gone, aware of the others'

raised eyebrows. Then she allowed herself a small smile. 'Well, he's been asking for it for a long time.'

'Men like Harris make me worry about what is in store for the press in the future,' said Milner, as he and Lonsdale strolled at a leisurely pace along the Strand together. Cook and Hulda had gone to their homes in different directions. Gas lamps threw insipid pools of light onto the pavements, and there was a damp, chill feeling that suggested more drizzle was in the offing.

'In what way?' asked Lonsdale.

'That, before long, we'll all be ordered to climb up drainpipes to spy on public figures and their illicit loves, or fight each other for statements from the bereaved at the scenes of accidents.'

'The press will never sink so low,' said Lonsdale firmly.

'It will,' insisted Milner. 'Reporters will become jackals, feeding off the famous and the infamous, grubbing about in the gutters for ever more vile and filthy tales.'

'Lord!' breathed Lonsdale. 'You're in a melancholy mood tonight.'

'Your current story is a case in point,' Milner went on. 'Stolen body parts and murdered prostitutes. It's all too horrible. It will create an appetite for ever more sordid stories, and we will descend into the pit of sensationalism.'

The two men walked in silence for several moments.

'Are you interested in what Hulda and I found in our search today?' Lonsdale asked. 'Or will it be too horrible?'

Milner sighed. 'Probably – but proceed anyway.'

'She found several items in the February papers,' said Lonsdale, pulling his notebook from his pocket. He strained to read aloud in the poor light:

> *An inquest was held yesterday concerning the deaths of Frederick Kempster, aged twenty-eight, and Edmund Corlett, aged twenty-six, who were burned to death on Tuesday morning at a fire that occurred in Southampton Row, Holborn, on the premises of Messrs Morson and Sons, manufacturing chemists. Mr Kempster was the*

manager of the retail department, and Mr Corlett the first
assistant.

'Surely you're not suggesting that every fire in London has a sinister motive?'

'Just listen.' Lonsdale read on:

The evidence indicated that the only explosive upon the
premises was benzoline, of which not more than ten gallons
were kept at a time, and that was stored in a vault. All
the fires were put out the previous night, a gas jet being
the only light left on the premises. When the fire was
discovered it had full command of the premises. No explan-
ation could be given for its origin. Both men were badly
crushed by the collapse of parts of the building, obliging
the bodies to be identified by the keys in their
possession.

Milner stopped walking and looked at Lonsdale. 'You think they are victims, too?'

'There's more. According to *The Daily Telegraph*, a similar fire occurred a week later at the Thornycroft shipyard in Chiswick, where one person's head was mutilated beyond recognition. And shortly after that, several papers carried accounts of how the entire upper body of a workman disappeared in a violent explosion at a vinegar works in Peckham.'

'*Four* other cases?' breathed Milner.

'*Possible* cases,' corrected Lonsdale. 'But those are only the ones we've found so far. There may be others. Many others.'

'Then you are right to pursue it,' said Milner grimly. 'Vile it may be, but if you can catch the perpetrators and save lives . . .'

Before they had walked much further, both Lonsdale and Milner were assailed with a great feeling of weariness. A hansom drove near, and Lonsdale hailed it. 'Pimlico,' he told the driver, pushing Milner into it. 'Fifty-four Claverton Street.'

He waved at the disappearing cab and looked for another. But most hansoms were engaged, because the theatres were just letting out. After several unsuccessful attempts, he decided to walk towards Oxford Street in the hope that the area away from Trafalgar Square might have fewer customers for the cabs. As soon as he turned from the colourful bustle of the Strand and its amber gaslights, everything seemed colder and less friendly. Despite being used to traipsing around the city at night, Lonsdale felt that St Martin's Lane seemed black and sinister, and he could not shake off the sense that he was not alone. But each time he glanced behind him, he saw nothing amiss. The gradual lessening of the traffic noise as he moved away from the main thoroughfare made his footsteps echo, and once or twice he thought he heard a second set behind him. He began to doubt the wisdom of his decision to leave the main streets.

He glanced behind him again, abruptly. There! A shadow flickered briefly at the periphery of his vision before fading into the darkness of a doorway. There was indeed someone on his heels. He walked faster and, when he came to a particularly dark section, ducked to one side. Then he waited, heart thudding, to see what his pursuer would do. He was not disappointed. Seconds later, a shadow slipped past, and he heard a litany of ripe curses as his stalker saw he had been given the slip. Lonsdale's arm shot out of the gloom and grabbed him by the scruff of the neck.

'Still following me, Jamie?' he asked softly, gratified to see the alarm on the boy's face.

'Steady, old pal,' gasped Jamie, wriggling free. 'You fair set me old ticker racing like a pigeon's. Why're you leaping out on me like that?'

'Why are you still following me?' retorted Lonsdale coolly.

'Because I was worried,' explained the boy. 'You said you'd find out about me pals, and I'm just making sure you do it – and that I can warn you if them other coves are about.'

'Have you seen any of them since?'

'Ol' Big Arms,' replied Jamie. 'He followed you to that oyster bar, but he likes a drink, and by the time you left he was three sheets to the wind. He's still there. You can go back and see for yourself, if you don't believe me.'

'I do,' said Lonsdale, recalling the burly man in a cloth cap. Not an informant waiting for a reporter after all.

He walked to the nearest gas lamp and studied the lad in the light. He was shabbier than when they had last met, and his stolen clothes looked as though he had lived in them every second since. The cuffs of his trousers had been trodden into the muck of the streets, and his hat looked ready for the rag-and-bone men. Jamie sniffed, and ran the back of his hand over his nose, and Lonsdale saw the dirt deeply ingrained in his skin. The boy sneezed, then sniffed again, wetly.

'A cold?' asked Lonsdale sympathetically, holding out his handkerchief.

'New-moan-yer, I 'spect,' said Jamie, taking the proffered linen and dabbing his nose very carefully before offering it back. 'Comes of following folks around in the cold and wet.' He regarded Lonsdale challengingly, and the reporter laughed, thinking he had some gall to blame him for his sniffles.

'So, what do you want from me this time?' he asked, waving the handkerchief away. Jamie secreted it carefully in his pocket, and ran his sleeve across his nose instead.

'You to give me a job.'

Lonsdale stared at him. 'A job? You mean at the paper?'

'I could do it,' Jamie assured him. 'I can go places where you can't and blend in. Like I'll find out about that Walker tart for you.'

'No,' said Lonsdale immediately. 'That's too dangerous. However, there *is* something you could do. Did you hear about a fire in the chemical factory in Holborn? Two men – Frederick Kempster and Edmund Corlett – were killed back in February. I want to know what kind of people they were.'

'What kind of people?' asked Jamie, confused. 'You mean whether they liked doxies or boys?'

'Nothing so colourful. Find out if they had families, and, if so, where they live. I want to know if they were quiet or loud, rough or respectable. Ask their neighbours.'

'Why?' asked Jamie doubtfully. 'It doesn't sound like much of a job.'

'It is,' said Lonsdale. 'It's very important. And when you've finished in Holborn, there may be work for you in Chiswick and Peckham.'

Jamie listened avidly while Lonsdale explained what he

wanted him to do, and his eyes gleamed. 'Really, so I'll be a reporter?' he asked.

'An investigator,' said Lonsdale, wondering what information the boy would bring back. *Would* there be a connection between the death of quiet, shy, decent Donovan and the two men in Holborn? Or was he grabbing at straws that weren't there? Regardless, Jamie's enquiries would save him time if it was a wild-goose chase, and if it was not, well, he could always go back and ask the same questions himself.

'All right then,' said Jamie, and held out a grimy hand. 'But I need money for expenses.'

Lonsdale handed him a florin and some pennies. 'Start tomorrow. You know how to find me. And there will more when you tell me what you've discovered – whatever you find out. You'll be paid regardless. Just be careful.'

'I'm always careful, old pal,' declared Jamie.

SEVEN

Wednesday began poorly for Lonsdale. He had slept uneasily and was woken well before six, roused by the raucous shouting of a coalman outside. An early breakfast in the kitchen, under the disapproving eye of Mrs Webster – who did not believe it was proper for a gentleman to eat at the table used by the servants – ended in disaster when Lonsdale accidentally knocked a bowl of porridge from the hands of the younger of the two maids. It splattered across the floor and the lower half of her uniform.

On arriving in Northumberland Street, he went straight to the archive, where Hulda joined him not long after. But her presence proved more tiresome than helpful, and he began to wish he had chosen one of the others to help him – quiet, clever Milner or shy young Cook, neither of whom would have interrupted him ten times an hour with irritable sighs and grumbles.

'I'm going to Bermondsey tonight,' he said eventually. 'To

see what I can find out about Cath Walker – her friends, her life, her dreams. It'll make the story more real, should we ever get to write it.'

'Oh, we'll write it,' said Hulda confidently. 'And if you're going to Bermondsey, I'll be with you.' She raised a hand to quell his immediate objections. 'It's not negotiable, Lonsdale. I'm coming.'

Lonsdale could tell from the determined jut of her chin that she meant it. They returned to their work, and he was pleased that the notion of an escapade to some of the city's most notorious slums had given her food for thought, because she was quiet for a long time. In the end, it was he who broke the silence.

'Hah!' he exclaimed in the mid-afternoon, by which time his shoulders and neck were cramped from his labours. He held up a paper. 'I think this might help me.'

'Don't you mean "help us"?' Hulda asked archly, 'or are you trying to pre-empt my part of this investigation?' He bit back a brusque reply and noticed that despite the dust and cobwebs that covered her usually pristine clothes, there was something attractive about Hulda. Lonsdale found himself staring at her, almost as if for the first time. He could not help but think that she was unusually pretty and would be enticing if only . . .

'Don't just sit there gaping like a fish, man. Tell me what you've found, so *I* can assess if it's relevant.'

The spell had been shattered, not for the first time, by her opening her mouth, and he felt his customary reservations about her flood back. But, he told himself after reflecting for a moment about the advantages of working with Milner on the investigation, his and Hulda's disguise as a couple had been successful in Wyndham Street, and he would probably be better served with Hulda in Bermondsey for the same reason. Annoyed nevertheless, he turned his chair back to the table.

'Well?' she said, looming over him. 'What is it?'

'A letter to the editor in *The Times*,' he replied. 'Back in February, a man wrote about what he considered an inadequate investigation into the death of his son.'

Hulda leaned over Lonsdale's shoulder to read what was on the table:

Sir – In the absence of the precise nature of William Willoughby's demise on the railway line, the French authorities have issued a verdict of accidental death, although they acknowledged in private correspondence the possibility of suicide. The English police, rather than pressing for answers, have stated that the case is out of their jurisdiction.

In response, I make an appeal for help, to beg that a more thorough investigation is carried out on behalf of a young man so horribly and prematurely taken from those who loved him. The close relationship of a father with his only son allows me to state with certainty that he did not end his own life. Nor would he engage in 'larks' that would see him accidentally killed on a railway line.

Moreover, the manner in which his poor body was found and the high degree of anatomical knowledge shown by the crime speak clearly of his life being taken by others. The initial French investigator speculated that my son was attempting to avoid individuals who had followed him. I believe that a full investigation would reveal the complicity of such individuals, and I pray that the authorities will pursue this topic with vigour.

I am, Sir, your obedient servant,
Edward St John Willoughby.

'This is very sad,' said Hulda, looking up. 'But I don't see—'

'Now read this,' interrupted Lonsdale, handing over a second paper. 'It's from the week before, and is a brief report on the son's body being discovered in France.'

Scotland Yard has received a communication from the French police respecting a death on a railway near Boulogne. It is stated that on the morning of 17th January the body of a young Englishman, about twenty-two years of age, was found on the railway line between Nesles and Camiers. The remains were somewhat disfigured, and had the appearance of having been run over by two trains. The top of the head was cut clean away . . .

Hulda looked up at Lonsdale. 'Is this . . .' Then she bent her head without waiting for his reply and continued to read:

One item of underclothing was marked 'W. J. Willoughby'. The medical evidence does not show whether the young man met his death by murder, accident, or suicide, but the guard of the train states that the victim was accompanied by two other Englishmen. One spoke French well, and was about forty years of age, with a thin brown moustache. The other was large, between forty-five and fifty, and had a long beard tinged with grey. The trio appeared to be friendly, and were seen laughing. The guard last saw the party together shortly before Étaples. Anyone knowing any of these men is requested to contact Scotland Yard.

'Here's the final piece about it,' said Lonsdale. 'Dated five days after the initial report and two days before the letter to the editor.'

Hulda read:

The French authorities are now satisfied that Mr Willoughby died accidentally. The door of his carriage was not properly fastened, and it has been suggested that he opened the window to lean out, and fell to his death. It has now been shown that he was the only occupant of the carriage at the time, his companions having alighted at Étaples. His watch and chain remain missing, but vagrants have been spotted in the vicinity, so it is concluded that the items were stolen after the victim's death. The deceased's father has contested the verdict, on the basis that the injuries sustained are inconsistent with being hit by a train, particularly pertaining to the head. The French authorities have expressed their deepest sympathy for his loss, but remain convinced that further investigation will serve no purpose.

'The French police are worse than ours,' she said, looking up at last. 'He was with friends, he was on his own. He jumped, he was pushed, he fell. They have no idea. And if there is a question about the injury to his head – it is similar to that inflicted on Donovan – well, all I can say is that trains do not remove cerebra. Not surgically, at least.'

'We don't know that's what happened to him,' said Lonsdale. 'But we're going to find out. I'll contact a friend at *The Times* and ask for the father's address. His letter suggests he'll be willing to tell us everything he knows.'

'When shall we go?' asked Hulda yet again, as they sat in the reporters' office. 'It's almost six. Surely the layabouts of Bermondsey and their whores will be awake by now?'

Cook blushed at her coarseness, but Lonsdale ignored her. He had already told her several times that there was little point in going before ten, as people would be more willing to divulge information in the cosy camaraderie of a pub in the late hours than they would when they were alert and sober. He tried to concentrate on the letter he was writing to Willoughby, and couldn't help but think he was already reaching the depths Milner had predicted: requesting an interview with a bereaved parent. But it wasn't like that, he told himself – he was doing the right thing.

After a while, Hulda grew restless, and began to poke around in Voules's belongings, moving his pens, ink and pencils so he would be unable to find them. She fidgeted with boredom, then tried to start a conversation with Cook, and finally became exasperated and went home to change.

Returning to the archive, Lonsdale laboured on until well past nine o'clock, after which he changed into some grubby clothes he had brought with him and joined Cook for a snack in the reporters' office.

'You're filthy,' the younger man said. 'Perfect for going to rough taverns in Bermondsey. But are you sure you don't want me to come? I know The Friederichs is a veritable gorgon, but I don't see her being much use in a fight.'

Lonsdale was not so sure about that. 'There won't be any fighting,' he said. 'But I'd better go. If I'm late, she might decide to trawl the taverns on her own.'

'She might,' agreed Cook. 'But be careful, Alec – for her as well as yourself. She might be the Prussian Governess, but she's *our* Prussian Governess, and I'm fond of her.'

Outside, a blanket of yellow-grey fog hung over the city. It had been thickening all day, so that by mid-afternoon it had been necessary to turn on the gaslights, and the street traffic had become very snarled. The air reeked of soot and smoke, and carried a sharp chill that was unusual for the spring.

As Lonsdale pulled shut the office door in the dim light of the overhead lamp, a woman swayed towards him, swinging her purse. She was clearly drunk, and Lonsdale thought she needed to take herself in hand unless she wanted to be arrested for prostitution. She stopped next to him, closer than was decent.

'Can I call you a hansom, madam?' he asked, edging away.

'It's me, you idiot!' snapped Hulda in a hoarse whisper. 'Who did you think I was? A whore?'

Lonsdale was at a loss for words. She had exchanged her usual skirts and stays for a dress that fell in thick folds to the floor. Her fair hair was bundled up into a peculiar turban-like hat, and a bright neckerchief was knotted around her throat. To keep warm, she wore a shawl that was fastened at the front with a cheap brooch. It was not so much her clothes that had led him to jump to the conclusion that she was touting for business, but the undulating walk she had adopted.

'It occurred to me it would look odd if a well-dressed lady was seen in company with a ruffian like you,' she added, when Lonsdale had nothing to say. 'So, I thought I'd wear the clothes I use for cycling.'

'You cycle?' asked Lonsdale, glad he had not congratulated her on her disguise if this was an outfit she liked to wear in public.

'Of course! How else would I get to archery on Saturday afternoons? Hansoms can't be had for love or money at that time, and walking is such a waste of time. Do you cycle?'

'Not unless my life depends on it. Metal wheels on cobbles . . . they don't make for a comfortable journey.'

'That's why I like horse manure on the streets,' confided Hulda. 'There's nothing like it for softening the surface.'

As no suitable response came to Lonsdale's mind, he changed the subject. 'I recommend we take a hansom to Great Dover Street, and walk the rest of the way.'

'Walk?' objected Hulda. 'Why?'

'Because the kind of people we need to meet tonight can't afford hansoms, and if we arrive in one, we'll stand out like a bishop in a brothel from the start.'

Hulda peered at him in the gloom. 'You seem very sure about the way the seedier areas of London work. Have you done this many times before?'

'That, Friederichs, is none of your business,' said Lonsdale loftily. In fact, his first commission with *The PMG* had been to write a series of articles on the Billingsgate Fish Market, which had led him to frequent some of the less salubrious areas of London. He was surprised she did not recall the pieces, since they had caused a vigorous debate between Morley, who maintained that Lonsdale's descriptions of poverty were exaggerated, and Stead, who stoutly asserted they were not.

They flagged down a hansom and gave the driver directions. Hulda's outfit and Lonsdale's dirty clothes were evidently convincing, because the driver demanded to see their money before he would accept their custom.

In the cab, both covered their mouths and noses with their sleeves, to avoid inhaling the moist, sulphurous fog. The gas lamps hardly penetrated the fug, and it was only on Blackfriars Bridge, where new electric lights had been installed, that they could see more than two or three feet ahead. The black sludge of the Thames could just be seen sliding fast and sleek through the arches below.

Eventually, they reached Great Dover Street; as soon as his fares alighted, the driver beat a hasty retreat to the more affluent areas of the city. Lonsdale and Hulda continued deeper into the slums, walking down roads that were foul with dirt and refuse. Hulda adopted a curious hopping gait as she struggled not to step in anything vile.

Eventually they reached Westcott Street, where Cath had rented a room. It was narrow, with tall houses on either side, reducing the road to little more than a dingy tunnel. There was a lamp at each end, but it was mostly the domain of darkness and fog. Hulda and Lonsdale walked along its entire seedy length to get a feel for the place. At the far end, a lamp lit a sign that read, 'Board School'.

'A school? Here?' asked Hulda.

'Like the one in *Nicholas Nickleby*. A home for orphans, probably,' said Lonsdale. 'Here we are, in the great capital of Victoria's Empire, and this is how we look after our wards of state. Hardly makes you proud, does it?'

'Walker lived at number twenty-nine,' said Hulda, looking away in disgust. 'It's over there.'

Lonsdale approached the house, but there was no reply to his knock. He stepped back and peered up, noting that the eaves were rotting and most of the windows were boarded over. The place looked abandoned. Something fluttered on the ground at his feet, and when he bent to retrieve it, he saw it was a notice of eviction – the building had been condemned as structurally unsound.

'Mrs Tanner gave this as her permanent address at the inquest,' objected Hulda when he showed it to her, 'and that was only a few days ago. Did she lie?'

'Not necessarily. The notice is dated yesterday, so she was doubtless in business here until the very last minute . . .'

As he spoke, the door opened, and a boy darted out, loaded down with lead pipes. He gave Lonsdale and Hulda a friendly nod as he passed.

'Ain't much left now,' he said helpfully. 'Better hurry.'

'Where's the nearest alehouse?' Lonsdale called after him.

The boy nodded to a spot past the Board School. 'Just down there – the Jolly Tar.'

'I can't imagine why he'd be jolly around here,' muttered Hulda. 'Still, I see why you want to go – it would have been Walker's local, and we know from the inquest that she plied her trade in taverns.'

The Jolly Tar was crammed to bursting, but exclusively with men. As Lonsdale and Hulda entered, all conversation stopped, and every eye in the room turned to them in what Lonsdale could only describe as naked hostility. To persist would be reckless, so he left abruptly, pulling Hulda with him. As the door closed behind them, the buzz of conversation resumed.

'Are they all going to be like that?' asked Hulda uneasily.

'I hope not,' said Lonsdale. He thought for a moment. 'At the inquest, Mrs Tanner said that she last saw Cath at the Dog and Bone on Minto Street. Let's try there. I think I can find it – I looked at a map before we left.'

Lonsdale had been in areas of chronic privation before, but few were as mean, poor, and hopeless as the area between Westcott and Minto streets. They traversed alleys into which even the police seldom ventured, lined with lodging-houses of the worst type, catering to costermongers, mudlarks, robbers, pickpockets and prostitutes. They were teetering, half-ruinous buildings that looked less safe than Mrs Tanner's lodgings – but were still in use.

They turned into a passage about twenty-yards long and three-feet wide. At the end of it was a rectangular court, illuminated only by the light from upper-storey windows. Slimy wet mould grew on the few paving stones that had not been prised up and spirited away, and on the rubbish that littered the yard like bizarrely shaped gravestones. It stank of urine and decay, and rats scurried in the shadows, brazenly feeding on a dead dog.

'Here?' asked Hulda, gripping Lonsdale's arm tightly. 'Are you sure?'

Lonsdale struck a match, and in its momentary flare he saw an old horse trough filled with all manner of putrid rubbish. To his right were three latrines, open to the elements, the pit below them overflowing and topped by a layer of scum. A bucket of filthy water was set for those individuals inclined to rinse their hands. Lonsdale was not surprised that cholera and typhoid regularly ravaged the population.

The match went out, so Lonsdale groped his way forward, right arm extended to feel his way ahead and left hand holding Hulda's. He moved gingerly until he felt a clammy, dirt-encrusted wall. A small arch halfway along gave access to a tiny, stinking alley that led into Minto Street. Evidently it was an important watering hole, as it was heaving with beer houses, gin palaces and taverns of every description. Despite it being eleven o'clock, the road was busy with people walking in pairs or alone, some weaving, some strolling, a few moving purposefully.

'Why are all these children out?' asked Hulda, retrieving her hand now they were in a better-lit place. 'Why don't they go home?'

'Some people make money by letting out their rooms for immoral purposes at night,' explained Lonsdale. 'Or the mothers are prostitutes who need somewhere to take their clients. The children will go home in the morning.'

Before he could add more, Hulda pointed to a decaying sign of a rather wicked-looking dog holding what looked unpleasantly like a human femur. She strode purposefully towards it, ignoring Lonsdale's suggestion that they look through the windows first, to avoid a repetition of their first experience. She put her hand on the door handle, and glanced back at him.

'I'll do the talking,' she said. 'You just stand and listen.'

The Dog and Bone was tightly packed, with men, women, and even children collectively exuding a breathtaking stench of sweat, unwashed clothes and cheap tobacco. Underlying all was the warm aroma of horse manure, brought in on the patrons' shoes. A fire popped and hissed in one corner, adding its own pollution but doing little to provide warmth. The walls were brown and splattered with stains, and the sawdust on the floor had not been changed in months.

A woman wearing a black wig reeled into Lonsdale, wafting gin-laden breath into his face as, simultaneously, he felt her hand slide into his coat pocket. He had taken the precaution of hiding the small amount of money he had brought in the lining of his jacket, so he was not unduly concerned about theft. He could not deny, however, that being frisked so brazenly was disconcerting. He eased away, then almost tripped over a child so small that she had to use both hands to hold her jug.

'Watch it!' she snarled, as the mild stout known as 'entire' slopped over the rim. 'This costs money!'

She raised the jug to her lips and quaffed a good part of it with all the ease of the experienced drinker. Then she wiped her lips on her sleeve before joining two other children under a table.

Hulda reached the bar and perched on a stool, where she was immediately surrounded by men, several of whom offered to light the cigar she pulled out and clamped between her teeth. Lonsdale's heart sank, and he wondered whether she had considered the fact that it cost more than these men would earn in a day. Thankfully, none of them seemed to notice, and he watched in growing alarm as she affected an appallingly bad cockney accent and began to hold forth. Whether because they were interested in what she had to say, or because she was by far the most attractive woman in the room, she soon had quite a following.

Lonsdale edged as close as he dared and watched as she artfully steered the conversation around to Cath. To his astonishment, her admirers vied frantically with each other to answer her questions. All the while, Hulda looked from one to the next, giving each the impression that she had never met anyone more interesting in her life.

'It was a shame about Cath,' said a short, stocky fellow with scarred hands that suggested he worked in a steel foundry; his friends called him Frank. 'We all liked her, if you know what I mean.' He treated Hulda to a leering wink.

'She was a good friend,' agreed Hulda in her terrible accent. 'More like a sister, really.'

'And old Joe,' said another, raising his frothing tankard of four-ale in tribute. 'I'll miss him, too.'

'Joe?' asked Hulda guilelessly. 'You mean Joe Johnson? Was she still knocking around with him?'

'I don't know any Joe Johnson,' said the tankard man doubtfully. 'Who's he?'

'Must have been before your time, Bob,' suggested Frank. He beamed at Hulda, keen to win her favour. 'Was he a skinny fellow, lived in Long Walk and died of the consumption?'

'Maybe,' hedged Hulda, too clever to agree to something that might trip her up later.

'You must be older than you look, if you remember Cath with him,' said Frank, giving Hulda a dig in the ribs with his elbow; if Lonsdale had taken such a liberty, he was certain Hulda would have responded with violence. As it was, she simply listened. 'We're talking about Joe Greaves, who she walked out with more recent-like.'

'Oh, Joe *Greaves*,' exclaimed Hulda. 'The one who worked on the railway?'

'No,' said Bob. 'That's Joe Hayes. He died about five years ago, hit by a train.'

Lonsdale resisted the urge to point out that being named Joe was dangerous in Bermondsey.

'Joe Greaves worked on the coal barges,' said a short, bald man. 'Up London Pool way. Good job, too. It's a wicked shame that someone did away with him. He had a wife and children.'

'Poor things,' sighed Hulda. 'Perhaps I should visit them, seeing as me and Cath were close.'

'She'd like that,' said Baldy, although Lonsdale could not imagine why the widow could possibly want to see a friend of the woman her husband 'walked out with'. 'She still lives in the same place.'

'The workhouse?' asked Hulda, sipping her second gin from a thick, greasy glass.

'Don't talk daft!' Frank said, while Lonsdale cringed – there were only so many mistakes Hulda could make before even the most drunken of admirers would suspect something amiss. But he was underestimating Hulda's charm. 'Mrs Greaves wouldn't be at the workhouse with what her Joe was making on the barges. She lives in Mermaid Court, over by the Zion Chapel; number ten.' Frank smacked his hand on the bar to gain the attention of the landlord, then gestured for Hulda's glass to be refilled, while Hulda beamed at him and blew a thin stream of cigar smoke up at the ceiling.

'Makes you sick, don't it?' came a low voice at Lonsdale's side. He turned to see a sad-eyed woman sitting next to him. She wore a cheap sateen dress, which had faded from black to brown. She had a pale, thin face, and greasy hair with nits nestling at the roots.

'It does,' agreed Lonsdale, and turned to watch Hulda again.

'See? Even you're at it,' said the woman spitefully. 'As long as she's here, no one else will get a look in. I been working here for six years, and now some north bank tart comes swanning in and takes all my regulars. And Frank's been buying her quarterns of gin like they're free. It ain't right.'

So, thought Lonsdale, Hulda might be able to wrap men around her little finger, but she had only made enemies among the women. He decided to leave her to it and work on the ladies instead.

'She's only here because Cath died,' he said reassuringly. 'She'll leave soon.'

'She'll be back,' predicted the woman, eyeing Hulda with raw jealousy. 'The likes of her knows a good thing when she sees it.'

Lonsdale was sure she did, but he was equally certain that she would not consider it to be the clientele of the Dog and Bone.

'Drink?' he asked.

'Well, yes,' said the woman, pleased. 'And to show I got more taste than she does, I'll have a Scotch.' She spoke the last word at quite a volume, sliding her glass across the bar for the landlord to fill. 'Come on, Bill. The gentleman here is buying.'

'Right you are, Tilly,' said the landlord. 'Large one, is it?'

'Of course,' said Tilly, regarding him askance. 'What else?'

When the glass had been filled so high that there was a meniscus across the top, Tilly put both hands on the bar for balance and lowered her lips towards it. Lonsdale watched entranced as, with a soundless slurp, her lips made contact: not a drop was spilled, although he suspected that if one had, she would just have licked it off the counter.

'Did you know Cath?' asked Lonsdale when the glass had been drained and the whole process repeated. 'I met her a couple of times.'

Of course, he thought, once was when she was dead, but there was no need to mention that.

'Of course I knew her! Poor lass – throat slit like an animal to slaughter. It happened up in Regent's Park, although God knows what she was doing there. Always did have ideas above herself, Cath. Ain't so grand now, is she?'

'What ideas?' asked Lonsdale.

'What are you, a peeler?' asked Tilly, loud and suspicious.

Several heads turned in his direction, and Lonsdale realized that he was asking too many questions, instead of steering the conversation subtly like Hulda.

'Do *I* look like a peeler?' he asked with as much indignation as he could muster.

'Yeah, you could pass for one, actually,' said Tilly. 'But if you say you're not . . .'

'I do,' said Lonsdale firmly.

Tilly grimaced. 'They were in here last week asking about Cath. Of course, they don't care about her now, not when they got the music-hall man's killer to catch.' She smiled suddenly. 'Did you ever see him? He had this wonderful turn with a bicycle, an umbrella and an accordion. His place was at the Wilton Music Hall, over on Sayer Street.'

'He was good?'

'The best – folks came all the way from Hampstead to see him. And that explains why Cath and Joe are getting ignored.'

'Did the three of them know each other?'

Tilly laughed at the notion. 'The likes of Philip Yeats doesn't mix with the likes of us, no matter how grand Joe and Cath thought they was with their flash money and smart clothes.'

'I thought Joe was a bargeman. What flash money?'

'Lord, sir! A woman could die of thirst in here.'

Lonsdale put two shillings on the counter for the remainder of the bottle. Tilly hooked dirty fingers around it and held it close to her chest. She tipped forward on her stool, and Lonsdale was not sure whether she was going to kiss him or pass out in his lap. Neither would have been welcome, but all she did was lower her voice and start to talk.

'Joe had a good wage from the barges – sometimes ten shillings a week! But lately he had extra. A lot extra. So did Cath.'

'Where did this extra come from?'

'I wish I knew,' said Tilly resentfully. 'Because neither of them could do anything I can't, and I'd like some cash myself. All I can tell you is that they had meetings in different parts of the city – and when they came back, they always had money.'

'Do you know where?'

'No, but if you find out, will you tell me? If you do, I'll share what I get with you.'

'Thank you,' said Lonsdale politely, suspecting that Tilly would be wiser to stay away from the whole affair.

Leaving the Dog and Bone was more difficult than arriving, because Hulda's throng of admirers had grown while Lonsdale had been entertaining Tilly. He eased his way through them and nodded to indicate that it was time to go. Hulda, however, had been an interesting diversion with her stories and wit, and the men who encircled her were enjoying themselves. When she tried to take Lonsdale's arm, he became the object of some venomous looks, while she was propelled back onto her stool and ordered to tell them another tale, like the one about the bishop's daughter and the jar of Macassar oil.

Fortunately, Lonsdale was not the only one who wanted Hulda out of there. So did Tilly, who was more than happy to help oust the pretty rival from her domain.

'When you hear me holler, grab the doxy and run,' she ordered. 'Some might follow you, so nip into the doorway around the corner. They won't bother looking for long. It's a rotten night, and it's nice in here.'

Idly, Lonsdale wondered what her home was like if she considered the Dog and Bone 'nice'.

Tilly took one more gulp from her bottle, then tottered towards a table, which she climbed onto unsteadily. She almost fell, but was steadied by eager hands. Whatever she was about to do, Lonsdale had the sense that she had done it to good effect before, as Hulda was already losing her admirers. Suspecting the diversion would not last long, Lonsdale edged towards Hulda.

When it came, Tilly's yell created a sensation. Heads whipped around, and men began to cheer. Lonsdale darted forward, grabbed Hulda, and steered her towards the door.

'What's she doing?' demanded Hulda, trying to pull away. 'I want to see.'

'I don't think you will,' predicted Lonsdale. 'Now, move – unless you want to be here all night.'

Not everyone was diverted by Tilly, however, and a couple of men cried their indignation when they saw what Lonsdale was doing. He barged outside, hauling Hulda unceremoniously down the alley and into the doorway Tilly had mentioned. Several men followed, but Tilly was right – they did not linger long before returning to the shabby tavern. Lonsdale heaved a sigh of relief, while Hulda regarded him furiously.

'That was unnecessary,' she whispered curtly. 'I was enjoying myself – and so was my audience.'

'Perhaps so, but I suspect it wouldn't have been long before they lost interest in your stories and demanded a different kind of entertainment.'

Hulda's eyes narrowed. 'What do you mean?'

Lonsdale stared at her, not sure whether she genuinely wanted an answer or was merely trying to embarrass him. He realized he did not understand her at all. She swore, was more outspoken than was seemly, and she smoked. Yet there was a curious, contradictory innocence in her.

'Things might have become unpleasant,' he hedged.

'It was unpleasant the moment we stepped inside,' sneered Hulda, then sighed. 'But it was worth it – we have a name for Walker's dead friend. Shall we go and see the widow now?'

But Lonsdale demurred. They had escaped from the Jolly Tar and the Dog and Bone, but their luck would not last forever. 'Tomorrow, at a more decent hour.'

'But you've been saying all day that *this* is the time to deal with whores and ruffians.'

'Mrs Greaves is – or was – a wife and mother. We've no reason to believe that – although poor – she has anything but the best character. So, we should call on her in the evening, not late at night. If we want information from her, we shouldn't start by treating her with disrespect.'

Hulda pulled her shawl more tightly around her shoulders. 'I wish I had seen what your woman was going to do, though. I might have learned something.'

'I doubt it was anything you'd want to try yourself,' said Lonsdale. 'Incidentally, she told me that at times Greaves and Cath had extra money that had nothing to do with their regular work.'

Hulda nodded. 'Frank said the same. Greaves would swagger into the tavern and buy drinks all around, even though it wasn't payday. People asked him how he could afford it, but he wouldn't say. Walker didn't share her windfalls – instead, she bought herself new clothes and drank whisky rather than gin.'

'When we learn who paid them and why, we may know why they died.'

Hulda nodded. 'Let's hope that Widow Greaves will know, so that tomorrow will see us with answers at last.'

Lonsdale peered into the shadows to ensure none of Hulda's suitors were still there. The alleys seemed safe, so he led the way to Minto Street, aware that while the road had been crowded when they arrived, it was now virtually deserted. Before he could step into the street, Hulda grabbed his arm.

'Someone's over there,' she whispered. 'In the shadows by the Fountain and Grapes.'

'I don't see anyone . . .' said Lonsdale. But, even as he spoke, he saw a flash of silver in the dim yellow light that spilled through the thick glass of the window. Hulda was right.

'Oh, it's a policeman,' he said in relief. 'I can see his buttons and the striping of his cuffs. He . . . My God! It's Iverson!'

'How can you tell?' breathed Hulda. 'Can you see his face? I can't.'

'No, but I recognize his posture and shape. It's him, Hulda, I'm sure of it.'

'So what are we going to do? Can we take him into custody? With this, perhaps?'

She produced a handgun with a long barrel. Lonsdale gaped at it, stunned not only that she should have armed herself so, but that she had kept such a massive thing concealed all evening. It was too large to have been in her handbag.

'Where'd you get that?' he asked.

'It's a family heirloom.' All Hulda's attention was on Iverson. 'Damn! He's too far inside the doorway for me to get a clear shot.'

'You can't just kill him,' gulped Lonsdale, horrified.

Hulda glared at him. 'Of course I won't *kill* him – just give him a fright, so he surrenders without a struggle.'

Instinctively Lonsdale knew it was a very bad idea. 'We should let the police deal with him.'

'But they've been hunting him for months with no success. Come on, Lonsdale, we can't just walk away. Imagine what your friend Peters will say if he learns you had Iverson in your sights and let him go.'

'What do you have in mind?' asked Lonsdale reluctantly.

'We trap him in a pincer-like movement,' she said firmly. 'I'll stay here – you get on his other side. Then we pounce. What could go wrong?'

A lot, thought Lonsdale, but nodded agreement.

'But for God's sake don't tackle him until I'm ready.'

Hulda pulled a face that indicated she would do what she liked. 'Well, go on, then,' she hissed when he still hesitated.

He set off at a run, terrified that if he took too long, she would do something rash. He skidded on mud, and when he reached out to steady himself, he felt a wall, moist and sticky with filth. Wiping his hand on his trousers, he hurried on. Eventually, he reached a point where the Fountain and Grapes was between him and Hulda, its yellow lights spilling through the fog like phosphorus eyes. He peered out carefully and saw the mist had thickened in the few moments he had been gone. He could see Iverson's doorway, but not him. Was the fugitive still there? Lonsdale could not tell. He began to inch forward, his hands balled into fists, ready for action. He froze as he trod on broken glass and it cracked under his foot. He tensed, expecting Iverson to come out of the shadows, but nothing happened. He took another step towards the doorway, and then another, then jumped to the doorway ready to lay hold of his quarry. But Iverson had gone.

Lonsdale glanced around wildly. He still could not see Hulda's hiding place through the fog. He groped in his pocket for his Alpine Vesuvians, and lit one with unsteady fingers. He held it up, half expecting Iverson to be crouching in the shadows at the back, but the doorway was empty. He experienced a gamut of emotions – relief, frustration, but strongest of all disappointment, and a sudden pang of concern for Hulda.

What happened next was a blur. There was a sharp crack as more broken glass snapped under a heavy boot, and something struck him hard across the shoulders. He fell forwards and out of the corner of his eye saw Iverson holding a truncheon in one hand and a knife in the other.

As Lonsdale put out his hands to scramble to his feet, he felt a sack of rubbish. He grabbed it and swung it hard at Iverson's knees. It exploded, sending foul-smelling kitchen waste and a cloud of cold ashes scattering across the alley. Iverson staggered, then charged, slashing wildly with his knife. Lonsdale raised an arm to protect himself, and felt the knife nick him as it sliced through his coat. He scrambled upright and his left fist shot out at Iverson's chin. Iverson staggered backwards two steps, then circled to his right.

Lonsdale dived at him and managed another punch, this time to Iverson's chest. But Iverson fought back like a wild animal, flailing with the dagger with one hand, while the other tried to grab Lonsdale's throat. As they grappled, Iverson's face was briefly illuminated by the tavern's lights, and Lonsdale saw his eyes burning like coals, dark and filled with rage.

Lonsdale twisted away, and landed a third punch, but Iverson grabbed his coat, pulling so hard that both men lost their balance on the slimy, rotting vegetables from the sack. Despite his bulk, Iverson was fast, and while Lonsdale twisted away from the knife, he lashed out with his foot, catching the reporter on the side of the head. Lonsdale fell again, and a meaty hand hit him twice in quick succession. He was dimly aware of a knife beginning to descend.

The gunshot sounded like a cannon in the enclosed space of the doorway. Lonsdale blinked to clear his vision and was aware that Iverson had gone. He heard receding footsteps, and then a clamour of voices – among them, Hulda's strident tones. He sat up, disconcerted to find himself surrounded by people.

'Drink this, mate,' said a voice, which turned out to be that of Barman Bill from the Dog and Bone. He crouched next to Lonsdale, offering something dark brown in a glass. 'It'll see you right, and it only costs a penny.'

Dimly Lonsdale realized Hulda had very wisely returned to the scene of her recent triumph and asked them for help – Frank and Bob were there, as well as Tilly and half a dozen others. Hulda appeared over the barman's shoulder and gave him the required coin.

'Drink it, Lonsdale,' she ordered. 'You're as white as a sheet. Fright, I imagine.'

She patted his shoulder condescendingly, then looked with disgust at the muck that stained her fingers, while Lonsdale sipped what might have been brandy. Whatever it was, it burned his bleeding mouth. He climbed to his feet, assisted by several helpful hands, and allowed himself to be guided back to the Dog and Bone, where Hulda ordered him a pint of 'best'. He grimaced his revulsion at the taste, but Tilly was there to help.

'Put a drop of this in it, to take away the taste,' she suggested kindly, giving him a very small tot from the bottle he had bought her.

'Why were the police after you?' asked Frank, taking the stool next to him. The hostility he had experienced earlier, Lonsdale noted, had gone now he had been engaged in fisticuffs with a uniformed policeman.

'He's wanted for a burglary in Mayfair,' explained Hulda proudly. 'The peelers have been after him for weeks.'

Lonsdale listened in mute horror while she fabricated an elaborate tale about a highly implausible crime, which had her audience agog. She then confided that he had another equally impressive crime planned in Knightsbridge, but that, unless he wanted to lose his opportunity to carry it out, they should be on their way.

'Although we'll pay our respects to Mrs Greaves before we get down to serious business,' she said.

'Hulda, no,' whispered Lonsdale. 'Not tonight.'

She ignored him, and they left the Dog and Bone amid nods of approval. Several men shook Lonsdale's hand, and Bob slapped him on the shoulder in a congratulatory fashion. Frank offered to escort them to the Greaves's house, and Lonsdale found it easier to accept the offer than to argue. He and Hulda were proudly introduced to everyone they met – an astonishing number, considering it was past midnight – as the woman who shot at the police, and the man wanted for a burglary in Mayfair.

'That'll teach the peelers,' said Frank gleefully. 'They must want you bad, because they know they're not welcome around here. We only ever see them if there's a murder.'

He stopped outside a tall, filthy building with boarded-over windows and a front door that hung loose on its hinges, and told them that the widow lived on the top floor. Hulda thanked him.

Frank gave her a leering smile, then addressed Lonsdale. 'If you ever want to do the steelworks, I know where the cash is kept.'

'That might be useful,' said Lonsdale vaguely.

Frank scowled. 'They're laying me off in a couple of weeks – they got a machine to pour the metal now. I wouldn't mind paying them back for tossing me out on my ear after twenty years.'

'He'll be in touch,' promised Hulda. 'Good night.'

'No,' said Lonsdale firmly, as Hulda aimed for the stairs. 'Not tonight – it's too late. We're going home.'

He expected her to argue, but she only began to walk to where the hansom had dropped them what felt like ages before. Her acquiescence told him that, for all her bravado, he was not the only one who had been unsettled by the events of the evening.

EIGHT

The next morning saw Lonsdale emerge from his bed stiff, bruised, and dull-witted from lack of sleep. Ignoring the maids' horror at the filthy bathwater and ruined clothes, he snatched a hard-boiled egg from the kitchen table and ate it as he walked to Northumberland Street for another day in the archive. Tired and sore he might be, but there was no time for lounging at home.

'Hulda tells me you're going back to Bermondsey this evening,' said Milner that afternoon. Aware that Lonsdale had not left the basement since he had arrived, he had come to bring him a cake baked by Cook's mother. Hulda had stayed for most of the morning, then had left at Stead's request to produce a story about the eruption of Mount Etna. She had asked how he was, awkwardly and formally, then had busied herself without another word.

'We're going to see Greaves's widow,' said Lonsdale, barely looking up to acknowledge Milner's kind thought.

'Are you sure that's wise?' asked Milner soberly. 'Hulda says you were almost killed there yesterday. Moreover, the killer's still free, and he may try again.'

Lonsdale disagreed. 'We fought because I was trying to lay hold of him. It was a chance encounter, and not one that will be repeated.

'I'm not so sure,' said Milner quietly. 'Doesn't it strike you as odd that, with the entire police force looking for Iverson, he hasn't been caught? And isn't it peculiar that you and Hulda are the only ones bothered about linking these odd deaths? And didn't Superintendent Ramsey tell the coroner, the police surgeon and Inspector Peters not to bother about Walker and Greaves?'

Lonsdale looked up at him, feeling his eyes gritty from tiredness and dust. 'I'm not sure what you're trying to tell me.'

'That Iverson – said to be insane by some – might not be mad at all, but following orders from a senior officer.'

Lonsdale frowned. 'You think someone in authority is involved in a business that involves Greaves being poisoned, Cath's cut throat, mysterious meetings, and missing cerebra?'

Milner shrugged. 'I cannot answer, but the whole affair is very odd.'

Lonsdale continued to stare at him. 'What made you come up with this? You said not long ago that it was not going to be important. Now you say there's a conspiracy.'

Milner was sombre. 'You've been down here all day, so you haven't seen the latest reports from the news services. There was a report from the Exchange Telegraph that caught my attention. Here.'

> *Harry Cannon, aged fourteen, mysteriously disappeared in the fog last night. While walking along the river to his home in Limehouse, accompanied by his brother and sister, he sat down near the Shadwell Dock Stairs, promising to catch up with them. He was last seen speaking to a man described as being short, strongly built, with thin hair and a long, uneven beard. A search has been made along the river, but nothing has been seen or heard of him.*

'Your workhouse lad described a man like that waiting in the background while his friends were enticed away,' said Milner when Lonsdale had finished. 'And now read the addendum to the report, which was released an hour ago.'

> *Cannon's brother and sister were not concerned at the time, as when their brother sat down, the man in question was speaking to a police constable. They did not see the*

policeman's number, but stated that he was a large man
with a scar above one eye.

Lonsdale decided that six o'clock was the best time to call
on Mrs Greaves – a time when most of her daily chores would
be done, but before she had settled down for the evening. The
city was busy, as people finished work and travelled home,
but it was a pretty evening, with a clear blue sky and the sun
casting long shadows. They alighted from the hansom and
Lonsdale set a brisk pace to Mermaid Court. It was even less
attractive in the cold light of day – windows broken and
patched, and the roof pitted with holes. The walls bulged
precariously and the whole place was in such terrible condi-
tion that Lonsdale wondered if it should be condemned as
unfit for human habitation.

Inside, the odour of urine, mildew and dirt made Lonsdale
want to gag. Even Hulda's brazen confidence wavered when
they stepped inside. Moisture oozed down the walls in a fine
green film, and the floorboards were dark with filth. A dead
kitten lay on one step, its bedraggled fur matted with blood.
Rats skittered in the shadows; the little corpse would not remain
there for long.

'Come on,' muttered Hulda. 'Let's get this over with.'

Her jaw jutted purposefully as she made her way towards
the stairs, hand on the gun in her bag, acting not so differently,
Lonsdale thought, to some desperado in the American West.

It was not easy to reach the top floor. The banister had been
stolen and the stairs were rotten – some were missing altogether,
revealing a drop to the floor below. As they rose, the stench
became increasingly foul, as overflowing chamber pots stood
on each floor, presumably to save the residents the trouble of
going down to the communal latrines.

Each floor boasted six rooms. Lonsdale peered into one and
saw a filthy floor and walls with mould. There were at least
five people asleep there. From another came the sound of heavy
breathing, as a couple snatched some desperate pleasure. Hulda
faltered, and Lonsdale pushed her gently, to urge her to continue.

'Close your eyes and think of England,' he whispered.

'If I close my eyes, I'll fall and break my neck,' she muttered, then gave a sigh of relief when they reached the top-floor landing. 'Here we are at last. Now where?'

The rooms in the attic had no doors, but some privacy was granted to the tenants by filthy blankets, which were pinned over the frames. Lonsdale pushed one aside and glanced in. It was occupied by an elderly crone who crouched by a dead hearth, her toothless jaws muttering indecipherable words. The next one was uninhabited, and the third belonged to the Greaves family.

The room was almost bare. The fireplace housed a pile of smouldering embers, and a log lay in front of them to act as a fender. There was a chair against one wall, along with a shelf that held a battered saucepan, a piece of dry bread, and what appeared to be horse bones, almost certainly salvaged from the glue factory. Against the opposite wall was a pile of sacks, greasy and evil-smelling, which served as a bed. On them, ragged, begrimed and bare-legged, perched a girl of about four.

A woman sat on the chair, rocking a second child who was painfully thin and was missing several front teeth. Something about her reminded Lonsdale of a weasel. A pink scalp shone palely through wisps of fair hair, and her clothes were stiff with engrained grime.

Lonsdale knocked on the doorframe. 'Mrs Greaves?'

'I'll pay you tomorrow,' said the woman tiredly. 'I'd be out working tonight, but my little one's sick.'

'We haven't come for the rent,' said Lonsdale gently. 'We're here to say how sorry we were to hear about your husband.'

Fear and confusion flared in her eyes. 'Who are you? What do you want?'

Hulda pushed her way inside. 'I'm a friend of Cath's,' she declared. 'A couple of weeks ago, she said that if anything happened to her, I was to see you got this.'

She held out her hand to reveal a plain silver ring. Mrs Greaves's eyes opened wide with astonishment.

'She gave you that for me? But why? She'd never done nothing like that before.'

She reached out slowly and took the ring, as if afraid a sudden movement might make it disappear. She bit it between yellow molars, and then walked to the window to inspect it in the light.

'It's silver,' said Hulda, 'so don't let anyone give you less than thirty shillings for it.'

'Thirty shillings!' breathed Mrs Greaves. 'Then I'll get my furniture back! They took it two days ago for the rent, as I ain't been able to pay nothing since . . .' Her voice tailed off.

'It'll buy medicine for the baby, too,' added Hulda comfortingly.

'So what do you want?' asked Mrs Greaves, gripping the ring hard, as if she were afraid Hulda might demand it back. 'People don't give stuff away unless they want something.'

'Information,' Hulda replied briskly. 'People have been saying that Joe often had lots of extra cash. Where did he get it from?'

The woman's eyes narrowed suspiciously. 'Go away! I don't want to talk to you!'

Lonsdale stepped forward, poking Hulda in the back to warn her to be quiet. 'Don't be frightened,' he said gently. 'All we want is for whoever killed Cath and Joe to be brought to justice. Can you tell us anything to help?'

'Why should I?' demanded Mrs Greaves, suddenly tearful. 'Especially for Cath. It was her what got Joe killed.'

'How?' asked Lonsdale.

'She was always in the Dog and Bone, wearing new clothes and drinking her whisky. She took a shine to Joe and said she'd take him to people who'd give *him* money, too.'

'And did she?' asked Lonsdale.

She nodded. 'Every so often he'd come home with a sovereign or a guinea. He'd give me a shilling, but that was all. His friends at the Dog and Bone did better – it was drinks all round for them.' Her voice was bitter.

'Where did this money come from?' persisted Lonsdale.

The younger child began to cry, so Mrs Greaves sat back down, bouncing it up and down on her knee.

'From somewhere he went after work,' she said. 'He wouldn't tell me where. He usually came back in the small hours, mad drunk.'

The child gave up screaming, and grew still. Mrs Greaves regarded it suspiciously, then poked it to see whether it moved. Satisfied when it did, she looked up at Lonsdale.

'Did anyone else earn sudden, inexplicable amounts of money?' he asked.

'Oh, yes, but they all came to bad ends. I told Joe he'd go the same way, but he wouldn't listen. Now look at him.'

'Do you know their names?' asked Lonsdale, hopes rising.

'First was Len Baycroft – he disappeared last summer. Mind you, none of us miss *him* – he was a nasty piece of work. Then there were the Johnson sisters, Long Lil and Bill Byers, but I ain't seen none of them for a while.'

'Did Joe – or any of them – ever say anything to make you think whatever they were doing was dangerous or illegal?'

She gave a sharp bark of laughter. 'No, but no one would hire the likes of Joe, Cath or Len if they wanted angels. Of course what they were doing was against the law, although none of them would tell me about it, so I don't know what they did for their money.'

'Were any of them worried or afraid at any point?'

Mrs Greaves thought carefully. 'I think Cath was. She had a blazing row with Joe the day they were killed.'

The baby drew breath for another howl, so she stood up quickly, to allow more room for bouncing.

'What about?' he asked.

'It was something about telling someone something. She said they should, he said they shouldn't. They were still arguing the last time I saw them.'

The baby vomited suddenly and spectacularly, and Hulda only just leapt out of the way.

'Now look what you done,' said Mrs Greaves. 'That's enough. I want you out.'

Almost immediately, a thickset man with a large black beard appeared.

'Are they bothering you, Helen?' he asked. 'Do you want me to throw them out?'

'We're just leaving,' said Lonsdale, before the man could oblige.

Mrs Greaves's burly protector shadowed them down the stairs, and watched as Hulda set a rapid pace down Mermaid Court.

'You're going the wrong way,' said Lonsdale, as she turned a corner.

'I know,' muttered Hulda. 'But I want to get away from that place as quickly as possible. It was worse than Hades!'

Lonsdale took her arm and guided her back towards London's more civilized face, glancing back every so often to ensure Mrs Greaves's friend was not following them. Because he was looking for a man with a beard, he failed to spot the small, clean-shaven man who pulled his Müller cut-down low against the gathering chill of a clear evening, and began to dog their footsteps. Behind him, in a silent procession, were five others.

'So, we make progress at last,' said Hulda as they walked along Great Maze Pond, a road along the side of Guy's Hospital. The daylight had almost gone, and the gas lamps were lit, but a thick fog had rolled in from the river while they had been with Mrs Greaves. Lonsdale pulled the collar of his top frock up around his neck to keep out the gathering chill.

He nodded. 'Cath told me that at least six people had died, and Mrs Greaves gave us names of five who are missing. They are doubtless the same.'

'So, when Donovan was killed, Walker decided she'd put a stop to whatever was going on, and worked on Greaves to support her. But both were killed before they could talk.'

'The five people Mrs Greaves mentioned seemed to have one thing in common,' mused Lonsdale. 'None of them was missed. Her comments suggest that she just woke up one day and realized she hadn't seen them for a while. The same is true of Jamie's friends – he's the only one who cares about them disappearing. And Donovan lived alone, with no friends or family.'

'I see where you're going with this, Lonsdale. You think someone is targeting the unwanted and unloved, and that Walker and Greaves were involved in it until she decided she had had enough – although her conscience took a while to prick, if she was paid as much as Widow Greaves seems to think.'

Lonsdale took a detour around a deep puddle. 'It was kind of you to give Mrs Greaves that ring,' he said.

'I assumed she wouldn't tell us anything unless we won her over. And I felt sorry for her in that disgusting place.'

'At least she'll put it to good use, getting her furniture back.

Her husband would have . . .' Lonsdale stopped suddenly. 'What was that?' He peered back into the darkness of the swirling fog.

'I didn't hear anything,' said Hulda.

They stood silently, but all they could hear were sounds from the nearby Barclay Perkins Brewery. The business of producing ale was a round-the-clock concern, and clanks, hisses and the restless whinnies of drays could all be heard emanating from behind a glass-shard-topped wall.

They had just started to walk again when Hulda exclaimed, 'I know the answer!' She slapped her forehead dramatically. 'And it's obvious!'

Before Lonsdale could respond, he heard running footsteps behind them. He whipped around to see six scruffy men hurtle out of the gloom. Hulda scrabbled for her gun, but two of the men were already on her, grabbing her arms before she could reach it. She kicked out furiously, and one attacker doubled over. But the other four advanced on Lonsdale, one of them brandishing a broken bottle.

Unlike in his other recent encounters, this time Lonsdale was prepared to fight. The man with the bottle lunged, so Lonsdale stepped neatly to one side, seized him by the collar, and used his momentum to bowl him into one of his comrades. Both went sprawling, and while the others' eyes were fixed on their fallen colleagues, Lonsdale landed a right cross directly in the face of one of them, breaking his nose and dropping him as if he were poleaxed. The other he felled with a sly kick to the groin. Meanwhile, the man with the bottle picked himself up and advanced again. Lonsdale feinted to one side, then launched an attack of his own, landing three short right jabs that left him reeling.

He glanced over to see how Hulda was faring. It was a mistake. The man he had kicked used his inattention to grab him around the knees. When the other two moved in, Lonsdale ducked the first punch, then lost his balance, falling backwards over the man who clung to his legs. As he landed, his scrabbling fingers encountered a spoke from a broken cartwheel. He rolled away, jumped up, and swung it at the man who was trying to grab his legs again. There was a sickening crack as wood met head, and the man collapsed into a puddle.

The remaining two assailants both drew knives. One, more confident than his crony, feinted to his left and then lunged at Lonsdale, who flinched backwards as the blade whipped past his face. The fellow grinned, tossing the weapon from hand to hand in a display of careless dexterity. He lunged left, narrowly missing skewering Lonsdale, who jerked hard to the other side. Thinking the reporter was still off balance, he lunged again, but Lonsdale landed a heavy blow with his makeshift cudgel, making the knifeman howl in pain. Lonsdale advanced on him, but before he could strike again, the man hurled his knife in a last-ditch attempt to kill and fled. The remaining man followed suit.

When Lonsdale looked over to Hulda, it was to see her brandishing her revolver with a menace that any eighteenth-century highwayman would have envied, while her two assailants also took to their heels.

'Are you all right?' Lonsdale asked her.

She nodded. 'Although I would feel better still if this damned thing had not jammed and I could have disabled one. Then we could have questioned him before taking him to hospital.'

'Right,' said Lonsdale, not sure whether he should be relieved or disappointed.

'Their leader was the one who threw the knife,' Hulda went on. 'The fool thought I would be easy prey and decided to lend his own talents to dispatch you. It was a serious mistake on his part. I heard one of them call him "Pauly" when they ran off, although I'm not sure if that was from "Paul" or was a last name.'

'Regardless, let's leave before they return,' said Lonsdale, uncomfortable with the way Hulda was shaking and prodding at her pistol. 'We should be able to catch a hansom from the front of the hospital.

He led the way quickly, although his one attempt to remove the firearm from her irritable attentions earned him such a glare that he did not try it again. He was glad to see a hansom outside the hospital and glad also that the entrance was so brightly lit and busy. No one would attack them there. Then he remembered what she had been saying before they were attacked.

'You were about to tell me the answer to all our questions,' he said, waving to the cab, then opening the door to help her in.

'I was,' she said, closing the door and calling her address to the driver. 'But it'll have to wait until tomorrow, because I need to think about it.'

'No!' cried Lonsdale. 'You cannot make me wait. Besides, this is the only cab, and who knows where I might find another. Can't we share?'

'We live in different directions, Lonsdale, and I'm too tired for messing about with detours. I shall see you tomorrow.'

With wordless disbelief, Lonsdale watched the hansom disappear into the fog.

It was some time before Lonsdale found another hansom, by which point he was seriously considering visiting Hulda's home and making a scene in front of her parents, landlord, or whatever other unfortunate individuals were forced to endure her company. He thought about her claim to have solved the mystery, and wondered what her explanation could possibly be.

He did not reach home until midnight. Going straight upstairs, he threw his dirty clothes in the linen basket and washed quickly, and not very carefully, in some cold water in the long, narrow bathroom that had been installed on the same floor as his bedroom. Then he threw on an old, comfortable dressing gown and went downstairs. The sitting room smelled of expensive cigars, and Lonsdale recalled with a pang that Jack had invited Emelia's family to dinner, and had asked him to join them. It had seemed like a good idea at the time, and the prospect of seeing Anne was delightful. But, with everything that had happened in the last two days, it had completely slipped his mind.

Blocking out the prospect of a tirade from Jack, he meandered into the drawing room. There was still a red glow in the embers of the fire, so he poked them about and added another log. He then poured himself a large brandy and sat in Jack's favourite armchair. Running all the new information through his mind, he heard the clock of Trinity Church on Bishops Road chime one, but he had fallen asleep long before it tolled again.

*　　*　　*

There was a brief moment of bewilderment when Lonsdale
woke the next morning, and he opened his eyes to something
other than his bedroom ceiling. Then he heard the servants
chatting on the floor below, so supposed he had better be up
and about, too. He stood and stretched, stiff from a night in the
chair and aware that his bruised knuckles throbbed painfully.
He supposed 'Pauly' and his friends would also be sporting
some impressive bruises that day.

He was hungry, so he made for the kitchen, drawn there by
the warm aroma of fresh bread. The kitchen was steamy from
the clean clothes hanging from frames on pulleys that were
hoisted high up to the ceiling. Every Thursday was laundry day
in Jack's household, so all had been washed, beaten, boiled and
wrung the previous day. Lonsdale thought with disgust of the
filthy items in his bedroom, which would now wait nigh on a
week to be cleaned.

The housekeeper was sitting near the fire, reading *The Daily
Telegraph* – one of three newspapers Jack had delivered – before
it was ironed and sent upstairs for his breakfast. She jumped
guiltily to her feet when Lonsdale arrived.

'Sorry to disturb you, Mrs Webster,' he said, taking a seat at
the large, scrubbed wooden table in the centre of the room. 'Do
you mind?' He thought she well might, as the kitchen was
chaotic. Dirty pans were everywhere, while the daily battle with
'blacks' – the small pieces of soot that blew inside the house
from every door and window – had obviously not yet been initi-
ated. Hillary was chatting at the door with the milkman, and,
judging from her giggles, the topic was not of matters dairy.

Lonsdale felt a surge of irritation that they should take advantage of his brother's benign nature. Jack's staff had a relatively
easy existence – as long as meals were on time and the house
superficially clean, Jack tended to leave them to their own
devices. However, their days of idleness were numbered, as
things would change when Jack married Emelia.

'May I help you, sir?' asked Mrs Webster, regarding him
oddly.

'Is there anything to eat?' he asked, and then chastised himself
for such a foolish question. Of course there was something to
eat: it was a kitchen. 'Something that's ready now?'

'You should've said if you needed to be up early, sir,' she said, hastily scrambling to oblige.

'Not much in the paper,' said Lonsdale, lingering only because he knew they wanted him gone – the atmosphere was rather frosty. 'Other than Ireland, of course. Hah! This is interesting! Lord Frederick Cavendish has been named Chief Secretary. I expected it to be Joseph Chamberlain.'

Mrs Webster looked at him out of the corner of her eye. 'Were you expecting to see something particular, sir?'

Lonsdale thought it an odd question. He treated her to as searching a glance as the ones she was shooting at him. Then she handed him a plate of fried potatoes and what looked to be curry.

'That was left over from Mr Jack's meal with two legal associates yesterday,' she said. 'I don't like foreign food myself – all them hot spices lead to violent tempers. Shall I carry that upstairs for you, sir?'

'I'll eat it here,' said Lonsdale, sitting at the table and smiling after she made a show of chopping some onions. At least she would earn her keep for a few minutes that morning. 'Crikey!'

He had taken his first bite of curry and could well believe that her cooking could lead men to do violent things. Seldom in his life had he tasted anything quite so powerful, which was a considerable achievement, given some of the places he had visited.

'Tasty, is it, sir?' she asked.

'Very,' said Lonsdale. His mouth and lips burned, and he had the feeling that if he spilled any on the table, it would sear a hole and drop through onto the floor. 'How much chilli powder did you put in it?'

'About a pound, sir. It's what gives it that lovely red colour.'

'I see,' said Lonsdale, wondering whether Jack had managed to eat any of it, and if it had later interfered with his evening entertaining Emelia's family. 'Is there any bread?'

She quickly cut him some, although she did not change knives, so the slice she gave him tasted of onions.

'Lamson, who poisoned his nephew with aconite, is in the news again,' she said chattily. '*The Telegraph* has letters he wrote to those relatives he didn't have time to kill. Fancy a doctor poisoning his crippled nephew just for – oh! Sir!'

Lonsdale followed Mrs Webster's surprised gaze to where Jack stood at the door.

'Good God, Alec,' he exclaimed. 'I shall send for a doctor forthwith!'

A short while later, Lonsdale and Jack sat in the morning room, where, over a more appropriate breakfast, Lonsdale told his brother what had happened the previous night. The services of a medical man had not been required, as a glance in a mirror had revealed to Lonsdale that he had been less than assiduous with his ablutions the previous night and that one side of his face remained a dark blue-black. He supposed it explained why the staff had behaved so oddly towards him, and why Mrs Webster had asked what he was expecting to see in the papers – clearly she thought one might carry word of a brutal assault.

As Lonsdale told a horrified Jack of his experiences, he took an antimacassar from one of the armchairs, dipped the end in a vase of flowers, and washed his face.

'Well, thank the Lord for that!' exclaimed Jack, seeing his brother's sinister-looking injury vanish. 'However, this affair has gone quite far enough. I never approved of you entering the news trade, and nor did Father. But we accepted your decision, and I think we've been more than patient. We were wrong.'

'But it was only—'

Jack silenced him with an imperious hand. 'While you might care nothing for your own reputation, you should at least consider ours. A scandal could damage my practice, and it could ruin the reputations of your father and brother in the Church. They might find themselves ousted from their current livings to some vile backwater.'

'The Church would never do such a thing!' objected Lonsdale. 'And—'

'Being attacked twice in two nights *proves* that what you are doing is dangerous and sordid. And worse yet, to allow a woman to accompany you . . .'

Lonsdale could see how that might appear to an outsider. He

thought about the other women he knew – not least Emelia and Anne – and could not imagine embarking on such an adventure with them. To hide his chagrin, he wiped his face again with the antimacassar, then realized with a guilty start that he had ruined the thing, and that it was one lovingly crafted by Emelia. Reasoning that she had already given Jack enough of the things to furnish Buckingham Palace, and one would not be missed, he set it furtively on the mantelpiece, from whence he assumed one of the staff would dispose of it later.

'It is hard to believe that you are risking your life for a story,' Jack went on, pretending not to notice what was happening to Emelia's lacework.

'It isn't *just* a story,' Lonsdale said softly. 'Cath Walker was murdered while she was trying to right a wrong. She deserves justice.'

Unexpectedly, Jack softened. 'I can see that's important. But if you want my blessing with this wretched career, you *must* promise to be more careful. In other words, try to emulate the dignified Mr Morley, who manages to be a journalist *and* maintain his respectability and his reputation as a scholar and a gentleman. I shall be married soon, and can you imagine what Em would have said if she had come downstairs and seen you looking like some Bermondsey bully-boy?'

'Nothing,' replied Lonsdale shortly. 'Because when you're married, I won't be living here. I'll need to find rooms of my own – which is another reason I must make a success of this story. I need *The PMG* to hire me full time.'

'Nonsense,' said Jack. 'You know that you can stay here for as long as you like.'

'Emelia will have something to say about that,' said Lonsdale ruefully. 'She and I disagree on so many things that you'd never have a moment of peace.'

'That, unfortunately, is true,' said Jack. 'Speaking of which, Em was vexed when you failed to appear last night. So was I, while Anne was openly disappointed.'

'Was she?' asked Lonsdale keenly. 'Then perhaps I'll call on her to apologize.'

'Please don't,' said Jack sternly. 'I suspect you'd receive a chilly reception from my future father-in-law, and I should be on hand to mediate. Sir Gervais is a difficult man, and I won't have you upsetting the apple cart.' He grinned suddenly. 'He spent most of last night complaining that my house smelled of India.'

'I'm not surprised,' said Lonsdale, grinning back, glad the momentary spat was over. 'Mrs Webster gave me some of her curry this morning. It was . . . powerful.'

Jack nodded. 'She blamed you when I told her it was inedible. She claimed the recipe was one that you'd brought back from Afghanistan.'

'But I've never been to Afghanistan, and none of my recipes call for a *pound* of chilli powder, I assure you.'

Before Jack could answer, the front doorbell rang, and a moment later Hulda was shown in.

'What do you want?' Lonsdale asked coolly, having neither forgotten nor forgiven her selfishness over the hansom the previous night.

'Alec!' breathed Jack, and turned quickly to Hulda. 'Forgive our poor manners, madam. We're unused to visitors at such an early hour.'

'Friederichs,' Lonsdale said with ill-disguised hostility, 'may I introduce my brother, Mr Jack Lonsdale of the Inner Temple. Jack, this is Miss Hulda Friederichs, reporter from *The PMG* and dangerous company.'

She did not rise to the bait, but stared down at her hands, folded demurely in her stole. Lonsdale's suspicions rose – Hulda was never demure unless she had an ulterior motive. All sweet charm, she accepted Jack's offer of tea, and then made a series of polite remarks on the house's décor.

Lonsdale felt his temper rise at her flagrantly transparent attempts to appear the upright, well-behaved lady. 'What do you want, Friederichs?' he asked curtly.

'It's . . . personal,' replied Hulda, blushing shyly. Her lower lip trembled, and, with horror, he saw she was about to cry.

Immediately, Jack was at her side to present her with a clean handkerchief. 'Calm yourself, madam, and tell us how we might help.'

'I need to speak to your brother,' said Hulda, and gave a brave little smile. 'Alone.'

'Impossible! Leave you unaccompanied with a single man? Your reputation—'

'It's quite all right, dear Mr Lonsdale,' said Hulda, closing her eyes and touching her forehead with the back of her hand in a dramatic gesture Lonsdale had only ever seen used in bad comedies at the theatre. 'I trust your brother with my honour.'

'Very well,' said Jack, standing reluctantly. 'I'll be across the hall if you need anything.'

'Never mind *her* calls for help,' hissed Lonsdale. 'You're more likely to have one from me!'

As soon as Jack closed the door, Hulda's façade of timid vulnerability disappeared. She abandoned her chair and went to the table, where she began to help herself to the remains of their breakfast.

'What a stuffed shirt, Lonsdale! I wouldn't tell him too much about our work if I were you. He might faint.'

'He's a good man,' said Lonsdale stiffly. 'And if you came here to insult my family, you can—'

'No, no,' interrupted Hulda quickly. 'I'm sure he meant well. Do you have any preserves?'

She began removing the lids of various pots and dishes to see what was inside.

Lonsdale's patience began to wear thin. 'What do you want, Friederichs? I'm going to cover an exhibition at the British Museum in a minute, so tell me what you need and go.'

'You're an ungracious beast, Lonsdale,' said Hulda, unperturbed. 'I came to apologize, if you must know.'

'Apologize?' asked Lonsdale suspiciously.

'I should have let you share the cab, especially since you put up such a splendid fight against those ruffians. And I should have told you what I'd reasoned. But the truth is, once I'd started thinking about it, my solution didn't work, but I was loath to admit it.'

For several seconds, the only sound was the chiming of the grandfather clock in the hall.

'You confess you were wrong?' asked Lonsdale.

'You're not making this very easy,' grumbled Hulda reproachfully. 'Yes. I was wrong, although if you tell anyone else, I

shall deny it. I was wrong to abandon you last night, and I have
not solved the case.'

'So where does that leave us?'

'With Bradwell,' said Hulda, taking a large bite of toast.

'Bradwell?' echoed Lonsdale warily.

Hulda waved the toast at him. 'Would *you* know how to
remove a cerebrum? I wouldn't. But he would – maybe he's
conducting some kind of macabre experiment on corpses.
Superintendent Ramsey is suspicious of him – you told me that
he thought Bradwell might have taken Yeats's cerebrum, as it
went missing while in his care.'

'But it was Bradwell who started our investigation by pointing
out that Donovan was missing a cerebrum. If he was the thief,
why draw attention to the crime?'

Hulda waved an airy hand. 'Yes, there are problems with my
theory, so it needs further investigation. I suppose it's what the
Americans would crudely call "a hunch".'

Lonsdale was bemused. 'But I thought you liked him. He is
certainly enthralled by you.'

'He is, but that could be a ploy to confuse us – all gushing
admiration for *The PMG*'s most astute reporter.'

Lonsdale ignored her hubris. 'So your suspicions are based
on the fact that he works in a mortuary and has access to
corpses.'

'And that he has a family to support, but his post at Bart's
is poorly paid. He *needs* a second income, yet he chooses to
work for the pittance offered by the Metropolitan Police – he
could earn a fortune in private practice. Why?'

'Perhaps he isn't very good with living patients.'

'I checked,' said Hulda. 'He's excellent, according to his
colleagues. It is my contention that Bradwell chooses to be a
police surgeon because it allows him to use corpses as subjects
for some dark and sinister research. Moreover, a couple of
months ago, I visited the City of London Police mortuary – the
one on Golden Lane. It was well staffed and brightly lit.'

'So?'

'I learned that Bradwell was offered a post there, but that he
declined it. I'm no connoisseur of such places, but Golden Lane
is a lot nicer than the mortuary he runs. Why opt for dirty, old,

under-funded, when he could have new, bright and clear? It makes no sense – unless he happens to like working with a single assistant, rather than a team, and in a place where visitors rarely tread.'

Lonsdale could not believe that the man who had been so helpful would transpire to be the culprit, but supposed there was no harm in humouring her.

'Then shall we pay him a visit and see what he has to say for himself?'

'Unfortunately, he's taken his family to Brighton, and won't return until next week.'

'Brighton? Why would he go there? Especially now, when we need his expertise?'

'Exactly,' said Hulda, with satisfaction. 'The plot thickens, eh, Lonsdale?'

Shortly after Hulda had left, jaws still working on the toast she had filched, Lonsdale received a letter from the father of William Willoughby, the young man who had been killed in France. Willoughby Senior was elderly and unable to travel to London, so Lonsdale was asked to meet him in Brookwood, the closest village with a train station to Willoughby's home in Bisley.

To expedite matters, the envelope also contained a first-class ticket for the ten thirty a.m. train the following day, a Saturday. Willoughby also promised a longer letter would arrive before Lonsdale left the next morning. Lonsdale was pleased, hoping that the interview would provide information that would allow him to develop an alternative solution to the one Hulda had proposed. He disliked – and was generally sceptical of – the notion of Bradwell being involved in anything untoward.

NINE

Lonsdale left the house and went directly to the British Museum, where he spent much of the morning at the 'Religions of the Empire' exhibition. Afterwards, feeling he would make better progress alone than in the reporters' room, he went to the Museum Tavern across Great Russell Street. He ordered shepherd's pie, which he ate while he wrote a review of the exhibition.

When he had finished, Lonsdale hurried to Northumberland Street and handed the article to Stead. The assistant editor read it quickly, the fingers of one hand drumming his desk, while the other hand dipped into a dish of sultanas. His jaws worked rhythmically and he nodded approval of the piece at the same time. Idly, Lonsdale wondered how he managed to carry out so many completely independent movements and read at the same time.

Stead finished, then assumed his customary position – feet on the desk and chair tilted back at a precarious angle. Sultanas sailed through the air towards his mouth, but before he could say anything, there was a perfunctory knock at the door and Hulda entered. Without so much as a nod or greeting, she launched into her suspicions regarding Bradwell.

'No!' snapped Stead, slapping a hand on the table, sending sultanas cartwheeling across the room. 'This accusation is absurd! I know Bradwell.'

'But the evidence,' began Hulda.

Stead raised one arm, closed his eyes, and tipped his face towards the ceiling. Not even Hulda could ignore such a peculiar posture, and she faltered into silence.

'You're grasping for solutions willy-nilly,' he said, standing and beginning to pace. Lonsdale leaned down to retrieve some of the sultanas before Stead ground them into the carpet, dropping them back into the bowl. Eventually, Stead sat again and began to eat the fruit that Lonsdale had picked up. 'The notion of Bradwell using corpses to conduct unsavoury experiments is too ridiculous to entertain.'

'So what should we do now?' asked Hulda. 'Write up the facts that we've uncovered so far, and leave our readers to form their own conclusions?'

'Facts?' demanded Stead. 'You have no facts – just gross speculation or downright slander.'

'Not so,' objected Hulda indignantly. 'We know that Walker *did* have information about missing people, and we have learned some of their names. We also know that Donovan is connected to them, and that Iverson is involved.'

'Yes, yes,' said Stead impatiently. 'But you don't know *why*! What you can report at the moment isn't the essence of a great story. We need to know *why* they went missing, and *why* someone killed Donovan and desecrated his body.'

He tipped the last of the sultanas into his hand from the bowl. He gazed at it, slightly puzzled. 'How curious! I thought I had more of these. Have you two been eating them?'

'There are few things more repellent than a sultana,' replied Lonsdale in distaste.

'In that case,' said Hulda, 'I recommend we travel to Brighton and—'

'No!' snapped Stead crossly. 'Leave Bradwell alone. What happens now is that Lonsdale will continue trawling the archive, while you, Miss Friederichs, will write about the Americans' disastrous North Pole expedition.'

'Which one?' asked Hulda sulkily.

'The one where the ship sank, two-thirds of the crew are either dead or missing, and reporters from *The New York Herald* are racing all over Siberia interfering with the search for survivors,' said Stead. 'So off you go.'

While Hulda went to the reporters' office, Lonsdale – knowing she would be down in the archive within minutes to rant about Stead's interference – left the building and hurried to Scotland Yard, hoping for a word with Peters. But the inspector was out, so he turned to retrace his steps, hoping enough time had lapsed to spare him a tirade from Hulda.

Had he not been so preoccupied, he would have noticed the tall, well-dressed gentleman gaping at him as their paths crossed, Lonsdale leaving the building and the man on his way in.

The man watched Lonsdale hurry away with a combination of disbelief, anger and frustration. How could the reporter still be alive, given that he had been assured that no fewer than six men would make certain he could not continue any investigation? Yet he was, and moreover he was clearly still actively pressing his enquiries – given that there could be no other reason for his presence at the Yard. *The PMG* knew little so far that could prove awkward, but it was only a matter of time before that changed. And once that happened, there would be serious repercussions.

But the man had no intention of letting matters go that far. Full of resolve, he entered the building for his meeting.

Lonsdale spent much of the afternoon conducting his search through recent newspapers, uninterrupted until Milner walked in shaking his head.

'The Prussian Governess won't stop grumbling about Stead,' Milner said, leaning against a filing cabinet, then inspecting the dust on his sleeve with annoyance. 'Even though he gave her the North Pole story.'

'Would you have liked it?' asked Lonsdale, glad of the interruption, as his hours among old papers that day had yielded nothing new and he was bored, tired and disheartened.

'My goodness, yes!' said Milner. 'A rival paper sends its own expedition to the Arctic, and it ends up an unmitigated disaster? Who wouldn't want to write about that? Even the relief expedition was a catastrophe, needing yet another relief expedition to save *it*! It certainly has a great deal of drama and, if nothing else, it's a chance to snipe at Harris.'

Lonsdale carried a pile of copies of *The Daily Telegraph* to the table, then wiped his hands on his trousers. 'It does sound more appealing than grubbing around in this lot.'

'Don't give up,' said Milner, perching on the table. 'I've been mulling over what you told me, and I think I was wrong to say the matter would be horrible, but not important.'

'You do? What changed your mind?' asked Lonsdale hopefully.

Milner gave a self-deprecating shrug. 'Just a feeling. It seems to me that you may have not just a single killer, but a group of them with a common purpose.'

'What common purpose?'

'Now that I cannot tell you – not yet. But I'll keep pondering and perhaps something will occur to me. Incidentally, a message from Francis Galton arrived a few minutes ago. He wrote that five o'clock will be a good time for you to arrive at his house today, and he has invited you to stay for dinner afterwards.

Lonsdale grimaced. He had forgotten about Galton's invitation, and was not in the mood for more tedious stories or admiring a collection of dried grasses, in which he had no interest whatsoever.

'A reporter should be interested in everything,' said Milner, reading his mind. 'Cheer up, Alec. Perhaps he will tell you something about his cousin Darwin. Then you can write it up, and Morley will have to give you a permanent job here. But meanwhile, you'd better go home and change soon. You can't arrive at his house dressed like a ragamuffin.'

Lonsdale dressed carefully for his meeting with Galton, selecting a black lounge coat and matching evening trousers of doeskin, offset with a light grey waistcoat. Galton lived in a handsome house at a corner of Rutland Gate, just south of Hyde Park. The door was white with shiny brass fitments, and Lonsdale had hardly taken his hand off the knocker before it was answered by a haughty butler with an amply bejowled face. Lonsdale was shown into Galton's study, a large first-floor room with an enormous table in the window. The overflowing bookcases reached the ceiling; the desk was piled high with notes, letters and manuscripts; and even the parquet floor was cluttered with teetering columns of papers and pamphlets. The walls boasted portraits – photographs or sketches – of Galton's famous friends: men like Darwin, Thomas Henry Huxley and Herbert Spencer.

'Lonsdale,' said Galton, with a movement that dismissed the butler and reached for Lonsdale's outstretched hand in one motion. 'We shall talk here, because Mrs G is in the drawing room, having tea with her ladies.'

Lonsdale sat and glanced around. On a table near his elbow were sheets of paper covered with curious diagrams, comprising arches in-filled with complex patterns. Galton saw him looking at them and came to sit next to him.

'Those are fingerprints,' he explained. 'Well, thumbprints to be precise.'

'Really,' said Lonsdale, trying to think of an intelligent response to something so manifestly peculiar. 'What are they for?'

'They will be the most powerful weapon the police have ever possessed,' declared Galton. 'Sir William Herschel has been collecting these in Bengal for almost two decades, and he has thousands of them. They do not change with age, and they are unique to an individual – so if you pick up that glass and leave your fingerprints behind, they'll prove you touched it just as surely as if you wrote your name.'

'But they all look the same,' said Lonsdale, studying the sheets.

'Not to the trained eye,' said Galton grandly. 'There are arches, loops, whorls and compounds, as well as an almost endless possibility of differences, with circles, spirals, ellipses, plaits and twists – each one different to any other. There are no external bodily characteristics comparable to these markings, Lonsdale. The limbs and body alter in the course of growth and decay. The colour, quantity and quality of hair, the number of teeth, even eye colour, change. There is no persistence in any visible parts of the body, *except* these minute ridges.'

'I've never heard of this before,' said Lonsdale. 'How do you collect them?'

'A light coating of ink on the thumb,' replied Galton. 'Then this is pressed on a piece of paper. I aim to index them, so they can be consulted and used to catch malefactors. But you didn't come here to discuss my detective work, fascinating though it is. You came to look at African grasses.'

On the contrary, Lonsdale thought fingerprints were far more interesting than decades-old plants. He tried to think of a way to avoid them, but Galton went to a bureau and began to remove a number of shallow trays. Lonsdale's heart sank. There were dozens of specimens, and he was sure Galton planned to provide him with the life history of every one.

Galton had just opened his mouth to commence, when the door opened and the butler arrived with a silver tray bearing fine porcelain cups. Galton muttered under his breath while the man served them, then drained his in a single swallow. He indicated that Lonsdale should do likewise, so they could give their full attention to the grasses.

'I met a colonel in the Gold Coast who had cups just like these,' Lonsdale said, in a last-ditch attempt to delay the inevitable. 'He was later committed to a lunatic asylum.'

Galton chuckled. 'Not as a consequence of making your

acquaintance, I hope. Of course, there's a very narrow margin between sanity and insanity. Did you happen to notice the size of his head?'

Lonsdale blinked. 'I beg your pardon?'

'You should read my books, like your charming brother. Men with large heads, like me, have greater intelligence than those with small ones. We are also less likely to go insane.'

'But surely, the size of a man's head must relate to the size of the rest of his body,' said Lonsdale.

'I've measured more heads than you can imagine,' said Galton sternly, 'and I can tell you that many small people have large heads, and many large people have small heads. The correlation isn't to the size of the body, but to the *intellect*. Have you never noticed that our Prime Minister, Mr Gladstone, is amusingly insistent about the size of *his* head?'

'No,' said Lonsdale noncommittally. 'I can't say I have.'

'He asked me once if I'd ever seen such a large head, to which I replied that he must be very unobservant, as it was in no way remarkable – well shaped but of average circumference. He was devastated until I admitted that I was jesting with him. He does indeed have a large head, although not as large as my own, of course.'

'Hmm,' said Lonsdale, wondering if the two of them had been drinking at the time, as it sounded altogether a peculiar conversation. 'Is there anything that you can tell from the *shape* of a head as opposed to its size?'

'I've seen nothing to suggest that head *shape* relates to specific abilities,' Galton went on enthusiastically, 'but things can certainly be learned from variation in the *size* of body parts, the skull included. My current work is on anthropometry – you know, relating body size and shape to certain types of moral and social behaviours.'

'Really?' asked Lonsdale, beginning to wonder if Galton was wrong about men with big heads being immune from insanity. 'And yet we all know that appearances can be deceptive.'

'My conclusions go well beyond anything as simple as *appearances*,' said Galton with rank disdain. 'I include not just analysis of specific body parts, but weight, height, strength, breathing capacity, reaction times, sight, hearing and quantitative judgements. And I correlate all these with tests and interviews for intelligence and morality.'

'How do you test for morality?' asked Lonsdale, as Galton lifted a tray of grass lovingly from its drawer.

'By posing questions that assess a person's ethical, religious and social character.'

Lonsdale was sceptical, but decided not to say so. 'I see.'

'Perhaps you do,' said Galton. 'But I should have to measure your head to be sure. Measurement will tell us everything we need to know about the human species. Measurement and scientific assessment. Have you heard of my "beauty map" of the British Isles?'

'No,' said Lonsdale warily, wondering what was coming next.

'Whenever I travel, I carry a cross of paper and a pin with which to prick it. Every beautiful girl, I record by pricking a hole in the upper end of the cross; the average ones are recorded on the cross arms; and the ugly ones on the long lower arm. Ergo, I can tell you that the incidence of pretty girls is highest in London and lowest in Aberdeen.'

'According to *your* concept of beauty,' Lonsdale pointed out. 'Aberdonians might have a different one.'

'Then they would be wrong,' said Galton shortly.

Deciding that dried grasses might prove less contentious, Lonsdale asked about them with as much ardour as he could muster.

Galton was delighted in the sudden interest in his collection, and, in repayment for his feigned enthusiasm, Lonsdale saw dinner moved back half an hour so that Galton could finish his lecture. Before long, Lonsdale was looking forward to meeting Louisa Galton as if she were his saviour.

However, dining with the Galtons transpired to be a peculiar experience. The dining room was long and thin, with photographs on all the walls. A large black sideboard held tiny blue and white Japanese dishes, and a Zulu bead pot was used as a receptacle for the fire tongs and poker. The table was set for three.

Louisa was a small, sickly lady who ate little and complained a lot, while Galton chatted about population statistics and

African flora, neither subject of which required any input other than occasional eye contact. After a few moments, Lonsdale realized he was holding two conversations simultaneously, although neither Galton nor his wife seemed to resent the other's interference. Had he not been there, Lonsdale suspected the discussion would have been much the same.

'The kitchen maid is with child,' confided Louisa in a hoarse whisper during the consommé Desclignac. 'I'm sure the butler is responsible.'

Service being in the fashionable *à la Russe* style, the butler was standing near the door, and Lonsdale was certain he must have heard the accusation, although his impassive features revealed nothing.

'There are more species of grass than any other type of plant,' announced Galton in a voice more suited to the lecture hall than the dinner table. 'Barley, wheat and rice are grasses, you know.'

'I'll never be able to replace Potter, if I let her go,' continued Louisa. 'I don't know what I'll do. It's most inconsiderate of her.'

'Maize is a grass, too,' said Galton sagely. 'It's been cultivated for thousands of years.' He picked up a piece of bread and waved it. 'People were eating food like this when they were still living in caves and hunting mammoths.'

'Are any of your servants in the family way, Mr Lonsdale?' asked Louisa. She stole a venomous glance at the butler. 'I couldn't find my silver hairbrush this morning, and one can't help but wonder *what* one would find if one searched the servants' rooms.'

The butler stepped forward to manoeuvre a fillet of salmon à la Belle-Ile onto her plate. He seemed competent, but Lonsdale could not but help notice that he left a trail of sauce drops down her back. The master of the house was subjected to no such indignity, and Lonsdale suspected that the servants disliked Louisa every bit as much as she disdained them.

'All populations – animal and plant – share a normal distribution,' droned Galton. 'Like humans, most individuals are normal, while others are so far removed from the usual that you wonder whether they're the same species.'

'Servants are a different species,' declared Louisa confidentially, when the remains of the fish had been removed and replaced by fricandeau de Duc de Cambridge. Lonsdale noticed that her veal was considerably more singed than his or her husband's.

'When I was in southern Africa, I ate maize meal in a village once,' said Galton. 'It comes in a paste. You roll it into a ball, push a dent in one side with your thumb, and use it to scoop up meat grease. After the meal, the natives allowed me to measure their heads.'

'I came across an interesting case recently,' said Lonsdale, during a rare lull in the conversation, when both Galtons were concentrating on sawing through their leathery lamb. This was mostly concealed by a rather oily gravy that spilled across the tablecloth when anyone tried to ply a knife. 'A man was murdered, after which the killer removed his cerebrum.'

He glanced up nervously, suddenly aware that such a statement was hardly the kind of topic enjoyed by the average household over dinner. The Galtons, however, were far from average, and neither seemed disconcerted by his choice of subjects.

'Oh, yes,' said Galton, waving his knife. 'The cerebrum is a fine organ. It's what separates us from the monkeys, you know. Have you ever seen a monkey's cerebrum, Lonsdale?'

'Not that I recall,' replied Lonsdale, wishing he had kept quiet.

'That Potter has no brain of any kind,' said Louisa, giving the butler a glare. 'If she had, then she wouldn't have allowed herself to fall pregnant.'

'A scientist can learn a great deal from a cerebrum,' said Galton, slicing a potato in two with the neat precision of a surgeon, and eating one half so quickly that Lonsdale thought it might not have touched the inside of his mouth before it was swallowed.

'The butler doesn't have a brain, either,' whispered Louisa. 'He has a good position here, and he'd never secure himself another if I dismissed him for tampering with the maids.'

'The cerebrum is the seat of the soul,' announced Galton. 'It was once thought to be the heart, but we now know that the heart is merely a muscle, and does nothing but pump blood around the body. The cerebrum, however, holds the very essence of our humanity.'

Lonsdale was relieved when Galton turned to the subject of his cousin Darwin, whom he had previously refused to mention. His wife, meanwhile, began a tirade on their coachman's gambling habits.

'It reflects badly on us, his employers,' she said bitterly. 'What if he gets into debt, and undesirables come knocking on our door? The scandal would be almost as grave as if news of Potter's pregnancy leaked out.'

'But if Potter is with child,' said Lonsdale, speaking for only the third time since the meal had started, 'then people *will* find out. It will show.'

Galton went into a fit of coughing, but as soon as his wife and guest gave him their full attention, he miraculously recovered, and began to hold forth on the different methods used for drying peas.

'Do you like peas, Mr Lonsdale?' asked Louisa, then forged on before he could answer. 'The servants do, which is why they are such a rascally horde. No good can come of eating peas.'

'Chickens eat peas, but then a chicken's crop is a remarkable organ,' interposed Galton. 'Have you ever looked at one under the microscope, Lonsdale? But of course you have! You are a Cambridge man, are you not?'

The time passed slowly, despite the fact that the butler served the roast quail and its accompanying salad, and then the Boodle's gentleman's pudding, at impressive speed. The moment the port had been removed, Louisa retired, leaving the butler to serve coffee to Galton and Lonsdale.

'Don't smoke?' said Galton, as Lonsdale declined a cigar. 'My constitution wasn't made for smoking or London fogs. I've had to go to Switzerland to get away from them. But, speaking of Switzerland, I made some intriguing scientific measurements there. Fill up your glass – you'll be interested in this.'

It was almost eleven o'clock before Lonsdale was able to escape. He did so armed with a baboon skull Galton thought might remind him of Africa. He walked through Kensington Gardens, feeling the meal settle in his stomach like molten lead, while the teeth of the ape formed an uncomfortable lump in his coat pocket.

When he arrived home, the first thing he heard was Emelia's nasal voice emanating from the drawing room, despite the late hour. He tried to sneak past without being seen, but she heard him and came out to demand that he play the piano. He opened his mouth to refuse, but closed it when he saw Anne was there, along with a pair of elderly aunts who had accompanied the young ladies for decency's sake. As it was late, both were sound asleep.

'A sonata,' demanded Emelia imperiously, and then named the fiendishly difficult 'Grande Sonate' by Alkan, which was well beyond Lonsdale's modest abilities. He thought he saw gleeful spite gleam in her eyes when he started to demur.

'No, play Haydn's "Sonata in C Major",' said Anne. 'Alkan is too taxing for the listener at this time of night. Come, Alec, I'll turn the pages.'

Lonsdale did as he was told, enjoying her easy company. She looked particularly lovely that night, in a long, silky dress of pale blue that drew attention to her long neck and fine skin. Emelia he was quite happy to ignore.

'Em and Annie will come dine on Sunday after church,' said Jack, speaking too loudly, as he usually did when he had had too much to drink. 'Join us, Alec.'

Anne smiled. 'Please do.' Lonsdale inclined his head to accept, pleased when Anne smiled with what appeared to be genuine delight.

'Excellent!' cried Jack. 'I'll ask Mrs Webster to make something special.'

He drained the brandy in his glass and Lonsdale saw Emelia's dark brows draw downwards, leading him to suspect that it would not be long before after-dinner drinking was forbidden. He could not imagine why his sensible, rational brother had chosen such a gorgon, but supposed it was love. He hoped it would last, or both of them were going to be unhappy.

'Why don't we visit the botanical gardens at Kew afterwards,' suggested Anne. 'There's an exhibition of African grasses.'

She smiled sweetly at Lonsdale, who wondered if Jack had put her up to it.

'How about the British Museum instead?' asked Lonsdale. 'A new wing has just opened and there is a copy of the Magna Carta, letters written by Queen Elizabeth, and some of Darwin's original manuscripts.'

'Who's Darwin?' asked Emelia.

Lonsdale regarded her doubtfully, not sure whether she was teasing. Her puzzled expression told him that she was serious. He was amazed at her astounding ignorance: it could not be easy to be so unaware.

'The chap who described the evolution of life-forms,' explained Jack. 'He was very controversial – particularly with clerics.'

'Oh, he's the one who claimed to be descended from a monkey,' said Emelia in distaste. 'We don't want to see his nasty scribblings, do we, Annie? That sort of thing belongs in a Penny Dreadful.'

'*On the Origin of Species* is a great scientific work,' said Jack, startled.

'It is tedious in the extreme,' proclaimed Emelia firmly. 'And I want to do something *fun* anyway. How about a Punch and Judy show?'

'You choose Punch and Judy over Darwin?' asked Lonsdale, unable to disguise the disdain in his voice. Emelia's expression turned ugly.

'Punch is a subversive maverick, and his political opinions are an interesting commentary on modern society,' put in Anne quickly, thus saving her sister from further embarrassing herself, and Lonsdale from saying anything he might later regret.

'How was your evening with Galton?' asked Jack, also eager to change the subject. 'Did he tell you anything about his new book?'

'Boring,' muttered Emelia under her breath.

'He mentioned that—' began Lonsdale, but stopped when Emelia gave a small scream.

'He has a skull in his pocket!' she shrieked, pointing at Lonsdale's coat.

Lonsdale regarded her in astonishment before realizing that the baboon skull from Galton could be seen poking out of his pocket. He pulled it out, to show her it was a baboon, but she backed away in alarm.

'Ugh! Disgusting!' she cried. 'Keep it away from me.'

'It's interesting, Em,' said Anne, taking it from Lonsdale and turning it over in her hands. 'Look at these teeth.'

'I shan't,' snapped Emelia, folding her arms with a pout.

'Damn funny thing to keep in your pocket, Alec,' muttered Jack, while Lonsdale thought that Emelia might well possess less inside her skull than the baboon had.

'I never realized how massive their canines are,' said Anne, handing it back to Lonsdale, 'or how tiny the brain case. I wish we had a human skull, so we could compare.'

Lonsdale was half tempted to promise to find one, but had no wish to provide Emelia with more reasons to dislike him. It was a pity, he thought, that the two women were sisters, as any attempt to further a friendship with Anne would necessarily throw him into company with Emelia, and he would have to endure her quite enough when she married Jack.

'Shall we say the Chelsea Physic Garden for Sunday, then?' asked Anne, and Lonsdale was pleased she seemed to want the outing to go ahead. He smiled at her, and she blushed and looked away.

'As long as it's not raining,' said Emelia. She rested her hand on Jack's arm and smiled coquettishly; Lonsdale saw his brother melt. 'Alec and Anne can discuss skulls, and we can talk about our wedding.'

'I'm sure we can find something more interesting than skulls,' said Lonsdale, noting with pleasure that Anne seemed to regard the prospect with as much delight as he did.

The next morning, the train from Waterloo rumbled through the Surrey countryside and toward Brookwood station, where Lonsdale was to meet Willoughby Senior. It had been a scramble to make the train, as he had overslept after his late night. The promised letter from Willoughby had arrived, but it was only when the train was moving that Lonsdale was able to read it. What he learned caused his heart to beat faster. At last! He was about to get the answers he needed!

The Manor House, Bisley, Surrey

Dear Mr Lonsdale,
I am grateful for your letter and for your understanding of the distress and pain caused when my only son, the beloved child of my old age, was taken from me in so brutal a fashion.

You kindly offered to visit me to discuss my son's fate and the subsequent lack of interest in it by the French and our own police. The train ticket I have already sent you will give you passage from Waterloo to Brookwood, and I will have a coach awaiting you on your arrival. For your convenience, the driver will take you to a local establishment, The Volunteer in Brookwood. I will be awaiting you there, and we will have some four hours together before you must catch your train to London.

In your letter, you asked about certain specifics of William's death. I shall provide you with a detailed account when we meet, although I can answer two of your questions briefly here.

First, I can tell you few details about my son's recent activities. He completed his degree at Oxford last June, then returned home for the summer. I had expected him to follow me into law, and with the foolish indulgence of a doting parent, allowed him a summer of idleness and leisure. Thus, imagine my surprise when, in September, he announced an intention to accept a post as a pre-doctoral researcher in London, and that he would be moving there directly. I was naturally concerned by the haste with which he jumped to an alternative career to the one I had envisioned, and my concerns grew when he declined to provide me with details. My insistence appears to have driven a wedge between us; nothing of the kind had ever entered our relationship before.

From that time, we grew more distant. I was not inclined to visit him without an invitation, which I never received. The mystery of my son's altered character was also of interest to Inspector Peloubet, the officer in charge of the investigation into his death.

Your second query related to the manner of William's death. I sent Dr Quayle, the family's physician throughout the entire twenty-two years of my son's life, to make such examination as would be permitted by the French authorities. He reported that my son was found lying next to a railway track, the top of his head cut off. The French authorities concluded that a train ran over his head, his body being flung to one side by the impact.

This raises several questions. Would not the wheels of a train crush a head, rather than slice off the top? How could William jump or fall from a train, yet land with his head on the track? Does this not indicate that my son's head was mutilated by other means, and his body placed near the tracks as if by 'accident'? Moreover, if one were to fall from a moving train, would there not be other injuries? No such injuries were observed by Dr Quayle.

Now I come to the most horrifying element of the tale: one section of my son's brain had been removed. The French authorities believe this to be consistent with injuries caused by the train. Dr Quayle disagreed, and is of the opinion that someone killed William, cut off the top of his head with a long, sharp knife to remove part of his brain, and left him on a railway track to disguise the fact.

I hope these facts will convince, rather than dissuade you from exploring the matter further. I enclose a family photograph of William, taken in happier times, in the hope that you will see the hopeful promise in his sweet face and feel my concerns about his death should also become your own.

I wish to express my fervent thanks for your offer of help.

I am, Sir, your obedient servant,
Edward St John Willoughby

The photograph had been cut from a larger picture, and showed a youth of twenty or so, with light hair and a smooth face. There was indeed something hopeful and endearing about the youthful features, and Willoughby Senior was right in that his son did truly make a jump from faceless victim to a person in Lonsdale's eyes.

Lonsdale returned to the letter and read it again, and then a third time. By the time the train rattled into Brookwood, he was beside himself, not just with anticipation of answers about to come, but also with a resolve to see justice for William.

He alighted on a platform at a pretty place, with painted pots bursting with spring flowers and a cluster of attractive little brown and white cottages where the stationmaster and his staff lived. After the clanking, hissing train had gone, Lonsdale stood for a moment to savour the peace and collect himself. A pheasant issued its croaking call, and Lonsdale could see it strutting around a field, resplendent in its russet-bronze feathers.

He went outside and was pleased to find a trap waiting for him. The driver opened the door for him, then climbed into his own seat, and encouraged the horse to a lively pace. Within minutes, after little more than a mile, the driver drew up outside a nondescript tavern.

Lonsdale stepped into the main taproom to find two workmen standing at a long bar, talking to someone on the other side of a door behind it. As Lonsdale approached, he realized that they were addressing the publican, who was heating mutton chops for their midday meal. There had been a time when it had been common for workmen to bring in a cut of meat in a cabbage leaf for the publican to cook, in return for the men buying a quart of porter or four-ale. Lonsdale felt a momentary sadness that such a pleasant custom was disappearing.

'Harry,' called one of the men at the bar. 'You've a gentleman out here.'

The publican stepped into the doorframe and looked enquiringly at Lonsdale, who said he was looking for Edward Willoughby.

'You'll be wanting the saloon bar, then,' said Harry. 'Take the staircase to the first floor, go down the hall, and it'll be on your right.'

Lonsdale followed his instructions, and entered a room with attractive dark wood walls, plush carpeting, and two comfortable leather chairs, one of which was occupied by a tall man, impeccably dressed. His hair was neither long nor short, and his sideboards and thin moustache were neatly trimmed. He had a pleasant but unremarkable face. He rose as Lonsdale entered.

'Thank you for coming.' He extended his hand. 'Francis Willoughby.'

'You seem familiar,' said Lonsdale, frowning.

Willoughby smiled. 'Yes – you might not remember, but we met a year ago at the Oxford and Cambridge Club.'

Lonsdale had the sense that they had met more recently than twelve months before, yet poor Francis was so undistinguished that Lonsdale knew he might have passed him a dozen times in the street and not noticed. Then something occurred to him. 'Francis Willoughby? My appointment was with *Edward* Willoughby.'

'He's my father. Please take a seat – I'll explain everything.'

With a knock, the landlord entered with two glasses of beer and a tray of food. Lonsdale wondered if he had been waiting outside, listening.

'Well?' asked Lonsdale when Harry had gone. He did not touch the proffered meal or drinks, and had the sinking sense that answers that had seemed so near his grasp were about to be snatched away.

'My father is not a well man,' began Willoughby. 'He has a weak heart, and my brother's death has been a terrible shock. Those of us who care about him decided that it would be best if I met you in his place, to prevent him from becoming overexcited.'

'Surely that should be his decision – not yours?' said Lonsdale.

Willoughby gave a tight smile. 'I'm a doctor, Mr Lonsdale, and I consulted both my father's regular physician – Dr Quayle – and the heart specialist who treats him. It was a decision made by all of us in his best interests.'

'Your father agreed to this?'

'He doesn't know,' said Willoughby, gently apologetic. 'When you fail to arrive, he'll assume you've been delayed or have decided against listening to the ramblings of an old man broken by grief. He'll go home, where I shall continue my efforts to help him let poor William go.'

Lonsdale looked around him. 'So this isn't The Volunteer? The man in the trap outside the station effectively kidnapped me to bring me here, while your father waits elsewhere?' He did not try to conceal his frustration.

'Please forgive the dramatics, but I hope you can appreciate that I won't endanger my father's health,' said Willoughby politely but firmly. 'It might be a story to you, but it's my father's future at stake.'

'I understand,' said Lonsdale, trying to be as agreeable as possible, since he was not going to see the man's father regardless. 'But I have reason to believe his concerns about your brother are justified. Certain injuries . . .'

'Then share your suppositions with me, and I will try to answer any questions you have.'

Lonsdale disliked the situation he was in and was full of suspicion. 'How do I know you are who you claim to be? Your father's letters – both to me and *The Times* – said that William was his only son. He did not mention you.'

Willoughby sighed sadly that Lonsdale should doubt him. 'I can show you documents bearing my name, I suppose. And I have a family photograph . . .'

He removed it from his wallet, much folded and fingered, showing two men sitting side by side. Lonsdale recognized them at once: one was William, the other the man who sat opposite.

Lonsdale handed it back. 'So why did your father say William was his only son?'

'He and I had a falling out some years ago,' said Willoughby, re-folding the photograph and putting it away. 'It was what one might call a mutual disinheritance. My recent re-entry into his life was brought about by the death of my brother – my half-brother, actually.'

'So you and he are reconciled?'

Willoughby grimaced. 'Let us say we are working to that end. Unfortunately, the hurt we inflicted on each other will take time to mend. But I love him and will do all I can to comfort and protect him.'

'I see.' Lonsdale was uncomfortable hearing such intimate details. It felt like the prurient prying that Milner feared reporters would soon have to undertake for their stories.

'The cause of our disagreement was his shameful treatment of my mother,' Willoughby went on. 'They had been married for more than twenty years when he divorced her for a younger woman – William's mother. He hurt her and ruined her reputation, simply for selfishness. William was born seven weeks later.'

'Hmm,' mumbled Lonsdale, beginning to be embarrassed by the confidences.

'I was seventeen at the time,' Willoughby went on, oblivious. 'And I sided with my mother – the innocent party. But although my disgust at my father and my dislike of his new wife intensified, I was fond of my new half-brother. When my mother died, I washed my hands of my father and his woman, but remained in touch with William. Then, when William went up to Oxford, away from my stepmother's poisonous interference, he and I were able to become friends.'

'Your father didn't know?'

Willoughby shook his head. 'William and I both decided it would be easier for all concerned if he didn't. I had no wish for William to lose his father, as I had done. However, in the last four years of his life, I knew William better than his parents did.'

Lonsdale took a sip of beer. 'Your father mentioned a falling off of his relationship with his son. Was that why?'

William smiled. 'Of course not. What happened was that Oxford turned William from a cosseted, smothered boy into a man. He grew up, Mr Lonsdale – outgrew the need to tell his papa every little thing. I had nothing to do with it.'

'Is his mother still alive?'

An expression of pain crossed Willoughby's face. 'She decided against spending her life nursing an elderly husband, and left for greener pastures when William went to Oxford.'

Lonsdale wanted to ask his questions and leave. The Willoughby family troubles were not relevant to how William had died in France. He eased the discussion to more practical matters. 'How did you know your father planned to meet me?'

'He mentioned it to Dr Quayle, who told me.'

'Are you familiar with your father's investigation into

William's death? That he believes William was followed to France and murdered?'

'Yes, of course, but there's no evidence to support his claims.'

'On the contrary – he has the evidence of Dr Quayle, who travelled to France at his request and examined your brother's body.'

'Dr Quayle did not go to France alone. Do you think I would sit back and do nothing if I thought someone had deliberately hurt William? I went with him, and I saw the same things that he did.'

'Which was that William's cerebrum had been removed?'

Willoughby made an impatient sound at the back of his throat. '*That* did not happen. First, William's poor head was far too badly damaged to allow any such assessment to be made. And second, Dr Quayle would never have reported such a ghoulish detail to my father. I can only assume that this has come about due to the strain. Hearing it makes me wonder if he's lucid enough to understand what Dr Quayle said at all.'

'So Dr Quayle said nothing about a knife being used on William?'

'The only knives involved were the scalpels employed by the pathologist at the mortuary,' said Willoughby firmly. 'The top of William's head was severed, and parts of his brain were missing, but to say it had been surgically removed . . . it is a nonsense!'

Lonsdale was not sure what to think. 'There have been other cases of missing cerebra recently . . .'

Willoughby initially looked sceptical, but seeing how serious Lonsdale was, his face showed actual relief. 'Thank God! That explains where my father got the idea. I was afraid it might have derived from some sickness of his own mind. He must have read about it in one of the less responsible papers, and thought that as William's brain was also damaged . . .'

Lonsdale shook his head. 'That's impossible, because several of us at *The Pall Mall Gazette* are the only ones other than the police who are aware of the details of those cases.'

'Then all I can imagine is that my father misunderstood what Dr Quayle told him. Perhaps Dr Quayle indicated that part of the brain was gone, and my father made the leap to assuming that meant it had been taken.'

Lonsdale supposed that made sense, and with bitter frustration saw answers slipping further away. And yet the picture of William's youthful face drove him to ask his last questions.

'Was William's death an accident then?'

'It was not suicide. He had no reason to terminate his life. It was, I believe, a tragic accident. And let me add that my father's criticisms of the French police are unreasonable. They assessed the situation carefully and minutely, and I believe their conclusions: that William was killed by a train, his body being thrown aside by the impact.'

'Is it possible to fall from one moving train, be hit by another, and sustain no injuries other than to a head?'

'But William *did* suffer other injuries. Dr Quayle and I found significant bruising to his chest, legs, and back.'

'So what do you think happened?'

Willoughby looked away; the subject was painful. 'That William fell out of the train because he leaned on an insecurely fastened door, that he suffered serious bruising in that fall, that perhaps he staggered back to the tracks before passing out with his head on or next to the tracks, and that he was killed when another train hit his head as it passed later. And that, Mr Lonsdale, is a much more plausible explanation than my father's.'

'I guess it is,' acknowledged Lonsdale reluctantly.

'Are you free to share with me any of the details of these other cases that you thought my father might know about?' asked Willoughby. 'I'm just wondering if I might be able to see a connection.'

And because he did not want his journey to Brookwood to have been a total waste of time – and as Willoughby was a medical man – Lonsdale told him about the other deaths he had been investigating. Willoughby was a good listener, and Lonsdale outlined every detail of the cases, including his suspicions that incidents in Holborn, Peckham and Chiswick might also be related.

'I see now why my father's letter brought you running,' said Willoughby when he had finished. 'But to answer your earlier question, I have no idea why anyone should want to steal a fellow's cerebrum. However, I seriously doubt the business has anything to do with the medical profession. You would do better to look among the criminal fraternity for your culprits.'

'Probably,' admitted Lonsdale. 'Just one more question: do you know what "research post" William took in London?'

Again, Willoughby winced. 'None, as far as I know. I strongly suspect he was in the city enjoying its delights, and the claim of employment was to avoid our father's censure. He deplores idleness.'

The two men sat in silence. After several moments, Lonsdale stood to leave. 'Thank you for your candour. My condolences on the loss of your brother.'

The trap was waiting, so he climbed in and nodded to the driver to take him back to the station. Willoughby watched him go and, had Lonsdale glanced back, he would have seen the mask of poised suffering slip to reveal something else altogether.

On Sunday night, Anne lay in bed and stared at the ceiling, but all she could think about was Lonsdale, and the time they had spent at the Physic Garden. He had not returned from Surrey early enough to join Jack, Emelia and her on Saturday, but after church on Sunday the four of them dined together and had a lovely afternoon. She and Lonsdale were officially acting as chaperones for the betrothed couple, but she remembered nothing at all of what they had said or done. All she remembered was Alec – his slightly awry hair, his laughing eyes, and his bright, intelligent conversation.

They had sauntered lazily around the garden and, at one point, when Jack and Emelia had followed a bend in the path before she and Lonsdale reached it, he had taken her hand and held it gently. She remembered the warmth of his hand, and the light, affectionate squeeze he had given hers before he had let go. Then, when he had helped her to the carriage – at the end of the most glorious evening she could remember – he had turned towards her. Their lips had been scant inches apart, and she had desperately wanted to kiss him. Smiling, she slipped into a contented slumber.

TEN

Lonsdale arrived so early at Northumberland Street on Monday morning that he was there before anyone else. Eager to speak to Stead, and knowing the assistant editor crossed the Hungerford Bridge each day from his house at Wimbledon Common, Lonsdale went to meet him. He headed towards a cavern that led to Villiers Street under the South Eastern Railway Terminus – lit by a single lamp at each end, and wet with mineral-rich moisture dripping from stalactites in between. Just as he was entering it, Stead appeared, trudging with a slouching step and bent shoulders, and a large leather satchel swinging from his right hand. Next to him was Milner.

'Wonder of wonders,' said Stead. 'First Milner calls at my house at six. Now you meet me before seven.'

Without waiting to hear what had drawn Milner – never an early riser – from his bed at such an hour, Lonsdale told them both about his foray to Surrey. Stead barely listened.

'I appreciate you have the bit between your teeth with this cerebrum business, Lonsdale, but it will have to wait, I'm afraid. All our attention must focus on the tragic events of Saturday.'

'What events?' asked Lonsdale.

But they had reached the office, and Stead sprang up the stairs without answering. Lonsdale looked at Milner for an explanation.

'On Saturday, Lord Frederick Cavendish, the new Chief Secretary for Ireland, arrived in Dublin,' Milner explained. 'That evening, he and Under-Secretary Burke were walking in Phoenix Park when they were set upon by four men armed with knives and murdered within sight of the Viceregal Lodge.'

'Members of the Irish Republican Brotherhood?' asked Lonsdale, hating the thought of what such an outrage would mean for the continued troubles in Ireland.

'Probably, although no one has yet claimed responsibility. Because yesterday was Sunday, almost nothing's known, but the public will soon be clamouring for information, and we'll be expected to provide it. Morley has already set up a meeting with Gladstone, his close personal friend. We'd better go upstairs.'

In all his time at *The PMG*, Lonsdale had never seen everyone so intent on a single story. Milner was sent to Dublin, and every other member of staff was allocated a different aspect of the crime. Nothing else seemed to matter.

Thus it was not until Wednesday, when the furious activity had abated, that Lonsdale had time to return to the archive. The first thing he did was to address an issue that had been niggling at the back of his mind ever since he had boarded the train from Brookwood. Willoughby Senior claiming that William's brain had been taken was just too much of a coincidence at a time when similar incidents were occurring, and Willoughby's explanation for the 'confusion', although possible, simply did not feel right. Lonsdale suspected that a second attempt to see the father would be no more successful than the first, so he decided to approach Dr Quayle – to ask for a detailed account about William's body and *exactly* what he had told Willoughby Senior.

It took a while for Lonsdale to compose the missive, as he needed to mention his correspondence with the father and his meeting with the son, without betraying his doubts about what the younger Willoughby had told him. But at last it was done, and he took it upstairs to be posted, before returning to the drudgery in the archive.

He had been working steadily for several hours when Hulda arrived with a visitor. She looked tired after the frenzy of the Phoenix Park murders, but her eyes had not lost their customary gleam. Lonsdale was somewhat startled to see Jamie in her wake. The boy's once-fine clothes were even more rumpled and stained, but he was grinning in triumph.

'I found what you asked,' he said proudly, 'and I'm here to make me report.'

'Very well,' said Lonsdale, indicating the archive's only other chair. 'Take a seat and tell us what you've discovered.'

'No,' said Jamie, turning to Hulda with a clumsy but sincere bow. '*Ladies* sits. Gentlemen stands.' Hiding her amusement,

Hulda inclined her head in gracious thanks and perched on the edge of the seat.

'Are you hungry, Jamie?' Lonsdale asked.

'She bought me a pie, didn't she?' he said, nodding toward Hulda. 'She ain't nearly so stiff as she looks.'

'You won't get another if you don't watch your tongue,' Hulda snapped brusquely, although a smile twitched at the corners of her mouth.

'Right,' said Lonsdale. 'Frederick Kempster and Edmund Corlett. What have you learned?'

'Neither had any family or friends,' Jamie replied, 'except each other. They shared rooms, and kept to themselves. Their neighbour says they was dolly boys.'

'Homosexuals,' translated Lonsdale for Hulda's benefit. 'And probably ostracized by their families so, like Donovan, they were alone.'

Jamie nodded. 'No one went to their funerals, and no one collected their belongings – those are still at the police station. I asked to see them, but the peelers wouldn't let me.'

'Right,' said Lonsdale, thinking the boy had some gall to try.

'No one could say how the fire started,' Jamie continued. 'But I think it was deliberate, like the one that did for Donovan. I gave a penny to the mortuary guard, and he let me see them. Neither had no head – it was like they'd been squashed right off.'

'You inspected the bodies?' asked Lonsdale, aghast.

'I'm a thorough reporter, me,' said Jamie with haughty pride. 'But there's more, old pal. While I was visiting me mates at the workhouse, they told me that *he's* been seen again, doing his stuff.'

'Who?' asked Lonsdale. 'Iverson – the big man with the scar?'

'No, the blacksmith-like feller. His appearance has changed because he shaved off his beard. But he's got the same snake tattoo on one of those big old arms.'

'What did he do, exactly?'

'Me mate – Roger – he said Big Arms went off with a woman called Agnes over in Hackney after they'd been making eyes at each other all night. It's been a week now, and she ain't been seen since. I figure she thought she was catching herself sommat good, but got caught instead. And she's as dead as me mates.'

'Has her disappearance been reported to the police?' asked Lonsdale.

'Sure, but they said they couldn't do nothing.'

'And you're absolutely certain?' asked Lonsdale. 'Big Arms is the same man we talked about earlier?'

Jamie nodded firmly. 'Roger said they all calls him Captain, because he has the same name as the pirate.'

'What pirate?' asked Lonsdale. 'Drake? Bluebeard?'

'No, the one from Bristol. Morgan. Henry Morgan. That's Big Arms' name.' Jamie grinned, delighted with his success. 'So now I'm ready for the next job. Chiswick, you said.'

Lonsdale explained what he wanted, and urged Jamie to be careful. He then gave him two shillings, one for the job just completed and one for the next. Jamie tossed them in the air, caught them, and raced up the stairs to begin at once. Hulda regarded Lonsdale sceptically.

'He's a child. Are you sure you should use him like this?'

'No,' admitted Lonsdale, 'but from what he told us, I think he'll be safer in Chiswick than anywhere frequented by Big Arms Morgan.'

'So have you discovered anything yourself, or have you left it all to your helpmeet?'

'I've found out that a milkman – John Poole – who's due to attend court tomorrow, has disappeared. He's accused of stealing canisters put out by other milkmen, and was supposed to report to the police each evening. He hasn't for several days.'

'You're clutching at straws,' said Hulda. 'Maybe he just absconded.'

'Well, it's a minor charge, but if he runs away, he could end up behind bars. His barrister insists that he was keeping to the terms of his bond because he was so frightened of prison. He and the police are baffled. Have you found anything?'

Hulda fumbled in her handbag and pulled out a newspaper. 'I asked a friend in Brighton to keep an eye out for any murder or disappearance that might occur in the area after Bradwell went down there. Here is yesterday's *Brighton Herald*.'

The body of Teresa Godley, aged fourteen, was discovered
yesterday after a fire at a beach arcade. She had gone
missing a week ago after being released until trial
following her arrest with her brother for stealing a gold
chain and watch and two pounds from a man named Frank
Wood. Her body was burned beyond recognition, but she
was identified by the chain taken from Mr Wood.

'Are you ready to investigate Bradwell now?' Hulda asked.

When Lonsdale arrived at Northumberland Street on Thursday morning, he headed to the reporters' room to collect Hulda, so they could investigate her contention that Bradwell's 'holiday' was connected to the death of Teresa Godley. But before he had reached the top of the stairs, Stead called out. Lonsdale stuck his head into the assistant editor's office, and saw him sitting on a stack of newspapers. His back was to the door, his feet were on the mantelpiece, and he was rhythmically beating the sides of his trousers with a long-handled clothes brush.

'Ah, Lonsdale,' he said, leaning back until his head was almost upside-down, and regarding the reporter in a most unorthodox fashion, 'I understand you had plans with Hulda today, regarding poor Bradwell. It's therefore with some pleasure that I destroy your nefarious intentions by telling you what I told her fifteen minutes ago: the two of you will be needed here all day, because Mr Morley, Milner and I shall be attending the funeral of Lord Frederick Cavendish.'

Stead spun around, looked his reporter up and down, and held out the clothes brush. 'You need this more than I do.' He scratched his thick beard. 'I'd like you to write a note on last night's storm. There's been damage throughout the south.'

When Lonsdale reached the reporters' office, the most serious storm appeared to be in Hulda's face. She was furious, and Lonsdale could tell from the flushed, angry features of Voules that he had experienced the sharpness of her tongue. He glanced at Lonsdale as he entered, and resumed reading the morning papers. Wisely, Cook had retreated to the furthest corner.

'Stead can be most irritating,' she said angrily. 'Rather than investigating Bradwell, we're forced to remain here. I should *never* have told him what we were planning.'

'A mistake I wouldn't have expected from you,' said Cook, rashly joining the discussion.

'Easy for you to say,' she hissed. 'All you do is gallivant around speculating about assassination. But just exactly what have you learned about the Phoenix Park murders, eh?'

'Not much,' agreed Cook, in a manner that indicated he was not going to give her the satisfaction of an argument. 'It'll be a long investigation.'

'But no more difficult than ours,' said Hulda grumpily. 'And at least the Phoenix Park murders don't have Stead slowing down the investigation.'

Lonsdale arrived home at Cleveland Square that evening to find Jack just bidding farewell to Emelia and Anne, who had joined him for late-afternoon tea. Anne's face lit up when she saw Lonsdale, which was not lost on Jack, who gave his brother a meaningful wink. Emelia saw the wink, but did not understand it, and looked from one to the other in confusion. 'Surely you don't have to go just yet?' asked Lonsdale, sorry that he had taken a leisurely walk through the parks instead of the more direct route. 'Do you have plans for this evening?'

'We're expected home – Mother and Father are hosting a dinner party,' said Anne. 'We need time to dress.'

'And we're dining at the United Service Club tonight, Alec,' Jack added. 'We were invited by Taylor, who is in London on leave. He's moved up the ranks since he and I were young together, and you can't have seen him for years.'

Lonsdale sighed ungraciously.

'It's gratifying to see you disappointed to miss my company, Alexander,' said Emelia blithely. 'I've been labouring under the impression that you didn't like me, but now I see I was wrong.'

'Yes,' said Lonsdale hesitantly, not sure how to respond.

'What would you like to do this coming Sunday?' asked Anne, addressing Jack, but glancing at Lonsdale. 'A picnic in Greenwich Park?'

'Oh, no,' said Emelia with a shudder. 'There would be too many ants.'

'Hampton Court might be nice,' suggested Lonsdale, speaking to Anne.

'Rather than making a major outing of it, we could dine here,' Jack said. 'And then we could stroll to Hyde Park to watch the boating. The Serpentine is famous for its model yachts.'

'That sounds dull,' said Emelia. 'Toy boats are for children.'

'Not necessarily,' said Lonsdale, thinking about Donovan's love of watching them during his half-days off. Suddenly, Jack's idea seemed very attractive. 'It might be interesting.'

'I suppose Annie and I can find something to amuse ourselves while you grown men play,' said Emelia sulkily.

'Don't worry, Em, I'm certain we'll all have an enjoyable time,' said Anne, and smiled happily.

Lonsdale had not been home long when he received a message from Stead. Due to public and legal pressures, it had recently been decided that the Hampstead Smallpox Hospital would cease admitting smallpox patients and would concentrate instead on treating scarlet fever and diphtheria. Stead wanted Lonsdale to ascertain whether this change was due to the wealthy residents of Hampstead using their political influence to override public health concerns. Stead also had a new assignment for Hulda, and Lonsdale was just as glad he would not be there when she found out that her goal of looking into Bradwell had been delayed again.

When Lonsdale awoke on Friday morning, he felt as though he had not slept at all. For much of the night, he had been plagued by unsettling dreams, and, although he could not remember them, he still had a lingering sense of unease. But he felt considerably better after three cups of tea and a large plate of bacon and coddled eggs, and, despite a light rain, he was soon walking to the Midland Railway Station to take the 10.05 a.m. to Hampstead.

Late that afternoon, having interviewed administrators at the hospital as well as the locals who were among its greatest adversaries, Lonsdale took the train back to London. He dozed fitfully throughout the journey, sleep alternating with wondering if a response had arrived from Dr Quayle. Reaching the Midland

Station, he began to move along the platform with a wave of humanity from another train that had arrived simultaneously. Someone behind bumped him hard with a large bag, and he turned his head around in annoyance.

A glimpse of a figure further back, however, drove all other thoughts from his mind. Iverson was not wearing his police uniform, but a dirty black jacket of the kind favoured by dockers. His eyes met Lonsdale's. Turning quickly, Lonsdale knocked into a hurrying businessman. By the time he looked up again, Iverson had gone.

Once outside the station, Lonsdale decided that rather than heading to Northumberland Street, he would go straight home, in the hope of finding Anne and Emelia there again. He was disappointed to discover the house empty except for the servants. He retired early to his rooms and sat near a fire, reading and dozing.

He woke Saturday morning pleasantly refreshed and found Jack had already left. Lonsdale wandered down to the drawing room, where he read *The Morning Post* and *The Daily Telegraph*. He was just perusing more speculation about the Phoenix Park killings when Dillon, the butler, opened the door to admit Hulda.

'Are you all right?' asked Hulda without preamble. 'You didn't come to work yesterday, and there was no sign of you today. Are you ill?'

Lonsdale poured her some tea. 'It's good to know you care, Friederichs.'

'I wouldn't want anything to happen to you in the middle of our investigation,' she said stiffly. 'Have you made any progress, or have you just been lounging about?'

He told her about his dull day in Hampstead, finishing with, 'but I saw Iverson at the Midland Railway Terminus, although he disappeared before I could reach him.'

Her eyes widened. 'He seems to be everywhere. I have news also: Peters sent a message yesterday saying that O'Connor has apparently absconded with an unspecified sum of money.'

'O'Connor the mortuary assistant? Perhaps we should see what Bradwell can tell us about it. He must be back from Brighton by now.'

'Great minds, Lonsdale. I've heard that he *is* back, and I want to know if he had a role in the murder of Teresa Godley. Shall we go?'

They arrived at the mortuary to find its windows boarded over with fresh wood and its door secured with a strong, new lock.

'Have the Metropolitan Police finally provided sufficient funds for Bradwell to make his building safe?' asked Hulda, rattling the door. 'He *will* be pleased! But quick – stop that hansom before it gets away. He's not here, so we need to locate him at the hospital.'

St Bartholomew's Hospital was a substantial complex, comprising a number of large brick and stone edifices and a mass of outbuildings. Lonsdale and Hulda were directed on a complicated route along corridors, across patches of scrubby grass, and up and down stairs. Hulda was beginning to become frustrated when they finally found the surgical section, with its brightly lit operating theatres. Bradwell, just leaving a recovery room, was not pleased to see them.

'How may I help you?' he asked stiffly, leading them into a grimy corridor away from his colleagues. 'Much as meeting you is a pleasure, Miss Friederichs, I am busy today.'

Lonsdale noticed that his face was paler than it had been and his hands were unsteady – his sojourn in Brighton had evidently not been the restorative jaunt he had hoped.

'We wanted to ask you about O'Connor,' said Hulda. 'Where is he?'

'I don't know,' said Bradwell. 'I haven't been to the mortuary in days, so I can't answer questions about what the staff do without me. Is there anything else? I have patients waiting.'

'But you must know,' insisted Hulda. 'You worked with him for . . . how long was it?'

Bradwell shook his head quickly, glanced up and down the hall, and then looked her squarely in the eyes. 'Please, Miss Friederichs, I'd love to help you, but I've an operation to perform in ten minutes. Now, if you will—'

'Have the police asked you about O'Connor's disappearance?' persisted Hulda.

'Of course, but I'll tell you what I told them: I haven't seen him in days. I've been in Brighton, you know, with my family.'

'So what did you do there?' asked Hulda. 'Meet any local young girls?'

Bradwell blinked. 'Pardon?'

'One was murdered,' said Hulda. 'Teresa Godley.'

Bradwell raised his eyebrows. 'Yes, I read about it in the newspapers.'

'She was found dead after a beach arcade was set ablaze.' Hulda forged on. 'Sounds rather like what happened to Donovan, don't you think?'

Bradwell gaped at her in horror. 'You can't think that *I'm*—'

'Is it a coincidence that you leave for Brighton and a similar murder occurs there?' she pressed relentlessly. 'We don't know if Godley had her cerebrum taken out, but we *will* find out.'

'Good,' said Bradwell unsteadily. 'I hope you do. But remember who first mentioned the excised cerebrum to Lonsdale. What possible motive would I have to do so if I were involved?'

'That's a good point,' said Lonsdale to Hulda.

'But I'm afraid I can no longer help you on this case or any other,' Bradwell said. 'I've resigned my post with the Metropolitan Police.' He shrugged. 'I'm tired of long hours for little pay in a broken-down building. Bart's offered me an appointment that'll suit me much better, and I'll be able to spend more time with my family. Now, please excuse me. My patient—'

'Has someone threatened you?' asked Lonsdale, moving to block the surgeon's way as he turned to leave. 'Is that why you're so frightened?'

'I'm not frightened.' Bradwell glanced around uneasily again. 'But I do have a wife and children to think about.'

'So someone *has* threatened you?' pounced Hulda.

'Please stop,' begged Bradwell, the fear now obvious in his face. 'Leave me alone!'

He turned from them and strode down the corridor.

'Well,' said Lonsdale thoughtfully. 'That's not the ebullient, friendly man I met a few weeks ago.'

'No,' Hulda agreed. 'Something's terrified him.'

'I wonder if Iverson reached him,' said Lonsdale.

There was no more to be done, so while Hulda returned to *The PMG*, Lonsdale went to see Inspector Peters. The policeman's willingness to talk to Lonsdale – without chastising him about interference – indicated his own investigation was not going well.

'I had another encounter with Iverson,' Lonsdale told him. 'Yesterday at the Midland Railway Station.'

'Really?' asked Peters, raising his eyebrows. 'Are you certain it was him?'

'Oh yes. Positive.'

'Then we have a most peculiar problem,' said Peters, puffing clouds of blue-grey smoke. 'Because I saw Iverson, too, the day *before* you did. He was floating face down in the Thames. He was very dead, and had been for some time.'

Nothing Lonsdale could say would induce the policeman to believe he had seen Iverson. The inspector simply pointed out that a large moustache and a scar often made quite different men appear similar, especially when only a fleeting glance was possible. The two parted on friendly but sceptical terms.

Upon arriving home, Lonsdale was initially disappointed not to find a response from Dr Quayle, but then he heard Jack talking to the sisters in the sitting room. He felt a surge of pleasure when Anne looked as delighted as he felt when he joined them.

'What happened to you?' demanded Emelia. 'We came to invite you to Pagani's, only to find that you had left with another woman.'

'Not another woman,' Lonsdale said. 'Just Friederichs. She's a colleague.'

'A pretty one, though,' remarked Jack, watching Anne mischievously.

'If you like that sort of thing,' responded Lonsdale stiffly, disliking his brother's teasing.

Emelia had watched the exchange with a puzzled frown. 'Do you have many female colleagues?'

'Just the one,' replied Lonsdale. He turned to Anne. 'Let's not talk about Friederichs. I'm sorry I wasn't here. Did you enjoy Pagani's?'

'It would have been better with you there,' said Jack bluntly.

'No,' contradicted Emelia. 'It was better *without* him. The three of us never argue when we're alone, but we often do when he's here.'

'I like a lively debate,' countered Anne.

'I had planned to stay home today,' Lonsdale said, 'but Friederichs suggested that we locate a certain doctor at St Bartholomew's, and—'

'You went off the moment another woman beckoned?' snapped Emelia. 'Without leaving a message to say where you had gone?'

'Why would I leave a message, when I was out for an undetermined period following up on my investigation?' Lonsdale asked reasonably.

'So you didn't want anyone to know where you had gone?' Emelia looked him up and down in some disgust. 'How often do you disappear with that kind of woman?'

'Steady on, Emelia,' said Jack, startled by her venomous tone. 'There's no need to react like that.'

'Please, Em,' said Anne softly, mortified by her sister's outburst and trying to make peace. 'Tomorrow's the day that we're all to go to the park together, and as there's a red sky outside, the weather should be fine. I think we should have a picnic there, rather than eating here.'

'I don't want to go,' said Emelia waspishly. 'Not with him.' She eyed Lonsdale malevolently.

'Why not?' demanded Lonsdale. He had had enough of Emelia and her unpleasantness. 'I've done nothing wrong by having a female colleague, and I don't know why you would have so unfairly taken against her.'

'I see,' said Emilia stiffly.

'She's a perfect lady,' he stormed on. 'And would never stoop to besmirch the reputations of those she doesn't know.'

'Well,' said Anne in the awkward silence that followed, 'I've heard there are lots of ducklings on the Serpentine this year.'

'I shan't go,' said Emelia sulkily. 'I don't like ducks.'

'Don't be silly,' said Jack, rather sternly. 'It'll be pleasant to spend an afternoon in the sunshine, and I will have Mrs Webster prepare us the picnic Anne has suggested.'

'Or you can stay here, and we'll tell you about it when we come back,' suggested Lonsdale.

'Very well, I'll come,' said Emelia, yielding when she saw that Jack and Anne were ready to go along with Lonsdale's suggestion. 'But Alexander had better not decide to run off—'

'How about a little music before we go,' interrupted Anne.

The four trooped into the drawing room, where Anne selected a lieder by Brahms. Lonsdale was ordered to play the piano, while Anne and Emelia sang. Lonsdale did not like Brahms, but was prepared to suffer as long as Anne was happy. Emelia, he decided, could go to the Devil, and he brazenly risked more censure by attacking Jack's brandy. Emelia watched sullenly, but said nothing.

Lonsdale woke the following morning when his brother burst into his room and threw open the curtains, letting in a stream of golden sunlight.

'Don't you know it's Sunday?' groaned Lonsdale, trying to pull the covers over his head. There was a brief tussle when Jack tried to haul them off him. 'It is the one day we can sleep in. Why are you up so early?'

'Because it *is* Sunday,' said Jack, beaming happily. 'We're going to church, then we're going to have a pleasant afternoon in the park.'

The prospect of a day with Anne pleased Lonsdale. He promised himself not to give the murders a moment of thought, but to enjoy the glorious spring day. He dressed with more than his usual care, and Jack had to drag him away from the mirror.

After enduring an unusually long and complex sermon, and five fervently patriotic hymns, the brothers strolled back through Kensington Gardens. They had just arrived home when they were hailed by a familiar voice – Hulda. Lonsdale regarded her in astonishment. She was sitting astride a bicycle, wearing a skirt short enough to reveal a full four inches of leg above the ankle.

'You're looking unusually smart today, Lonsdale,' she said, dismounting and wheeling the contraption towards him. 'Are you going out?'

'To Hyde Park, with my fiancée Emelia and her sister Anne,' said Jack cheerfully, oblivious to her provocative apparel. 'It's an excellent day for a picnic.'

'I was going to ask if you wanted to come cycling,' said Hulda, crestfallen. 'I'm sure you know cycling is good for the constitution.'

'I don't think my constitution would survive long on that thing,' said Lonsdale, eyeing the bicycle doubtfully.

'Well, don't exert yourself, then.' Hulda gave her bicycle a shove, and flung her leg over it to mount in much the same way that Lonsdale had seen men do. She was around the corner at a furious speed before Lonsdale could tell her about Peters claiming Iverson was dead.

'She's quite a lady,' said Jack ambiguously, watching her disappear.

When Emelia and Anne arrived, the four of them walked to Hyde Park's Italian Water Garden, and picnicked near the statue of Jenner.

'Emelia and I have been discussing taking her parents to Raunds, so they can meet Mother and Father,' Jack told Lonsdale as they ate. 'We were thinking of August. Would that appeal to you, Alec?'

'Certainly,' he replied. 'I've not seen Mother and Father nearly as much as I expected when I returned to England, and I'm sure they'd enjoy meeting the Humbage family.' He was certain they would be hospitable and kindly, although – based on Jack's descriptions – he suspected his gentle, intellectual father would be disappointed in his future in-laws.

'Good, it's settled then,' said Jack. 'But look – the sun's going behind a cloud. Shall we go for a walk before it turns cooler?'

But it was already too late: as soon as they began to stroll along the Serpentine, a chill breeze picked up. Some of the clouds drifting towards them were heavy and dark; despite Anne's prediction of fine weather, a downpour was in the offing.

Jack and Emelia walked ahead, arm in arm like a married couple, while Lonsdale and Anne dawdled behind. Anne talked about her childhood in India, then, seeing several women in three-quarter-length dolmans, switched to a commentary on fashion. After a moment, she stopped suddenly and turned towards him.

'I can't believe that I'm blathering about fashion! I'm sorry. I'm not usually so silly.'

Lonsdale smiled and reached for her hand. 'I don't think you are silly, and if we were somewhere on our own, I'd kiss you, Annie.'

'And if we were somewhere on our own, I'd let you.'

He smiled at her, and they continued walking, hand in hand. Ahead, Lonsdale could hear Emelia's strident voice as she held forth about the price of satin. He wondered how Jack – or Anne – could bear to spend so much time with her.

Anne, on the other hand, was such easy company – unlike Hulda, whom he found himself also thinking about, to his surprise. He compared them: Hulda was strong, flaxen-headed and driven, like some Viking, whose sole aim was conquest, while Anne was slim, also light-haired and eager, although just as serious and intelligent. But, despite his growing attraction to Anne, Lonsdale could not but help notice that she was not as challenging as Hulda – in both the positive and negative senses.

They had reached the part of the Serpentine that was used as a boating lake. There was a wooden pier on which sat a number of men and boys, many proudly displaying tiny craft and happily criticizing those of others. It was here that Donovan came on his days off. Lonsdale gazed at the boat owners, wondering if any had known him.

'Come on,' he said, springing up the steps that led to the pier, and forgetting his intention to put Donovan's death from his mind for the day.

Anne hesitated. 'You want me to go with you? With all those men?'

It had not occurred to Lonsdale that Anne – independent and curious – would hesitate, or that she would be alarmed at the prospect of people discussing model boats.

Stemming his impatience, he offered her his arm. 'I'd like to see the boats more closely.'

'No.' Anne was firm. 'You go, and I'll wait here. I don't feel comfortable clambering out there.'

Lonsdale hesitated. It was ungentlemanly to abandon a woman, even in as public a place as Hyde Park. But it was only for a moment, and the pier was only a few yards from the shore.

One of the men saw him looking, and beckoned him over in a friendly fashion. Lonsdale's mind was made up. He walked briskly onto the jetty, and stood facing the bank so that he could still see Anne. She was well away from the water, and Lonsdale wondered if she were frightened of it. But his attention was not on her for long, as several men were more than pleased to show him their boats.

'An acquaintance – a chap named Donovan – recommended I come here,' he said after he had admired and complimented their vessels. 'He often told me how splendid your boats were.'

'Donovan,' sighed one, shaking his head sadly. 'Poor codger died in a fire. He was a lovely fellow, too. He came here without fail every Sunday and Wednesday, although he never had a boat himself. Said he didn't have the talent to make one, but I think he'd have done all right, if he'd tried.'

'He came twice a week?' asked Lonsdale, watching carefully to make sure that Anne was not being disturbed by an elderly man with a cane, who was strolling past her.

'Usually, but he was less regular just before he died,' said a young man with a peculiarly shaped felt cap. 'He was taking part in some survey or other.'

'Was he?' queried the first man. 'I didn't know that.'

'Well, you know Donovan,' said Felt Cap. 'He wouldn't tell anyone anything. I asked him where he'd been, but he just said something about business. I said it must be pretty important to keep him away from the boats, but he wouldn't tell me anything else.'

'Quite right, too,' said the first man. 'You'd no right asking him questions. He was a private man, was Donovan.'

'He was a bit *too* private, if you ask me,' said Felt Cap. 'It wasn't normal. And I only asked so I could look out for him, like friends do. I thought I ought to find out what was keeping him away from the boats.'

The first man shook his head again. 'It must've been sommat important, that's all I can say. And you're right – friends *do* look out for each other, and he had no friends except us. The snobs at Salmon and Eden never cared about him.'

'Did you find out what kept him from coming here?' asked Lonsdale, all his attention on them, Anne forgotten.

'I did,' said Felt Cap, unable to disguise his pride. 'You see, Harold's boat sank, and Donovan took off his jacket to help him get it back.'

'He did,' acknowledged Harold sadly. 'I wouldn't have got *Endeavour* back if he hadn't helped me. What did you do, Fred? Look in his jacket pockets?'

Fred looked offended. 'What do you think I am? I don't rummage through people's things. But I did notice a piece of paper sticking *out* of one pocket. Because he was a friend – and I look out for friends – I looked to see what was on it.'

'What did it say?' asked Harold, keenly interested.

'There was a date,' said Fred. 'It was in his fancy handwriting – Wednesday the nineteenth of April at three o'clock.'

Lonsdale's interest quickened. That was when Donovan had told his colleague at Salmon and Eden that he was going to watch the boats. He had died the following morning.

'So did Donovan come boating that day?' he asked. Harold shook his head. 'The last time we saw him was the Sunday before. What else did this piece of paper say, Fred?'

'After the date and time, it said, "survey at the Imperial sommat or other Institute, Brunswick Gardens." That's where he went instead of coming here.'

'The Imperial Statistical Institute?' asked Lonsdale, recalling reading about a grand opening of such a place in the distant past.

'That's the one!' exclaimed Fred.

Lonsdale was disappointed. He could not imagine that an appointment at some obscure academic department could have anything to do with Donovan's death.

'Did he say what he was going to do there?'

'No, but he was furious when he saw me with the paper in my hand. He snatched it away and said it was none of my business, and that I shouldn't tell anyone, or I'd put him in an embarrassing situation.'

'And have you told anyone else?' asked Lonsdale.

'Not until now – you can't embarrass the dead, can you? Anyway, I didn't see why it should be cause for embarrassment, but then it struck me. It probably wasn't this statistical institute he was visiting, but a hospital. Men's diseases – you know. He must have had a tart somewhere.' Lonsdale was glad Anne was not with him.

'You think he had the clap?' asked Harold in wonderment. 'Never! Not him.'

'Can you think of a better explanation?' demanded Fred. 'Can you see old Donovan missing an afternoon here to talk about numbers or some such thing?'

'Maybe he was having money problems,' said Harold. 'He lived in a fancy house on Wyndham Street, but when his father died, he didn't inherit as much as he thought he would, and his windows needed replacing. He told me his neighbours are the type to complain about a bit of shabbiness, and that he'd have to fork out for them to be replaced.'

'So he may have taken paid work at the Institute,' mused Lonsdale, 'to pay for house repairs?'

Yes,' said Harold firmly.

'No,' said Fred at the same time. 'He had the clap. And if he *was* short of money, it was because he needed it for his fancy piece.'

Lonsdale left them debating and turned to hurry back to Anne. But she was not there.

Lonsdale looked around quickly, trying to see where she could have gone, but she was nowhere to be seen. He ran to the end of the pier and was about to start asking passers-by if they had seen her, when he spied both sisters with Jack on a bench.

Emelia gave Lonsdale a nasty look when he rejoined them, but Anne just laughed and did not seem to mind that she had been abandoned.

'Really, Alec,' muttered Jack crossly as they began to walk home, Emelia and Anne lagging behind when they stopped to admire some bluebells. 'How could you leave Anne alone?'

'Hardly alone! I could see her the whole time.'

'Not the *whole* time, or you would have noticed her coming to sit with us,' said Jack pointedly. 'You should be more thoughtful. They had a brother who drowned when they were young, so neither of them likes water.'

'How was I supposed to know that, for Heaven's sake?' Lonsdale asked, although he felt mildly ashamed of his neglect.

'These are two *ladies*, not the frontier women you met in Africa. Or Hulda Friederichs, for that matter, who, if you don't watch out, will have you riding bicycles and chaining yourself to railings in favour of women's votes.'

'What's wrong with letting women vote? They do comprise half the population.'

'A year ago, I would have agreed,' said Jack. 'But do you really want the likes of Emelia deciding the future of our country? She doesn't read the newspapers, and has no idea what's happening in the world.'

'I'm sure the same is true of a lot of men, but they're allowed to do it. Besides, some women are extremely well informed. Look at Friederichs, who knows more about British politics than virtually any man I know – including you. And Anne is no dullard.'

'No, she's not.' Jack gave Lonsdale a playful jab in the ribs. 'Pretty girl, Anne. Good family, too. You could do a lot worse than her.'

Lonsdale was not about to confess his regard for her, because he knew he'd never hear the end of it. He changed the subject back to Emelia.

'If you think Emelia can't be trusted to vote, why in God's name are you marrying her?' There. It was out, and there was no turning back. Lonsdale realized he was holding his breath.

'A man needs a woman, and she has everything I require,' said Jack simply. 'And I love her.'

Lonsdale was spared from responding, as several penny-sized spots appeared on the path and Emelia screeched her horror.

'Rain!' she shrieked, as if it were acid dropping from the sky rather than water.

'Dash it all!' exclaimed Jack. 'I was hoping to reach home first. Can we make it to those trees, do you think?'

They trotted across the grass to a small copse, considerably hampered by Anne's uncontrollable giggles. The sky was now a solid mass of grey, and the rain that fell was the kind of downpour that might set in for the rest of the day. Lonsdale offered to fetch a hansom, more to escape Emelia's grumbles than from any sense of chivalry.

'I'll bring it down Carriage Drive, so you can just come over when you see me arrive.'

'Don't forget us then,' said Anne, as the drips came through the branches onto her hair.

Lonsdale began to hurry across the grass to where there were always hansoms for hire. Other strollers were thinking along identical lines, but he was faster than most, as ladies in fashionable sheath and tie-back dresses moved slowly.

He reached his destination ahead of the crowds and hailed a carriage. But they had gone no more than a hundred yards when he heard a loud crack. The horse screamed at the same time that the carriage lurched forward, throwing Lonsdale headfirst against its interior wall. His mind reeling, all he could think was that someone was shooting at him.

ELEVEN

'You all right, mister?' the driver asked. Lonsdale tried to clear his wits. 'The axle snapped when we went over a pothole. Sorry if you was thrown about. If it makes you feel any better, the underside of me carriage looks worse than you do.'

Lonsdale climbed out and inspected the damage. Rain drummed on the umbrellas of the people who clustered around watching. A policeman hurried over and asked him to wait while he helped the driver to disengage the horses. Several people asked if they could help, and one gentleman invited Lonsdale to share his umbrella.

Eventually, after shuffling impatiently while the policeman made ponderous notes about the accident in his pocket book, Lonsdale told him that he had to go. Then it took a while for him to find a replacement carriage. He directed the driver to the trees under which Jack and the sisters had sheltered, but they were no longer there.

Grimly, knowing he was in for lectures from both Jack and Emelia, he told the driver to take him home. When he reached

Cleveland Square, Dillon the butler informed him that the others had not returned. For a reason he couldn't put his finger on, Lonsdale began to feel uneasy.

Using the same cab, he gave the driver the Humbages' address – Gordon Square in Bloomsbury – and told him to hurry. Progress was agonizingly slow, as the traffic was heavy because of the rain. After what felt like an age, Lonsdale was deposited at the door of the handsome, five-storey affair with window boxes, yellow shutters, and twin marble columns leading to a front door. He flung a handful of coins at the driver, and ran up the steps. His knock was answered by a maid, who gasped as he thrust past her into the hall.

'Are Jack and Anne here?' he demanded, darting down the corridor and looking through open doors as he went. In one, an elderly woman regarded him with obvious interest. 'And Emelia?' he added as an afterthought.

'Alexander!' came Emelia's shocked voice from behind him. 'Whatever's the matter with you? You're frightening our grandmother.'

He turned to see Emelia and Anne coming down the stairs, from where they had evidently been changing into dry clothes. He sighed in relief.

'Thank goodness you're safe,' he said. 'I wasn't sure where you'd gone.'

'Where *we'd* gone?' demanded Emelia, glaring at him. 'You were gone for an age, but our neighbour, Sir Henry Hartley, saw us and offered us a ride in his own carriage. Jack insisted that we accept.'

'So where's Jack?' asked Lonsdale. 'Did you leave him behind?'

'Who might you be, sir?' interrupted an imperious voice from the top of the stairs. 'Anne? Emelia? Who is this ill-dressed fellow? What is the meaning of this unseemly commotion on the Lord's Day?'

'It's Jack's brother, Father,' said Emelia, giving Lonsdale a warning look. 'Here to ensure we arrived home safely.'

'Is he now?' asked Sir Gervais, in a voice that dripped hostility. He was a tall man, with stern features, vast mutton-chop whiskers, and a manner that indicated he was used to having his own way. He wore a silk smoking jacket and had *The Pilgrim's Progress* tucked under his arm, a tome that Lonsdale considered one of the dullest ever written. Evidently, Sir Gervais had been reading it aloud to his household, as a bevy of servants emerged to stand at his heels.

With them was a large, squat woman whom Lonsdale took to be the lady of the house. Lady Humbage wore a heavy, uncomfortable outfit that would not have improved her enjoyment of the afternoon, as it looked hot, stiff and restrictive. No wonder Emelia was such an ignoramus, thought Lonsdale: her parents had turned literature and education into an ordeal. He wondered how Anne had survived.

'He looks drunk to me,' said Lady Humbage, coming to take the arm of the old lady, who had emerged from her room to watch. 'Go and sit down, Mother.'

'*Are* you drunk, sir?' asked Sir Gervais, reverently placing the Bunyan on a small table before descending the stairs with a majesty of which the Old Queen would have been proud.

'He's always like this,' said Emelia petulantly. 'And, this afternoon, he abandoned Annie to the attentions of crude men on the banks of the Serpentine and then ran off alone, leaving us without a carriage.'

'He did *what?*' exploded her father, glowering at Lonsdale as if he wished to thrash him there and then.

'Em is teasing,' said Anne, giving her sister a sharp glare. 'We had a most pleasurable walk together, and then – with my blessing – Alec went to interview some men for a story he's writing.'

'You abandoned my daughter? And what do you mean, "for a story"?' His voice oozed contempt.

'Look at him,' said Lady Humbage, before Lonsdale could defend himself. 'His hair is uncombed and he's dripping on the Persian rug.'

'It's raining,' said the old lady tartly, speaking in a voice that was unexpectedly strong. 'Of course he's dishevelled. But he's not drunk. I know a drunk when I see one.' She smiled enigmatically, leaving Lonsdale to wonder whether the family's roots were as respectable as Emelia and her stiff, pompous parents would have everyone believe.

'You're right, Grandmother – he isn't drunk,' said Emelia, trying to bundle Lonsdale towards the door. 'But he *is* leaving.'

'Stay,' countered the old lady, extending Lonsdale a warm smile and holding out a gnarled hand. 'A visitor kind enough to brave a wet Sunday must not be allowed to escape so easily.'

'I agree,' said Anne quickly. 'He should stay.'

'He's busy,' said Emelia. 'He has work to do.'

'On the Sabbath?' asked Sir Gervais coldly. 'The day the Lord instructed us to rest? What kind of heathen are you, man?'

'No kind, indeed, sir,' responded Lonsdale shortly. 'As a matter of fact—'

'Alec's father is a rector,' interrupted Anne, trying to salvage a degenerating situation.

'Well, obviously,' said the old lady dryly, 'if he's Jack's brother.' She chuckled softly.

'A rector who failed to teach his son that cleanliness lies next to Godliness,' intoned Sir Gervais. 'It's hard to believe he's related to Jack.'

'Yes,' agreed Lady Humbage. 'Breeding is important, and one can tell a good deal from families.'

Emelia blanched, as she realized doubts were being cast on Jack because of her unwarranted hostility to Lonsdale. He felt a twinge of malicious satisfaction.

'How can you account for your actions towards my daughter, and then for bursting in on us during our devotions?' demanded Sir Gervais.

Lonsdale adopted a pompous voice of his own, speaking loudly enough to ensure he would not be interrupted. 'I regret the weather has made it difficult for me to appear my best. I have the utmost regard for your daughters, and I would never intentionally put them in the way of verbal unpleasantness or physical harm. My arrival here was based on concern for them and my brother, who left the park before I could bring them the transport I had secured.'

'Don't take that tone with me, sir,' blustered Sir Gervais. 'By God, if there weren't ladies present—'

'Oh, go and sit down, Gervais,' ordered the old lady crossly. 'You'll give yourself a seizure. You, too, Agatha.'

'Where's Jack?' Lonsdale asked of Anne.

'Jack's a charming fellow,' said the old lady, before Anne could answer. 'One brother a rector, another in the Royal Navy.' She smiled at Lonsdale. 'And now I meet the baby of the family.'

'Alexander was in the Colonial Service,' said Emelia, to repair any damage she might have caused. 'Weren't you?' There was desperation in her eyes.

Lonsdale nodded his head obediently. 'Jack?' he asked.

'Walking home,' replied Anne gently. 'Don't worry. He'll be wet, but a drenching will do him no harm.'

'Stay for some rum punch,' ordered the old lady. 'I have a recipe that will put some colour back in your cheeks.'

'Go back to the sitting room, Mother-in-law!' snapped Sir Gervais unpleasantly. 'He is not here to listen to the prattle of elderly women. Or to imbibe sinful substances.'

'Pity,' sighed the old lady, genuinely disappointed.

'Perhaps another time,' said Lonsdale gallantly.

'Good day, sir,' said Emelia's father and, without another word, he turned and stalked back upstairs, his wife and servants in his wake.

'Goodbye,' called the old lady wistfully, as Lonsdale aimed for the door. 'Do call again.'

'Hopefully we'll see each other soon,' put in Anne.

'I'm not pleased with your treatment of that antimacassar, Alexander,' hissed Emelia, anger erupting again now her parents were no longer present.

'What antimacassar?' asked Lonsdale, bewildered by the sudden change of topics.

'You obviously wiped your dirty hands on it,' continued Emelia. 'It was ruined, and it was one of a set that took me a month to make.'

'It fell out under the trees while Jack was looking for his handkerchief to wipe spots of rain off Em's face,' said Anne, laughing at Lonsdale's guilty look. 'At first, we couldn't imagine why he had such a filthy rag, but then she recognized the stitches.'

'Jack said he had put it in his pocket because he thought he'd have a replacement made,' said Emelia. 'As if I wouldn't notice the difference between my lacework and someone else's! You men must think us stupid.'

'He told you *I'd* ruined it?' asked Lonsdale, thinking it unlike his brother to land him in trouble quite so shamelessly.

'Of course not,' said Emelia, scornfully. 'When I demanded to know what had happened to it, he said he had found it on the mantelpiece and that one of the servants must have damaged it. But from the way he blustered, I knew he was protecting *you*. Now go. I don't want Father to have second thoughts about what kind of family he's letting me marry into.'

Lonsdale walked down the steps to find the driver of the carriage still looking for coins in the mud.

'You don't know how much there was, do you?' he asked unhappily. 'Only I'm not sure I've got it all, see. People don't usually lob money at me.'

'Sorry, I don't,' said Lonsdale. 'I hope it was enough.'

'It'll suffice,' said the driver smugly. 'In fact, I'll take you back to Bayswater for free if you like.'

He had a final prod in the mud with the whip, and then they were off, travelling sedately along the tree-lined streets.

Lonsdale rubbed his head. Was he mad, tearing all over London and making bad impressions on Jack's intended in-laws? He decided he had better be careful, or it would be Jack he would have to worry about, not some crazed killer.

When Lonsdale arrived home, he was surprised when the door was opened before he reached it – the servants were not usually so assiduous. He was even more surprised to see Hulda in the hall.

'Your butler told me that you'd shot in and out again with no explanation,' she said. 'I was concerned.'

'I went to see Emelia and Anne,' said Lonsdale vaguely, and turned to Dillon. 'Is Jack home?'

'Not yet, sir.'

Lonsdale went to the drawing room. Hulda followed and sat opposite him.

'Jack should be home by now. Where could he be?'

'His club?' suggested Hulda. 'The place where men go to do things mere women are not permitted to witness?'

Lonsdale ignored the barb. 'Anne said he planned to come home.'

'Well, he would say that, Lonsdale,' said Hulda. 'He'd hardly confess that he aimed to spend his evening drinking and playing cards. Why are you so worried? Has something happened?'

'No,' admitted Lonsdale, not sure how to explain the irrational fear that had been with him ever since he had come home to find the place empty.

Hulda fumbled in her bag for an Esmonda cigar. 'A hansom knocked me from my bicycle just after noon,' she said quietly. 'It would have run me over had I not rolled out of the way.'

'Hulda!' exclaimed Lonsdale, appalled to think he had been so engrossed in his own concerns that he had failed to notice her. He looked her over quickly, noting that her hands were scraped and that there was mud on her skirt. For a woman of her impeccable appearance, this was unusual indeed. 'Are you hurt? Can I fetch you anything?'

She shook her head, but her voice was unsteady. 'I was on my way to a special Sunday archery session when the attack came. I'm damned if I'll allow a maniac to interfere with something I enjoy, so I picked myself up and continued. I was a little alarmed, but once at the butts, I could protect myself by treating any comers to an arrow in the heart. After practice, I came here.'

She seemed subdued, and he sensed she was still in shock.

'Did you see the driver? Was it Iverson?'

'No, but someone just as interesting.' She blew out a large ring of smoke. 'I believe it was the man who attacked us near the hospital – the one we think is named "Pauly".'

'But he didn't harm you?' he asked again, thinking that for Hulda to admit to being 'a little alarmed' probably meant that she was terrified.

'Just my pride. I had to submit to the indignity of being helped to my feet and fussed over by a group of men. But there is more important news.'

'What could be more important?' he asked uneasily.

'I met Wheatley, *The PMG*'s business reporter, just before I was knocked over. He told me that the police had sent a note to Stead saying that a body had been found in Shepherd's Bush.'

Lonsdale waited while Hulda blew a stream of smoke towards the hearth.

'It was Poole, your missing milkman,' she said. 'He was *sans* cerebrum.'

While rain splattered against the window, Hulda and Lonsdale sat by the fire. The flames sent a comfortable orange glow around the room, and snapped and popped in a way that always made Lonsdale think of toasting teacakes when he was a child. He might have enjoyed sitting there, talking quietly while the storm fussed outside, were they not discussing a series of brutal murders, and had he not been worried about Jack.

'Poole wasn't killed where he was found – in an alley – because there wasn't enough blood, apparently,' said Hulda, sipping her tea. 'And because a number of people saw the corpse and that its cerebrum was missing, the police have not tried to conceal it.'

'Leaving him in an alley,' said Lonsdale. 'The killer is getting audacious.'

'And perhaps selective. Greaves's and Walker's cerebra were left intact when they were killed in Regent's Park, but Donovan and Yeats, the music-hall entertainer, were despoiled.'

'There's no pattern, is there? Some victims he mutilates, and others he doesn't.' Lonsdale felt dispirited, unable to see a way forward.

'Let's think this through,' said Hulda. 'Iverson – I think we can safely name *him* as our culprit, given he had been seen, and his past record – has been killing people and taking their cerebra. Obviously, there's a limited number of times he can do this and escape, as there would be a public outcry, and the police would mount a major hunt. So, he concealed what he did in his early victims.'

'And Iverson is *not* dead, as Peters claims,' said Lonsdale. 'I know what I saw at the train station. He's alive and he has help – men like Morgan, whom Jamie mentioned.'

'I believe you,' said Hulda. 'I'm also sure he's the man we want. So, he's been killing people and removing parts of their brains . . .'

'The five people Cath Walker claimed are dead are so well hidden that their bodies have yet to be discovered,' said Lonsdale. 'And the removal of Donovan's and Yeats's cerebra was also cunningly concealed.'

'It was only because Bradwell was observant that it was discovered,' said Hulda. 'Which brings up the question of him – Bradwell.'

'Well, he was so thoroughly rattled that he disappeared on an impromptu holiday with his family and resigned his position as police surgeon. I don't think he's involved, but I do think he's been warned not to help us any more.'

'Spineless!' sneered Hulda contemptuously.

'Better spineless than brainless,' said Lonsdale.

'Perhaps we shouldn't be looking at Bradwell, but at his assistant, O'Connor,' suggested Hulda. 'He went missing during the time that Bradwell took his holiday.'

'He may have disappeared because he was also intimidated,' said Lonsdale. 'And he fled to save his life. There's nothing to say he's involved. But speculating is taking us nowhere. Let's go back to facts.'

'Well, we know Walker decided to put an end to it – not by telling the police, because if Iverson was involved, so might other officers have been. I have not forgotten that high-ranking officers came to warn us against investigating, and when we did it anyway, we were attacked.'

'So her only other option was the press,' said Lonsdale, 'hoping that the resulting furore would see Iverson and any cronies arrested. But she was murdered herself before she could do more than pique our interest. The killer poisoned Greaves first, then he cut Cath's throat. But that's odd, isn't it? Why poison one victim and slit the throat of another?'

'It *is* odd,' agreed Hulda. 'Everything about the case is odd. Indeed, at the risk of sounding defeated, I wonder if we shall ever have any answers.'

When the drizzle brought an early dusk, Hulda went home, having refused to let Lonsdale accompany her. A few minutes later, Inspector Peters was shown into the drawing room.

'You've heard the news, I take it?' Peters asked. 'Another victim relieved of his cerebrum?'

'Yes,' said Lonsdale, noticing the rings of tiredness around the inspector's eyes. 'Iverson strikes again.'

'Iverson's dead,' stated Peters firmly. 'I've known the man

for twenty years, and I can assure you it was *his* body we dredged from the Thames.'

'But I saw him on Friday,' insisted Lonsdale. 'And it *was* him – the same man I saw at Donovan's house fire, and who attacked me in Bermondsey. Unless you think a different man happened to have a scar through his eyebrow and be wearing the uniform of PC six-nine-six-D.'

'Regardless,' said Peters, in a way that showed he clearly thought Lonsdale was mistaken, 'he seems not to like you much.' He pulled his pipe from his pocket and began to tamp down the tobacco. 'I wonder whether we might put that dislike to use.'

'Meaning?'

'I'll be blunt. These murders are random – there's no pattern in location, time, choice of victim, or anything else. Ergo, it'll be almost impossible to catch the culprit. You don't need me to tell you that the milkman's fate will hit tomorrow's headlines like a mortar shell. We must lay hold of this maniac before we have mass panic.'

Lonsdale nodded. 'But what do you want from me?'

'Our evidence suggests that the same man or group of men are responsible for these deaths, and I'm inclined to think that he or they have also made attempts on your life.'

'Oh Lord!' gulped Lonsdale. 'You want me to wander about the city in the hope that he'll come after me?'

'Exactly,' said Peters, without the trace of a smile. 'Of course, you'll be closely followed by my best officers, and I'll be on hand to make sure nothing goes wrong.'

'But what can you do if he shoots at me from a distance?' asked Lonsdale. 'He might still escape.'

'He might,' agreed Peters. 'And he might kill you. But I'll make damn sure he doesn't get your cerebrum.' He could tell his last statement was not much comfort. 'I know I have no right to ask, Lonsdale, but you won't be safe until he's under lock and key anyway.'

'True,' said Lonsdale, 'but even so . . .'

'Of course, there have also been attempts on the life of Miss Friederichs,' said Peters slyly. 'Perhaps she'll—'

'*No!*' Lonsdale was horrified at that notion, sure she'd

volunteer in an instant. He took a deep breath and looked into Peters's gloomy features. 'Keep her safe and I'll do what you ask.'

'Thanks,' said Peters. 'I know there's little I can say that'll be of comfort, but please believe that my men *will* give all they have. And I'll send a message to Superintendent Ramsey, who will get someone to go to Miss Friederichs' home to watch over her.'

Lonsdale recalled seeing natives in Bechuanaland leaving tethered goats as bait for lions. Now he would be put in the same position.

'What do you want me to do?' he asked grimly.

Peters studied the backs of his hands, and Lonsdale sensed he was not happy either. 'You'll need to act normally – it's no good me suggesting a walk down the Strand if you never usually set foot there. Our man would know something was amiss, and he might not go for the bait . . . for you. What do you normally do on a Sunday evening?'

Lonsdale swallowed hard. 'You mean we start *now*? Tonight?'

'Unless you'd rather wait for him to come to you.'

It was a fair point.

'I was about to go to the Oxford and Cambridge Club to see if my brother's there. He should have been home by now, but . . .'

'Would you take a hansom?'

'If I can find one. It's usually relatively easy at Westbourne Terrace. What will you do? Follow in another?'

'In another two or three. We could arrange to have a man in one with you, although I suspect that would reduce the chances of the killer showing himself.'

'I'll go alone,' said Lonsdale. 'If Jack's not at the club, I'll go to his chambers at the Inner Temple – Number Three Paper Buildings.'

Peters stood. 'It's ten minutes before eight now. Give me half an hour to organize my men, then leave the house and go about your business. Walk normally.'

'What do you mean?'

'Not too slowly and not too quickly. Don't look around for him, but at the same time, be vigilant. When you reach Westbourne Terrace, approach the hansom with a driver wearing a flower in his buttonhole. He'll be one of ours. Go directly to your club, not stopping for any reason. Is that clear?'

'Perfectly,' said Lonsdale. 'If I find Jack, I'll stay for a while and come home with him. No, I won't! I don't want him involved. If he's there, I'll go to Northumberland Street. If he isn't there, I'll take the same hansom to the Inner Temple.'

'Very well. I won't wish you luck, because that simply implies an element of good fortune. But I'll warn you to take care. And no deviating from the plan.'

Lonsdale nodded understanding. 'But what if he's watching the house now? He'll see you leave and his suspicions will be raised.'

Peters gave a grim little chuckle. 'Credit us with *some* sense, man. I entered by the back door, and I'll leave the same way. No one will see me.'

Lonsdale glanced at the clock in the hall as Peters took his leave, and wondered how he would pass the next thirty minutes. His clothes were still damp, and hardly suitable for the club, so he went upstairs to change. He opened a trunk in a spare bedroom that he had turned into a rather messy storage area. There, wrapped carefully in a well-oiled cloth, was the revolver he had carried in Africa.

He studied the weapon for a moment. It had been given to him by an officer who had been killed in Wolseley's campaign against the Ashanti. Lonsdale had learned to shoot well but, even a decade later, he could not look at it without thinking of his friend. He loaded it, put it in his pocket and headed downstairs.

Finally, it was time to go. He left the house and walked as purposefully as he could towards Westbourne Terrace. His heart pounded when a drunk staggered across the street, but he forced himself to breathe normally again when he recognized one of Peters's men. He reached the line of hansoms, and looked for a driver wearing a flower in his buttonhole. With horror, he saw there were two: one sporting a bunch of daisies, another a drooping daffodil. One fingered the daisies and winked.

Lonsdale gripped his revolver in his pocket and climbed into the cab. Then they were away, the horse trotting briskly. At one point, another hansom pulled level with theirs, and, for a horrifying instant, Lonsdale thought Iverson would lean out and shoot him. He clutched his own weapon harder, but the driver slowed and the other carriage rattled past.

After what seemed an eternity, they arrived at the club, where the doorman told Lonsdale that Jack hadn't been there that day. Lonsdale returned to the hansom.

From a window of the smoking room, a tall, slim man watched Lonsdale arrive and leave. He sighed irritably and threw down his newspaper in disgust, causing another member to glance up in annoyance at the disturbance. The man at the window fixed him with such a cold, harsh look that the fellow blanched. By the time the tall man looked out of the window again, Lonsdale's driver was awaiting his instructions.

'Where to, sir?' asked the driver, when Lonsdale gave him none.

How stupid, thought Lonsdale. If he were acting normally, he would be expected to give directions to the driver, even though they both knew where the next stop would be.

'Inner Temple,' he called, sitting back and trying to relax. The hansom headed for the Strand. It was late enough that the streets were clear, and they made good time. They turned into the pleasant courtyard outside the library. Lonsdale glanced both ways before alighting and then headed for Jack's chambers. A sharp yelp made him spin round.

There was nothing to see. The driver slouched in his seat with his head down against the drizzle, and the horse stamped restlessly. Then Lonsdale looked more closely. The driver was sitting very still. As the horse jolted the vehicle, the driver slowly tipped forward and pitched out of his seat to the ground.

Lonsdale did not wait to see more. He turned and raced to the nearest building, which was the library. It was locked, although he could see lights at the windows, so he knew there were people inside. He pounded on the door, but his yell to attract attention was choked off as a strong arm snaked around his neck so tightly he could barely breathe, followed immediately by the touch of cold steel against his throat.

'Now, then, sir,' came a calm, reasonable voice that Lonsdale recognized instantly from the scene of the fire at Donovan's house. 'We don't want to be making a racket and disturbing these good folk reading, do we?'

It was Iverson. Lonsdale tried to struggle, but could not remember having ever been in such a powerful grip. Then he felt his captor tense in anticipation of the sharp stroke that would slice through his neck.

'Wait!' he croaked, trying to gain some time. 'Was it you? Did you kill them all?'

'Now who might you be meaning, sir?' asked Iverson, with unseemly interest.

'Poole,' said Lonsdale, feeling the grip ease very slightly. Where was Peters?

'Certainly, I killed the milkman,' said Iverson, sounding chillingly pleasant. 'He was quite a challenge. I went to see him in uniform, but he wouldn't speak to a policeman. So I went back in my civilian clothes, and the problem was solved.'

'But there was no problem with Donovan, was there?' said Lonsdale, playing for time. 'That was flawless.'

'Practice makes perfect, they say, and that was definitely one that filled me with pride,' said Iverson, as if claiming to have helped a lady across the road, rather than confessing to a murder.

'And Yeats – the entertainer who was murdered?'

'Murder is such an unpleasant word,' said Iverson, his voice becoming harsher. 'I think "sacrificed" might be a better way of putting it.'

'Sacrificed?' gasped Lonsdale, visions of a Satanist coven flashing through his mind. 'Sacrificed to what? To whom?'

'So many questions! I can hardly keep up with them. Sacrificed to the cause, of course. Just as you are about to be. That *will* happen tonight – it's been made quite clear.'

'By whom?' asked Lonsdale, wondering if Iverson really was receiving instructions from someone else, or if he was one of those who 'heard' mysterious voices. 'Who's making you do these things?'

'Depends what things you're referring to,' he replied enigmatically. 'But it doesn't really matter, does it? Not to you. Not now.'

Lonsdale tried to jerk away, but Iverson held him too tightly. Suddenly the door to the library opened and a short, balding barrister with thick glasses stepped out.

'Is someone knocking?' he asked. His jaw dropped in horror when he saw the knife.

The interruption made Iverson loosen his grip fractionally, which was enough for Lonsdale to lift one leg and stamp down as hard as he could on the policeman's foot. Iverson gave a sharp hiss of pain, and his arm flinched upwards, scoring a shallow nick in Lonsdale's neck. But his wrist ended up near the reporter's face, so Lonsdale sank his teeth into it. The knife fell to the ground, and Lonsdale twisted and drove his elbow into his attacker's chest. Iverson let go entirely, and Lonsdale slithered away from him, fumbling for his revolver.

But before Lonsdale could take aim, Iverson produced a truncheon and struck out with it, cracking it down on Lonsdale's forearm, making him drop the gun. It skittered into the bushes. He swung again, and Lonsdale jerked back to avoid the blow, then ducked behind one of the Corinthian pillars.

'Stop this at once!' blustered the barrister.

Drawing attention to himself was a mistake. In an instant, Iverson scooped up his knife and grabbed him by his coat, pulling him close to his chest.

'Let him go,' shouted Lonsdale, as Iverson put his knife at the little lawyer's throat. 'He has nothing to do with this, and they haven't told you to sacrifice *him*, have they?'

The policeman looked at Lonsdale with a mixture of hatred and wonder. 'In some ways, it's a shame you have to die, Mr Lonsdale. You *do* appreciate what we do. Most people would still be talking about "killing", when we both know they're "sacrifices". But as to your question, I don't think it appropriate that a civilian should be asking such things of a member of the force.'

'My apologies,' said Lonsdale, at a loss as to how to deal with someone so patently insane, but hoping to keep the terrified barrister alive until Peters came. 'It was clever, the way you killed Greaves and Cath. How did you manage it?'

'That wasn't me,' said Iverson, 'although I *would* have done it. She was going to tell you about me. They wanted her killed quickly, but I was busy collecting another sample.'

'Who?'

'Someone who is hidden in a place you won't find, no matter how hard you look. Anyway, one of my colleagues did it.'

'Who? Pauly or . . .' Lonsdale broke off, trying to remember the name Jamie had given him. 'Morgan. Was it Morgan?'

'You know Morgan? That *is* a surprise. But then, if you know us all, shouldn't you be able to tell our work apart? Certainly, you don't think my sacrifices are like those of the others?'

'Others? How many of you are there?'

'Now, Mr Lonsdale, I know you journalists like numbers, but it wouldn't be polite to tell other people's secrets, would it?'

'What are you doing with the cerebra?'

'I give them to the people I work for, of course. That's why the sacrifices were made, after all. They told me to strangle or slit the throat, but never to poison. It might pollute, you understand.'

'I see,' said Lonsdale, speaking loudly to mask the sound of the police rattle in the distance. 'And did they tell you what they were doing with them?'

'I wouldn't want to know,' said Iverson with a shudder. 'It's a disgusting business, if you ask me. I think they're quite mad, personally. Morgan is mad, and so is that nasty little tyke in the Müller cut-down—'

'Pauly?' interrupted Lonsdale.

Iverson nodded. 'Even the people in the hospital thought *he* was mad.'

Desperately trying to keep Iverson talking, Lonsdale thought about the people whom Mrs Greaves had said had disappeared. 'Did these mad people tell you to sacrifice the Johnson sisters and Leonard Baycroft?'

'Baycroft?' snapped Iverson, his manner suddenly changing and a hint of real menace in his voice. 'What do you know about him?'

The knife jerked up, and Lonsdale saw that he had made a mistake. He moved out from behind the pillar, but before he could come any closer, Iverson drew his blade with great force across the neck of the barrister, and let the dying man drop to the ground. Without pausing, he leapt at Lonsdale.

TWELVE

S hocked by the casual brutality of the attack, Lonsdale darted back behind the pillar, trying to keep it between him and Iverson, who lunged at him, knife in one hand, truncheon in the other. He wondered how long he would be able to duck and weave, when the penalty for failure would be his life. Then another police rattle sounded nearby. The police were nearly there!

'Peters!' Lonsdale yelled. 'Here!'

Iverson's face twisted with hatred and he swung his truncheon. Lonsdale ducked away from the blow aimed at his head, and heard the wood splinter as it struck the pillar. Iverson grunted in pain as the shock of the blow travelled up his arm.

'You tricked me,' Iverson hissed. 'You kept me talking, so Baycroft would get me.'

He saw the police racing towards them and, abandoning his prey, turned to flee. Lonsdale tore after him, and managed to snag a corner of the rough serge uniform jacket, but Iverson whipped around, lashing out with a punch that sent Lonsdale sprawling, while the killer disappeared towards the Temple Gardens.

'Are you all right?' Peters yelled, as he ran up.

'Where were you?' demanded Lonsdale, climbing to his feet and hurrying to retrieve his gun from the bushes.

'He killed my men!' Peters's customary poise was gone, and he looked almost as insane as Iverson, hair in disarray and blood on his hands. 'He crashed his hansom into ours, killing Evans, then came here and stabbed poor Kemp to death.'

'But why—'

'To distract us so he could get to you!' snarled Peters. 'He played us like fools! Where in God's name is the bastard?'

'This way!' Lonsdale set off in the direction Iverson had taken, Peters and half a dozen constables at his heels.

Peters put on an immense burst of speed when he saw their

quarry in the distance, and Lonsdale was hard-pressed to keep up. Iverson was little more than a dark blur, running with a speed that belied his heavy physique. A helmet was flung away, followed by a cloak; unencumbered, Iverson began to pull away from them.

'Cut him off!' screamed Peters frantically. 'He's heading for the river! Cut him off.'

Obediently, the men peeled away to either side. There was only so far Iverson could run before the river stopped him, at which point he would either have to turn left or right. Policemen were already fanning out to both sides, while Lonsdale and Peters were directly behind.

Iverson scaled the wall at the end of Temple Gardens and disappeared from sight on the Victoria Embankment. Two policemen were already scrambling over it, Peters screaming at them to hurry.

Lonsdale reached the wall and vaulted to the top, kneeling there for a moment to use its height as a vantage point. Policemen were everywhere, heads turning this way and that as they hunted for Iverson among the shadows of the trees. Carriages clattered past, obscuring Lonsdale's view.

'We've lost him,' he gasped as Peters struggled up beside him.

'No!' yelled Peters, pointing. 'Look! He's heading for the river, like a rat returning home!'

A flicker of movement behind one of the trees betrayed the burly form scrambling over the wall that separated the Victoria Embankment from the river. Lonsdale tore after him, causing a hansom driver to swerve. Oblivious to the driver's curses, he reached the wall and leaned over it. The river was at low tide, revealing a thin ribbon of silty beach. Iverson was stumbling along it, slowed by slippery debris and sucking mud.

'Hah!' muttered Lonsdale grimly. 'He makes a mistake at last.'

He raced along the road until he was ahead of Iverson, making better time than the killer on the flat, paved surface, then climbed the wall. As Iverson pounded past below, Lonsdale dropped on top of him, allowing his full weight to land on his quarry.

But Iverson seemed invincible. With a roar of rage, he flung

Lonsdale off as though he was made of feathers. Then he swung round with his broken truncheon, catching Lonsdale a blow that knocked him clean from his feet and into the stinking waters of the Thames. By the time Lonsdale had struggled back to the beach, Iverson was some distance away.

'He can't escape,' he gasped as Peters staggered past. 'Where can he go?'

'The sewers,' Peters cried in desperation. 'There's an entrance ahead. Once he gets in there, we'll never catch him.'

Lonsdale stumbled on after him, wet clothes dragging him down and the foulness of the Thames in his mouth. He tugged the gun from his pocket.

'Stop, or I'll shoot,' he yelled, aiming to loose a couple of rounds to let Iverson know he meant it. He thought the threat made Iverson falter, then realized the killer was actually wresting with a heavy metal grille. Lonsdale aimed skyward and pulled the trigger, but there was only a sharp click. He tried it again with the same response, cursing himself for not having checked it before he went out. He had not used it in years, so why would it work now? He shoved it back in his pocket and began running again, each breath rasping painfully in his chest. The mud made him feel as though he were running in treacle.

Ahead, Peters was straining every fibre in his body to reach Iverson before he got the grille open. Lonsdale heard a distant screech of protesting metal, and Iverson looked back at his pursuers before disappearing from sight. It was dark, but Lonsdale could have sworn he saw him smirk.

'No!' yelled Peters, his voice cracking in despair.

Inside the sewer, Iverson felt he was free and safe. He knew the tunnels like the back of his hand, and needed no lamp to guide him. He took a convoluted route that he was sure his pursuers would never follow, then stopped to listen. In the distance, he could hear Peters organizing his troops, but Iverson was not bothered. They wouldn't catch him now. He reached a cavernous tunnel and groped in an alcove for the lantern he had left there for just such an occasion. He lit it and splashed on through a stinking soup of sewage and rainwater.

Suddenly, there was a sharp sound ahead. Iverson stopped

in alarm. Then there was an agonizing pain in his chest. A second bang followed, and a second centre of pain. Slowly, disbelievingly, Iverson set his light on a nearby ledge and looked down at himself. Blood was pouring from his chest. He tried to straighten up, but the wounds were draining his energy as well as his blood.

Suddenly, hands wrapped round his throat. He had no strength to fight, and was pushed against the wall and then down to the bottom of the passage. Water filled his shrieking mouth.

Peters watched as his men carefully pulled the body out of the water and laid it on a ledge, next to the lamp that someone had left there so conveniently. It illuminated the dead man's face. Now the chase was over, Peters had lost the wild look that had so transformed him, and was once more his impassive self.

'Do you recognize him, Lonsdale?' he asked.

'It's Iverson,' replied Lonsdale. 'You can see the number on his collar – six-nine-six-D.'

'He's wearing Iverson's uniform,' acknowledged Peters. 'But, as I told you, we fished Iverson out of the Thames days ago. This is Leonard Baycroft from Bermondsey, whose speciality was robbery with violence. He liked to break into houses, and if the residents put up a defence, he liked it even more. He was a vicious brute, and London will be a safer place without him.'

'Baycroft,' echoed Lonsdale. 'He was one of the people who Mrs Greaves said had disappeared. I mentioned his name when I was trying to keep Iverson – I mean this man – talking until you arrived. He accused me of trying to keep him talking until Baycroft came to get him.'

'But he *was* Baycroft,' said one of the constables in puzzlement. 'What was he on about?'

'The ramblings of a deranged mind,' said Peters. 'His crimes had been growing more violent for some years, and the most recent time we arrested him – last summer – we asked Dr Bradwell to assess him. Bradwell said Baycroft was no longer sane and recommended he be sent to an asylum before he killed someone. The judge ignored the advice, and, based on the one charge we could prove at the time – although we knew he had perpetrated a lot more crimes – sentenced him to six months in Newgate instead.'

'He was released in December,' said a constable. 'We knew it was only a matter of time before we came across him again.'

'December was when people started to disappear,' mused Lonsdale. He recalled the other names that Mrs Greaves had mentioned. 'The Johnson sisters, Long Lil, Bill Byers and Baycroft.'

'And we don't know if Baycroft killed them, or whether there is some other reason for their disappearance,' said Peters. 'Did he say anything else?'

'He mentioned other murders – said we wouldn't find the bodies,' replied Lonsdale. 'And he said he had "colleagues" who killed Cath and Greaves – Pauly and Morgan, I suppose. He also claimed the stolen cerebra were for "them", but he didn't want to know what "they" did with them.'

'In other words,' said Peters, 'he was not responsible for his own actions – any wrong-doing was someone else's fault. It's not the first time I've heard criminals claim this.'

'You think he was making "them" up?' asked Lonsdale. 'He was actually acting alone?'

'Yes and no. I don't believe there's some grand enterprise in operation, with arch-criminals delivering orders to minions. However, I am sure Baycroft had help. Our search is far from over.'

'And you are sure this isn't Iverson?' Lonsdale felt he had lived with the spectre of the man for so long that it was somehow unsatisfactory that he should transpire to be someone else.

'Quite sure. Iverson had a scar on his forehead, but it looked nothing like this.' Peters pointed to the jagged cut on Baycroft's eyebrow. 'I suspect this was self-inflicted, probably when he decided to assume Iverson's identity.'

'But why would a robber impersonate a policeman?' asked Lonsdale.

'For the authority it gave him, and for access to people and places that would otherwise have been closed to him. It worked – you believed he was one of us.'

'But why Iverson?'

'Almost certainly because he was ill and easy prey. Not to mention that Iverson would have needed money – I imagine he sold Baycroft the uniform.'

'Or Baycroft murdered him for it.'

'Poor Iverson killed himself. There were no marks of violence, although Bradwell says he was poorly nourished. He was ill, poor, and clothed in little more than rags. We failed him miserably. If Baycroft was alive, we'd be able to confirm all this. But now it's just speculation.'

'Which brings us to the question of who shot him, down here in the sewers,' said Lonsdale.

'Someone who knows his way around. We heard the shots, but it took us how long to find the body? Twenty minutes? The killer could have gone anywhere.'

'Can you tell anything from the body?' asked Lonsdale. 'I confess the gunshots meant nothing to me – whether large bore or small.'

'Definitely large,' said Peters. 'Whereas the blood smears on the wall suggest there was a bit of a struggle between Baycroft and his assailant.'

He began to organize a makeshift stretcher, using his men's cloaks, carefully knotted together. Lonsdale watched, alert for another attack, but the sewers were eerily silent, the peace broken only by the soft gurgle of water and solids oozing towards the pumping station by Chelsea Bridge.

'Tell me about these other men,' ordered Peters, as four officers each grabbed a corner of the stretcher to carry Baycroft's body outside.

'Morgan is short, powerfully built, and has a tattoo of a snake on one arm. Pauly led a group that attacked Friederichs and me. He's slight, with dark brown hair and a moustache that's half brown, half grey. He swears almost constantly. Baycroft said he had spent time in a hospital or an asylum.'

Peters started. 'That's Thomas *Pawley*! P-A-W-L-E-Y. He's a murderous fiend, and he *has* been in a number of asylums, most recently Bethlem, from which he escaped. You say he's the man who attacked you?'

'Twice.'

Peters groaned. 'What a mess! Just when you think you might be getting near a solution, it all slips away.'

Peters had sent for Bradwell to examine Baycroft's body. When Lonsdale expressed surprise that the surgeon was still on the payroll, Peters said he was serving two weeks' notice. They waited for him on the narrow beach, Baycroft's body lying on the mud at their feet. It was not long before he arrived, and Lonsdale immediately noticed the change in him. Gone was the nervous pallor; he was back to his ebullient self. He greeted Lonsdale and Peters enthusiastically.

'You got him, then? Thank God! I told you Baycroft was dangerous, Inspector.'

'Especially to you,' said Lonsdale. Both Peters and Bradwell regarded him uncertainly.

'I know why you went on your sudden trip to Brighton. And why you resigned your post so abruptly.'

Peters looked perplexed, but Bradwell sighed and gazed up at the sky. When he looked back down again, his face was sombre.

'I made a grave error in judgement,' he said to Peters. 'And I overstepped my duties as a police surgeon. It cost me dear . . .'

'Explain,' ordered Peters and, when Bradwell hesitated, added, 'Or do you want Lonsdale to do it, given that he seems to know already?'

Bradwell took a deep breath and began. 'I started to think about the nature of the murders, and I made a list of suspects – criminals I'd examined in the past with certain mental abnormalities. In the medical trade, we call it *dementia praecox*. Baycroft was on it.'

Peters frowned. 'That doesn't sound like overstepping the mark to me. It sounds like initiative.'

Bradwell winced. 'Yes, but then I did something stupid. I decided to speak to them before passing the list to you. I thought my medical training would make me better equipped for it. I was right!' He gave a bitter laugh. 'I managed to trace Baycroft, and saw immediately that he had lost touch with reality. He had delusions, hallucinations, and his cognitions were accompanied by severe emotional disturbances.'

'So what did you do about it?' asked Peters.

'I made an appointment for him to come and see me at the hospital the following day.' Bradwell shrugged apologetically.

'Did he come?'

An anguished expression crossed Bradwell's face. 'He visited my wife instead, and said that if I attempted to contact him or mentioned him to the police, he'd kill our children.'

Peters made an exasperated sound at the back of his throat. 'We could have taken your family somewhere safe. Why didn't you ask us for help?'

'I had every intention of doing so. But first, I escorted my wife and children to Brighton. My plan was to see them safely installed in a hotel, then take the next train back. But I had no sooner left the hotel when there he was – Baycroft.'

'He had followed you to Brighton?'

Bradwell nodded miserably. 'He was leaning against the seawall, smirking. I'd been so careful to ensure we hadn't been followed, yet there he was. I realized there was nothing I could do without endangering my family. I *had* to do what he demanded.'

'And what was that?' asked Peters.

'To have nothing more to do with these murders, and give up my post as police surgeon.' Bradwell shrugged. 'So I did.'

'And what's happened *since* you resigned?' asked Peters, pulling out his pipe.

The surgeon sighed. 'I put my family in an isolation ward at Bart's, claiming they had diphtheria. My wife and I agreed I should tell you everything, because neither of us thought we should put our own safety over the lives of others any longer. I was on my way when I heard you'd got him.'

'What about O'Connor?' asked Lonsdale. 'Was he was aware of any of this?'

'Of course not,' said Bradwell. 'I was told he'd absconded with money from the mortuary – although I find that difficult to believe.'

'*What* do you find difficult to believe?' asked Lonsdale. 'That there was money to abscond with, or that O'Connor would take it?'

'Both. There's nothing to steal, and once, when I left ten

shillings sitting out on my desk, O'Connor put it safely in a drawer and reminded me to take it the following day. He was odd, but no thief.'

'Odd in what way?'

'Well, wanting to be a mortuary assistant for a start,' said Bradwell. 'It's hardly a rewarding occupation – low pay, dismal surroundings, frequently harrowing duties. He just happened to turn up when I needed an assistant, and now he's moved on.'

Peters gaped at him. 'Are you telling me that you hired him without checking his credentials? The mortuary is a police facility, man! We must observe certain security precautions.'

'He had written references,' objected Bradwell. 'And I was having trouble finding someone to do it. He was basically an itinerant who wanted a job for a few months. Come August, I expect he'll be in Kent, picking hops.'

'I suppose such people do exist,' acknowledged Peters. 'And I can see why men aren't exactly queuing for that post. By the way, a further review shows that nothing was actually taken from the mortuary. As you say, he appears to have been an honest man.'

By the time Lonsdale finished giving his official statement, it was the early hours of the morning. He trudged home wearily, and lay down on his bed, intending to rest for a moment before undressing and sluicing the muck from his skin, but he fell asleep almost at once. He awoke after eight to the sound of the servants moving about downstairs.

Rubbing sleep from his eyes, he walked down the stairs and knocked at his brother's room. When there was no reply, he opened the door and saw the bed had not been slept in.

'Where is Jack?' he asked Dillon, who had appeared at the top of the stairs.

'He failed to come home last night, sir. But I knew not to expect him for dinner, as he had an appointment at six o'clock.'

'An appointment at six on a Sunday?' asked Lonsdale in surprise. 'With whom?'

'I don't know, sir. Might I suggest you check his diary? Perhaps after your bath?'

Lonsdale glared at him. If his own days were numbered in the house, then so were the butler's, because Emelia would not appreciate his smug condescension. Nevertheless, the idea was a good one, so Lonsdale found Jack's diary and flicked through it.

'Sunday,' he muttered. 'Six o'clock, Regent's Club re Imp Dem Ins with O.'

What was Imp Dem Ins, and who was O? And why would Jack be going to the Regent's Club? It was one of the newer establishments, located on Regent Street, away from the exclusive atmosphere of the St James's area known as 'Clubland'. He was sure Jack had never been there before. Moreover, six o'clock on a Sunday was a peculiar time to meet anyone, and dinner was unlikely to last until morning, although it would not be the first time Jack had drunk too much and accepted an offer of a room for the night.

Lonsdale went upstairs to wash away the stench of the Thames. He threw his clothes in the linen basket, on top of the last ones he had ruined. Perhaps Louisa Galton had been right to complain about the difficulty of finding good help, he thought, and if he ever dined with her again, he could match her stories of lazy servants.

He sat on the edge of the bathtub as a thought struck him. Galton! Had part of the solution to the murders been staring him in the face all along? The scientist had spoken at length about fingerprinting, and only hours before, Peters had commented on Baycroft's blood being smeared on the sewer wall. Could Galton glean anything from it? Were there prints that could lead to Baycroft's killer?

As he considered, Lonsdale realized that Galton might have answers to other aspects of the case as well – he certainly knew about the human brain. He not only had sophisticated theories about its development, but had conducted studies. To Lonsdale, the cerebrum seemed an odd organ to take, but perhaps Galton could explain why someone might want one.

Then again, Baycroft had been insane. For all Lonsdale knew, the man might have believed that by taking cerebra he would be able to absorb intelligence. Maybe he was even eating them. Still, Galton might be able to help him understand even that.

Lonsdale decided that he would put everything else aside and try to see the scientist.

After a hurried bath and dressing in clean clothes, he penned a quick note to Stead and Morley, outlining what had happened and telling them he was going to see Galton. He gave it to Jack's valet with the order it be taken straight to *The PMG*. He then left the house at a run, waved down a hansom, and promised the driver double if he took him to Rutland Gate as fast as he could. Determined to have the money, the man whipped his horse into a gallop, and there followed a frantic journey full of jolts, angry yells from other road users, and urgently clattering hooves. They arrived, Lonsdale shoved money at the man, hoping he would spend some of it on extra oats for his lathered horse, and hammered on Galton's door.

The great man was shuffling papers into a series of boxes when his guest was shown into his study. Lonsdale reached out to shake his hand, but his host's limp appendage returned little pressure, and the reporter quickly withdrew his own.

'I'm just filing my notes for *Human Faculty*,' said Galton grandly. 'Material of this importance can't be treated with too great a care.'

'I quite agree,' said Lonsdale. 'But I wanted—'

'Louisa is away,' interrupted Galton. 'She will be sorry to have missed you. She told me your conversation was a delight.'

As Lonsdale could not recall her having listened to a single word, he could only suppose that she preferred the kind of discussion where she was the only participant.

'I need your help, sir,' he said urgently. 'Lives depend on it.'

Galton looked pleased. 'Then sit down. We'll have tea while I save the day. And not just out of one of those asinine thimbles of Louisa's. We'll have man-sized receptacles.'

In the next hour and a half, while drinking tea served in what appeared to be plant pots, Galton gave the reporter a penetrating assessment of the structure and functioning of the human brain.

'I can think of no one who has conducted more research into cerebral functions than I have,' Galton declared. 'And I certainly can't see any benefit in collecting them. But you say this man Baycroft was mad. Perhaps that is your answer – he was possessed of the lunatic belief that owning the part of the brain that controls sensory processing allowed him to absorb its power. Similar beliefs have been shown to exist among some of the cannibals along the Congo River.'

Lonsdale felt that information led him nowhere, and he was further disappointed to learn that, unless Baycroft's murderer had placed his fingertips on the sewer wall, there was unlikely to be evidence that could be interpreted by the scientist. Moreover, even if he had, if the prints were smudged – and the entire area had been one large smear – they would be useless. Lonsdale sighed. He was faced with more dead ends.

'You are hungry,' declared Galton. 'We shall dine.'

Lonsdale was not hungry at all, and itched to leave, to visit the Regent's Club and ask after Jack, but he still had questions for Galton, as the very faintest glimmer of a solution was beginning to grow at the back of his mind. He realized he needed to stay, as he could not be sure of a welcome if he declined the invitation and tried to resume the conversation later.

'You'll observe that no grace was said prior to this meal, unlike the last time you were here,' said Galton between mouthfuls of radish soup. 'Louisa insists on prayers before meals, but I avoid them. Unless I am analyzing them.'

'You analyze prayers?' asked Lonsdale warily.

'To determine whether they are answered. The scriptures, of course, express the view that blessings, both of long life and a spiritual nature, should be requested in prayer. I have compiled a table of the mean age of death for males of various occupations. It shows that the clergy and missionaries, who should be good at prayer, have lifespans less than that of doctors, who do not have time for them. Meanwhile, lawyers, who are a godless horde, live the longest of all. Ergo, prayers are futile.' He beamed proudly.

Lonsdale could see a lot wrong with that thesis.

'But doesn't your assessment ignore the fact that some pray for others, not just petition the Almighty for a longer life?'

Galton's eyes fixed on Lonsdale. 'If such prayers had any influence, don't you think that insurance companies would make allowance for them? But they ask no questions about their customers' religious habits, nor do they take into account the risk to ships and buildings owned by pious individuals. Members of the civilized world must give up this childish belief in the efficacy of prayer, and be guided by an understanding of demographics and statistics.'

The last sentence grabbed Lonsdale's attention. 'Demographics and statistics,' he echoed. 'Are they the same?'

'Of course not. Demographics is a new field of science and refers to studies of the life conditions of people as shown by the statistics of their births, deaths and diseases.'

'There is an Imperial Statistical Institute,' said Lonsdale, recalling what the boaters had seen on the paper in Donovan's pocket.

'It closed last year,' replied Galton. 'But there is an Imperial Demographic Institute. It's fairly new, and is located at the end of Kensington Gardens, on Brunswick Gardens.'

Lonsdale's mind was in a whirl. Jack's diary had read 'Imp Dem Inst'. It had to be the same place. Moreover, Donovan's appointment had been the day before he died, so the chances were that he had gone to the Demographic Institute, and the boaters, unfamiliar with the term, had misremembered. His stomach churned. Was Jack in danger? He wanted to dash to the place immediately, but forced himself to wait. First, he had to find out as much as he could.

'What is its remit?' he demanded.

Galton looked up in surprise at the urgency in his voice.

'I haven't had extensive dealings with the place, as I consider its director an egotistical dogmatist, but I imagine data are being compiled that will become relevant to my studies on eugenics—'

'Eugenics?' interrupted Lonsdale curtly, wishing the man would speak plain English.

'A term I've coined in *Human Faculty*. If I tell you what it means, it will spoil the surprise when it's published.'

'Please,' begged Lonsdale. 'Believe me, I wouldn't ask if it wasn't a matter of life and death.'

'Life and death,' mused Galton. 'Very well, then. Eugenics is the science that deals with improving the human race. Its aim is to further the ends of evolution more rapidly than if events were left to their own course. First, we identify the characters we want to propagate, then we see about promoting them and eliminating useless rivals.'

'But sir,' cut in Lonsdale, 'how can you reconcile a desire

to expedite evolution by directing it to a predetermined end? It contradicts the notion of natural selection.'

'Eugenics won't *control* natural selection, but will assist it. Helping the weak and preventing suffering is all very well, but eugenics will improve the life of our entire community. We must, for example, breed *out* feeble constitutions and immoral instincts, and breed *in* those that are vigorous and noble. Eugenics cooperates with natural selection by ensuring that humanity is represented by the fittest individuals. What Nature does blindly, slowly and ruthlessly, we may continue providently, quickly and kindly.'

'From what I've observed,' remarked Lonsdale dryly, 'humanity is already doing an admirable job of continuing itself.'

'That's not the purpose of eugenics,' responded Galton. 'Quite the reverse, in fact. Improving a race depends on increasing the *best* stock. That is far more important than repressing the worst. Eugenics encourages the best characteristics to be passed on to future generations.'

'But how will you dissuade your "lesser stock" from reproducing?' demanded Lonsdale, not realizing he was sounding exasperated. Eugenics was as mad a theory as anything Baycroft had believed, and here he was listening to Galton go on about it while he should be finding out what had happened to Jack. 'Besides, other than the occasional extraordinary men, aren't people rather similar?'

'Such a lack of understanding!' spat Galton, annoyed in turn. 'Those who believe in natural equality are deluding themselves. I've no patience with the hypothesis that all babies are born alike – they aren't. Furthermore, the British man *is* superior to any others. It's a fact.'

Lonsdale was shocked by the imperial arrogance. 'I hardly think—' he began.

'So we must control breeding,' interrupted Galton, 'or the intelligent, thoughtful and prudent members of society will be outnumbered by the ignorant and non-thinking, and therefore bring utter ruin upon our country. It may seem monstrous that the weak should be crowded out by the strong, but it's still more monstrous that the strong should be crowded out by the incompetent and unfit.'

'And this is what the Imperial Demographic Institute is exploring?' asked Lonsdale. 'How to manipulate some ideal devised by an elite few? Eugenics?'

Galton looked at him as if he were an unruly school child. 'Consider the gain to our nation if the practice of eugenics were applied. Our race would be less foolish, less frivolous, and politically more provident. We should be better fitted to fulfil our vast imperial opportunities. And able men would thrive.'

Lonsdale had had enough, and also felt an urgent need to find Jack. 'I am sorry, sir, but I simply must go to an appointment at *The PMG*,' he lied, standing abruptly. 'But thank you for sharing your fascinating theories, and I shall look forward to reading *Human Faculty* when it's published.' Mind whirling, he left Galton.

As Lonsdale walked out of Galton's front door, he decided to go straight to the Regent's Club to ask about Jack. He hurried up Rutland Gate towards Kensington Road.

Questions and answers poured into his mind in equal measure with every step. The relevance of eugenics to the murders had been apparent the moment Galton explained it. Could it be that a group of scientists was conducting investigations not unlike Galton's, but going a step further and looking at their subjects' cerebra? What if Baycroft's 'them' was not a delusion? What if someone really had ordered him to steal cerebra – someone who had already collected other data from his subjects, and who had paid them for their time, so they were able to make house repairs or buy whisky?

What if that same someone hoped to match his results to the part of the brain where the answers originated? Baycroft had confided that he had been ordered not to poison his victims lest he pollute the organs. Is that why Baycroft had been shot? Because he had not managed his 'takings' properly?

But certainly legitimate scientists would never condone such an unethical study, and the results could hardly be published. Any such information would be worthless, for who could ever admit how he had come by it? And yet, did the results *need* to be published? Could they not be given to those able to act on them? There were genuine fears that the rising numbers of poor would rebel against the wealthier classes. Wilson from the zoo had talked about it, for example. But whereas Galton proposed a fairly sedate rate of change, Wilson had wanted something done fast. Would other, like-minded, people try to put such a plan into practice now?

Or were strain and tiredness causing his imagination to run riot? No one would seriously consider implementing such a scheme. Yet someone *was* killing people for their cerebra. He decided to go to the Imperial Demographic Institute to see what he could discover the moment he had assured himself that Jack was safe and well.

'Lonsdale! Lonsdale, here!' A voice cut through his thoughts as he turned onto Kensington Road, and he looked around wildly. It was Hulda, sitting in a carriage and motioning to him. He found himself wondering if Peters had been true to his word and had had her watched over for the night. 'I've been waiting for you here, because I didn't want Galton to see me sitting outside his home,' she said. 'Get in.'

'I must go to the Regent's Club to try to find Jack,' he replied.

'Morley sent me to collect you,' she said. 'You've been summoned to his office – Superintendent Ramsey was sending Inspector Peters over to speak to you. I have some other news as well.'

'After I find Jack. I need—'

'No, *now*,' she interrupted. 'Besides, *The PMG* is not that far from the Regent's Club, and it will be quicker for you to get in now, even with the stop there, than to walk the whole way.

Knowing she was right, Lonsdale acceded to her demand, and the hansom shot off. As it raced along Knightsbridge Road, he began to tell her what he had learned from Galton and how it helped explain the pattern of events. But after several minutes, she suddenly interrupted him again.

'A gentleman was killed around one or two o'clock this morning,' she blurted, 'and his cerebrum taken.'

'But Baycroft was dead by then.'

'Nevertheless,' said Hulda, 'it has happened again.' Lonsdale felt his stomach churn, but didn't have time to speak before Hulda added: 'We're there. Now come upstairs.'

The first floor was in its usual controlled chaos. Morley's door was closed, a murmur of voices emanating from within. Stead was distributing fresh orange peel into various containers – which he insisted counteracted the smell of the printing presses – while simultaneously dictating an article for the final edition. Lonsdale slipped into the reporters' office behind Hulda but, before he could close the door, Morley emerged from his office, looking grave. 'Do you have a moment, Lonsdale?'

Lonsdale followed him inside, with Hulda at his heels. Peters was there, looking grey from lack of sleep. Morley gestured for Lonsdale and Hulda to sit, but Lonsdale refused. He had a very bad feeling about the look on Peters' face.

'There's been another murder,' said Peters. 'It happened while you were at the station giving your statement. The victim was a barrister, judging from the papers with the body. We don't yet know his name, but you told me last night that your brother was missing. Have you seen him this morning?'

'No,' whispered Lonsdale. He felt sick. 'He didn't come home last night.'

'We found this with the body.' Peters held out a dirty rag that Lonsdale saw with horror was Emelia's spoiled antimacassar. He did not need to tell Peters he recognized it: the answer was clear on his shocked face.

'I'm sorry,' said Peters gently. 'That was all the killer left, other than some miscellaneous court papers.'

'The Imperial Demographic Institute,' said Lonsdale numbly. He gazed at the antimacassar but could not bring himself to touch it. 'Jack wrote it in his appointment book. He went to discuss it with someone at the Regent's Club at six o'clock yesterday evening.'

'The Regent's Club?' asked Peters. 'That's a strange place for a gentleman of your brother's standing to go. But what is this Institute? Where is it?'

Lonsdale tried to force his stunned brain to work. What had Galton said? 'Brunswick Street. No – Brunswick Gardens.'

'Right,' said Peters. 'Now go home, Lonsdale. Can I have your assurance that you won't go to this Institute or the Regent's Club? We can't risk losing our culprit because you storm into these places and start demanding information.'

Lonsdale nodded, barely hearing. Peters patted his shoulder, then was gone, leaving Lonsdale with the antimacassar.

The journey to Cleveland Square was a blur. Lonsdale was dimly aware of Hulda sitting next to him, but he heard nothing of what she said. He looked at the familiar streets in a daze, feeling as though he were in the grip of some terrible dream.

Once home, the butler took Hulda's umbrella and cloak, then reached out to remove Lonsdale's hat, seeing he was not going to do it. Dully, Lonsdale aimed for the morning room.

'There you are,' said Jack, looking up from the remains of a meal. 'I do hope you two haven't been doing dangerous things again.'

'God's blood!' breathed Hulda, gazing at him. 'What are *you* doing here?'

'I live here,' said Jack curtly. 'Where else would I be?'

Lonsdale lurched over and enveloped Jack in a hug, bewilderment, relief and shock vying for attention in his mind. He wanted to yell at his brother for giving him such a fright. Instead, he pulled the antimacassar from his pocket and held it out to him.

'Where in God's name did you get that?' demanded Jack. 'I thought it was lost.'

'It was found with . . .' began Lonsdale, but could not bring himself to say it had been retrieved from a corpse.

'If you have any sense, you'll keep your dirty fingers away from Emelia's lacework from now on,' advised Jack. 'She's not as stupid as you think – she knows you had something to do with it.'

'You lost it?' pounced Hulda. 'When? Please think. This is important.'

Jack frowned. 'It fell out of my pocket at the park – which is when Emelia saw it – but I put it back in my coat. But the coat – and the antimacassar with it – disappeared last night.'

'Where did it disappear?' demanded Lonsdale, finally regaining some of his composure.

Jack was becoming irked. 'Can't a man spend a night away without being the subject of all this commotion? What's wrong with you?' He glowered in a way that, along with the dark circles under his eyes, told Lonsdale he had a headache, almost certainly from having had too much to drink.

'We should tell Peters,' said Hulda briskly and, without further ado, sat and penned a note informing the inspector that he now had an unidentified body. Once the butler had gone to deliver it, Hulda stood with her hands on her hips.

'Right,' she said, all business. 'Lonsdale needs to eat. He's white as a ghost. Tell your people to prepare devilled kidneys, curried potatoes, and scrambled eggs with a healthy shake of black pepper. Tasteless food is no good for a man recovering from a shock. Besides, I cannot bear it, and I'm hungry, too.'

Jack hastened to relay the 'request' to the kitchen. 'Now tell me what's going on,' he said.

Lonsdale did, falteringly at first, but with more conviction as his shock receded. The food helped – Hulda was right about that.

'And now you,' he said to Jack when he had finished. 'Where have you been since you vanished from the park without leaving any hint about where you might be.'

'I wasn't aware that I was under any obligation to do so,' said Jack stiffly, but then relented. 'I was with John Otherington at his club – the Regent's. It's a grim old place, with lazy and incompetent staff. Anyway, the upshot is that they gave someone else my coat, leaving me with some shabby thing.' He shuddered. 'I think Otherington has mine, and I shall demand it back later.'

'The "O" in your diary referred to Otherington?' asked Lonsdale.

'You looked in my diary?' Jack was outraged. 'A chap's diary is his own personal business!'

'It was an emergency,' said Lonsdale, unrepentant.

'Well, I don't see why you were worried,' said Jack, miffed. 'I sent a message to tell you I might be very late back. There was a lot to drink, you see.'

'Then you should choose your messengers more carefully – it never arrived.'

Jack grimaced. 'I hired a lad from the Regent's. I told you it wasn't a decent place.'

'So why did you go?'

'Because Otherington – a clerk from work – invited me. He's a lonely sort of fellow and I felt sorry for him, so I accepted. He's damned hospitable – one drink led to another, and . . . well, you know how it is.'

'So you've been drinking all night?' asked Hulda in distaste.

'Not at all!' said Jack defensively. 'I spent a good part asleep in the reading room. Naturally, I assumed Otherington would stay with me, as it's considered poor manners to leave a chap slumbering in a club that isn't his own. But he didn't.'

'He abandoned you to go home?'

Jack nodded. 'But he drank even more than I did, so that explains the lapse in manners. Regardless, I suspect he donned my coat in a drunken stupor, leaving me with his ratty old thing.'

'Then poor, drunk Otherington is probably the man the police found dead,' said Hulda.

Jack turned white. 'Otherington is *dead?* No! We were getting along like a house on fire last night! I was beginning to like the man. Please don't say it was for my coat . . . a better one than most members of that place owned!'

'No, the coat was irrelevant,' said Lonsdale. 'Did Otherington tell you about the Imperial Demographic Institute?'

Jack gaped at him. 'How did you know that? Yes, he blathered on about some survey he was participating in there.'

Jack listened with growing horror as Lonsdale explained his theory: 'I think someone there has embarked on a two-tiered study. The first is a battery of tests to ascertain the religion, morals, intelligence, etc., of the subject. The second compares these results to the subject's cerebrum.'

'A cerebrum?' echoed Jack. 'How? Those are inside their heads.'

'Not once the likes of Baycroft, Morgan and Pawley have been issued with orders to collect them.'

'Then Otherington got it badly wrong,' said Jack soberly. 'He said the work there is sensitive, and the government wants it kept quiet. He said it's noble stuff, of paramount importance to the future of the Empire. I was on the verge of volunteering when he'd finished waxing lyrical.'

'What did he tell you exactly?'

'That there are tests for solving mathematical and logical problems, and interviews about religious and ethical matters. There's also a physical examination, where they measure your height, weight, hat-size, and so on. Otherington swore me to secrecy – the scientists running the programme say that if people know what they'll be asked, it'll ruin the objectivity. Gentlemen and ladies are trusted to be discreet, but there's a deferred payment for the rest to stop them from talking. If they blab, they don't get paid.'

'Perhaps they should have made a deferred payment to Otherington, then,' said Lonsdale dryly.

'We should go to this Imperial Demographic Institute,' determined Hulda. 'It sounds more sinister than anything I've ever encountered, and *The PMG* should tell people what it's up to.'

'But I promised Peters—' Lonsdale began. He stopped when there was a knock at the front door.

Moments later, the butler delivered a message addressed to Jack, who opened it, then frowned in mystification before handing it to Lonsdale.

It was a pleasure to interview you and find out what was inside your head. Thank you for visiting the Imperial Demographic Institute.

'But I never went anywhere near the place,' said Jack, shaking his head. 'And nor will I now.'

'It isn't meant for you,' said Lonsdale, knowing exactly what was going on. 'It's for me. And it's not a thank you, either. It's an invitation.'

'Explain, Lonsdale,' ordered Hulda.

'Whoever wrote this thinks Jack is dead,' said Lonsdale. 'They're goading me, hoping I'll storm over in a rage, so they can finish what Baycroft failed to do.'

'Lord!' breathed Jack.

'And I was wrong when I said that that the coat was irrelevant. I've no doubt that they would have claimed Otherington eventually – you said he was a lonely sort of chap, and they have a preference for such folks. However, this note tells me that you *were* the one they wanted – Otherington was killed because he was wearing your coat. Now they are daring me to go there in order to do something about it. Doubtless they hope Friederichs will accompany me, so they can be rid of both of us.'

'But once they killed him, they would have realized Jack wasn't the victim if they knew Otherington,' objected Hulda.

'But it doesn't matter if it was me or not,' said Jack, suddenly understanding. 'All that matters is that Alec *thinks* it was me.'

'But how would they know what he's thinking?' asked Hulda, unconvinced.

'There's only one way,' said Lonsdale. 'Someone knows that Peters told me of Jack's murder. So it must be Peters or Ramsey who is working with them. I'd like to say I trust Peters, but he *was* agonizingly slow last night.'

'Ramsey is a pompous, upper-class ass who cares nothing for the victims,' said Hulda. 'He interfered with Walker's inquest so that some basic questions wouldn't be asked. He delayed Greaves's inquest indefinitely. And he ordered Peters not to investigate their murders. He's done nothing but sidetrack and obstruct the investigation from the start. *He's* the snake in the cradle.'

'So, what are you going to do?' asked Jack.

'Go to the Demographic Institute—' began Hulda.

'No,' said Lonsdale decisively. 'That's what they're expecting. We'll go tomorrow – our delaying will confuse them. For now, we'll drive by in a hansom to get a feel for it, which will make our trip tomorrow safer. If Peters is there, we can stop and tell him what we've reasoned.'

'But surely not everything – in case he's involved!' Hulda was horrified.

'Of course, not everything. Enough so he'll be able to help if we need him, but not so much that he knows we suspect him or Ramsey.'

Hulda grinned and gave him a rather painful thump on the arm. 'We're very near the end of this. And then we'll have a story to rock London!'

THIRTEEN

B runswick Gardens, just west of Kensington Palace, was a shady street dominated by a medieval church and large, graceful Georgian terraces with pillared entrances, wrought-iron railings and shuttered windows.

The driver had been ordered to traverse the street as slowly as possible without attracting the attention of the police. Well before they reached the Institute, Lonsdale and Hulda could see these were out in number. Peters was talking to three, while others were conducting house-to-house enquiries and swarming in and out of the building in the middle of the street.

The Demographic Institute was more modern than its neighbours, and boasted an elegant edifice of carved white marble, blind arcading and a splendid portico. There were tall windows on all three floors, and the building was entered through an impressive arched doorway at the head of a flight of wide stairs.

Before Lonsdale could stop her, Hulda had jumped from the still-moving carriage and was striding towards Peters, arms swinging purposefully.

'Did you receive my message?' she demanded. 'The body you found wasn't Jack Lonsdale. Indeed, it wasn't even a barrister – it was a clerk.'

Peters regarded her lugubriously. 'Do you know his identity?'

'John Otherington,' replied Lonsdale, who had just caught up with her. 'I don't know his address, but the Regent's Club will.'

'I doubt it,' muttered Peters dryly. 'I've rarely met a less-competent group of individuals.'

Nevertheless, he nodded to one of his men, who clambered into the carriage that had brought Lonsdale and Hulda and clattered away.

'Aren't you going to ask us how we know?' demanded Hulda, regarding him through eyes that were narrowed with suspicion.

'I assume because Jack Lonsdale returned home and answered

some questions,' said Peters, maddeningly unflustered. 'But we agreed you were to stay away. You've been a great help, but we can take matters from here. Go home, Lonsdale, and take Miss Friederichs with you. I promise to keep you informed of any developments.'

'We can prove the people here are involved in these murders,' said Lonsdale. 'If you'll let us.'

'Not now, thank you. When it's over I shall listen all you like. Now please go home.'

'Is there a reason we can't stand here and watch?' demanded Hulda, growing more indignant by the minute.

'There's nothing *to* watch,' said Peters. 'There's nothing untoward happening in there, and Superintendent Ramsey has instructed me to pester the scientists no further. He informs me that his orders come from the highest possible authority.'

'From God?' asked Hulda archly. 'Ramsey must be powerful indeed!'

The ends of Peters' moustache quivered in amusement. Lonsdale recalled that Otherington had told Jack that the government wanted the Institute's work kept secret, but Lonsdale found Ramsey closing the investigation sinister – particularly as Peters could not have had time to conduct a thorough search.

At that moment, Ramsey emerged from the building, his assistant Chief Inspector Leonard at his heels. Ramsey glanced briefly at Lonsdale and Hulda, snapped something to Leonard, and strode off in the other direction.

'We've just heard that the "highest authority" has deemed this place off limits,' said Hulda accusingly, turning the full force of her personality on Leonard as he approached. 'Who is it? The Home Secretary? The Prime Minister? The Queen?'

'I understand it was more of a corporate decision, madam,' replied Leonard, not at all discomfited by her temper. 'The Institute has been conducting important research for several years, and no one wants to see its findings harmed by unwarranted publicity.'

'Poppycock!' snapped Hulda. 'Something very odd is going on here, and I mean to find out what.'

She began to flounce towards the entrance, but Leonard caught her arm in a grip that was gentle but firm and stopped her.

'Please,' he said. 'I must insist you leave now. If Superintendent Ramsey sees you interfering, he'll have you arrested.'

Lonsdale hastily offered his arm to Hulda, and was surprised when she accepted it and allowed herself to be led away. Leonard followed them down the road until he could flag down a hansom.

'I'm sorry,' he said, offering his hand to help Hulda climb inside. 'But we have our orders.' He turned to the driver. 'Take the young lady home, please. Longridge Road. And no stopping.'

Hulda sat rigidly in the carriage until it had turned several corners.

'Driver!' she called imperiously. 'Pull over.'

'The gentleman said not to,' objected the driver. 'And he gave me a shilling.'

'I'm about to be sick,' said Hulda icily. 'You have ten seconds before the inside of your hackney will never be the same again.'

The hansom immediately halted, and Hulda scrambled out. She straightened her skirts, patted her hair into place and looked around haughtily. It was obvious to anyone that she was the picture of robust good health, and vomiting was not on her immediate agenda. Lonsdale climbed out more slowly.

'You needn't bother to wait,' she said loftily. 'I might be some time.'

The driver cracked his whip and the carriage moved away. Apparently, there were limits to what he would do for a shilling, and taking on Hulda was well beyond them.

'Now what?' asked Lonsdale. 'We can't go back there. Peters is—'

'Peters is powerless!' snapped Hulda. 'Ramsey *is* behind all this! How did Leonard know where I live? I don't give my address to just anybody. He knew it because *Ramsey* told him, and Ramsey doesn't want us investigating.'

Lonsdale sensed she was right. 'So we'll visit the Institute ourselves, but I stand by what I said earlier. We go tomorrow when they won't be expecting us.'

'Very well.' She began to walk away, then stopped. 'I want you to promise me one thing, however.'

'What?'

'I shall have my gun. Bring yours as well.'

That night three people thought seriously about how Lonsdale and Hulda would slip into the Imperial Demographic Institute. On Longridge Road, Hulda carefully cleaned and loaded her pistol, and laid out the clothes that would serve most effectively in helping her to conceal it.

At Cleveland Square, Lonsdale cleaned the muck of the Thames from his pistol, and pondered ways to invade a place he imagined was fairly secure. Would they have to smash locks or break windows? Slowly, he began to gather a range of tools that might be needed.

Not far away, in Chesham Place, a third man wondered what the reporters would do. He had no doubt that Lonsdale would come to the Institute, and was equally certain that Hulda would accompany him, especially after the note he had sent to Cleveland Square. It was a shame they had to die the next day: they were obviously intelligent and resourceful, and, despite being a nuisance, had earned his grudging respect. Moreover, Lonsdale had seemed quite a gentleman when they had met. Under different circumstances, the forces that brought them together might have made them friends.

The man jotted down some private thoughts in his diary, as he did each evening. He recalled how, more than a dozen years before, with the aid of one short letter, he had conceived the plan now nearing fruition. He wondered what destiny had brought Lonsdale into his otherwise well-ordered world. It was interesting how destiny had brought the two of them together: one soon to be world-famous, the other – like so many – to have his cerebrum in a jar.

'We need to know as much as we can about this place,' said Hulda, surveying the Demographic Institute from a discreet distance the following day. 'If we sit under the trees in the churchyard, we can observe comings and goings and make sure it's safe to go in.'

The plan sounded suitably cautious to Lonsdale, although it obliged them to push their way into the middle of some thick bushes for an unobstructed view of the Institute entrance. It would not be comfortable to stand there for long, thought Lonsdale, and it became less so when Hulda wedged herself next to him.

Their surveillance began around nine in the morning. Dozens of people from all walks of life came and went, but there was only one policeman in sight: a lone constable at the front door. As slipping past him was out of the question, Lonsdale suggested looking at the back. This was reached via an alley behind the Kensington Dispensary, a narrow lane flanked by tall walls pierced by locked gates through which rear gardens could be glimpsed. The Institute's had a door banded with steel, above which glinted broken glass. The wall, too, was topped with sharp, protective wire.

'For a research facility, these people seem remarkably conscious of their security,' mused Hulda.

'I could throw my coat over the barbs to climb over it,' suggested Lonsdale, eyeing the precautions uneasily, and wondering what had led him to be pondering how to burgle a government-approved research foundation.

'That never works when I try it,' said Hulda, drawing a surprised look. 'What about through a neighbour's garden?' Lonsdale went to the nearest gate, but it was locked, and looked sturdy. The one on the other side was also locked, but the bolt snapped under his hefty kick. He ushered Hulda inside, and closed it quickly behind them.

The wall that divided the neighbouring garden from the Institute's was tall, but a well-placed compost heap allowed them to hoist themselves up to peer over the top. They looked into a rectangular yard, mostly paved, but with a tree and a bench that would be pleasant in summer. It appeared to be deserted. Lonsdale jumped down, and helped Hulda do the same. Carefully, they crept towards the back door.

'Do you think we should come back at night, when the building's empty?' whispered Lonsdale.

'I doubt it's ever empty. We've seen a huge number of people enter. But that works to our advantage. We shall claim we're participants in a study if anyone challenges us.'

The back door was locked, but a window was open. They

climbed into a small room with a low ceiling and untidily stacked shelves. Lonsdale inched open the door and listened. Voices came from a room at one end of a corridor, while a flight of steps stood at the other. They headed for the stairs.

At the top was a hall that led to the front door. When someone opened it, they saw the policeman outside. To their left was a large room that looked like a lecture theatre, while to the right were a series of doors. Lonsdale ducked back as one opened and a young couple walked by, the man twisting his hat nervously in his hands.

'They look like subjects for the study,' breathed Hulda. 'Come on.'

She and Lonsdale trailed the couple to a large room, well appointed with chairs and tables. Others were already there, drinking tea or reading the newspapers provided. Hulda sat and pulled Lonsdale down next to her, snatching up a paper and using it to hide their faces. He peered over the top. There were about fifteen people present, comprising a curious cross-section of society. He ducked behind the paper as a man in a white laboratory coat entered the room. He spoke to an elderly man, who nodded and followed him out.

'We can't stay here,' he said uncomfortably. 'If someone asks who we are, it'll be obvious we don't belong.'

'But we haven't seen anything incriminating yet. Let's try some more doors.'

She linked her arm in his and marched back into the hallway, head held high. Her confidence was convincing, as no one asked where they were going. They reached the end of the hall and selected a door that led to a narrow corridor. Hulda tried one of the doors that led off it, but it was locked, as was the next one, and the next. Lonsdale took the opposite side, and they worked their way down. Then Lonsdale lurched suddenly into an office when a handle unexpectedly turned.

Hulda pushed past him and tried the desk drawers before turning her attention to the cupboards.

'They're locked,' she hissed in frustration. 'Can you break into them?'

'Are you mad? It'd be too noisy. We need to come back later. Let's go before someone catches us.'

'You've left it a little late for that,' came a voice from behind them. Lonsdale and Hulda spun around to face a tall man, who smiled at them from the doorway, although there was neither amusement nor friendliness in the expression.

He stepped into the room, followed closely by three hefty louts, who wore white laboratory coats that looked odd on their beefy frames. One held a lead tied to a growling Alsatian with yellow fangs and a mean look.

'I have been expecting you, Lonsdale,' he said. 'I knew you'd understand when I sent the note to your brother's house. And I knew you'd come. I assumed you'd be here too, Miss Friederichs. You do realize that you've put me in a most awkward position.'

'We apologize,' said Hulda, smiling ingratiatingly. 'And now we'll be on our way.'

One of the thugs closed the door, while another stepped in front of her, and the dog obligingly growled.

'I'm afraid not,' said the man. 'You'll have to stay for a while – quite a while.'

'Is that so?' snarled Hulda. 'And who are you, anyway?'

'We dined together in Surrey,' said Lonsdale. 'His name is Francis Willoughby.'

The tall man contrived to smile, although it was an expression that chilled Lonsdale, and reminded him of a crocodile he had once seen in Africa. He heartily wished he'd listened to Peters and left the Imperial Demographic Institute to the police, as he was sure of one thing: he and Hulda would not escape the place alive. And who would ever know what had happened to them? They had told no one what they planned to do, on the grounds that the police had ordered them to stay away. How reckless they had been!

'Yes, when you met me, it was as Francis Willoughby,' he said. 'Although my name is Weeks: Professor Nathaniel Weeks. You won't know of me yet, as my research is so far unavailable to the general public.'

'Your research?' said Hulda scathingly. 'Is that what you call it?'

'Work of vast importance, Miss Friederichs.' Weeks looked

back at Lonsdale. 'As you've reasoned, I am investigating what the famous Mr Huxley has recently called "the struggle for existence in human society". I prefer to think of it as "human Darwinism" – that is, man's relation to Darwinian principles.'

'Why have you been following us around?' demanded Hulda, not at all worried by the situation in which she found herself. Lonsdale admired her audacity and courage. 'I remember you buying collar studs at Salmon and Eden.'

'An excellent memory, although "following us around" is overstating matters. I watched you once or twice, but not for long – I am a busy man. But I *am* impressed with your memory, Miss Friederichs – when I met Lonsdale in Surrey, he couldn't place me at all. But to return to your question: you are of interest because you've presented problems for my work.'

'What work?' asked Lonsdale. 'You mean . . . murdering people for their brains?'

'I needed them,' replied Weeks simply. 'My team and I have tested and studied hundreds of people for intelligence, decision-making, moral and social behaviour, emotions, and more. We've studied lawyers, dockers, physicians, Members of Parliament, beggars, vicars, clerks, railwaymen, scientists, shopkeepers, naval officers and ratings, even reporters. But it didn't go far enough.'

'So you decided you needed their cerebra as well,' surmised Lonsdale.

'Quite,' said Weeks. 'I have seventy representative samples in jars downstairs, if you'd care to see?'

Seventy! Lonsdale was appalled.

'No, thank you,' he said quickly, lest Hulda accepted. 'You claim the government supports your research, but it would never condone murder.'

Weeks smirked like a mischievous child. 'Obviously, we don't tell them *everything* about the project. But there's nothing more terrifying to a politician than civil unrest, which is what they fear we'll have if our population continues to expand at its present rate. They grasped my promise of a solution with desperate hands.'

'You told them you could solve overpopulation and inherent civil unrest?'

Weeks nodded. 'Galton's reputation is such that when I claimed *he* was collaborating with me, I gained instant credibility. But I have more genius in my little finger than he has ever had in that great thick skull of his. I would *never* work with that boring, pompous old man.'

'So you lied to the government about him?'

'I massaged the truth a little, but the ends justify the means. Galton's not only unable to see a practical way forward, he's inexplicably squeamish. I've developed the pragmatic solution that was beyond him. I'm providing valuable information on human behaviour and thought, not at an individual level, but on an entire population. In order to control demographic growth, we first need to understand it. How can you hope to comprehend such a complex organ as the cerebrum without matching test results with physiology?'

'But—' began Hulda.

Weeks overrode her. 'It's obvious that a lawyer and a flower girl think differently, yet no one knows why. I will.'

'But the nature of your work means you can never tell anyone,' argued Lonsdale. 'What's the point of it?'

'Oh, I shall tell them,' said Weeks. 'And then I will be hailed as the greatest scientist who ever lived. Greater even than Darwin. I have many supporters; men who realize that the laws of evolution have been the laws of the jungle – cunning, brutishness, ruthlessness – and they have rewarded the wicked and punished the righteous. There are many who feel this is horrifying, and that something must be done.'

'Men like Wilson of the Zoological Gardens?' asked Lonsdale.

'Why, yes – Wilson is with us.'

'And Superintendent Ramsey?'

Weeks threw his head back and laughed. 'He'd be the last man I'd include in my coterie. He lacks intelligence, courage, or freedom of thought.'

Lonsdale was about to ask more, but there was a knock on the door. A man in a white coat entered.

'Inspector Peters is here. Dr Sorenson feels you should be the one to talk to him.'

'Thank you, Dr Hancock,' said Weeks. 'I'll go and meet him now. My guests will have to wait in my office until I've finished.'

Lonsdale and Hulda were bundled out into the hall, but any hopes of escape were quickly quashed by the three louts, who took their arms and marched them upstairs.

Weeks's office was a beautiful, wood-panelled room. One wall was filled to the ceiling with books; another was dominated by three large, well-spaced windows, which Lonsdale noted were nailed shut. On the wall behind the fine walnut desk were certificates of Weeks's various degrees and qualifications, as well as a letter, all in specially constructed frames. Their guards left them there and shut the door behind them. Lonsdale dropped to his knees and looked through the keyhole. They were outside with the dog, and he sensed there was nothing they would like more than the chance to pummel him if he tried to escape. But he and Hulda had one advantage: they still had their guns. Hulda read his mind.

'See what we can find out, Lonsdale,' she whispered. 'Then we'll shove the evidence in our pockets and shoot our way out. Now *hurry*! I don't think Weeks will be long.'

Lonsdale quickly began to browse through the papers on Weeks's desk. After only a few moments, he gestured to Hulda.

'This looks like a master ledger,' he said. 'There are hundreds of pages of statistics and test results. Some tables note where the subject lives, whether he has completed his tests, and there are other columns that I don't understand.'

Hulda scanned the entries. 'Norma Johnson, Adele Johnson, Frederick Kempster, Edmund Corlett, William Byers, Teresa Godley, John Poole, Patrick Donovan . . .'

'And a lot more we've never heard of,' said Lonsdale. 'What's this column – "Collected"? There's just one letter for each entry: B, C, M, P or T . . .'

'There's a B next to the Johnson sisters and one next to Poole. Don't you see, Lonsdale? B is for Baycroft. Next to Kempster there is a P – Pawley. It records who collected the cerebra – which means there are far more people taking them than we ever imagined.'

'There probably *are* seventy entries with letters in that column,' said Lonsdale. 'But what about the rest? I assume they're still alive, but for how long?'

'We don't need cerebra from *everyone*,' said Weeks sourly from the door, making them jump with the stealth of his entry. 'But I must say that you are behaving more like a reporter and less like a gentleman, Lonsdale – going through the papers on a fellow's desk.'

Lonsdale did not bother to point out that his antics were a lot more gentlemanly than murder.

'As long as we're discussing what we've found, why is "Francis Willoughby" on the diploma from Oxford?'

'Isn't it obvious? I was born Francis Nathaniel Willoughby, but I later adopted my mother's maiden name – Weeks. These days, my father knows no more about me than he does the Mountains of the Moon. But I've kept a close watch on *him*, because I'll inherit his fortune when he dies.'

'So you didn't meet me out of concern for his health?'

'I would never have any concern for that vile old bastard. His valet is secretly in my employ, so I was familiar with your correspondence, and he was given a note expressing your regrets that you couldn't accept his invitation, as your research had shown that William died in a foolish accident. He might come to believe it in time, although he's right to be suspicious, of course. Meanwhile, I was able to persuade you that the business in France had no bearing on your cases.'

'But it actually did? You mean William *was* murdered?'

'Of course. His cerebrum is downstairs with the others. You see? I have fooled you every step of the way. You have been so out of your depth – I could even tell that you would come back from our meeting and write to Dr Quayle to see if he would support my version of events or my father's. I couldn't allow him to tell you the truth, so I had his butler bribed to forward the letter to me when it arrived – Quayle never saw it.'

'But he would have confirmed your father's story?'

'Certainly – but he never had the opportunity, because I am prepared for every eventuality. You need the cool, calculating mind of a scientist to carry out an audacious plan like mine.'

'So it's true that you stole your brother's brain!' breathed Hulda, appalled.

'My *half*-brother,' corrected Weeks. 'And I wouldn't say stole, Miss Friederichs. After all, I *was* next of kin, and he *was* dead.

Morgan had seen to that. A little too enthusiastic about that kind of thing is Morgan, but he *is* conscientious.'

'Why kill William?' asked Lonsdale.

'Well, if you must know, he was a problem. I gave him a job here, but he wasn't really suitable – not enough courage in his convictions. He wanted to leave, but that was impossible. He knew we'd never let him go – not with the secrets he was familiar with – so he tried to run.'

'And he's just one of the people you've had butchered?' asked Hulda coldly.

'Not "butchered", Miss Friederichs. All our subjects are treated with surgical care. Baycroft worked in the kitchens at Newgate, where he became proficient with the heads of sheep and pigs. That expertise first drew my attention to him while I was gathering data there. My other collectors, I trained myself. All are skilled in the delicate processes required.'

'If Baycroft was useful to you, then why did you have him killed?' asked Lonsdale.

'Because he was becoming mentally unstable,' explained Weeks. 'He dreamed *you* were going to drown him – rather like Morgan ultimately did. His irrational fears led him to engage in progressively riskier behaviour. For example, he tried to have you killed – telling Pawley that I wanted him to do it. I didn't mind the concept, but I hadn't approved the action. So he had to go.'

'I don't understand how you could have taken seventy cerebra with no one noticing,' said Hulda. 'It would be impossible.'

Weeks looked smug. 'We conceal our work in a variety of ways: fires, explosions, a quarry landslide, and of course train accidents.'

Lonsdale looked at Weeks and thought he and Baycroft had a lot in common – both were happy to discuss their monstrous acts and expected to be congratulated on their efficiency.

'You took a lot of trouble over Donovan,' he said. 'It was almost impossible to tell he had been strangled. One of your collectors killed him, took his brain, then ran into the street yelling that the house was on fire. Then he ran back inside, sealed off the front door with the chest, and locked the back door on the way out to ensure the body was incinerated, leading to the assumption that the fire was caused by a blocked chimney.'

'That was me, actually,' said Weeks. 'I couldn't trust Baycroft to imitate Donovan well enough. I was extremely convincing, despite being much taller than my subject.'

'You weren't as good as you think. One of Donovan's neighbours heard the difference in your voice – she thought it meant Donovan was drunk. And your cool, calculating scientific mind missed the detail that his chimney had been swept the previous week.'

'I wondered why you visited his sweep,' said Weeks. 'He'll be one of my subjects, by the way. He's perfect – an old man slipping ever more deeply into debt. It'll be assumed he couldn't pay the rent and fled his creditors.'

'Why kill the music-hall entertainer, Yeats?' asked Lonsdale. 'He seems a little high-profile.'

'And so he was. He was killed in a street robbery – nothing to do with us. But as he'd been part of the study, it seemed a shame to waste a good cerebrum.'

'Where does Cath Walker fit in?' asked Lonsdale.

'Her job was to entice subjects to come here.'

'You mean poor people, so desperate for money that they'd do anything for a bed for the night?' asked Hulda. 'Or men, thinking of sex? And, in so doing, signing their death warrants?'

'Let's not be emotive, Miss Friederichs. You can't allow the scientific process to be hampered by sentimentality. Walker was a whore. She just whored for me in a different way. Then she brought me Greaves, and he was *very* useful.'

'What did he do?' asked Lonsdale. 'Dispose of bodies in the river?'

'Exactly! He was a bargeman, who knew where to drop corpses. But then he asked for more money, and said Walker was trying to persuade him to go to the press with the "whole story". As if *they* understood the whole story.'

'She must've realized she wouldn't be allowed to live once the study ended,' said Lonsdale. 'She probably thought telling me was her last hope. If her story were to be publicized, you'd be arrested, and she might escape. But I imagine when Greaves betrayed her to you, you thanked him for his loyalty, and then slipped arsenic into whatever you gave him to drink.'

'Finest French brandy,' said Weeks. 'I reckoned he'd be dead before you arrived at Regent's Park, and my timing was, as usual, impeccable.'

Lonsdale could see through the window that Leonard and Peters were bickering on the street below. He glanced at the three thugs outside the office, and noticed the fingers of one of them twitching in anticipation of violence. It was time for him and Hulda to pull out their guns and put an end to the horrible affair. But there was one thing more that he wanted to know, and he was certain this would be his only chance to ask it.

'Why did you try to kill my brother?'

'Try? If I'd wanted Jack dead, he would be dead. It was Otherington's cerebrum that I wanted, so I sent one of my collectors for it. It was only later that I realized he had been wearing Jack's coat and that such a misunderstanding would lead you a merry dance. Which it did! I also knew how you would respond to my note. You *are* predictable.'

'And you,' retorted Lonsdale, 'are insane.'

'Hardly,' said Weeks, annoyance creeping into his voice. 'You just lack the intellect to understand my work, which will be admired for centuries to come. The world's greatest mind tells me that my research will cause just as great a watershed in scientific thought as *On the Origin of Species* did when it was published twenty-three years ago.'

'The world's greatest mind?' sneered Lonsdale in disgust. 'No reputable scientist would endorse you.'

'Darwin would!' Weeks shouted, his voice quivering with agitation. He strode over to where the framed letter had pride of place on the wall and took it down. 'Look, Lonsdale! Darwin himself – *blessing* my work!'

Lonsdale and Hulda looked at the letter in its thick gilt frame, dated 3 December 1869.

> *My dear Galton,*
> *I have been reading your book* Hereditary Genius, *and I*
> *do not think I ever in all my life read anything more*

interesting and original. You have made a convert of an
opponent, for I have always maintained that, excepting
fools, men did not differ much in intellect, only in zeal
and hard work. I see now that education and environment
produce only a small effect on the mind and that a man's
natural mental abilities are derived by inheritance. Your
contention that human intellect and talent are therefore
subject to natural selection and can be improved – whether
by nature or by our own concerted efforts – is compelling.
I congratulate you.

    Yours most sincerely,
    Charles Darwin

'But this wasn't written to *you*,' said Hulda, bewildered. 'It was to Galton! How did you get it?'

'I took it from Darwin's home before he sent it. It was just sitting there for me to find. When I read it, everything became clear! Even then, Galton was expounding the theories that have led to what he calls eugenics. The letter proves Darwin *knew* that was the way forward. All I had to do was to carry it out!'

'But it is unethical!' cried Lonsdale.

'Just the opposite!' said Weeks. 'Darwin realized that progress depends on the survival of the fittest. But as modern medicine helps the sick, and governments support the weak, there's nothing to check the inferior stock. But *I'm* attaining an understanding of the true differences among individuals and the determining features of natural selection. Through *my* work, humanity will secure ultimate perfection. The shouldering aside of the weak by the strong, and the dominance of the superior races – these are the decrees of natural selection, and these are what *my* work will guarantee.'

Lonsdale saw that Weeks had done nothing but twist Darwin's and Galton's theories into pathetic, evil visions. 'You're not a scientist,' he said in disgust, 'just a self-righteous, murdering lunatic.'

Weeks glared. 'It's been interesting talking to you, but now you begin to bore me. Your efforts to interfere with my work have failed, but you can be assured that your cerebra will be added to my collection today – to advance my great and noble theories.'

'Wait,' said Lonsdale. 'Who's been protecting you, other than Wilson. Who?'

'Enough,' said Weeks, and gestured for his thugs to enter. 'Remember that a squashed organ is no good to me.'

He strode off, slamming the door behind him.

Lonsdale glanced at the three louts, as wicked, mirthless grins crept across their faces. He stuck his hand inside his coat, but the biggest jumped at him, knocking him backwards before he could reach his gun. He followed with a swing, but Lonsdale ducked and came back with a right cross that sent him reeling. Meanwhile, as another grabbed Hulda, she sank her teeth into his arm. The dog began to bark frantically, snapping the air with its dripping fangs. Its owner let it go, and chaos ensued.

The dog was poorly trained, and entered the melee little caring whom it bit. It delivered a sharp nip to its owner's ankle, then sank its teeth into the calf of the man Hulda had already bitten. The man yelled and kicked out, catching it on the nose. The dog yelped, and retreated under Weeks's desk. With the owner's attention briefly diverted, Lonsdale landed a hefty blow to his stomach, driving the air from his lungs so he dropped to his knees. He followed it with an uppercut to the jaw, which dropped him senseless. Meanwhile, there was a thump as Hulda's attacker slumped to the ground. Out of the corner of his eye, Lonsdale saw her holding a heavy paperweight that had been on the desk.

Having recovered sufficiently to determine he wanted no more, the first man made for the door. Lonsdale leapt at him, pushing him hard against the wall, and proceeded to deliver a series of short jabbing punches to his head until he, too, slid to the ground.

'We're becoming quite proficient at this,' said Hulda coolly. 'Now, let's find Weeks!'

Lonsdale pulled out his gun, then paused. 'No, we fetch Peters and Leonard,' he said, dropping it into the outside right pocket of his coat. 'We've done enough.'

They left Weeks's office and ran down a flight of stairs.

'That way,' shouted Lonsdale, and they went through a set of doors leading to the front.

'Leonard!' gasped Hulda, spotting the policeman standing in the hallway talking to a man in a white coat.

Leonard looked up in astonishment, while the other man turned round slowly.

'O'Connor!' exclaimed Lonsdale.

'*Dr* O'Connor *Sorenson*, actually,' said the mortuary assistant. The Irish brogue was gone, and in its place was a drawling upper-class accent. 'But not at your service.'

'Chief Inspector, arrest this man!' ordered Hulda imperiously.

'I don't think so,' said Leonard, pulling out a revolver. 'Much as I'd like to oblige a lady of the press.'

Hulda gaped as Leonard pointed his gun unwaveringly at her.

'Professor Weeks said he'd taken care of you,' said Leonard, 'but he spoke too soon. That comes of having others do your dirty work.'

'You?' breathed Lonsdale. He glanced at the door – could he run out to reach Peters?

Leonard shook his head.

'I wouldn't, Lonsdale. I'll shoot you and Miss Friederichs. And then shoot the constable outside. It will be easy to explain away – you are trespassing in direct contravention of police orders.'

Lonsdale sensed that Leonard was a far more dangerous adversary than Weeks, and that he and Hulda would not escape a second time. After all, Leonard had more to lose if *The PMG* exposed what was happening at the Institute – Weeks would use influential friends to escape justice, but Leonard had no such connections.

'Now,' said Leonard, 'I doubt Weeks will be overjoyed to see you again, but go through that door.'

Lonsdale glanced at Hulda; both were still armed, but attempting to reach their weapons was too dangerous. Leonard would kill at least one of them before they could stop him.

'I told you to go through that door,' said Leonard when neither moved. The look on his face indicated there was no alternative. O'Connor led, and Leonard brought up the rear.

They went through a lecture theatre and beyond to a series of offices, in one of which was Weeks. His eyes became hard and cold, and he looked at Leonard for an answer.

'You might be a great scientist, Weeks,' said Leonard, 'but you don't know anything about hiring the right men for this kind of job.'

He stood to one side of Lonsdale, the gun in his left hand. Lonsdale eased closer to him, wondering what the chances were of jumping him before he could fire. Slim, he decided. He glanced out of the window, and saw Peters talking to several constables.

'Don't expect help from that quarter,' Leonard said, watching him. 'All the windows in the front of the building are specially made, and you won't attract attention by breaking one. You could hit one with a rock and it wouldn't shatter. Besides, *I* don't make mistakes.' He waved with his gun towards a cabinet that stood next to a desk on the other side of the room. 'Stand over there and keep your hands where I can see them.'

'So it was you all the time,' said Lonsdale. 'Not Peters or Ramsey.'

'Neither has the vision to understand what Professor Weeks is doing,' responded Leonard shortly. 'His research will make a great step forward for our society.'

'But you're a policeman,' objected Lonsdale. 'You should want to help those who can't protect themselves.'

Leonard sneered. 'We'll help them into a better world all right – the next one.'

'So, you protect Weeks and his project?'

'Working with that idiot Ramsey makes it easy. He listens to all my suggestions and follows them slavishly, because he knows I'm cleverer than he is. I only have to say he wants something, and it happens. I can act as though I'm trying to be helpful, while subverting anything that threatens us.'

'He's been invaluable,' said Weeks smugly.

Leonard glanced at O'Connor on his left and Weeks on his right. 'Can you keep them here if I give you the gun? I need to get rid of Peters – he's almost as much of a menace as they are.'

'We'll keep them quiet,' said Weeks confidently, as

O'Connor pulled a long, thin knife out of a cabinet. 'Hand me the gun.'

As Leonard reached over to pass Weeks the pistol, Lonsdale groped for his own revolver. Without taking it out of his pocket, he pulled the trigger. The bullet shattered the strengthened glass of the window and everybody in the room froze.

'Down,' yelled Lonsdale to Hulda, dropping behind a desk and pulling out the gun. But before she could react, O'Connor grabbed her hair and thrust the knife against her throat.

'She'll be dead within seconds,' he hissed.

'So will you,' said Lonsdale, levelling the gun at him from behind the desk.

'Which makes three,' said Leonard, aiming at Lonsdale. He spoke urgently. 'Kill her now, Sorenson, and they'll both be dead before Peters gets here. I'll clear everything.'

'I'll do it,' said Weeks. 'I have an MP visiting tomorrow, and I don't want a mess on the Turkish rug he gave us.' He stepped in front of Leonard to reach O'Connor, and in that instant Lonsdale fired again. The bullet hit O'Connor's right shoulder and he dropped both the knife and his hold on Hulda.

Leonard shoved Weeks, sending him sprawling to the floor, and then leapt at Lonsdale over the desk. Lonsdale tried to re-aim, but Leonard landed on him, knocking the pistol away. In a moment, Leonard had jammed his knee onto Lonsdale's chest and grabbed his throat with a two-handed grip. They struggled for a moment before Leonard's vice-like clamp began to suffocate Lonsdale. Disobeying the instinct to pull the hands away, Lonsdale let go of Leonard's wrists, and swung with all his remaining strength up into his groin. The policeman screeched, released Lonsdale, and fell on top of him.

'What's going on?' Peters shouted, as he raced into the room, brushing by Weeks at the door and looking around wildly. The first thing he saw was Hulda, skirt awry and pointing a huge revolver at O'Connor, who was groaning and bleeding profusely. The second was Lonsdale, who pushed out from underneath Leonard, grabbed the chief inspector's left arm, and brought it up behind his back. Two constables who had momentarily detained Weeks let him go as they came to help their superior.

'Leonard is one of them, Peters,' shouted Hulda. 'Weeks is escaping! Get him!'

'Now, Miss Friederichs,' said Peters, infuriatingly slow on the uptake, 'put down that gun. Constable, see to the chief inspector.'

'It's true, Peters,' Lonsdale said, breathing heavily. 'Leonard *is* one of them.'

'Arrest them, George,' Leonard gasped. 'They shot Sorenson, then tried to kill me.' He began to reach for his gun.

'Don't move, Leonard,' said Hulda, pointing her gun at him.

'Miss Friederichs!' shouted Peters. 'Disarm! Let me sort this out.'

'No,' she shouted frantically. 'Lonsdale! Don't let Weeks escape!'

Lonsdale tore from the room. An open door at the far end of the corridor told him which way Weeks had gone. He leapt down the narrow spiral stairs beyond, three at a time. At the bottom was another door. He burst through it and found himself in a long, cold room lined with shelves. He didn't pause to look at the dozens and dozens of glass jars, but plunged forward, and into what was apparently a dissecting area. A man sat at a bench, chopping something up on a piece of white polished marble; he did not look up as Lonsdale raced past.

Then Lonsdale was outside, exiting through the now unlocked door they had seen earlier at the rear of the building. Weeks was nowhere to be seen. Lonsdale dashed to the gate, but it was locked. There was no other way out, so he could only assume that Weeks was doing what he himself had already done – climbing through someone else's garden. He pulled himself up onto the wall he had scaled earlier, just in time to see Weeks disappearing over the one beyond it.

He leapt off the wall, and ran across the neighbouring garden. The next wall was high, but his running start helped him reach the top and haul himself over. What he saw from the top filled him with horror.

The 'garden' surrounded a gaping hole with silvery lines at the bottom, and the house to which it was attached was just an empty façade. It was the Metropolitan Line's vent, through which underground trains ridded themselves of excess steam.

There was a maintenance ladder attached to the side, down which Weeks was climbing.

Lonsdale heard a yell from behind and saw Peters and his men were running after him. He could not wait for them to catch up. Weeks had boasted about his supporters, and if he was not caught now, pressure would be brought on the police to abandon the search. He jumped off the wall and raced to the ladder. Weeks was almost at the bottom, and Lonsdale saw him drop the last few feet and disappear into the tunnel. Placing one hand on the rusty metal, Lonsdale swung down.

The ladder groaned, and he felt it ease away from the wall. Frantically, he grabbed at the rim of the pit, but then it steadied, and, knowing it had held Weeks, he began to climb down. One rung disintegrated under his feet, so that, for a moment, he was suspended by his hands. His feet scrabbled for the next rung down.

He knew that the longer he took to climb down, the greater the distance Weeks would be able to put between them, so he struggled to move faster. He was almost at the bottom when he discovered the last part of the ladder had rusted away completely. Weeks had evidently known it, indicating it was not the first time he had used the thing, but Lonsdale was unprepared. With a screech of tearing metal, he plunged into empty space, still clutching a rusty bar.

Lonsdale landed with a crash, the stench of engine oil and steam rising about him. From above, he could hear Peters shouting, but the echoes made it impossible to decipher what the inspector was saying. He climbed to his feet, and stared at the black tunnel down which Weeks had vanished. A long way in the distance was a tiny pinprick of light marking Kensington Station. He listened intently for the rumbling of a train, but the tunnel was silent. As he looked down the line, he saw a flicker of light. Weeks had struck a match to illuminate his way – he had been groping his way in the dark, and was not as far ahead as Lonsdale had feared. Now the professor had decided to abandon stealth for speed.

Lonsdale shot off down the tunnel after him. He could hear the tap of Weeks's feet and the rasp of his breath. Lonsdale increased his speed, then fell over an uneven tie, bruising his knees and scraping his hands. He lit a match of his own and started to trot, the glow from his tiny light making eerie shadows on the walls.

'Weeks!' he yelled. 'You can't escape!'

He heard the scientist laugh in derision. Lonsdale continued running, concentrating on the pinprick of light that marked Kensington Station. His breath came in ragged gasps as the foul, stale air of the tunnel choked him. He felt himself grow dizzy, and he stumbled again.

He forced himself to move on, each step becoming more of an effort. He felt a blast of cooler air on his cheek. He blinked, and saw the lights from the station were a good deal closer now, and that Weeks was not very far ahead of him. He staggered on. And then he noticed the rails beneath his feet beginning to tremble. Glancing back, he saw a great round light. A train! He ran faster, feeling the shaking increasing beneath his feet, and hearing the dull rumble of metal on metal, growing louder and louder.

Lonsdale ran harder, knowing that to fall now would mean death. The train was lighting the entire tunnel, and there was a shrill whistle from the engine as the driver saw him. It screamed in his ears like a creature from hell. Then he saw one of the alcoves that had been built into the wall for workmen to use when trains went past. As the brakes were applied in a screech that Lonsdale thought would split his skull, he dived into the niche, and the train hurtled past in a shower of sparks.

He thought he was going to be sick. His lungs were burning, and he fought for breath, clutching at the sooty wall of the alcove as the train thundered past. Then it was gone and, glancing out, he saw a figure emerge from another alcove ahead, and make its way towards the back of the train, which was pulling into the station. Weeks was going to escape after all!

Lonsdale forced himself forward. Weeks had reached the train, and was climbing up the back. With a shock, Lonsdale saw he planned to lie on the top, and wait until he reached a place where there were no police, when he would calmly climb down. Then he would be free.

Lonsdale forced himself forward. He was almost there! He reached the back of the train and stretched up, snagging a handful of trouser leg. Weeks kicked backwards, and Lonsdale struggled to hold on. From behind him, he could hear running footsteps. Peters and his men were coming. Then, very slowly, the train began to move. Lonsdale knew that if he did not hold onto Weeks now, he would escape. The police were too far away to help.

He reached up with his other hand, hanging onto Weeks's ankle with all his strength as the train began to gather speed. Weeks kicked again and, this time, Lonsdale was unable to maintain his grip. He felt his hand sliding, and then he was down, tumbling onto the track.

Peters arrived just as the engine began to disappear into the tunnel at the other end of the station, breathing hard, his face streaked with sweat and soot.

'Damn!' he yelled, all exasperated fury.

Weeks was looking back at them with a gloating smile. He was kneeling on the top of the train, swaying slightly as it gathered speed. He raised his hand in a triumphant farewell.

Lonsdale closed his eyes tightly as the last carriage entered the tunnel. From the platform, he heard a woman scream. Weeks had misjudged the height of the hole.

Peters's men rushed towards the crumpled body, while Lonsdale pulled himself up onto the platform, away from the rails. Peters followed Lonsdale, watching his constables mill about the body that sprawled across the tracks in a bloody heap.

Lonsdale slumped on the platform and tried to catch his breath.

'I hope it dashed the bastard's brains out,' he said in a hoarse whisper.

Peters sat next to him. 'Oh, it did,' he said grimly. 'It did.'

EPILOGUE

'I find it utterly reprehensible that you won't let us tell the entire story,' raged Hulda. 'We exposed the plot at great personal risk, and now all we can publish is a watered-down version. We can't even use the perpetrators' real names.'

'Don't blame me, Miss Friederichs,' said Peters, pulling out his pipe and tobacco. 'It came from one of those "higher sources" you dislike so much.'

'Small wonder she's vexed, then,' put in Bradwell. 'If that's what higher sources do, perhaps they shouldn't be in higher places.'

It was Monday afternoon, six days after the fateful encounter at the Imperial Demographic Institute. For the first time since then, Lonsdale, Hulda, Peters and Bradwell were together, enjoying a meal at the restaurant in Derry & Toms.

'It was Morley who agreed not to print everything,' Peters said mildly. 'So some of your irritation should be directed *his* way. Not mine.'

'Morley has his reasons,' said Lonsdale. 'But it would be different if Stead were editor.'

'Something we may see before too long,' said Hulda enigmatically.

Lonsdale raised his eyebrows. 'Do you know something I don't, Friederichs?'

'A great deal,' replied Hulda. 'But as regards *The PMG*, I just sense a change in the offing. There'll be a seat in the Commons open soon, and Morley will be Gladstone's choice to fill it.' She smiled in anticipation. 'Then, with Stead in charge, we'll have some excitement!'

There was silence at the table for several moments, before Lonsdale spoke again.

'So, we all know that the Imperial Demographic Institute has been closed down and a number of individuals arrested, Inspector. What else can you tell us?'

'That Weeks kept most of the important documents elsewhere, and we haven't been able to locate them, and the ledger you mentioned had disappeared by the time we searched his office. That leaves us struggling to hunt down many of those involved. We found seventy-six cerebra in the basement, but we don't know if that was the total number of victims.'

'Has Leonard told you anything?'

'Not much – he feels I helped destroy his dreams. He says Ramsey and I are two of a kind – neither with the vision to understand the greatness of Weeks's plan. Sorensen has been more helpful, and answered some of the questions you wanted us to ask. For example, one of their colleagues was supposed to follow you home after the Walker inquest, so that Weeks would know where you lived. But he followed Miss Friederichs' hansom instead, so Weeks went to her house in the morning, hoping she would lead him to your residence. Instead, of course, he followed her to Salmon and Eden.

'Sorensen has also identified some of the low-level participants. We've caught two men who were involved in murders, although Morgan has disappeared. You heard about Pawley, didn't you?'

'No,' said Lonsdale.

'He was found on a Great Western train travelling without a ticket. He refused to pay so was taken into custody, where his identity was ascertained. He's been incarcerated in an asylum. He denies any involvement with Weeks, and says he'll break out at his first opportunity.'

'So, do you think,' asked Bradwell, 'that there are individuals who'll try to continue the scheme?'

'We seem to have the most important *active* participants,' said Peters. 'There are people like Wilson who believe in the concept, but didn't play a role that we know of – they're still free. But, without Weeks, I think we're safe from more of this madness.'

'And hopefully, we always will be,' sighed Lonsdale.

Lonsdale sat comfortably in the morning room at Cleveland Square and opened *The Observer*. He had three-quarters of an hour to spare before he and Jack were to meet Emelia and Anne.

He was looking forward to the afternoon considerably more than to dinner that night with Emelia's family. But he had found in recent weeks that he was prepared to put up with a great deal to please Anne.

Idly, he scanned through the news. The world seemed to be holding on for one more day. But the smile left his face when he read:

> *A gunpowder explosion resulted in a double fatality yesterday morning at 94 Old Bath Road in Bristol. After a fire in the upper rooms was extinguished, the lodgers, Mr and Mrs Hicks, were found on the floor with the upper portion of their heads blown off. An examination revealed a large number of canisters containing gunpowder and loaded cartridges. It was apparent that Hicks was filling cartridges when the explosion occurred. The police say there is no need for further investigation, and that the case is closed.*

Lonsdale felt himself shaking. 'The case may be closed,' he muttered. 'But it certainly hasn't ended.'

HISTORICAL NOTE

The account of the gunpowder explosion that killed Mr and Mrs Hicks in Bristol was true, as were all the news articles and many of the events described in *Mind of a Killer*. The quotations were taken directly from *The Pall Mall Gazette*, *The Times*, or other London newspapers. This is just one interpretation of what might have happened when this strange series of seemingly unrelated events took place.

In 1882, *The PMG* was a small but very influential London newspaper. Founded in 1865, it had been on the verge of financial collapse when Frederick Greenwood, the first editor, convinced his brother James to spend a night in the Lambeth workhouse and to write a series of sensational articles about the experience. The four instalments not only exposed the horrific conditions in workhouses, but also helped guarantee the paper's success by doubling its circulation in three days.

In 1880, the newspaper's ownership and political orientation changed, and John Morley (1838–1923), a much-respected intellectual and political commentator – called 'the last of the great nineteenth-century Liberals' – became editor. Morley left *The PMG* in 1883 after being elected to Parliament. He later twice served in the Cabinet as Chief Secretary for Ireland, having told Prime Minister Gladstone that if he could manage Stead, he could manage Ireland. He was also twice Secretary of State for India, and was created Viscount Morley in 1908, after which he became Lord President of the Council.

One of Morley's first moves as editor was to hire the Liberal firebrand W. T. Stead (1849–1912), from the *Northern Echo* of Darlington, to serve as assistant editor. Stead succeeded Morley as editor, and in the next seven years his 'New Journalism' introduced many innovations, brought American-style sensationalism to the British press, and demonstrated how the press could be used positively to influence government policy in the creation of child welfare and social legislation

– what Stead called 'Government by Journalism'. In 1890, Stead founded and became editor of the non-partisan monthly *Review of Reviews*, a position he held until his death in 1912 on *Titanic*.

Under Morley and Stead, the staff of *The PMG* was one of the most remarkable in the history of the press. Alfred Milner (1854–1925) served as a reporter and then Stead's assistant editor, before abandoning journalism for a career as a politician and colonial administrator. He was High Commissioner for South Africa and Governor of the Cape Colony, a member of the War Cabinet during World War I, Secretary of State for War, and Secretary of State for the Colonies. He was knighted in 1895 and created Viscount Milner in 1902.

Edward Tyas Cook (1857–1919) ultimately succeeded Stead as editor, and in 1893, after new ownership had changed *The PMG* to a Tory newspaper, he founded a new Liberal evening paper, *The Westminster Gazette*. He later became editor of *The Daily News*, and was renowned as the world's leading authority on John Ruskin – editing his writings, which were published in thirty-nine volumes. He was knighted in 1912.

Hulda Friederichs (1856–1927) initially joined *The PMG* as Stead's personal assistant, and thereafter became the first woman journalist in London engaged on exactly the same terms, with regard to work and pay, as the male members of staff. In 1893, she went to *The Westminster Gazette* with Cook and, three years later, became editor of the *Westminster Budget*. She wrote biographies of several important British figures of the time.

Clustered in the months around the death of Charles Darwin on 19 April 1882 were numerous incidents appearing in this book. For example, W. J. Willoughby was found dead on a train track in France, after two companions with whom he was travelling disappeared; the murderer Dr George Lamson confessed his crimes to his gaoler; the pauper Bingham died after being placed in a fumigating box; and Frederick Kempster and Edmund Corlett were burned to death at their factory.

The PMG also featured coverage of the death of Jesse James; the explosion at the Court Theatre, during a performance that the Prince of Wales was attending; an attack on a ship by a sperm whale; the riots in Camborne; the eruption of Mount Etna; and Milner's two-part story on 'nomads', explaining the way vagabond women selected men at workhouses. Other pieces of news included milkman John Poole being arrested for stealing milk, Teresa Godley being killed in a beach fire after being part of a group that robbed Frank Wood, and Thomas Pawley – an escapee from a lunatic asylum – being found on a Great Western Train travelling without a ticket.

Perhaps the most intensely covered news event of the time was the double-murder of Lord Frederick Cavendish and Thomas Henry Burke in Dublin's Phoenix Park. The resolution to these murders did not come until the next year, after the members of the 'Invincibles', a small, violent faction of Irish rebels, had been arrested. Ultimately, five were hanged and three given penal servitude for life, while James Carey, who turned Queen's evidence against them, was murdered while being smuggled by the government to Natal.

The other newspapers mentioned in the book all existed. At the time, *The Daily Telegraph* and *The Standard* had the largest daily circulations in the world. *The New York Herald* – which was widely disliked by the British press for its use of sensationalism – at times had the largest circulation in the United States and full-time staffs for both its Paris and London editions. The restaurants mentioned – including Craig's Oyster Bar, Pagani's and the Aerated Bread Company – were all successful at the time, as was Derry & Toms, the London department store. The homes that Lonsdale, Milner and Galton lived in can still be seen in London, although Galton's is much changed after being damaged by a bomb in World War II.

Galton was one of the great gentleman-scientists of his generation. He had travelled in Africa and then returned to Britain, where he achieved prominence for his investigations into numerous aspects of heredity and genetics. The originator of the concept of eugenics, he received the letter from his cousin Charles Darwin in December 1869. His book *Inquiries into Human Faculty and Its Development* was published to critical acclaim in 1883, and his later achievements included the founding of the anthropometric laboratory and being one of the fathers of fingerprinting. At this time, several of Lonsdale's other acquaintances – including Sir Garnet Wolseley (1833–1913), who was raised to the peerage as Baron Wolseley later in 1882, and Professor John Robert Seeley (1834–1895) – were also at the height of their powers and influence.